Issue 2

by Cambria Hebert

"A revolution is a struggle to the death between the future and the past."

—Author unknown

#REV
gearshark magazine

One

Drew

I was no quitter.

I refused to quit Trent.

So angry. I was so goddamned angry.

He was pushing me away when all I wanted to do was pull him close. It was almost laughable he tried to break up with me. I felt the laughter bubbling up inside me, ready to explode. It was like I was so incredibly infuriated I couldn't yell… I couldn't cry… I couldn't even speak.

But I wanted to laugh. The kind of laugh only villains in movies did. The kind that bespoke of internal madness.

That's what tonight was. Madness.

He was jumped. Beaten.

He told me he loved me.

Then he laid out intent to withhold that love.

Trent was trying to protect me. In his mind, he wasn't keeping the love he felt from me, but rather showing it in the best way he knew how. I respected that. I did.

But I wouldn't have it.

We'd gotten one week together. I wanted more.

I suppose thinking we could keep our relationship a secret was naive. Merely wishful thinking. When you loved someone the way we loved each other, it was impossible to hide.

It showed in every way.

Not just in the way we looked at each other. Or the way we spent every spare moment together. It showed in ways I never wanted to see until now. Ways I thought no one else would notice.

I'd been fooling myself.

It was the way he put ketchup on his plate so I could eat his fries. The way I automatically pulled the tomatoes off my burgers and slid them onto his plate. It was the fact that I went to him first whenever something happened I wanted to share. And the way we made each other's coffee exactly as we drank it.

Love is in the details. It's in the everyday. It's the way you treat someone when they aren't even looking and the way they fill your head when you're apart.

Of course people were going to see it.

Joey saw it almost from day one. Braeden and Ivy already knew. The reporter from *GearShark* knew from just one conversation…

Hiding our relationship was almost not an option.

Dissolving it wasn't either.

My hand throbbed and my knuckles were slick with blood when I slammed out of the room. I was so intensely frustrated I couldn't look at him another minute.

We weren't over. No way in hell.

But I needed a minute.

My mind was so clouded with anger I didn't see him. I didn't notice him at all until he cleared his throat. My body jerked to a stop and my head whipped around to see Romeo leaning against the wall as if he were resolved to be there a while.

I was sure he heard everything.

Trent and I had been yelling. And the sound of my hand going through the wall hadn't exactly been silent.

"Guess I don't need to ask how he is," Romeo said, straightening off the wall.

"You agree with him?" I challenged, my hand flexing. It was already fucked up from going through a wall, but I'd use it again if I had to.

"I understand why he thinks he's doing what's right."

At first, his words didn't sink in. They just pissed me off even more. All I heard was Romeo understood Trent. I growled low and stepped forward in an aggressive movement.

Romeo's eyes narrowed, watching me close, but other than that, his body language didn't change.

That's when I realized he was no threat. That's when I realized he was on my side.

"We're in a relationship," I said point blank. I kind of wanted to shock him. I wanted someone other than me to feel the sting of words tonight.

I also wanted a fight.

Just not with Trent.

Never with Trent.

"I know." The amusement in his tone took a little heat out of my oven. "You can't keep secrets like that from family. Family who really loves you."

I tilted my head to the side and regarded him. Was he saying he knew before he walked into this house a little bit ago? Was he saying he didn't care?

"You should probably get that hand cleaned up. You're bleeding on the floor."

I glanced down at the blood dripping off my knuckles.

"I'll talk to Trent." He went on.

Romeo stepped off the wall and toward the bedroom door. I moved fast, silently snatching his arm and turning him around. He didn't pull away or act like my roughness was a threat, but his muscles tensed beneath my arm, and I felt tension coil in his limbs.

"He cares what you think," I said quietly. "Your opinion matters. So if you aren't sure how you feel about our relationship or the fact there are two gay guys in your family, walk away. Walk away right now."

Romeo stared at me level, his blue eyes bouncing between mine.

"He's already fucked up enough right now. If you can't offer him the brother he needs tonight, I won't let you in that room."

Romeo's lips curved up into a knowing, almost pleased expression. "He pissed you off so bad you put your hand through a wall and he's pushing you away, yet here you are, standing guard at the door, protecting him."

"That wasn't an answer," I growled.

Romeo laughed beneath his breath. And then he answered.

Not with words.

In seconds, his arm was out of my grasp and he was hugging me. I hesitated, shocked he would just reach out and embrace me like this.

"Family takes care of family." His voice was muted. "I'm not sure if there's anything that could make me turn my back on family, but if there is, it ain't this."

When he pulled back, I looked him in the eye.

He meant it.

"Congratulations on finding a love worth fighting for."

I wasn't expecting this. It wasn't that I thought he wouldn't accept us, that any of this family wouldn't. It was the way they did it. The way they acted like it wasn't even anything to bat an eye at, like Trent and I were inevitable and they'd only been waiting for us to figure it out.

I wished it were that easy for me. For Trent.

"I thought the fighting was over," I said, suddenly incredibly weary. "But it's only just begun."

"You aren't alone." Romeo slapped me on the shoulder. "I'm going in now."

I nodded, knowing Trent was going to get the support he needed. I started down the hall. This time it was Romeo who stopped me.

"I know you're going to go after them," he said.

When I glanced back, he was right behind me, and his voice was quiet.

"Oh, yes," I intoned. "There's no way in hell I'll let what they did to him go unpunished."

Those bastards at Omega were going to pay for what they did to Trent and they were going to pay dearly.

"Me and B are with you."

I nodded. I wasn't sure what I was going to do yet, but I wasn't going to turn down help. The more painful the revenge, the better.

And if worse came to worse…

I'd have someone to bail me out of jail.

TWO

Trent

Don't count on it.

I put my faith in fate. I put all my proverbial eggs in one basket.

What do I get?

Don't count on it.

Fucking A.

Or maybe that's what I got for asking a magic eight ball for love advice.

Maybe I should have just smacked myself in the head with it. It would have been less painful.

I learned quite a few things in the moments after I broke up with Drew and he stormed out of the bedroom with a bleeding fist.

1.) Seeing him bleed was not something I liked.

2.) I wanted to call him back the second he walked out.

and

3.) Something else I wasn't quite ready to do something about.

Hurting him wasn't something I wanted, but this seemed like the best thing. Maybe doing this now might save more pain later.

What if it hurt forever?

What if the pain I was trying to spare us both was for nothing because it was pain just the same?

Pain was pain.

Pain hurt. It didn't matter if it were fists and physical blows or a broken heart and busted dreams.

I already knew what life was like trying to deny how I felt about Drew.

Misery.

Was I sentencing us both to misery because I was trying to do what was best for Drew…?

Or because I was scared?

It seemed there was misery in our futures no matter which choice I made.

Everything inside me ached with bleakness. I ached for the life I wanted and for the one I had.

I laid my head back against the headboard and stared at the eight ball still in my clutches. Maybe the melancholy I saw in our futures wouldn't be quite so grim if it were also woven with bliss.

Stolen moments in the dark, grazing touches as we worked beneath the hood of his car. Laughter, smiles… friendship.

Wasn't it those things that made life suck less?

Let's face it. Life is hard.

Anyone who said it's easy was one of two things:

1.) A liar.

or

2.) On damn good drugs.

I was reeling inside.

I was a knotted mess of confusion and hurt.

A light knock on the doorframe gave me a slight reprieve from my tortured thoughts. Leaning my head against the headboard, I rolled it toward the sound as Romeo stepped into the bedroom.

I stifled a wince when my body tensed. I knew he knew. Braeden probably told him as soon as he walked in the door tonight.

I was nervous about this conversation.

I never really said it, never really let on… but Romeo was important to me. It sounded odd because we were the same age, we were family, and because, well, I was taller than him, but I looked up to Romeo.

He always seemed so together. A rock. A man who always had his life on point.

I tried to be that way. Hell, most people probably thought I was. But inside, I often felt I was grasping a rope as I dangled off the side of a cliff.

"Hey." He began.

"Hey," I echoed, pushing myself up a little straighter in the bed.

His footsteps faltered when he turned toward me. "*Fuck*," he swore low. "They told me you looked like shit."

I laughed and then grabbed my side. "What a nice thing to say."

"That was nice. You look worse than shit." He folded his arms across his chest, the blue of his eyes only visible through narrow slits, but even half closed, he still appraised me entirely.

I wondered if he saw me any differently now that he knew.

Now that he knew beneath the bruises, cuts, and college athlete, my heart beat for another man.

"What happened, Trent?" he asked.

"I'm sure B told you."

"B wasn't there. I want to hear it from you."

I told him everything. About how the trouble I said I took care of at the frat hadn't really been over. I told him about Con and the shit he'd been saying to me for weeks. Anger bubbled up inside me when I retold how I was jumped, pinned down, and beaten by four guys that were supposed to be my brothers.

Sure, I was upset by all this. I was hurting inside because of Drew.

But I was also pissed.

Con knew he'd never win a fight against me alone or even if it were fair.

So he came with backup.

Motherfucker.

When I was done talking, Romeo rubbed a hand along his jaw and gestured toward the bed. "You mind?"

"I'm in love with Drew," I said, deliberate.

The side of his lips tilted up. "Yeah, I might have heard."

"You still wanna sit there?"

The small smirk left his face, and he sighed. Instead of dropping onto the side of the bed, he kicked off his shoes and climbed onto the mattress. The bed bounced a little beneath his weight as he took up Drew's side and mirrored my sitting position. When his back was leaning up against the headboard, he dropped his hands in his lap and looked in my direction.

"I didn't know I came off as a judgmental asshole," he mused.

"You don't. But you are a total alpha male and you know it."

"All the men in this house are," he retorted.

"Maybe, but I think we both know you're number one."

"Have you met my wife? She totally runs me."

I laughed. It was so true. Rimmel was less than half his size, and he was totally wrapped around her little finger. "Don't make me laugh," I grabbed my side again, trying to hold it still while I guffawed.

His eyes narrowed with my movement, and it served to help sober me up.

"You really didn't think I'd accept you?" he asked, bringing the rest of the laughter out of me.

I looked him in the face. "Honestly? I think I always knew you would, but I was scared to tell you. Scared if you didn't, it would crush me twice as hard because it would mean I was wrong about the one guy I always admired."

"I've always admired you. More so since I stepped in this house tonight."

Of all the things he could have said, that was probably the least likely I would have ever guessed.

My voice was rueful. "I just got my ass beat."

He waved that off like he wasn't quite ready to deal with that, like it paled in comparison to everything else we had to talk about. "You've always been a quiet guy. You're the observer. The friend, the guy who's always there but stays in the background. You're kind of like the funny sidekick in a TV show. People might not have come to watch you, but you're the reason they stay. That inner strength you all say I have? You got it, too."

I swallowed past the rocks in my throat. Not lumps of emotion. Rocks. "I'm not so strong, Rome."

"You're dying inside right now, aren't you?" he said, frank. The nakedness of his words made me feel uncomfortable. It was hard to show him just how much I loved Drew when I still wasn't used to admitting it to myself.

I glanced down at my lap and didn't reply.

"I watched you and Drew dance around each other for months and months. I was starting to think you two would deny each other forever. You made the first move, didn't you?" he asked.

I thought back to the night of our first kiss. The night I grabbed Drew's arm and felt him shake. I nodded once.

"Starting something with him took strength. Breaking it off with him tonight took even more."

"You heard?"

"I think the entire house heard." He joked. "And I saw him in the hall."

"How did he look?" I asked, forgetting about the throbbing behind my eyes and the sharp pain in my side.

"Just like you." He was silent a heartbeat, then said, "I imagine I looked the exact same way the night Rimmel found out about initiation and the dare to sleep with her. The night she got out of my car and walked away. I didn't think I'd ever see her again."

Oh, I'd see Drew again. And it would feel like salt being poured into a gaping, raw wound.

"I think my situation is a little different." I pointed out.

In his lap, Romeo began twisting the wedding ring adorning his finger. "Why's that? 'Cause you love a dude and not a woman? Man, have you met women? They're borderline impossible to deal with half the time."

I snorted. I learned it from his wife.

The humor left his voice when he spoke again. "I know something about loving someone you aren't supposed to. Someone no one thinks you should."

I looked up.

"I also know something about the person you love becoming a target for hate because you love them."

I was already reeling, but Romeo pushed me off kilter. Never had I thought about his love story with

Rimmel like that before. I guess I never really saw it from his point of view. All I ever really saw was the way they were together, how obvious it was they belonged together.

Made me feel kind of dumb for not seeing it sooner. After all, I had a front row seat to everything they'd been through.

"That was different, though." I disagreed, even though I saw his point. What was between him and Rim was nothing like what was between me and Drew.

"Why?"

I faltered a little. "Because Zach was crazy. Like seriously mental."

He nodded. "Yeah, he was. But hate doesn't care. Hate can turn anyone a little mental."

"Like Con." I surmised.

Romeo shook his head. "I'm not talking about that pecker head."

I grinned because that's exactly what Con was. A little pecker head.

"I'm talking about anyone who hates on people who are gay. Who loves someone of the same sex. Those people might not be quite as unstable as Zach, but they're just as dangerous. Anyone who uses the fact that a person loves another person as some kind of weapon or reason to be a douche bag isn't right in the head."

"So you get why I broke it off," I said, thinking about what he just said. Feeling his words down to my core.

All this time I'd been so focused on telling myself it was wrong to love Drew because he was a man. It wasn't wrong to love Drew.

What was wrong was the way some people saw that love.

As a perversion. As a twist of the devil.

"Yeah, I get it." Romeo replied. "But you're wrong."

My body jerked. "What?"

Romeo sat forward, his back no longer against the headboard. His waist twisted around and one hand landed on my bare shoulder. "I'll never turn my back on you. You're my family. No matter what."

That meant so much to me. More than I could probably ever put into words.

It made this even harder.

Because not only was I breaking up with Drew, but in a way, the rest of my family.

It was my worst fear.

It was the reason I hadn't wanted to tell Drew how I felt in the first place. I had been scared I would not only lose my best friend, but my family.

When Drew validated everything I felt for him, when he basically returned my feelings, I'd been so goddamned relieved because if he had rejected me, I would have had to walk away.

Away from him.

Away from Romeo, Braeden, Rimmel and Ivy.

That's what I had to do now.

I was the one choosing this. I was the one who didn't live here.

I couldn't be here, not right now anyway. I couldn't see Drew day in and day out and not be with him the way I wanted.

I couldn't watch him date again…

Searing pain cut through my chest. I wrapped my arms over my middle, trying to hold myself together.

There would come a time when Drew would date. A woman? Another man?

It didn't matter.

It wouldn't be me.

"You break anything besides the ribs?" Romeo asked, his voice concerned.

My heart. I shook my head.

"You don't turn your back on love." He went on without missing a beat. "Love isn't easy, not for anyone, but you don't push it away. You hold even tighter."

"There's always going to be a Zach for us," I told him. "More than one. I'm trying to protect him. I'm trying to protect his career."

"It's hard to protect someone when you aren't around."

There was a final note to his words.

Like someone who just gave the be-all, end-all closing argument and dropped the mic.

"Maybe my absence is all the protection Drew needs," I whispered.

"I think you know better than that," Romeo said. "But after a night like tonight, you're allowed to waver."

"I'm glad I have your permission," I said kind of surly.

My body hurt, my head hurt, and my swollen eye felt like the skin around it was stretched so tight it might burst.

"Just remember, all flags tremble in the wind, but they still keep flying."

I thought about making a crack about how he sounded like Dr. Phil or some shit, but I couldn't. Because in that moment, he was a voice of reason. He was like my deepest conscience speaking up after I told it to shut up too many times.

"So you really knew about us for months?" I asked, thinking of what he'd said earlier.

He grinned. "Dude, I had you guys pegged almost from day one."

"How?" I wondered.

"The way you watched each other when you thought no one else was looking. I thought maybe you two were going to finally figure it out at Christmas. Man, the way he watched you that night with Nova sleeping on your chest," Romeo mused. Then he seemed to snap out of the memory. "When nothing happened, I started to think maybe I was wrong."

He'd been watching me that night at the cabin? My limbs tingled a little just hearing it. I loved knowing I affected Drew in the ways he affected me.

"Is that why you've been riding me so hard about family lately?" I demanded.

He laughed low. "Yeah. I could feel you pulling back. I couldn't let that happen."

"Why didn't you just say something?"

"Because you can't tell someone they're in love with someone else. They have to figure it out on their own. Besides, I figured if I came right out and said it, one of you would run scared."

"Like I am now." My voice was grim.

"You aren't running. You're proceeding with caution." I opened my mouth to object, but he held up a hand. "Take a couple days. Let some of this sink in. You might feel different when half your face isn't swollen."

There was some noise out in the hall, and then Braeden walked in. "Mom's here." He stopped in his tracks and looked at us on the bed. "Get your own man, Trent. Rome's mine."

Romeo cackled, and I rolled my eyes.

"Don't be an idiot," Rimmel announced, appearing from behind B and smacking him in the middle. He rubbed at the area and scowled as she kept moving.

Romeo stood as she climbed onto the bed and wrapped an arm around my neck, gingerly pressing close. Her dark hair was up in some wild bun with strands sticking out and tickling my face. I wrapped one arm around her to return the hug.

"I love you," she whispered in my ear. "Those guys better pray they never meet me in a dark alley."

I chuckled as she pulled back so our eyes could meet (well, her eyes met my one good one).

"Seriously." She nodded sagely. "I'm a real badass."

I adjusted the black-framed glasses perched on her nose and smiled. "Toughest one in the house."

Her eyes suddenly filled, and it was like another kick in my gut. I couldn't take many more kicks tonight. "What's up?"

"Promise me something."

I leaned my head back against the headboard. "Okay,"

"Promise you won't just leave. You're my family. I don't like to lose my family."

Well, damn. The guilt trip was strong with this one. What made it worse was she had truth to back it up. Rimmel had lost a lot in her life already, and I truly believed the tears threatening were because she was worried she might lose more.

It hit me right in the feels.

I honestly didn't know everyone in this house cared about me as much as I did them.

Too bad it took so much to make me see.

"You and me are always gonna be family." I held up my pinky.

She laughed.

"C'mon, man!" B exclaimed. "It's one thing to be gay, but pinky swearing is for chicks!"

"You do it, too," Ivy said, stepping through the doorway. "So don't be acting like you don't."

"Burned," Rome sang.

"Aww, baby, why you gotta do me like that?"

I laughed and hooked my pinky around Rimmel's.

"C'mon, Smalls." Romeo wrapped one arm around her middle and lifted her off the bed. "Trent needs to get looked at."

"See you in the morning." She gave me a little wave.

I frowned. I wasn't going to be here in the morning.

Romeo seemed to read my thoughts, because he stopped and turned, moving like his wife weighed nothing at all. "Family meeting first thing."

God. What the hell was it with him and family meetings?

I think we pretty much just said it all.

"Just 'cause I'm gay doesn't mean I want to keep talking about my feelings," I said.

Out in the hall, I heard a very familiar laugh. I closed my eyes because the sound pierced my soul.

He was so close.

Yet so far away.

Romeo and Rimmel left the room, and B followed. Ivy pointed her finger at me, stern. "No more yelling and no more holes in the wall. I just got Nova back to sleep."

I swore beneath my breath. "I'm sorry, Ives. I didn't mean to wake the baby."

"You can pay me back by letting Braeden's mom look at you."

I groaned.

"And hey?" Ivy said from the doorway. "The next time you want to get in a fight, maybe just don't."

I smiled. It reminded me of the time last spring break when a bottle cap sliced her foot open and I'd said something similar.

Caroline Walker, B's mom and a professional nurse, passed Ivy on her way in. The thought of all her poking and prodding was enough to make me shrink against the pillows and pull the blankets up a little higher.

Well, that and the fact I was in my damn boxers.

"I told them not to call you."

She glanced at me and frowned. "Well, from the looks of you, it's good they did."

A small kit in her hand hit the table beside the bed, and she clicked on the overhead light to go with the lamps already on in the room.

"I'm really not—" I started, but the words died on my tongue. All my attention went to the doorway where Drew hovered.

He acted like he wanted to come in, but at the same time, he didn't. I knew the feeling.

I sat up a little so I could glance around to see his bandaged hand. I was glad it was taken care of. His eyes swept my face like they were hungry for a glimpse of me. A stark note of worry floated in the blue of his gaze.

I leaned back against the headboard and looked back at Caroline. "Thanks for coming."

I felt rather than saw Drew relax. Just knowing I was going to let her look at my injuries made him feel better.

It was all I needed to submit.

Caroline picked up the no-longer-cold cold-pack and carried it over to where Drew watched. "Would you mind getting him another one?"

"Sure."

Before he left, I felt his eyes again. I looked up, unable to ignore the silent call.

It was hard to remember all the reasons I broke it off with him when he looked at me like this. It was hard to justify my reasons.

It was definitely hard to love someone.

But with Drew, it was impossible to stop.

Drew

Never in a million years.

That's how often I thought life would lead me here.

Since the minute I was conceived, my life was planned out for me. Hell, it might as well have been back in the day when parents arranged their children's lives before they were even grown based on land agreements, family obligations, and money.

Even though I never really fought the ideals my parents upheld, I never really liked them either. Even so, if asked what I actually wanted from my life, my answer wouldn't have resembled this.

However.

Even admitting life was nothing like I ever planned or thought I wanted…

I learned something tonight.

I learned why I never really fought what my parents always pushed me toward. Up until now, there was never anything I cared enough about to fight for.

Then I met Trent.

I fell in love with my best friend.

It's a good damn thing I was a fighter.

I'd fight for him.

I'd fight for me.

I'd fight for us.

Downstairs, I tossed the now-warm cold-pack and reached into the freezer for an icepack. It would probably stay cooler longer. I didn't mind coming down and changing them out as often as needed, but every time I did that, I had to walk out of the room.

As angry with Trent as I was right now for breaking things off between us and with the guys who jumped him, anger wasn't all I felt. My insides were rattled.

Worried.

Scared.

I could literally feel some of my joints vibrating beneath my skin. It left me slightly unsteady, off balance. It was sort of like chugging a giant Slurpee and chasing it with a king-size candy bar. But instead of a sugar rush, I was having an emotional rush. My body was buzzed, reacting physically to all the angst of tonight.

I wanted to be with Trent, to be able to look at him whenever I needed to reassure myself he was here and okay. I wanted the constant reassurance he wasn't gone from my life, that we were still tethered together despite what he declared.

A guy knew he loved someone when all he could think about was being in the same room with them, even knowing they didn't want him there.

He wants you there, my subconscious whispered. Trent might say he didn't, but I knew different. I saw it in his eyes when I stood in the doorway of the room. I felt it deep inside.

"How's the hand?" Ivy asked, stepping into the kitchen.

"It's fine," I replied, pulling out a towel to wrap around the icepack. The scrapes and cuts from putting my hand through the wall were the last thing on my mind. "Thanks for bandaging me up."

"You're gonna fight for him, right?"

I followed the abrupt change in conversation with ease and abandoned the task in front of me. My gaze swung around to pin my sister with a steady look. "You think I wouldn't?"

Her elbows were resting on the island and her chin was in her hands. Perched on the top of her head was a high ponytail that was slightly crooked, and rogue strands of blond hair framed her face. "I think I want you to know I want you to."

I felt my lips curve up into a half smile. "Well, if you want me to."

My attempt to somehow lighten this entire night, my thoughts, this conversation was not received.

"It's been really hard for you, huh?" She straightened from the counter and stepped forward, toward me.

I'd been silent a long time. Never spoke about what I was and wasn't feeling. Never let on that maybe I was struggling with feelings no one else knew about.

Except, according to the fam, everyone knew.

Everyone saw the invisible pull between T and me. They felt the ripples in the air between us.

All this time, I'd felt alone; I had no one to talk to.

I wasn't alone. Neither was Trent.

I shrugged. "It's been hard, but it's also been really easy."

"Love is easy and hard at the same time," Ivy mused.

I nodded. Love was a conundrum, a paradox. Loving Trent was incredibly easy. I did it without thought, without effort. But everything that came with those automatic feelings—that's where the effort came in.

"You're really okay with this?" I asked. My sister had already given T and me her blessing. But maybe I needed some reassurance.

"With you being in love? I'm more than okay with it."

I pursed my lips and gave her a look. While I appreciated her pragmatic view, I didn't want it right then. I wanted a real conversation.

She made a rude sound and hopped up on the island to sit. "I was surprised when I first noticed the way your relationship with him developed. But the more I thought of it, the more I watched you both, it seemed so obvious."

I started to say something, but she held up her hand and gave me a *be quiet* look. "The right kind of love is supposed to bring out the best in people. It adds to your life, fills in all those gaps you didn't even realize were there. Trent does that for you, doesn't he?" She tilted her head to the side and watched me.

I nodded slow, realizing T did exactly that.

"Then it doesn't matter who you found it with. It doesn't matter he doesn't have boobs."

I laughed out loud.

She giggled, then turned serious again. "You found something some people wait their entire life for. I'd much rather you be happy and so in love with a man than have some mediocre relationship with a woman."

"Not everyone is going to see it that way."

"Are you worried about everyone or someone more specific?"

I glanced away, back down to the ice lying in front of me. My sister knew me well. "I don't want to tell him."

"We have great parents. They'd do anything for us, but they were always so strict," Ivy replied. "I think you felt their pressure more than me and Camden. You've been living up to Dad's ideals for a long time, Drew. I don't think I quite understood what it was like for you until you moved here."

"It wasn't terrible," I told her, but I couldn't disagree entirely.

"I regret not seeing sooner. I regret not being there for you more."

"Hey." I pushed away from the counter and moved to where she was sitting on the island. "Big brothers take care of little sisters, not the other way around."

She made a face like I knew she would. "That's the dumbest thing I've ever heard, and I've heard a lot of dumb crap."

"Well, you are married to Braeden," I muttered.

She smacked me in the chest, and I grinned.

"We're both grown adults. I'm not a little girl, Drew. You've always been there for me, and now it's my turn to be there for you."

"I love you, Ives." I wrapped an arm around her shoulders and pulled her to my chest. Both her arms locked around my back and squeezed. "And you are there for me. In all the ways I need you to be," I whispered in her ear.

She didn't say anything else for a few long moments, instead just pressing her face against my chest and hugging me.

I never really thought of it until right now, but being in a relationship with Trent didn't just affect him and me. It affected our entire family.

Suddenly, the family meeting Romeo declared we have in the morning didn't seem quite so unnecessary.

"I want to be there when you tell him," Ivy said, pulling out of my embrace.

I shook my head. "I don't know, Ives." It was going to be a hard conversation. She didn't need to deal with that. She didn't need to see a side of our father that was basically unknown. "I'm not sure I'm ready to tell Dad."

To tell anyone really. The people in this house were the only people I'd felt comfortable enough sharing with.

But I was beginning to think that choice was being taken out of my hands.

"No one in this house is going to say anything. You and Trent can decide how and when you want to tell people, and we'll support you. I'll support you."

I pulled her close again and pressed a kiss to her hairline. I was still rattled inside. I would be until I was with Trent and I knew he wasn't going to try and run. But this was good. Having some backup in the form of family went a long way in easing some of the havoc inside me.

As if Ivy understood those very basic feelings I never voiced, she said, "I never doubted you would fight for him. He needs you to."

I picked up the ice and nodded. "Yeah, I know he does."

"I'll see you in the morning," she said.

On my way out of the kitchen, I snagged the first aid kit and tucked it beneath my arm. Walking up the stairs, I couldn't help but think about all the times Trent fought for me and I didn't even know it. All the times he put the way I felt before himself. The weeks of verbal abuse from Conner at the frat he turned a deaf ear to and never said a word. Even the way he was fighting now, pushing me away.

A lot of people might argue right now that T was being weak.

He wasn't.

He was still the bravest guy I'd ever known.

That's why it was so important I fight for him now.

Even the bravest of men sometimes needed someone else's strength.

Four

Trent

Fractured.

Cracked.

Not whole.

Will heal, but never as it was before.

That was the prognosis for my ribs.

For my entire life.

Caroline didn't stay too long. She poked and prodded and asked a bunch of questions. None of them were personal. None of them were curious. It made me wonder how much B told her, if she knew the why I was like this.

When she was done, she listened to my chest one last time, asking me to breathe deeply and exhale. It hurt like fucking hell. 'Course, that was normal. Having a cracked rib or two was going to make it painful to breathe. Hell, I was lucky the rib didn't break all the way and puncture an organ—like a lung. If that were the case, I'd be in the hospital right now, not lying in Drew's bed.

I liked his bed.

I might even argue it was my favorite place.

Maybe being in the hospital would have been easier.

"Remember what I said." Caroline drew back and placed her stethoscope in her bag. "Anti-inflammatory, limited movement, and come to the hospital if you start to feel worse in any way."

"Got it." I agreed, hoping to head off another review of the long list of symptoms I needed to look out for.

"Keep those cuts clean." She went on and glanced at the butterflied gash at my hairline. "Ice the eye and maybe the lip."

She seemed to be rambling suddenly, like now that her instruments were put away and her official exam was over, she was becoming less robotic.

"I'm fine, Ms. Walker," I said gently and placed a hand on her arm. "Thank you for coming over, especially this late."

She smiled. "I'll always come," she said low. She covered my hand with her free one. "I'm so sorry this happened."

I made a dismissive sound. "I'm a tough guy. I can handle it."

"You shouldn't have to."

"How much did Braeden tell you?" I asked, curious.

"He didn't have to say anything. The look on Drew's face when I walked in the house said it all."

Everyone kept saying that.

Damn. Drew and I would suck ass at poker.

"He's pretty upset," I said for lack of knowing what else to say.

"It's hard to see someone we love in pain."

"Yeah, well the pain isn't going anywhere." I muttered, a thought I accidentally spoke out loud.

"You know what the best medicine for pain is?" she asked, giving my hand a squeeze before releasing me to stand.

"Beer?" I asked, hopeful.

She laughed lightly. "No," she argued. "The only thing strong enough to chase away pain is love."

"Love *is* pain," I told her.

"Yes. But some of our greatest pain becomes our greatest strength."

Maybe if anyone else had said that, I would have scoffed. Maybe I would have been able to justify her words so they didn't seem so profound.

But Caroline Walker knew great pain. Looking at her now, I knew all the strength and acceptance I saw in her eyes was a direct result of her past. Once upon a time, she'd been the victim of someone's love.

She'd almost died beneath the fists of his version of love.

If anyone in this world deserved to be jaded and against love, it was this woman. A woman who was beaten and abused, who had to rebuild not only her life, but the life of her young son.

Yet she wasn't.

Caroline stood here whole and strong, telling me, practically urging me, not to give up on Drew. If she could find it in herself to love and be loved after everything she lived through, then I couldn't possibly argue.

Maybe I should listen.

Humbled, I said nothing as she gathered up her things.

"I'll stop by in a couple days to check on you, make sure you're doing what I said."

"You don't have to do that. I promise I will."

"I know. But it will give me another excuse to see my granddaughter." She winked.

I smiled. "In that case, I might need a few checkups."

"I always knew I liked you."

I chuckled and it made me cough, which made me grimace. Damn ribs.

"Is he okay?" Drew's deep voice carried through the room, but it was his presence that filled it. With my hand still wrapped around my middle, I watched him enter.

He moved with purpose, not quite hurried, but not exactly relaxed. The shirt he was wearing still had smears of my blood on it from when he used it as a rag. It didn't bother me to see because it wasn't his blood and also because he didn't even think about stains or seemed grossed out they were there. He hadn't rushed from the room to change, to get me off him.

Like every part of me was welcome to him.

Even the bad parts.

I was showing a lot of bad parts tonight.

But I was also showing a lot of good. Protecting Drew was the best thing I could do.

His dark-blond hair was tasseled and wrecked, his hands filled with first aid supplies, ice, and a bottle of pain reliever.

Earlier, he hesitated on the threshold of the room, peeking in but not staying. Now he barged right in. The sound of my coughing was all it took to make him forget he was pissed with me.

I took a few shuddering breaths, trying to calm my strained chest as my eyes locked on him and refused to let go. He was so incredibly good-looking. A visual representation of everything I could ever dream of, all wrapped up in one blue-eyed, dimpled, scruffy-jawed package.

I already missed rubbing my palm over those jaws. They were shadowed and scratchy looking, like the stress from tonight had made the hairs go awry and stand on end.

"He's fine." Caroline assured him. "That's just a symptom of the rib fracture."

"So they're broken," Drew said, his voice calm and deadly.

Well, that wasn't a good sound.

"Not completely broken. Just cracked. That's a good thing. It will make the healing a little faster and will cause less complications."

"What about his head?" Drew asked, still watching me. His eyes were hungry, but they were also focused. He wasn't looking at me so much as measuring me, like he was trying to decide if I really was okay.

"No concussion," Caroline replied.

"Told ya," I grunted.

The sound of my surly voice snapped his eyes to my face. Everything else fell away when he looked at me like that—with his heart in his eyes.

It hurt, but it was the kind of pain I'd become addicted to.

Never ever had the words *I love you so much it hurts* been truer.

The push-and-pull effect I always felt with him took center stage and confusion tugged at my heart strings.

Caroline cleared her throat and stepped up toward Drew. "You should probably stay with him tonight. Watch him, you know, in case of complications."

Right in the center, in the deepest part of the blue, Drew's eyes flared. The tug-of-war turned in his favor, and I knew I'd lost this round. At least for tonight.

Caroline had just given him an excuse to stay close a little bit longer.

She'd given me one, too.

Hell. Even though I knew I didn't need a babysitter, tonight I wasn't going to argue. I was content to lose. It really wasn't a loss anyway; it was a reprieve.

"I'll watch him," Drew vowed, his voice slightly husky. When his eyes left me and went to her, the muscles in the back of my neck relaxed a little. "I'll call you if anything seems to get worse."

"Call anytime." Caroline agreed, giving me a parting glance. I could almost see the smile in her eyes. She thought she'd been clever setting us up for some time alone. She was, because neither Drew nor I would call her out on it. If we did, we wouldn't be able to pretend.

I was so incredibly tired of pretending.

On her way out, she shut the door behind her. It closed with an audible click.

The two of us stared at each other, neither moving.

Finally, his chest seemed to deflate with pent-up sentiment. "You broke up with me. I *don't* break up with you. Everyone in this house knows we're more than friends. Your beat-up face makes me want to pound a bottle of vodka—"

"Isn't that a happy little list." I was sarcastic because showing my true emotions in that moment made me feel far too vulnerable.

Drew shuffled all the stuff he was holding into one hand and held up the other, stopping me. "Can we just forget it all tonight?" His voice was weary. He sounded exactly the way I felt. "Can it just be like it was before, at least until morning?"

"How was it, Forrester?" I whispered.

A glutton for punishment. That was me. I knew exactly what it was like between us. It was being a part of something so much bigger than yourself. It was that feeling of rightness a person got when something settled in their gut. This wasn't going to make anything any easier.

It would only make it harder.

"It was complete."

I lifted my eyes back to his.

Those three words almost matched another three he said to me just hours before. I wasn't sure which were better. *I love you* or *it was complete.*

They both knocked me off center. They both grounded me.

His feet were silent on the carpet when he stepped forward. As he spoke, he set down the items in his hands, one by one.

"Just me and you. Just this room. Just the dark and the sound of your breathing. Us. Together."

I swallowed. *My God, I want that.*

"It doesn't change anything." I warned him.

"You wanna have it out?" Drew challenged without heat. "We will. And I'll win. Losing you is *not* an option."

I tipped my head toward the ceiling and closed my eyes. My face hurt. My chest hurt. My head hurt…

Losing you is not an option.

Suddenly, he was beside me, filling up his side of the bed. The heat he radiated and the familiar scent of leather and the Fastback was like the first taste of home a person got after too long spent away. My chin angled down when I looked at him, my eyes thirstily gulping up every feature.

"Here," he said quietly and lifted a wrapped ice pack between us. Gently, he pressed it against my swollen eye, and I expelled a sigh of relief.

"That feels good," I murmured, allowing the cold pressure to combat some of the burning tightness.

"I need this tonight." The naked candor in his voice had every cell in my body enraptured. "I need you."

He used the only thing in this entire universe that could sway me.

Him.

"Just tonight." I agreed, turning slightly so I could look at him with my good eye.

The second I moved, he adjusted, folding his legs in front of him between us, his knees brushing against my side. The ice pack against my face stayed firmly in place with the perfect amount of pressure. Not so much it hurt, but enough to do the job.

Honestly, I wasn't doing this just for him. I wanted it, too. Just having him beside me felt like bliss.

Ignorance is bliss.

Pretending is denial.

I hated both.

But in this moment, I hated reality more.

Drew's long-fingered hand slid across my abs. The muscles quivered beneath his touch. My eye slid closed as I reveled in the feel of him against me.

Funny how I'd only lived with his touch for a week, such a short amount of time in the span of my entire life. But it eclipsed all others. How quickly it became the most singular desired sensation I'd ever known.

No one would ever touch me the way he did. No one would ever electrify and soothe me at the very same time the way Drew did.

Carefully, he tugged at my arm still folded over my side. I fought the request a single second, in a slight moment of panic.

It almost seemed like my arm was holding my entire self together, like it was somehow a guard to the deepest part of myself.

It was too late to try and guard myself. Drew had already slipped past all my defenses.

My arm slid down and my palm fell open. He tangled our fingers together, wrapped his around mine, and rested them over my abdomen.

Beneath my fractured ribs, my heart ached. It ached with love and loss.

"Don't think about it," Drew whispered as if he could read my mind.

It was unsettling, and I glanced at him. My thoughts had always been my own. No one had ever been able to read them before.

He nodded. He could.

"Tonight is ours," he reminded me, the pad of his thumb stroking over the back of my hand.

I gave in completely. I surrendered it all.

Maybe I shouldn't have, but like I said… As much as I hated pretending, sometimes pretending was a beautiful lie.

Five

Drew

Trent was not easy.

In fact, Trent was about as easy as asking a hive of bees for their honey.

I wasn't talking about on the surface, because in that sense, T was easy. He got along with everyone (except Lorhaven) and he made everyone feel at ease in his presence. I used to think it was because that's just the way he was; he had that kind of personality everyone meshed with.

Maybe some of it was that. But it was more.

He was more. Trent had a quiet understanding about him. A quiet way of making everyone feel accepted. He left people better than when he found them. Whether it were as simple as a kind word, a smile, or a listening ear. His quiet demeanor wasn't a flaw; it worked to his advantage. Those who listened were far wiser than those who only spoke.

I'd been learning about him since the day we met. I hadn't always realized it or even known it was happening, but now I did. It was like being taught how to tie a shoe, not being able to get the hang of it until one day I created a bow.

Today was my bow.

It might be a little crooked, it might be a little loose, but it was a bow all the same.

Trent was so understanding because he himself wasn't understood. He had the ability to make people feel at ease with themselves because he knew what it was like to be conflicted. He listened because his mind was the loudest, and he accepted others because he himself felt unaccepted.

How much of himself had he sacrificed over the years? How selfless could one man be before it became detrimental to his own well-being?

The surprise in his hazel eyes when he realized I understood how he was feeling was genuine. So was the fear. It made me equal parts determined and sad. Sad because he was so used to protecting himself, silently observing, that he didn't know how to react when he realized all this time, I'd been silently observing him. It was glaringly obvious no one had ever taken the time to learn how the true Trent ticked.

Or maybe others had tried.

Others had failed.

I was determined. Determined to show him I wasn't like everyone else. I wasn't going to let him push me away. I was going to give him all the consideration he gave me.

Starting with tonight.

Though he'd never admit it, the fact he gave in and agreed to being here like this was proof he wanted me.

We just sat for a while, my knees pressed against his side as I held the ice to his face with one hand and wrapped the other around his. The sight of his injuries was physically painful for me. The bruises and the dried smears of blood were reminders of the way he'd looked when my headlights first illuminated his body in that parking lot.

I don't think a person can ever be prepared for that. For seeing someone they love—someone who had never been anything but strong and capable—look so broken.

Broken, but not beaten.

I think that hurt worse. Because even in the battered, unstable state he was in, I still saw him fight. He fought for balance; he struggled to stand. Even as he bled and hurt, he refused to lie down and give in.

Fuck Con.

Fuck the guys at Omega.

I might be a grown-ass man. I might not even go to that college. But I would never be too grown to protect my person. I would never be too mature to extract revenge. There were some things a man just couldn't lie down and take.

This was one of those things.

I was so angry I couldn't really think. I was too consumed with the man beside me to really formulate a plan.

But I would. And just like on the track, I wouldn't back down.

I wasn't sure how long we'd been sitting here, but it was long enough that the fingers on my hand holding the ice had gone numb from the cold. Slowly, I lifted the towel and lowered it off his skin.

"How's it feeling?" I asked soft, studying the still swollen and angry-looking black-and-blue eye.

"Better," he replied, glancing over.

His hair dropped over his forehead like it too was exhausted. Some of the strands fell across the bandaged gash. I reached out and pushed them back.

Trent's eyes closed with the touch, and my stomach dipped a little.

Even though I didn't need to, I repeated the action, pushing back his hair a little farther.

He sighed.

Reluctantly, I pulled my hand from his and snagged a bottle of water off the nightstand, uncapped it, and held it to his lips. He reached for the bottle, but I pushed his hand back and titled the plastic until cool water touched his lip.

Trent's hazel eyes fixed on mine as he drank, slow, cautious sips. When a drop of water escaped and trailed over the rounded softness of his lower lip and down across his chin, I used it as an invitation to lean over and swipe it away.

"My blood is on your shirt," Trent rasped, pulling back from the drink.

"I know."

"Kiss me." The request seemed to rip right out of him. You know that place I mentioned he never let anyone see?

With deliberate care, I capped the water and slowly set it aside. When I turned back, he was watching me, hunger and nervousness in his gaze.

It was a painful thing to want someone so much but to constantly deny yourself. It was even more so to let yourself believe the person you wanted so badly returned the desire.

I leaned forward, bracing my arm on the mattress on the other side of his waist, caging him in without touching him.

The back of his head hit the headboard, and his Adam's apple bobbed in his throat. The tip of my tongue wet my lips so they would slide right over his.

They did.

Oh, they did.

Trent held himself still; he didn't kiss me back. If I didn't know him, I might have taken that the wrong way, but I did know him.

I took his stillness right to my heart. It pierced like a clear piece of glass slicing right into that tender spot on the bottom of your foot.

He was taking something in that moment. Something just for him. Something he really wanted.

I was flattered. I was overwhelmed.

It was the first thing I'd ever seen him take.

Yeah, maybe it was just a kiss. But it wasn't. It was so so much more.

I poured everything into that kiss. Everything into my lips as I rubbed them softly over his. The one side was puffy, and I took a little care there, licking over it with my tongue, making sure it was good and slick so he didn't feel any kind of pain.

Between kisses, I would lift my head just a fraction of an inch and tilt my head a different way. The change in direction enhanced the kiss; it made certain I touched every last centimeter of his mouth.

He reveled in it. His body, which he'd held with stiffness and pain up until now, went boneless against the mattress. Small sounds I don't think he even heard vibrated the deep part of his throat.

I sensed rather than saw his hands fist into the sheets at his sides with restraint, as if it took everything in him just to take and not give back.

But, oh, he was giving. He was giving me so much by just reacting. If I hadn't already fallen in love with him, I would have right at that moment.

In fact, I think I fell a little harder.

It was a heady thing to be so incredibly wanted. To be the balm to a wounded soul, the answer to someone's prayer.

"Forrester." My name ripped from his lips when I sat back and shook out my trembling arms.

"Frat boy," I answered, and a second of panic almost ruined the moment pressing in around us. I wasn't supposed to call him that anymore.

Sure, he said he didn't like it, but we both knew that was a lie. He loved it when I called him that. It was a term of endearment, something only I ever got away with. But now, to him, it was a slur. A connection to the men who jumped him.

I felt my eyes widen. His own cleared; a little of the passion glazing over his body cleared.

"It was—" *An accident.*

"No." He stopped me and brushed the pad of his thumb across my lower lip. "You can call me that. You can call me whatever the hell you want, and I'll always answer."

"If it reminds you…" I began, and he shook his head.

"It reminds me of who I am to you. Only you."

"Only me," I echoed and went back for more of his lips.

This time, he kissed me back, his palms sliding over my jaw and holding. I smiled a little inside when he rubbed at the stubble and groaned.

The next thing I knew, he was holding my head and dragging his teeth down my jaw and kissing across my neck. I tossed my head back to give him better access as he sucked at the skin and made me moan.

The sound seemed to snap him out of his trance. His body stiffened and pulled back. My eyes sprang open, disappointed at the absence of his lips.

"Shit," he swore and pushed my head back so he could stare at my neck. He grunted. "No mark."

"That's disappointing."

Trent frowned. "I'm not gonna mark you where everyone will see."

"Right. 'Cause you don't want people to know you love me." My voice was bitter, and I pulled away from him.

"I don't want you to be punished for this." His voice begged me to understand.

My heart refused.

I shoved off the bed and paced the room. How easy it was to forget tomorrow. How easy it was to live in denial.

How easy it was for reality to come back and rip everything away.

Frustrated, I swung around. "I wanted that mark," I said angry. "I wanted something of you. Something I could look at..." My voice trailed away, and I shook my head.

"Something what?" Trent pushed.

I turned away.

"Something of me that would be here when I leave?" The pain in his voice was as real as the stuff building in my chest.

"Maybe," I whispered but didn't turn around.

"Come here, Forrester." The commanding tone in the words was almost undeniable.

I looked over my shoulder at him. I didn't see the bruises and the Band-Aids. I didn't see his scraped knuckles or the smear of red beneath his lip (guess I kissed him a little too hard).

All I saw was the look in his eyes.

I rotated, stepping toward the bed.

"Lose the shirt," he ordered.

With one hand, I yanked it over my body and dropped it at my feet. The second my knees made contact with the mattress, he moved. Without thought to his injuries, Trent palmed my waist and pushed me down. I didn't fight him one ounce, so it didn't cost him much strength.

Strong, defined thighs straddled my hips, and when his weight sank onto me, I bit back a groan because my cock was hard and the pressure of his body was heaven.

"Where do you want it?" he rumbled, dragging his fingers down my chest and across my sides.

"What?" All my attention was on his chest, his wide, strong shoulders.

He pinched my nipple lightly and rolled it around between his fingers. I groaned and arched up slightly, totally lost now. I had no idea what the fuck he was asking me, and I didn't care.

"Here?" he asked, trailing a finger along my hipbone. "Or here?" He gave my nipple another tug.

I made an incoherent sound and shut my eyes.

The nipple was still a hard pebble, tingling with desire when he let go and trailed up a short distance. "No," he whispered. "I think here."

Trent's big body came down, pinning me against the bed, and his lips locked onto my chest. On my pec, not far from the nipple he'd been teasing before.

At first, he swirled his tongue over the flesh and dampened it, kissing softly, and nibbled at the skin. Then the pressure increased as he sucked the entire spot into his mouth.

He was giving me what I wanted.

Both my hands locked onto his head. My fingertips dug into his scalp, and I pushed his face deep into my chest as he sucked.

"Don't stop," I growled, taking it all, even the tinge of pain when he obeyed and went deeper.

It was so satisfying, his mouth on me, knowing when he lifted his head, I would have a mark of where he'd been. I emptied my mind and just felt the pressure of him sucking, felt the pleasure/pain combination with soul-tingling emotion.

"Right there," I whispered and arched into him more.

I didn't want him to stop, but he did. Not all at once, but gentling so it was just a soft kiss before lifting his head.

"More, T," I demanded, refusing to let go of his head.

He chuckled briefly against my skin but then pulled back. "You're going to have a bruise for a week, man. No more."

It wasn't enough.

Trent pushed up off me, his body stiff, his movements controlled.

"*Fuck*," I swore. I was supposed to be taking care of him right now, not demanding shit.

"I'm fine." He started to laugh, but it turned into a gasping kind of cough.

Quickly, I slid out from beneath him and wrapped an arm around his waist, offering to take some of his weight as he settled back against the pillows.

"I'll get more ice," I said once he was still, and I reached for the towel.

"No," he caught my hand. "Stay here."

Guess I wasn't the only one who didn't want to let him out of my sight tonight.

I palmed the first aid kit and rummaged around, finding one last cold pack. I held it up like it was a trophy before rolling it around between my hands and bursting open whatever it was inside that made it cold.

Once it was applied to the black-and-blue part of his side, I left the bed again to change out of my jeans and into a pair of gym shorts.

I wasn't shy about it either. In fact, I felt his eyes when I fished around for shorts, so I tossed them on the bed and began unbuckling my jeans, almost like I was giving him a show.

Okay, not almost. I was.

I wanted to tempt him. I wanted to torture him a little. Make him see what he was trying to give up.

My thumbs hooked into the waistband, and I pushed down the material. I had to give it an extra tug to get them past my junk, which was still rock hard from him straddling my hips.

Even across the room, I felt the smolder in his gaze. His eyes locked on the most evident part of my desire and held.

Anyone who said cocks didn't have a mind of their own were liars. Sure, most of the time, they only thought about sex and pleasure, but never as much as when the person who won their loyalty was within reach.

Yeah, loyalty.

My dick was a loyal fellow.

No, you may not call him Lassie.

I was positive, even after tonight, tomorrow my body would only respond to Trent. It was only him I would want.

Realizing that was overwhelming. It was jarring.

In the beginning, it was confusing.

Confusion came from conflict. From not knowing what you wanted. From being unable to *admit* what you wanted.

I might not have been ready to tell my father about the person my heart chose to claim. I might not have even been ready to tell anyone outside this house, but it didn't make what I was feeling any less true.

Any less real.

I wasn't confused anymore because I knew.

Trent was absolute.

Hell, my dick was at attention and my boxers looked like a tent as it pointed to him. The jeans hit the floor when I let go, and I glanced at the shorts on the end of the bed.

Just tonight.

Isn't that what we said?

I wanted so badly to ditch the boxers and slip beneath the sheets completely naked, but I didn't. It wasn't because I thought Trent wouldn't like it (he was a guy; of course he would like it), but because he was hurting and now wasn't the time for messing around.

Even if all he was determined to give us was one more night.

I reached for the shorts, suddenly feeling incredibly grumpy.

"Can you hit the light? My fucking head hurts," Trent remarked.

I dropped the clothes and crossed to the light switch. The room went into shadows but wasn't completely dark because the lamp on my side of the bed was still on. I reached for it, too.

"Leave that one." He stopped me.

I frowned. "You still got a couple hours before I can give you more pain reliever. Maybe the dark—"

"I want to see you," he said in a rushed, quiet tone.

I didn't acknowledge the admission with words, but everything inside me quaked. I'd been with lots of women in my life. Getting one in bed was never a problem for me. I drove fast, had dimples and blue eyes… Plus, I was good in bed.

I wasn't being arrogant. Okay, maybe I was.

Even so, it was the truth.

So obviously, I'd had some good sex. My body understood what pleasure felt like.

But never before had I ever felt such a physical reaction to a person. No woman ever made my insides dip and tumble. No woman ever made my fingers shake and my breathing unsteady.

And it wasn't just when we were in bed.

All it took was the sound of his voice. A look. A single gesture.

Trent possessed some kind of ability to turn me inside out with the greatest of ease.

That's how I felt just then. Turned inside out. Shaken, not stirred. All because he wanted to look at me.

It was borderline insane.

But it was the best goddamned feeling I'd ever known.

"Careful." I spoke quietly and gripped the blankets to peel them down the bed. His legs were over them, and I had to slide them from beneath his body. When his hips thrust upward making room for the blankets to move, my sight zeroed in on the rock-solid bulge beneath his tight red boxer briefs.

The way the fabric molded to his shaft, I could see the slightly larger head on the tip, and it made my mouth run dry.

I cleared my throat and forced my eyes away, back up to his face. He wasn't watching me, but trying to disguise a grimace as he settled back against the mattress. A few curse words dropped into the air between us. I jetted forward and slid my arm and some of my shoulder beneath him. Almost instantly, he relaxed against me, allowing me to support all his considerable weight.

It was a weight I would bear willingly.

I'd bear it forever if he let me.

The thought was kind of like a bitch slap to the face. Sharp and stinging. Sometimes the truth hurt. Sometimes it took something heinous to really make everything completely clear.

I'd already known I was in love with T.

I'd fought my feelings for a long time.

We'd even begun exploring who we were to each other… And now he was hurt.

Beaten and aching.

The roughed-up shape he weas in made everything so incredibly clear.

I wanted him. For now. For always.

Trent would always be my ultimate adrenaline rush. Not even a car or racetrack could beat him. He'd crossed the finish line in my heart a long time ago.

"I love you." It came out like it was the first time I'd said it. Hell, it almost still felt like the first time.

Trent affected me profoundly. I wondered if I would ever get used to loving him or if it would always astonish me.

"Drew…" Trent warned, his voice wobbly and apprehensive.

My back and shoulder hit the headboard, but instead of easing my arm and side from underneath him, I settled back farther and spanned my fingers out at his waist, gently pushing so he would relax against me.

He did. He let me hold him. It was one of the first times we'd sat like this, with him in my arms this way. It was incredible to hold the very thing you loved most in your arms, to have it so close.

"Say it," I whispered. "Please, frat boy."

His back expanded against my chest when he inhaled. "I love you."

My eyes closed, and I was glad he couldn't see my face. I was the strong one right now, but his words… they broke me down.

My lips dropped, and I kissed the top of his shoulder as I softly looped my other arm around his waist so he was encircled.

We leaned our heads together and sat quietly while I listened to his breaths, silently making sure he was okay.

A few minutes later, he spoke. "It doesn't change anything."

I knew what he meant. I wanted to yell and put another fist through the wall. But I didn't move. I sat there calmly and held him.

How did I do it?

I realized.

I felt.

Beneath all the anger, I was calm. Calm because there was no way in hell our love wouldn't win out. We'd already been to hell and back just to make it to our first kiss.

Just because I wasn't confused anymore didn't mean Trent wasn't. He was battling inside himself. He was battling against the past and his future.

"We're not going to talk about that tonight." I stroked a hand across his hip.

Tonight wasn't caught up in the past or the future. Tonight was just the present.

And presently, I was going to love him.

Gingerly, I moved out from beneath him to pull up the covers around his legs. It wasn't lost on me his cock was still hard (I had that effect on him), and I knew from experience (he had the same effect on me) it was probably painful.

He was already in a lot of pain, but this kind of pain I could ease.

I released the blankets. My fingers moved up the top of his thigh and past the hem of his boxers. His breath caught when they kept gliding, angled toward his erection.

The second the weight of my palm covered it, he moaned. My fingers wrapped around it, performing a single jerk. A breath hissed between his lips.

"This too much for you right now, frat boy?" I whispered.

His eyes blazed with golden highlights and the heat of a thousand flames. He shook his head once, then said nothing at all.

I moved to my knees to carefully work the boxers down over his hips and legs. I threw them across the room, glad to be rid of the barrier between us, and dipped my head.

I wasted no time, but latched right on. With one hand fisted at the base of his rod I held him while I took him deep into my mouth. Trent shuddered, and I paused, leaving him deep inside my throat before slowly dragging my lips up. I kept up the same rhythm for a while. Taking him deep, then slowly letting him go, only to claim him completely all over again.

It was torturous. For him and for me.

His hand fisted in my hair and his other a pillow. When he started squirming impatiently, I changed tactics, not wanting him to move around too much. I released his shaft and climbed between his legs so I could gently massage his sack.

I loved the softness of the skin there, the delicate, vulnerable flesh. A man's balls were the most sensitive spot on his entire body. The urge to protect them was built in. The urge to cradle T's in my palms and take them lovingly between my lips was intense.

So I did.

He trusted me here, at this point on his body. I cupped them and kissed them. I suckled the skin until they tightened up with the need to release.

Occasionally, as I worked his balls, I rubbed his cock. I stroked it, teased it, and I fondled his head.

The sounds of pleasure he made only spurred me on and fueled my desire to give him bliss, to show him just how all in I really was.

I pulled back slightly, wrapped my hand completely around his dick, and began slowly jacking him. His hips rocked upward, and a low moan rumbled in his chest. I anchored my free hand around his hips and held him against the bed.

My tongue caressed its way down his taint and then circled around his puckered hole. His legs went stiff, and I licked again, this time fully, completely over his entrance.

My name broke through the silence of the room, and I stroked his cock again. On either side of my head, his legs began to tremble, and I took it as a sign to keep going.

We'd played around back here before; this wasn't the first time.

But this was the first time I was going full throttle with it, no hesitation, no asking… just straight to the tongue action.

Judging by the way his hand was flexed on the mattress, I would say he approved.

I made a sound, a gruff, satisfied tone, because I wanted him to know I liked this, too. I wasn't just doing it because I wanted to make him happy.

I did want to make him happy.

But this was also for me. Just like the mark he'd sucked onto my chest. It might be his pleasure right now, but these were my memories. Memories sustained even when pleasure waned.

His body relaxed into my caressing, and I used the tip of my tongue to explore his rim. The nerve endings here were sensitive and easy to please. I was surprised at the amount of full-blown pleasure a man could get from having his ass caressed by a tongue and fingers.

I wouldn't lie. It certainly made me curious as to what it would feel like to have Trent breach my body. The more I thought about it, the more intimate it seemed. No one had ever been inside me before, not like that.

But I wanted it. I wanted to be inside him, too. I wanted the honor of being the one person on this earth he trusted enough to let inside.

Inside his body. Inside his heart.

Gently, I speared him with my tongue, and he nearly came up off the bed. My laugh was throaty, and his cock jerked in my hand.

"Someone likes that," I murmured.

"I'm already tortured enough," he growled. "Finish me."

I took pity on him and let go of his cock and reached toward the nightstand. The first couple of times, I relied on T to have lube. It took me a while to get used to having it around.

Note: it didn't take any time at all to understand its pleasure.

But I was past that. I kept some here now, and I pulled it out.

"I'm not ready to finish you. I want more."

He started to rise up off the bed and grabbed his side.

"Lie back. You can't be moving around," I ordered.

He made a rude sound. "Why is it you decide to get all feisty and bold on me when I can't frickin' move?"

I tilted my head to the side and pondered the question. "Truth?" I asked, because hadn't we said we weren't going to talk about stuff tonight?

His voice was gentle. "Yes, Drew. The truth."

"Because seeing you on the ground tonight scared the shit out of me. Because seeing someone so strong and brave start to crumble was a giant wake-up call." I glanced into his eyes and then looked away. More quietly, I said, "Because you're only giving me tonight."

This time, he ignored the obvious protest in his body and shoved himself into an upright sitting position. He grabbed the bottle out of my hand and tossed it aside. When his palm cupped the side of my face, I pushed a little closer to it.

"No, Drew. I'm giving you my forever. I'm giving you my heart for my entire lifetime. I'm just not taking that from you." His thumb stroked over my cheekbone.

My stomach felt hollow, empty, like an arctic wind was blowing through.

"I don't want you doing things in this bed tonight that you aren't completely ready for. I don't want you to be down there because you think it will somehow change my mind."

"You act like me giving you the same thing, my heart *and* my body for my entire lifetime, is some kind of… hardship."

His hand fell away from my face, and I wanted to pull it back. But I couldn't. I hadn't even realized the truth behind my words, but they hit me like a bolt of lightning. Why was it okay for him to give me all of himself, but not okay for me to do the same?

"Don't you think I want that?" he asked. "I want that more than anything on this entire planet."

"I'm giving it to you and you won't take it."

"Because I want you to be safe. I want to protect you."

Frustration welled up within me.

"What hurts worse right now, your body or your heart?" I asked.

His forehead wrinkled. "What?"

"Your body or your heart?" I asked again.

His shoulders slumped. "I think you know the answer."

"Well, your heart isn't hurting from that beating. Your ribs endured a lot to protect what's beneath it. They cracked under the pressure, but they still held strong. They protected your heart. Seems like the beating they took was for nothing, because for all the sheltering they did, you are pretty fucking intent on pummeling it."

His face paled.

"You aren't protecting me right now, Trent. It isn't my body that needs the safety. Just like you, it's my heart, and it's taking a beating right fucking now." His eyes were stricken when I looked into them. "You're the one throwing the punches."

It was clear my declaration tormented him. The tone of his voice matched the look in his eyes. *"Drew."*

I nodded like I wasn't buckling under the weight of his inner struggle, like I didn't feel guilty for adding to it.

But all was fair in love and war.

If I had to fight dirty to keep him, then I'd be the dirtiest motherfucker there ever was.

"So what's it going to be, Trent?" I pressed. "Are you going to protect my heart *and* the love it holds for you, or are you going to walk away?"

Six

Trent

Body or soul.

I wished it were that easy.

He made it sound that way. He made it feel that way.

God, I love him.

On the surface, it seemed like a simple choice, but matters of the heart rarely were.

"It's not that black and white," I said, my voice gravely and deep. The guilt I felt just then, the all-encompassing urge to pull Drew into my arms and say to hell with everything else, was like trying to hold back an orgasm when the release had already begun.

"You won't let it be," Drew argued.

I guess it had been too much to think we could take an entire night and not get into this. We'd been fooling ourselves. But wasn't this what I wanted? Wasn't I tired of pretending?

Thick silence pressed in around us. He'd tossed me the ball. He'd laid down one epic argument and left me with a choice. I glanced at the mark I'd put on his chest, so near his heart. The heart he so willingly offered me.

I'd give him anything… but how could I take from him? Yes, he was offering, but just because something was offered didn't mean it was right to take.

But…

I was hurting him and I didn't want that.

"It seems like no matter what I do, you're going to get hurt," I confessed.

"There's only one kind of hurt for me that won't ever heal."

I pinched the bridge of my nose and exhaled. "Stop saying shit like that."

"Why? Because it bothers you? Because you know it's true?" His voice was argumentative, matter-of-fact.

"Of course it bothers me!" I shot out. "You're my weakness, Drew. You're the one person in this entire world I would do anything for."

"All I want is you."

"You have me," I said, weary, collapsing back against the headboard. I was exhausted and hurt in so many ways.

And I was naked.

This was a damn heavy conversation to be having without my drawers.

"Where's my damn boxers," I muttered.

"You don't need them," Drew replied.

I raised a brow. He lifted one back.

I fought a smile, but in the end, my lips curved upward.

The dimple in his cheek made an appearance, and I groaned.

"Please say you understand where I'm coming from," I pleaded.

"I understand you're an overprotective and bossy bastard."

"You flatter me," I quipped.

"We're talking in circles." Drew sighed. "I asked you a question."

"Just because the people in this house accepted us doesn't mean everyone out there will. How do I condemn you to that? How do I justify my love is worth the risk? It's not just your body, Forrester, I'm trying to protect. But it's your heart, too. What happens when you tell your father and he flips the fuck out? It's gonna crush you. What happens if your brother is sickened his brother likes dick?"

Drew's face tightened, and I knew what I was saying was crude and hard to hear. Good. It would never get easier.

"And what about your racing career, the one you're just starting? Do you think Gamble is gonna want a gay man as the face of his new sport? What if he drops you? What if you never get another opportunity like this again and you spend the rest of your life behind a computer, cut off from your father, brother, and maybe your mother? What happens when you go out and people whisper crude words, when they call you a fag and dick licker?"

He didn't say anything, just sat there and looked at me.

"You'll start to resent me," I whispered. "You'll blame me for all the shit you lost."

"Even if I lost every single one of those things you just listed, it still wouldn't add up to the single loss of you."

I was dumbstruck. So completely astounded. He told me he loved me. I knew it was true. What I hadn't realized was his love for me rivaled my love for him.

How did a man fight that?

I couldn't.

I was going to cave.

It was like all the reasons I put us through this were suddenly null and void.

"You know what I think?" he asked softly.

I gestured for him to speak.

"I think it's not just me you're protecting, but yourself."

Yes. But not from the bigots and the haters in the world. I was protecting myself from me. From all the things our relationship could do to Drew. As I said, it was he who was my weakness, and it was *his* hurt that had the power to destroy me.

"Protecting you is protecting me," I whispered.

"I really think you're the bravest man I've ever met," he confessed, almost shy.

I took it as some kind of affront, a challenge. Like he thought I was being weak by trying to push him away. "Pushing you away was brave, Drew. It took everything I had."

He nodded and reached for my hand. "I know. I don't want you to be brave for me, Trent. I want you to be brave *with* me."

"Look at me, Forrester." My eyes bore into his. "Look at my bruises and cuts. Look at the way people I've been friends with for years turned on me without even asking first if the rumors were true." I gave his hand a squeeze. "Are you up for this?"

He scooted forward on the bed, our legs bumping together. "I'm *asking* for it. I'm asking for you."

My chest felt tight, and it wasn't because of my ribs. I felt near to max capacity with emotion, as if everything we'd been through to get to this moment had been nothing but practice. My doubt and fear was waning, being replaced with a sensation of luck.

I was sitting in Drew's bed, beaten and bruised. Some people out there wouldn't accept us. Our life would never be as easy as it might have been if we just stayed friends.

It didn't even matter.

Our fingers were entwined together; his body carried the weight of mine more than once tonight. He was holding out his heart, extending it between us, offering me everything I honestly never thought I'd have.

He was so much more than I ever imagined.

How did I get so lucky? How was Drew able to look past my walls, past the façade I built for everyone to see? He saw me for who I was. For the man I was still discovering… I wasn't even sure who I would fully become.

But he seemed to see.

And he loved me.

"I can't say no to you," I whispered, my voice cracking halfway through. "Denying you anything would be like ripping out my own heart and abandoning it to the wolves."

Drew cupped his hand around the back of my head and made a sound I could only describe as intense relief. He wasn't smug he convinced me. He wasn't arrogant he'd gotten his way. When he pressed his forehead against mine and met my eyes, all I saw was gratitude.

Both our chests heaved a bit, and his fingers dug into my scalp where he held me.

"*Thank fuck*," he all but groaned.

I smiled. "If you think I'm protective now, it's probably going to get worse."

Now my defensive instincts weren't only concentrated on keeping him safe… but on my radar was *us*. Two men who shared a single heart.

Vicious wasn't even a strong enough sentiment to define how I was going to protect that.

"I don't care," he murmured, still holding my head against his. "As long as you're my person."

"And you're mine."

Drew's eyes darkened. "No more talking tonight, frat boy." Both hands grabbed my jaw and his lips covered mine.

He kissed me passionately, like we'd both jumped off a ledge into a bottomless well… His lips were the only ground I'd ever meet again. We tumbled together. Our tongues danced and caressed each other without hesitation. I rubbed my chin against his as we made out, the feel of his rough stubble causing tension to heighten inside me as my dick began to harden.

I didn't feel any pain, not even when we slowly lowered as one onto the mattress. His body covered mine, but he wasn't heavy. Drew supported all his weight on his hands and only allowed his chest and hips to brush me lightly. If my ribs weren't busted, I would have pulled him over me completely and reveled in the strength of his body.

Our hips started grinding toward each other as our cocks rubbed together. I palmed his hips and pulled them closer so his dick was pinned beside mine and there was no room to do anything but rock slowly.

His head fell to my shoulder, and I whispered, "I love you."

Drew moaned like the words only intensified his pleasure. Between us, his cock jerked. Abruptly, he pushed up, hovering just inches above me, caging me in.

I was far too big of a guy to ever feel that way, and between us, I was the protective one. But right now, I felt small. In this moment, it was as if Drew were the one protecting me.

"I want to be inside you," he declared with passion-thick words.

We'd yet to explore that far with each other; we'd barely even talked about it.

Once again, he read me. Once again, he saw my deepest thoughts and cut them off.

"This isn't just the heat of the moment." He paused. "Well, maybe a little. But we both know this is only a matter of time."

"No one said it has to be right now," I said gently, not wanting it to sound like a rebuff.

In truth, the idea of him entering me was something I thought about a lot. I wanted it. I craved it. Sure, I was curious, too. I wondered if it would be pleasurable for both of us or just the one on top. Thing was I couldn't imagine not liking anything Drew gave me. In fact, the mental image of him between my legs and filling my body made my mouth run dry and skin feel feverish.

"I want it to be right now." His eyes shifted between mine. "I…" He looked away and his jaw worked.

"Say it," I implored, rubbing my palm over his bicep.

"I want to give you the only thing I haven't yet."

"Then I'll have all of you." I liked that. I liked the commitment and trust doing something like that also represented.

He nodded. Seconds later, his expression turned a little sheepish. "And yeah… I want to claim you."

I laughed low, ignoring the pull in my chest. "Possessive bastard," I said fondly.

His straight, white teeth flashed, but it was no match for the dimple that came out to play. Without thought, I swept my thumb along the indent and pressed in, finally, finally finding out how deep that little charmer really went.

Turns out it was deeper than it looked.

It went all the way to my soul.

Drew lowered his body, supporting his upper half with his elbows, and dipped his lips. Our kiss was soft and slow. It made me feel as if I were floating underwater and everything around us was muffled except for his lips.

"Trent?" he asked against my mouth.

"Yes, Forrester," I murmured. "Take me."

When he swooped down to kiss me again, I felt the acceleration of his heart against my chest.

"I'll go slow," he whispered, pulling back. At my side, he paused, "You up for this? How bad are you hurting?"

"I'm not hurting at all," I uttered, reaching down to stroke his cock through his boxers. "You're a very good distraction."

His muscles moved beneath the smooth skin of his arm as he pushed the hair back off his face. His lips were slightly swollen and his eyes were already heavy with desire. His hand closed around the abandoned bottle of lube at the same time his tongue caressed my nipple.

The rock-hard pebble vibrated with pleasure as he nibbled at it while his hand traveled south.

Careful to avoid my injured ribs, Drew kissed his way down my body. At one point, I got a little choked up when he grazed directly over the fracture. The kiss was so soft it was barely there, like the brush of butterfly wings when one fluttered too close, then flitted away.

No one had ever treated me with so much thought and care before. It was almost my undoing.

Before settling between my knees, he tossed away the boxers. His cock sprang free with enthusiasm, and I closed my fist around it and licked my lips.

Gently, Drew pushed away my hand, pulling it up to kiss my palm before returning it to my side.

I was already wound tight, already quivering with need.

Or honestly, maybe it was nerves. This was a really big thing for us. I wanted it to be everything he wanted.

My body sank into the blankets with every stroke and lick he bestowed. I loved the way he swirled his tongue around the tip of my cock and licked at the sensitive spot just beneath my head.

When he pushed my legs wide open, I felt vulnerable, but then he was back to sucking me deep into his mouth while dragging his nails lightly over my inner thighs.

My tip starting weeping salty tears, and he lapped it up and whispered he liked the way I tasted.

Honestly, if this was all we ever did together, it would be more than enough. He satisfied me on a bone-deep level, the kind of satisfaction that stayed with me long after we left the bed, long after his hand released my cock.

I couldn't imagine it getting better.

Drew's attention moved downward, massaging and licking my sack. One finger caressed and teased my taint, rubbing so close to my anus but skirting away before I could sigh with pleasure. Tension and need built inside me. Like a cup in danger of spilling over, I felt silky drops of cum lubricate my head.

I barely registered the sound of the bottle opening, but I noticed when his hands left my skin. Seconds later, he came back, and I felt the warm sensation of slippery wetness coating my skin. I shuddered because it felt so wonderful, and Drew began prodding my ass gently.

I was no stranger to this kind of play; he'd done this before. I knew at first, there would be a moment of hesitation as my body opened up for him. I barely thought of that anymore because I knew once his slippery finger slid inside, it would find that magic spot, and my limbs would start to tingle.

My hands were shaking and my stomach fluttered when I reached for his head. My fingers threaded through his hair, and I pulled him down to me, thrusting forward. His lips slid over my dick and sucked deep.

At the very same moment, his finger delved deeper and rubbed against my prostate. I moaned low, and he started working my hole as he worked my cock.

It was sweet torture, the sensation of his hand and mouth in synch. When he slipped a second finger inside me, I rocked against it, inviting more. As he pumped me gently, his thumb caressed my taint and the sensitive nerves all around the area.

I hissed a breath, and there was a popping sound when he released my dick from his mouth and sat back.

"More?" he asked, his voice throaty.

"More." I pushed my ass against him. I felt the slippery smoothness of the lube as he added a generous amount and cautiously worked in a third finger.

I loved the care he showed. It was almost—*almost*—as good as the pads of his thick fingers nudging my prostate and making me quake.

I'd been slightly worried it might hurt, that three fingers would be too much.

I wanted more. I began rocking against him, begging.

Drew chuckled and, with his free hand, caught my cock to jack it slowly.

I gasped and nearly came up off the bed.

"You're going to come so hard tonight," he vowed, giving me a jerk.

I shuddered and fell back against the pillows. "I want more, Drew. Give me more," I begged and reached between us for his dick.

The feel of him pulling out of me was almost enough to make me weep. I'd grown used to the pressure inside, to having *him* inside me. Drew moved quickly and reached back into the nightstand and pulled out a foil-wrapped packet.

I snatched it out of his hand and ripped it open with my teeth. "Here." I crooked a finger at him, and he thrust his hips forward so I could grab his cock and roll the latex over his incredibly steely rod.

"Damn," I murmured, stroking it just because. "You're so fucking hard. You want this."

He made a sound. "I want this more than I've ever wanted anyone."

"Me, too." I released him and reached for my own length.

He made a tsking sound and pushed my hand away. His body hovered close, and he rubbed his sheathed cock against mine. Automatically, my legs spread and my hips lunged upward.

His tongue licked across my lips, and I forgot about my cock as we kissed deep.

Since I was ready and he wanted me to stay that way, his hand went back down to my ass, where he began teasing and fingering all over again.

I ripped my mouth free of his.

"Forrester," I growled.

"Me, too, frat boy," he murmured, sliding down my body. "I'm ready, too."

This could have been an awkward moment. This could have been scary and uncomfortable.

It wasn't.

We were best friends first. We knew each other too well for that to happen. I read him and he read me. It was like we were different chapters but of the same book. We had a deep enough connection and a strong enough sense of familiarity with one another to prevent any awkwardness from getting in our way.

Intimacy closed in like thick fog on a rainy morning. I shoved my legs wide, and he covered his thick and ready cock with lube. We were always very generous with the liquid. When he was done covering himself, he rubbed his slick fingers around my rim one last time before pumping my erection and making me pant.

Drew positioned against me, holding his rod at the base. "T," he rasped, "if you want me to stop—"

"I'm not gonna want you to stop."

He half smiled. "I will if you need me to."

"I know, Forrester."

I love you.

My body automatically stiffened when I felt the slick, swollen head against my sensitive skin. My teeth sank into my lower lip as I waited for that first push of penetration, for the second of pressure that came with his breech.

He didn't shove himself in, though. Instead, he rocked against my hole, back and forth, back and forth.

His hand closed around my cock, and he jacked me in the same rhythm.

"More," I asked.

He slid deeper.

A sound unlike anything I'd ever made before vibrated the back of my throat. My body stretched around him and loosened.

It felt…

Incredible.

"*Ohmymotherfuckinggod*," Drew rushed out. I could feel his body trembling, fighting to keep still.

"Drew?" I glanced up, making sure he was okay.

His eyes were closed, nothing short of bliss written on his features. Without thinking about it, he rocked a little deeper, and I moaned.

His eyes shot open with alarm, and our gazes collided.

Instead of telling him how much I liked it, I started to move, bearing down on his length and feeling every inch of him stretch and rub my inner walls.

"You squeeze me in all the right places," he murmured as his hands hit the mattress of either side of my hips.

"Move, Forrester," I urged. "Fuck me."

A growl ripped out of his chest, and his hips began to thrust.

Oh God, he was a beautiful sight above me. The way he moved was unlike anything I'd felt before. Even though it was tight, the pressure was delicious. He slid in and out, spearing me over and over with ease, and the silky moisture of the lube coated me in all the right places.

And then his swollen tip hit my prostate. My mouth opened, but no sound came out.

"T?" Drew stilled, looking down at me.

"Don't. Fucking. Stop," I ground out and shoved down on his dick.

His smile was brilliant, and he moved with renewed force. This time he was a little rougher, a little deeper, like he knew exactly where to hit.

I shuddered and grabbed for his hands. He only let me have one, linking our fingers together.

"I'm not gonna last much longer, man." He panted, pushing deep and holding himself there. "I want to see you come."

Before I could say anything, he grabbed my pulsing cock and worked it. His dick was still buried deep, and he rocked farther. His head came right up against my prostate, and my stomach muscles started to quiver.

"There," I rasped.

He repeated the same action with his hips and pressed the pad of his thumb against the base of my head.

My shoulders came up off the bed as an orgasm nearly ripped me in two. It was so powerful I felt a twinge of pain in my ribs, but even as I registered it, I forgot it.

One of Drew's hands slapped over my mouth just before I gave a yell as my body quaked and I emptied all over my chest.

God. Damn.

He left his hand over my lips until I collapsed against the bed, panting and sweating.

His hand left my cock and his hips started moving frantically, pounding in me, chasing the orgasm building in his balls.

I bore down until I felt them between my legs and a choked sound came out of his throat.

"Now." He jerked back, but I was ready for him and lifted my legs to lock them around him, pressing him deep once more.

"Trent, I can't hold it."

"Go," I told him. "I want it all."

His eyes flared, then rolled back in his head. I felt his cock pulse inside me, and a renewed sense of desire washed over me. Even with the condom, I felt his seed spill out as he trembled through the pleasure.

Even after the orgasm released him, he jerked with tiny aftershocks. Drew went boneless, all the tension left his body, and when his eyes found mine, there was wonder shining in them.

He swayed a little, like he was off balance. He was still inside me, and I wasn't ready to let that go.

"Come here." I grabbed for him and pulled him down.

He held himself stiff, not wanting to put his weight on my ribs, and I made a frustrated sound, wrapped both my arms around his body, and held him close.

"I can take it for a minute." I promised.

He sighed, and all his weight settled.

I wasn't sure what was better, lying here with him in a tangle of limbs, slick with sweat, or the orgasm that almost tore me in two.

Lie alert! I knew.

The orgasm.

But holding him like this was a close second.

A few minutes later, he lifted his head. "Please, frat boy. Please tell me you liked that."

"Uh, you're literally lying in my jizz." I patted his back. "And if you hadn't slapped your hand over my mouth, I'm pretty sure the entire house would have heard us."

"I don't even care," he muttered, his cheek pillowed on my shoulder again.

A rush of tenderness overcame me. Impulsively, I kissed his hairline. "I was worried you wouldn't like it."

It was the honest truth. It was the reason I never pushed for sex and wanted to take it slow. It was the reason I would have waited for years.

He laughed.

Seconds later, he rolled onto his side and faced me. I turned my head so I could look into his eyes. "I'd been nervous about it until tonight," he admitted.

I nodded, understanding. "Why not tonight?" I asked.

"I almost lost you."

Sometimes he spoke so honestly it made me ache.

"It made me realize the only thing I was truly scared of was anything you weren't around for."

I wanted to turn on my side and mirror his position, to bring my nose close to his. I couldn't because of my ribs, because I was sore from all the movement, but I would never admit that. I would never ever say anything to spoil what we just shared.

I settled for scooting a little closer, turning my head a little farther. I found his hand and grabbed on. "I asked the eight ball about us again," I confided.

His eyes widened. "What did it say?"

I made a face. "Don't count on it."

"Fucking eight ball." He chuckled.

"I'm beginning to think it has a problem with gays."

He threw back his head and laughed. The force of it made him roll away a little. When he glanced back at me, I nodded sagely, and he started laughing all over again.

I will never stop loving him.

Never.

He could kill a thousand people, run off with a woman, and steal all my money and my heart would still skip a beat for him.

When he was done laughing, he rolled close again.

"I learned something, too, though." I began. "The second that stupid answer floated to the surface, everything in me revolted. Even though it was the answer I wanted to see, I was hoping it would say different."

"Nothing like being told what you don't want to hear to make it crystal clear how you really feel," he surmised.

"For the record, I never really wanted to end things."

"I know." His eyes searched mine like he was looking for anything maybe I wasn't saying.

"This isn't going to be easy, Drew." I warned him again. I don't know why I felt the continued need to caution him about what being with me might cost.

His hand tightened around mine. "Like I said, the only thing I'm truly scared of is anything you won't be around for."

"I'll always be here for you." I promised.

"You and me against the world?" he asked, his tone lightening again.

I smiled. "I like our odds."

"And for the record." He began as he covered my package with his hand. "That was literally the best sex of my life. Good luck keeping me off you now."

Warmth spread through my limbs. It felt a lot like genuine happiness.

So when the voice in the back of my head began to whisper about all the things Drew and I had yet to face, I ignored it.

The sun wouldn't come up until tomorrow.

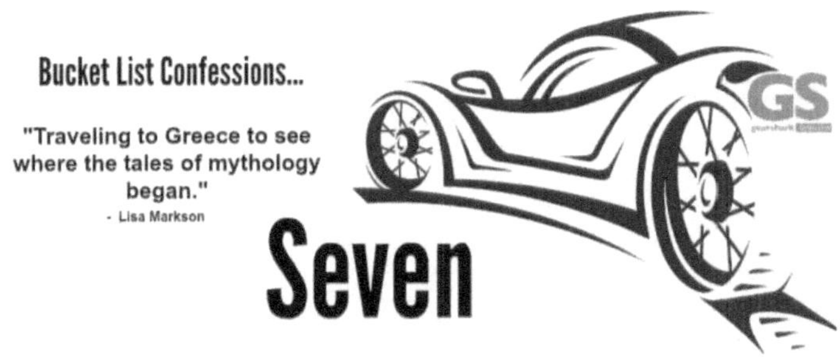

Drew

Morning came too fast. If I could have, I would've stayed in bed half the day. It was no secret I wasn't a morning person, but getting to wake up with T beside me made it even worse.

For the first time since our first weekend together, he didn't have to sneak out. I got to feel his body close by even as the sun's rays began peeking through the blinds.

Because of his injuries, I resisted the urge to wrap myself around him, and I knew he was used to doing the same. Instead, I settled for pushing along his side as tight as I dared so we were pressed together as much as possible without me jarring his body.

"Downstairs in thirty!" Romeo called through the bedroom door as he lightly pounded on the wood.

The only reason I heard was because it seriously disturbed my comfortable state.

When no one answered, Romeo knocked again.

"Okay," Trent called out, sleep thick in his tone.

Romeo stopped knocking and moved off down the hall. I groaned pathetically and rolled so I could face T. I kept my eyes closed, wanting to hold on to as much of the morning as I could before our family meeting so rudely interrupted.

Trent's laugh was deep as his palm settled over my jaw and rubbed at my stubble.

He wasn't kidding when he said he liked it. I'd never been one to keep the scruff very long, usually shaving for work, but not anymore. Anything tempted him to touch me was going to stay.

"I like not sneaking out at the crack of dawn," he murmured, still rubbing across my jaw.

"I like waking up to you," I told him, still reveling in his touch.

His lips replaced his hand. Softly they fluttered over my cheek and at the corner of my mouth. When he started to pull back, I grabbed his neck and kept him there, slipping my tongue into his mouth and kissing him deeply.

"Better than coffee." My voice was gruff when I let go.

"Something tells me you're still gonna need it," he mused, pushing back some hair that had fallen over my forehead. He touched me like I was cherished. Like he loved me so deeply I could feel it in his fingertips with every caress.

"I love you," I whispered, wanting him to know I felt the same.

"Thank you."

I smiled. Thanking someone when they said I love you wasn't likely a normal reply. In fact, I had it on pretty damn good authority if I said that to a woman, she'd probably try to corndog me.

Corndog = the official term for when a woman knees (or kicks) a dude in his goods.

T wasn't a woman. *Thank God for that.* And his response was perfect. He didn't take me for granted— us for granted. He was grateful for the way I felt, and he wanted me to know how much it meant that I'd handed over my heart.

He might have hesitated in taking it at first, but not for very long and not because he didn't want it. Trent was thankful I didn't give up even when he told me to.

"Think they'll notice if we don't go downstairs?" I asked, hopeful.

He made a rude sound. "Hells yes, they'll notice. Then they'll all be crowding in here, staring at us in bed together."

"Well, that's an unpleasant image," I muttered.

He grinned, and I was glad my eyes were finally open to see it.

"You can put off rolling out of bed for a few more minutes. I'm gonna take a shower." He started to push up off the mattress, and his mouth pulled into a taunt line.

All sleepiness vanished. I bolted up, and my eyes narrowed when I noted his stiff and slow movements.

"Fuck," I growled. "Hang on, frat boy."

Of course he didn't listen. I had to scramble to get up before him. I spider climbed over the bed and got out on his side. Once I was on my feet, he was in a sitting position with his legs thrown over the side.

I slid my shoulder beneath his arm and stood, bringing him with me. "All the soreness has set in, huh?" I asked, trying to temper my anger.

He made a gruff sound. "I'm just stiff. I'll be fine once I move around a bit."

I stepped back and looked him over. Forget tempering the anger. Just looking at him pissed me off all over again.

Not only had all his soreness set in, but so had all the bruises.

His eye was still puffy and swollen (though not swollen shut anymore); the skin around it was dark and mottled. His lip was cut and red, the corner of it still fat, and the cut on his ear was still fresh and raw-looking. I knew beneath the giant Band-Aid I'd put on his head, the gash there would probably still be raw and now bruised as well.

Since we were still naked, I was able to see the full damage to his chest and upper body. The bruise from where he was kicked in the shoulder was dark against his smooth skin and was a real contradiction to the muscles cording his body.

It was so goddamned unfair. If they hadn't jumped him, he would have wiped the floor with their asses.

His ribs—ha, his ribs. They were black and blue. Puffy in the center and clearly tender to the slightest of movement. He didn't seem to be having any trouble breathing, and I hadn't yet heard a cough.

That was good, I guessed.

There were also a few marks I hadn't noticed the night before, like the red dotted rash across the back of one arm. It looked like road burn from being pinned down on the driveway and beaten.

Basically, he looked like shit.

Sure, most of the wounds were superficial and he'd be fine in a week or less. But those ribs and the gash in his head would be there longer.

And every second they were, it would only feed my anger and thirst for revenge.

Yes. I was a grown-ass man. I had a college education, a career, and another career on the horizon.

It didn't matter who you were. There were some things in a person's life—a man's life—that were off-limits.

Trent was one of those things. I wasn't above revenge. Sometimes payback was inevitable.

"Can I borrow some clothes?" he asked, either not realizing how deadly I felt or pretending not to notice. "Mine are kinda ruined."

The idea of him in my clothes was enough of a distraction, and my temperature gauge went from boiling to hot.

"I prefer you naked." I stepped closer.

"Well, I can walk around in the buff all day if you want."

I made a face and showed my teeth. "No one sees you naked but me."

His lips tilted up into a half smirk, half smile. "Well then, Forrester," he drawled, "I'm gonna need some clothes."

He totally liked my possessive streak.

I stepped away to pull out some things, my favorite T-shirt and a pair of loose sweats that were slightly too big on me so they'd probably fit him perfectly.

Then I pulled out a pair of black Calvin Kleins.

He raised an eyebrow. "You're gonna let me wear those designer boxers?"

I returned his expression. "You like my designer taste in drawers, do you?"

"You wore those that night in the hotel, when we went to meet with Gamble," Trent recalled. The heat of his stare pierced me. "Do you know how long it took me to fall asleep that night?" His voice dropped as he stepped forward.

"Probably the same amount of time it took me." I matched his tone. We stared into each other's eyes, almost measuring one another, desire and electricity crackling through the room.

I cleared my throat and lifted the boxers between us, dangling them off my fingertip. "What do you say, frat boy? Wanna put your package in the same place mine usually goes?"

He snatched the underwear off my finger and fisted them in a tight grip. At the same time, one arm snaked around me and jerked me into his body. I tried to pull back, afraid of touching his middle, but he wouldn't let go.

"I'm gonna walk around with a stiff dick all day now because every time I shift and these fucking boxers touch my cock, I'm gonna know they did the same to yours."

I reached between us and cupped him gently. "Sounds like exquisite torture to me."

He lowered his head and claimed my mouth. He kissed me soft and slow, like right there between us, our cocks weren't stirring and our hearts weren't hammering.

He pulled back. "Thanks for the clothes, Forrester."

I caught his wrist. "Wait." I didn't want him moving around too much. "You should sit down."

He rolled his eyes. "I'm taking a shower."

I felt my lips thin.

He sighed. "I know you wiped up my cuts and shit, but I need to clean up. I need to wash my hair. Besides, the warm water will be good for my stiffness."

"Fine." I relented. "The Band-Aid on your head needs changed anyway."

"You inviting yourself into my shower?" His eyebrows lifted.

I was now. I nodded, grave. "You might need help."

He chuckled. "C'mon, then."

I rushed around to get some clothes for myself and then flung a towel laying on my dresser at T. Once it was around his waist, I opened the door and peered out into the empty hallway. Gesturing with my head, I stepped out, holding my clothes as a shield for my junk.

The second we were shut in the bathroom, Trent gave me a look.

"What?" I asked, reaching behind the curtain to turn on the spray.

"I needed a towel to walk down the hall, but you just strutted right along naked as the day you were born?"

"Pretty much." I shrugged and yanked the towel from around him.

"Asshole," he said fondly.

The shower wasn't as eventful as we both wanted it to be. We were under a time clock for the family meeting, and T really did look rough and I honestly didn't want him moving around too much.

If last night hadn't been so fucking awesome, I'd have felt bad about it.

But it was awesome. I wasn't lying when I said it was the best sex I'd had in my entire life. It wasn't just physical (though that part was bomb), it was the emotional connection between us as well. In that moment, we were tethered body and soul.

Once we were both clean (some parts cleaner than others *wags eyebrows*), I shut off the water and, to his frustration, helped towel-dry him.

"I'm not a damn invalid," he griped.

"Here, put on my underwear." I thrust the black boxers at him.

Once we were both dry and wearing boxers, I pushed the hair off his face and made him sit so I could re-bandage his forehead.

I sort of wished he'd gotten stitches. It probably would have healed faster.

"Hey," he rasped, grabbing my wrist and pulling it down. When my eyes met his, he said, "It's fine."

I didn't say anything, just finished applying some more antibacterial cream and another butterfly. Since he wasn't leaving this house today, I didn't bother with another large bandage over it, figuring the air would be better.

I dabbed a little more cream on various other scrapes and cuts. Then we both got dressed.

I was right. Seeing him in my shirt—my favorite shirt—was going to drive me crazy all day. The boxers might be his sweet torture, but watching his shoulders ripple beneath my shirt was mine.

The strength in his body was quite the turn-on.

"Yo!" Braeden called up from downstairs. "Get your gay asses down here!"

"Go ahead." I opened the door and motioned for T to go first. "I'm gonna grab the pain reliever out of the bedroom and bring it down."

He was still moving slow, but not as slow as when he first got up.

He was just stepping off the stairs when I jogged down. Without any thought at all, I hooked an arm around his waist and offered some support, moving toward the living room. He didn't lean on me, but he did grab the back of my shirt and bunch it in his hand.

In the living room, four sets of eyes turned on both of us. My feet stalled a little when I realized they were watching us… It was the first time we'd touched each other as more than friends in front of anyone.

And no, there was nothing even seductive about it. It was more me trying to help him move, but it was still more than we usually did. The second I reacted to being watched, Trent took it to heart. He let go of the back of my shirt and smoothed it out, cleared his throat, and stepped away.

Part of me was relieved, and that made the rest of me feel ashamed.

Ashamed because I didn't want to feel apprehensive about being open about how I felt about him in front of others.

"Don't be shy on our account," Romeo drawled from the couch. Rimmel was right beside him with her one-eyed black cat Murphy on her lap.

Damn. So much for hoping no one but Trent noticed my reaction.

I glanced around for my sister. She was smiling up at me from the floor where she and Nova were sitting on a big, fluffy blanket. The baby had a toy in her mouth and drool all over her hand. She was adorable.

Ivy gave me an encouraging smile. I reached for Trent's hand, linking them together. He glanced at me out of the corner of his eye. "It's okay," he whispered.

"So is this," I insisted, tightening the hold I had on his fingers and stepping forward, drawing him along with me. Maybe he understood better than I did what just happened. Hell, he seemed to accept it.

I didn't.

I wasn't going to do that to him.

To me.

Loving him was nothing to be ashamed of. I wouldn't put him in a neat little box I only opened when I thought no one was looking. He deserved more.

Braeden got up off the couch where he was lounging and slid into a nearby chair. Everyone already had mugs of coffee in their hands, and I knew Rome wanted to get down to family business, but I needed my damn caffeine.

Coffee was like gas to my car. I simply didn't start without it.

"I'm gonna grab some coffee," I told everyone when Trent was on the couch.

In the kitchen, I hurried to grab the brew and a bottle of water. I dumped a few pills into the palm of my hand and abandoned the bottle to the counter.

In the living room, Braeden and Romeo were debating some football play, and I held the pills over the back of the sofa for T to take. Once they were in his mouth, I handed him the water and moved to sit down beside him.

We didn't touch, but I sat close enough so the sides of our legs were pressed together. He set aside the water, and I sipped at my coffee.

Once I had a little in my system, I handed the mug to him.

He glanced between me and the mug. Then he took it and lifted it to his lips. I knew the second the brew hit his taste buds because his eyes came back to mine.

"This is how I drink it," he said out of the side of his mouth.

I hid a smile. "I was too lazy to make two."

I liked sharing my coffee with him. I liked eating off his plate. I liked anything that moved me just one centimeter closer to him.

"You two are like a damn Nicholas Sparks movie," Braeden announced, and T choked on the coffee he was drinking. "Stop it. We got shit to deal with. People to payback."

"You watch Nicholas Spark movies?" Romeo asked, blinking at Braeden.

Rimmel giggled.

"Maybe once," Braeden muttered.

"And you think we're the gay ones?" Trent goaded him.

I laughed. So did Romeo.

"Oh, for shit's sake!" he declared. "Ivy was all hormonal. Have you ever told a pregnant woman no?"

Ivy grinned from her seat on the floor, and Nova laughed. Trent's chuckle was rich and deep. I enjoyed the sound until he sucked in a breath and shifted.

I took the coffee from his hand and gently pressed my palm over his middle. I knew it wouldn't help, but I couldn't do nothing.

"I'll get some ice." Rimmel fussed and rushed into the kitchen.

Why didn't I think of ice?

Seconds later, she came back with a bag of frozen peas (no one ever ate them, so they made for good ice packs) and an actual bag of ice wrapped in a towel.

"Here," she said, leaning over Trent to place the peas against his side.

It wasn't lost on me that the second Rim leaned close enough to touch him, Braeden sat up quickly, ready to act.

I knew he was thinking of last night when Ivy tried to clean Trent up and I'd snapped at her for getting close. I still felt like shit about it, but it was a natural reaction. He was suffering, and I felt like a lion standing guard.

I caught B's eye and shook my head slightly. "I'm cooled off."

Braeden nodded and sat back, but his eyes remained sharp on his sister, like he wouldn't leave anything to chance.

"Is that okay?" Rim asked him, holding the ice against his side. If she noticed the undercurrents between me and her brother, she didn't acknowledge them. Instead, she was focused just on Trent. "Lower?"

Rimmel had an extremely caring and tender nature. It made her job running an animal shelter perfect for her.

Trent covered her hand with his and smiled. "Right here is good."

Rimmel smiled and pulled her hand from beneath his and gently put the second pack of ice against his eye. "Hold this there."

I took the coffee from him so he could do as she said. I would have laughed at him sitting there with ice all over and both hands holding it in different places. But his injuries weren't funny.

Trent seemed like he didn't want to put the ice on his face. I knew it probably made him feel like a wimp, but he didn't argue. No one in this house argued with Rim.

Romeo would kick their ass.

Besides that, it was hard to defy such an innocent face who truly just wanted to help.

"Just hold it on there for fifteen to twenty minutes." Rimmel drew back and stared down at him. "Sitting upright and icing it like this will draw out a lot more of the swelling. You'll be more comfortable."

"Thanks, sis." Trent nodded.

Everyone in the room reacted. Not really a physical reaction. Not even the kind of reaction most people would notice. But we were family; *we* noticed. We heard.

He called her sis. A three-letter word. No big deal.

Way big deal.

It was the first time—ever—Trent actually acknowledged the way he felt about our family out loud.

Yes, he called everyone in this house his family. Yes, he attended all the family meetings, and yes, he was one of us.

But…

He was the quiet one. The one who sometimes silently set himself apart.

A light bulb went on inside me. Around the mug, my fingers tightened.

He'd always done that because of me. The closer our family got, the more determined he'd been to draw a line, keeping himself just out of reach.

In case he had to walk away.

He confessed he fought his feelings for me a long, long time. He confessed he never thought I'd feel the same. All this time, the distance he allowed between us all… it was so he would hurt less when he had to walk away.

I rubbed a hand over my jaw, flabbergasted.

Last night had been hell.

Pure hell on Earth.

Now that the sun was up and we'd battled out the worst of it, I could look back on it with a little clarity.

Stars can't shine without darkness.

He never would have been able to fully accept his place in this family if I we hadn't gone through that fight—if I hadn't fought for our relationship.

He was totally mine now.

He was all in.

Acknowledging Rimmel as his sister was proof.

Everyone was quiet, sort of still (except for the baby; she was drooling all over her toys). Rimmel sniffled and pushed at the wild mane of dark, tangled hair around her face.

Trent looked up at her, almost timid.

"You called me sis," she whispered.

I read the self-consciousness in his body language. I practically heard him debating in his head. Obviously, he'd said it naturally, but once it came out, he realized all the shit I'd just sat here and understood.

"Is that okay?" he asked.

Rimmel made a choked sound and practically threw herself at him.

A few things happened at once.

Trent dropped the ice.

Rimmel flung her arms around his neck, and he hugged her close.

Romeo and Braeden both got up, both of them watching me. Romeo hadn't even been here yesterday to witness my caveman behavior. He didn't have to. All he needed to see was Braeden's reaction.

I waved them back and rolled my eyes. I wasn't about to interrupt their moment. This was way too important.

"Rim, baby, you're going to crush his ribs." Romeo reminded her gently after a few minutes.

She made a squeaking sound and yanked back, grabbing up the ice and holding it out to him. "Sorry."

Trent smiled. "Didn't hurt at all."

Rim went back to her seat beside Romeo and Murphy, and Trent went back to icing his face.

"We need names, Trent," Romeo said, getting right down to business.

Trent rattled off four names.

My fists clenched. I knew every single one of those fuckers. And now I hated them all. Judging by the looks on Romeo's and Braeden's faces, they knew them as well and felt the same way I did.

"First things first." I spoke up. "Trent will get all his shit out of that house and move in here. Once he's out, we can deal with Omega."

Romeo and B nodded.

Trent cleared his throat. "There's only one problem."

All eyes turned to him.

"I'm not moving out of Omega."

I must have just hallucinated. I could have sworn I heard him say he was going to keep living in that house. I laughed, because really, this had to be a joke.

Trent didn't laugh with me.

Realization dawned.

I wasn't hallucinating. He wasn't joking.

Trent was serious.

Eight

Trent

What the fuck?

Did this family think I was some quivering little boy? Did they really think I'd run into this house and hide behind them for protection?

No.

Hells no.

Yeah, yeah, I was broken down. I was bruised, cracked, and physically weakened. I looked like shit (not just their words... I looked in the mirror this morning), and my brothers weren't the type to just let this go.

But...

I might be down. I might even be vulnerable.

Even so, I was stronger than ever.

It's amazing what looking into the eyes of your worst fears would do for a man. Hell, those guys at Omega last night did me a favor.

They showed me their opinion didn't matter. That nothing anyone could say or do would matter. Drew and I were stronger than that. Than them.

Was I still hella concerned about what being gay would cost Drew? More now than ever.

I learned something last night, though, in the midst of the eight ball, the fighting, and the breaking up.

Even during the sex.

Oh my God, the sex…

Pull it together, Trent.

Drew and I were stronger together. I was stronger with him than I would ever be apart. He gave me strength. I gained courage from his love. I knew without a shadow of a doubt, this wouldn't be easy. A relationship with my best friend would be scrutinized, ridiculed, and, at times, make me feel like I'd done the wrong thing.

There was another side to that, though.

I would know unbridled happiness, unending affection, and a level of connection which I'd never have with anyone else.

Wasn't that something worth fighting for? Wasn't that worth enduring the shitty times?

Hells yeah.

This was a time I would need to fight.

Fighting didn't mean hiding.

"I'm still the president at Omega. Giving that up is what they want. I won't do it," I said, leaving no room for argument in my tone.

"Why would you want to be the president of a frat who would do this to you?" Drew spat.

He was getting agitated; it was to be expected. This was going to be hard on him. I was going to have to do what I could to shield him as best I could.

"It's not the entire frat," I rebutted. "It was four guys. If I turned tail and ran right now, everything I worked for over there for past few years would be for nothing. I will not just hand that house over to a bunch of Zach wannabes and walk away."

(Zach, aka the guy I replaced and the worst president in Alpha U frat history.)

"I agree," Romeo said.

I knew he would. He knew what that frat was like, and he knew walking away wasn't the kind of man I would want to be. If Drew wasn't so close to the situation, he'd see it, too.

Drew made a rude, angry sound.

I dropped the ice on my ribs and put a hand on his leg, giving his strong thigh a light squeeze.

"If I move out and abandon my presidency, it would be like admitting they were right. Like saying being gay is a reason to hide. Con's pissed because I took away his chance at presidency. He's challenging everything about me. My loyalty. My leadership." *My heart.*

"What are you gonna do, T?" Drew argued. "You gonna fight everyone who has a problem with you being gay?"

If I have to.

"It's not just about him having some man love," Braeden spoke up.

I swear, man love was like his new favorite saying.

"I know that," Drew said wearily.

"They think you're off licking your wounds" Romeo was thoughtful. "They expect you to show up and hand over the house. Con's probably working right now to discredit you even more because you aren't there."

I made a scoffing sound. "He's probably combing through the frat bylaws, looking for some kind of loophole he can use to get back into the game for presidency."

"What a douche." Braeden grunted.

"Why don't you just kick him and the other three out of the frat?" Ivy wondered out loud.

"It doesn't work that way," I answered. "Removing a member's charter is a lot harder than it sounds. Once they're in, it's really hard to boot them out altogether."

"Look how much it took to get Zach out," Romeo added.

Ivy's face darkened a little, and I regretted even bringing him up. Surely, hearing just the Omega name was enough to bring back horrible memories for her. And for Braeden.

I glanced at him, but he was watching Ivy, making sure he didn't need to step in and haul her out of the conversation.

Prada came prancing into the room and licked the baby's face. Nova laughed and grabbed the Chihuahua's ear and tugged.

"Easy," Ivy reminded her, but Prada didn't seem bothered. Instead, she lay down right beside Nova, who laughed her little baby laugh. Just like that, Ivy's face cleared and all the shadows of the past were gone.

"I could go to the dean. Show him my face… Tell him what's been going on." I went on, avoiding mention of Zach from now on. "It would be enough to at least put them on probation, maybe have them removed. Assault is illegal…"

"But?" Drew asked, sensing I didn't want to do that.

"But that's weak. That's a coward's way out. Omega handles their own. We have our own set of laws and justice set in place. Plus, this kind of thing would get press. So much on campus, it would probably make the local news. Omega doesn't need that kind of black mark, not after everything else. I didn't clean up that place just so I could trash it all."

And Drew didn't need to be dragged into it by pissed-off guys who got caught being bigots.

"You aren't trashing it, though. They are," Rimmel put in.

"It's about loyalty," Romeo explained to her. "Respect and taking care of your own."

"Why do men have to make everything so hard?" Rimmel wondered.

"'Cause they have big, dumb egos," Ivy added.

The girls laughed.

"So you're going to go back there, rat them out, and let the house turn on them," Drew surmised.

"Make their lives a living hell." Braeden nodded, approval lacing his words.

"Eventually," I replied, glancing at Romeo.

A ghost of a smile appeared on his face, and I knew he understood what I wanted to do. Hell, he'd probably do the same thing. It made me more determined.

"Trent," Drew growled.

I patted his thigh, and he growled again. Guess he didn't like feeling like I was appeasing him. I pulled my hand back and reached for the coffee.

He made it just the way I liked it, even though it was for us to share. Made it taste even better. The mug was practically empty, only enough to cover the bottom.

"Drink it," he said when he noticed me debating. "I'll make more."

I finished it off and set the empty cup in my lap. "I think sometimes the best punishment is making someone sweat. Letting them wonder when and how it's coming…"

"Devious," Braeden drawled, thoroughly entertained.

Drew stood and paced over near the fireplace. "So you want to go back home, act like nothing even happened, and let them get away with it?"

"I'm not going back home," I told him. "*This* is home."

He stopped pacing, and our eyes connected. There was a bit of relief deep in the blue of his irises. Just me reminding him he was my home made this easier to swallow.

"They won't get away with it," Romeo said. "But yeah. Go back. Have a meeting. You're gonna have to dispel everything he's probably saying right now."

"Won't be hard." I nodded. "My bruises will have some shock value. Everyone will be all riled up that I was jumped on Omega property. They'll want to start a witch hunt for the guys I *didn't see*."

"And then the guys who are being hunted will be looking over their shoulder and waiting for you to rat them out," Rimmel surmised.

"Exactly." I smiled. "Con and the rest won't be able to say one word against me because I'll be the injured one. I'll be the one who was wronged."

"And he did it to himself." Braeden laughed. "Fucker thought he would be getting his way. Instead, all those guys are getting is a free pass into hell."

"I wouldn't be surprised if the three who helped Con don't turn on him. Try to shove all the blame off on him," Romeo said.

"All four of them are getting what's coming," Drew growled. "I'll make sure of it."

"You can't go in there swinging," I told him. God, that scared me. I knew he was pissed, but they didn't fight fair. I was proof of that.

If Drew got hurt trying to avenge me…

I'd go ballistic.

I'd take the entire house down so hard there would be nothing left to rebuild.

Which is exactly why my plan was best. Did I want to go back there? No. Would I? Yes. Biding my time while those assholes squirmed and listening to the plotting of revenge from the others in the house against the ones who beat their president—that would give Drew time.

It would give him time to cool down; it would give me a chance to keep him away.

"They called me," Drew intoned, his voice low. "They fucking called me to come and get you. They wanted me to see you lying there. I picked you up off the ground. I saw the blood…" His fists clenched. "And you want me to let that go?"

His eyes were glacial when they snapped to mine. "Would you?"

He looked at Romeo and then Braeden. "Would you?"

I blew out a breath. Well, when he put it that way…

"Dude's got a point," B allowed.

"You can't just go beat up everybody," Ivy declared, standing up and putting her hands on her hips. "That doesn't solve anything."

"Romeo and Braeden can't get caught doing that." Rimmel worried, twisting her hands in her laps. "The press would be all over it. You too, Drew. You can't get in trouble."

"We aren't going to get caught, baby." Romeo assured her.

The girls gave each other a doubtful look, and I watched the worry and fear roll over their faces. I glanced down at Nova, who was still playing with an array of toys scattered around, and then I glanced at Drew, still looking murderous.

My heart clenched.

So much turmoil.

"Fine." Drew relented suddenly. Everyone looked at him. "I won't do anything irrational."

I stared at him. It was like he knew I was starting to spiral deep into that place inside me, the place that didn't want anyone to hurt because of me.

"We'll do this your way, frat boy."

I'm not sure I liked being appeased either. But it was better than the alternative.

"You know," Romeo drawled, "there might be a way we can do it both ways. Let them squirm and add a little hurt."

"Let's hear it, Rome." Braeden sat forward.

I patted the cushion beside me and motioned for Drew. He didn't hesitate coming to my side and sitting close.

I thought about linking our fingers together. I wanted to touch him, to reassure him… and maybe me, too. I didn't, though. I hesitated. I knew he was still getting used to the idea of us being "out" in front of our family.

I wasn't going to push.

I didn't have to.

Seconds later, he reached for me. His warm, thick fingers tangled with mine, and he pulled my hand into his lap.

Damn.

Such a little thing to make such a huge impact on my heart. My stomach quivered with nerves and excitement I tried not to show.

Be casual. I reminded myself. *Don't make it a thing.*

I did, however, glance at Drew at the same time he glanced at me. We smiled at each other.

My stomach trembled again.

No one else reacted to the fact we were sitting there holding hands. In fact, they didn't *not* react either. You know… when someone looks, then looks away quickly like they don't want to make it a thing, but it really is a thing?

There was none of that either.

It was just normal. Natural. Right.

I am so incredibly lucky to have these people.

Romeo sat forward and started talking.

I smiled.

Nine

Drew

It was a good plan.

I understood Trent's reasoning.

But I didn't like it.

What I did like?

An excuse to bash heads.

Thank you, Romeo.

Ten

Trent

House meeting. One hour. Be there. I sent the mass text to the entire frat.

Drew wasn't happy. He wanted me to stay another night. I wanted that, too, but it was Sunday. I had classes tomorrow. All the guys at the frat did, too. I couldn't put this off. If I walked around campus tomorrow looking like this, people would notice and start talking. I'd lose the shock value of being gone all day and then showing up looking rough.

I'd like to take a moment to say passing myself off as beaten or even roughed up was not something I wanted to do. *At all.* I could handle what happened to me. I'd been injured lots of times during football. I would heal. But this was necessary. Sometimes showing a little bit of weakness was better than being totally strong.

Plus, I wanted to put Romeo's suggestion into play.

It was a clever idea, one that would make me look good but at the same time secretly stick it to the four who jumped me. And, of course, it would quench certain people's thirst for bodily harm.

Certain people = Drew.

Surprisingly, I didn't feel like fighting back, not physically anyway.

I was tired of fighting.

For so very long, I'd been fighting. Longer than anyone even knew.

I just wanted to be happy. I wanted to be with Drew and make sure he was happy. More than ever, I was ready to graduate. I still wasn't one hundred percent sure what I would do once I did, but I would have a degree, and I was legit managing Drew.

We hadn't really discussed the details, but I knew I'd probably get paid. Even if it was just enough to live on, I'd be okay for a while. Taking some time off seemed kinda nice. Focusing on Drew, our relationship, and the new racing division sounded like heaven to me. It would be work. I planned on getting Drew as many opportunities as I could, but it was something I would enjoy.

Too bad we weren't there yet.

We had a lot of walls to break down. Walls to break through.

As I was lying on the couch, watching a movie with everyone (and Rimmel forced me to hold more ice on my face), I couldn't shut off my brain.

Drew and I were moving forward, taking small steps toward creating the life we wanted to have together but never thought we would. It wasn't going to be an easy life; we already knew this. That didn't mean I couldn't make it as good as I could. I wanted Drew to have everything. I was determined to give it to him.

What did that mean?

Change.

Facing fears.

Coming out.

Yeah. It was big. Bigger than me and Drew, bigger than our relationship. I didn't know if it would even be possible, but I was going to try.

I couldn't change the world or everyone's opinions.

But maybe I could change enough to make a difference in the life we would have together. I just wanted the bubble we lived in to be a little bit bigger, a little more comfortable.

Idealistic? Unrealistic? Brave?

No.

Selfish.

I wanted that for Drew, because giving him that would make me happy.

But how did one start a sort of revolution?

A couple ideas were floating around my head. There were a few platforms I could utilize and another pending revolution I could maybe tap into. It was worth a try. At the end of the day, I would at least know I gave it a shot.

Drew was quiet during the drive back to Omega. I didn't make much effort to talk. I knew he was still pissed off I was coming back here, and he was worried something like this might happen again.

It wouldn't.

I was on guard now.

My stomach twisted a little as we neared the house. I wasn't scared to come back, but I didn't want to be here. In truth, I felt betrayed. I'd given a lot of myself and a hell of a lot of time to this place. I felt it was all thrown back in my face.

Rationally, I knew it was only four guys and shouldn't reflect on everyone under the roof. But it did. If four of them felt this way about a gay member—a gay president—how many more of them would be disgusted?

It doesn't matter, I told myself. I wasn't walking in there and announcing tonight this happened because of a lifestyle choice.

I know that was ironic.

I was so determined to make the world Drew and I lived in a place where it was okay for us to love each other. Tonight wasn't the night to go there. I hadn't talked to Drew about it yet. I wasn't going to "come out" until he was okay with it. I could come out as gay and leave him out of it, but let's be real. Everyone would know who I was involved with.

They already speculated.

Judging from Drew's initial reaction to our family seeing us first touching (as more than friends), bringing it up right now was off the table. He needed some more time, and he was going to get it.

Do I need more time? I asked myself as we pulled up to the house.

A ton of lights were on inside, illuminating the grass and landscaping around the house. I even saw a sliver of light peeking through the heavy drapes in the dining room where we held our meetings.

Maybe I did need more. But honestly? More time wouldn't change anything.

I couldn't say I would ever be "ready" to face people's judgment. There are some things a person can never be ready for, but it shouldn't stop you from doing it. Waiting wouldn't change anything for me. I'd still feel the same way later.

I'd been digesting how I felt for a long time. I'd been trying to make sense of falling for my best friend almost since the day we met.

It came down to one thing.

Value.

I valued my relationship with Drew far more than I valued anything else. That deserved to be recognized. Even if it was the recognition I didn't want.

"Are you sure about this?" Drew asked, letting the engine idle as he stared out the windshield at the house.

"Yeah."

"I'll come in with you," he said for the hundredth time.

"No," I replied for the hundredth time. "Having you there will just make more tongues wag, and it's a house meeting. You aren't an Omega."

"Right."

I grabbed his jaw and pulled his head around. "Quit worrying like a damn woman."

One side of his mouth tilted up. "I'll see you tomorrow."

"Yeah. Let's have dinner. You can eat all my fries, and we can talk racing business."

"I like fries."

I released his jaw and laughed. "I know."

"See ya, frat boy."

I squeezed the top of his leg and popped open the door. On my way to the house, I looked in the lot at my Mustang. It was still there, pretty as ever. At least no one messed with it.

Drew sat on the road and waited for me to make it to the door. I knew he'd never just drop me off in a parking lot and drive off ever again. I couldn't even blame him. I would do the same.

Everyone was already gathered in the dining room for the meeting when I pushed open the front door. The familiar nerve-grating sound of Conner's voice set my back teeth on edge.

"…Just saying when he steps down, we need to make sure Jack is ready to assume the role as president." He spoke to the room.

You know how I said I was too tired to fight?

I just got a second wind.

This guy was really pushing me to my limit.

I dropped my chin and closed my eyes for second. Then I took in a deep breath and calmed down.

It wasn't the deep breath. It was the fact I caught Drew's scent. I opened my eyes and looked at the shirt I was wearing. His shirt. It smelled like him. Maybe it was weird, but having his shirt on, being able to feel connected to him in some way, was all I needed right now.

I moved around the corner and filled the doorway of the room.

"Who says I'm stepping down?" I boomed across the room.

Everyone turned toward me. Some low curses went through the room.

"Trent!" Jack gasped from beside Conner.

"What the fuck happened to you!" another brother yelled.

I made a point to place a palm over my ribs when I walked through the room to the podium. They still hurt like hell, but in any other circumstance, I wouldn't have acted like they did.

Con was watching me with fear and wariness in his eyes. I made sure when I looked straight at him, he would be able to see the anger and promise of revenge.

He moved out of the way immediately, and I turned away, dismissing him like the trash he was.

Jack stepped up to my side instantly. "Man, you look terrible."

"Let me guess," I said to him but spoke loud enough the entire room could hear. "Con here was making yet another case against me for not being here all weekend?"

Jack nodded, and some of the others shifted uncomfortably.

"I was being disloyal?" I asked, glancing around the room and then back to Jack.

One of the guys in the room cleared his throat. "He told us you were stepping down as president."

I lifted both my eyebrows. "Now where would he get that idea?"

I locked eyes with one of the men who helped jump me. He looked away immediately, a flush coloring his cheeks.

Aww, what's the matter? Is it hard to look at the damage you caused?

Good.

"Who did that to you?" the guy next to him demanded. "Were you in an accident?"

I glanced behind me at Con. A nervous expression crossed his face.

I balanced both hands on the podium. "This wasn't an accident. I was jumped by four men last night."

Everyone started talking at once, exclaiming and cussing.

I held up my hand, and the room fell quiet. "It was right outside, on Omega property. Right out there in the parking lot."

Looks of outrage became a common theme as I kept talking.

"I didn't see their faces." I shook my head sadly. "But I'm pretty sure this was a blatant attack on this fraternity. They were trying to send some kind of message, ignite some kind of war with this house and our brothers."

"They come after our president, they come after us all!" someone roared.

I nodded. "It's a sad fucking day, brothers." I called them that on purpose, reminding them we were united.

"This frat is being targeted. I don't know why yet. Or by whom. We can't let anyone on this campus think we're fair game."

"Omega rules!" one of the younger charters yelled, knocking over his chair in the process.

"I look worse than I am." I went on. "Some swelling, some bruises. A couple cracked ribs." I paused to meet two more sets of eyes… those of the men who were there last night.

They were looking very apprehensive.

I smiled, showing all my teeth. "They didn't do a very good job with their attack. You'd think four guys could work me over better than that."

"Pussies!" someone hollered.

"Oh, they definitely were." I agreed. "They had to gang up on me, hold me down, to get the job done."

"This is a bunch of horse shit!" one of the men I went through rush with exclaimed and stood. "We need to pay back these motherfuckers! No one messes with Omega and gets away with it!"

I let them all talk over each other while I stood back and watched them all whip themselves into a frenzy of anger.

What can I say? Men are predictable. Especially when their egos are at stake.

It was working to my advantage.

"I agree. We need to spread the word. Make it known that the attack on me and everyone in this house will not be brushed under the rug. We will not go crying to the dean." I glanced at Con, making sure he heard that part. "Here at Omega, we serve justice on our own terms!"

Everyone started cheering and hollering. It was like a pep rally for a football game.

"Brothers," I yelled over the noise. My head was still throbbing and my midsection was sore as hell. I wanted to go lie down, but this wasn't done. "Before the meeting is adjourned, I would like to make clear that I was in no way skipping out on the frat this weekend. I hit up a doctor and laid low… Wanted the attackers to wonder where I was, what I was doing."

One of the men who beat me cleared his throat. I smiled at him.

Oh, what a beautiful thing it is to be calm when people expect you to be enraged.

He actually looked scared.

I'm just getting started.

"I was also working on something, an opportunity for the fraternity. Something that will bring a lot more notoriety and good press to our house."

Everyone seemed interested.

"As you all know, I'm friends with Maryland Knights quarterback Romeo Anderson and also Braeden Walker." Everyone sat up a little straighter in their seats. "Since they're both also alumni of Alpha U, I knew they would want to be involved in what I was suggesting."

In truth, this was Romeo's idea. I was taking the credit because it would make me look good with the house and gain me some extra favor in case it was needed.

"What is it?" one of the guys in the back hollered.

I grinned, my puffy lip stretching uncomfortably. "Romeo and Braeden have agreed to play in a charity football game with Omega. The money raised from ticket sales and donations will go to a charity this house will choose through popular vote. I suggest Omega makes the charity one they support annually and, every year after this, organizes at least one event to fundraise and donate one hundred percent of the proceeds to said charity."

People started talking excitedly, and I lifted my hand. "In addition to Romeo and Braeden playing, they will be getting a few other Knight players to donate their time to come down and participate. Because of the popularity of the team here in their home state and Romeo's legendary reputation here on campus, this will be a very popular event and a chance to raise quite a bit of money."

"And get the Omega house back to being the most prestigious frat on campus!" Jack whooped from beside me.

Everyone cheered.

"I will set up a meeting with the Wolves coach here on campus this week and talk to him about scheduling a time for us to play the game, maybe get in some practices, etc. Teams will be divided up at a later date. Once all the details are worked out, I'll have another house meeting to keep everyone in the know."

"Props to our prez for not letting our rivals keep him down and for still striving to make this house better." Jack spoke to the room.

"I am not and will not step down from the presidency that I have held for almost two years. I remain true to the Omega brotherhood and will be until I give over the honor of president to Jack in just a few short weeks."

Everyone clapped.

I turned to Con. "Thank you, Conner, for looking out for the frat, for taking action when you thought we were leaderless."

Con swallowed, his eyes wide.

"But as you can see, I'm here. And I'd like to decree that if anything or anyone else should question my loyalty to the frat in the coming weeks, it is Jack who should step in and act as president."

Jack stepped forward. "Thank you, Trent. Men, keep your eyes and ears open for anything that might lead us to the scum who did this to our leader. Any information on their affiliation or motives will be rewarded. We will show this entire campus that Omega is not a house to be fucked with!"

Everyone went crazy again.

I banged the gavel, signaling the end of the meeting.

Con and his merry band of assholes left the room pretty quickly. I wasn't so lucky. I was the last one out, having to talk to almost everyone. I answered question after question. I replayed what happened over and over, joining in plotting and speculating.

Most people were inclined to believe this was the work of a rival frat. I didn't disagree with them. Eventually, I'd rat out the guys in this house. Until then, I'd let the rumors run wild.

By the time I was done, I didn't even have to make an effort to look pitiful because I felt pitiful.

"I'm gonna call it a night, guys," I said to the few remaining brothers. "I need some pills and my bed."

"You need anything, anything at all, just yell," one brother said and offered his hand. I shook it.

Another guy spoke up. "And don't worry about anything tonight. Get some sleep. No one will get in this house that isn't supposed to be here."

"Fuckin right," I drawled and shook his hand, too.

My ass dragged up the stairs. I wanted to go home to the familiar sounds of Prada running around, Braeden's sarcastic jokes, and Rimmel's hovering.

Most of all, I wanted to lie in bed with Drew. Maybe hold his hand.

I had a moment's thought outside my bedroom door to just say fuck it and drive back over there. But I couldn't. Not tonight. I had to be here.

As I was reaching for my keys in my back pocket (my door is always locked), I saw some movement out of the corner of my eye. I turned quickly to see Con hovering nearby.

I pinned him with a hard, cold stare. "You'll get yours," I vowed. "Can you guess when?"

He turned tail and ran like the little bitch he was. Fucking yanked my chain the guys actually thought I'd run out of this house and never come back.

I slid my key in the door and frowned. It was unlocked.

That peckerhead better not have been messing around in my room. I'd call him out here and now.

The door swung open, and all my attention went to the bed.

To who was sitting in the center.

Drew

Surprise stopped him cold. The dark lashes that framed his hazel eyes pulled wide, and the expression of relief written on his face made the back of my neck tingle.

I smiled, holding a finger up to my lips, reminding him to be quiet.

He recovered quickly, moving into the room, hastily shutting and locking the door behind him.

I wasn't sure how Trent would react to me sneaking into his room, especially after he told me he didn't want me to come in the house.

When the door first opened, before he saw me waiting, I recognized definite exhaustion clinging to him. For all the convincing he'd done that this was where he needed to be right now, it was painfully clear he didn't want to be.

It was pretty fucking heady when everything instantly changed the second his eyes found me. A complete three-sixty. The exhaustion evaporated and his hazel eyes lit up.

That crooked front tooth of his even came out to play.

I was so glad I snuck in.

"What are you doing here?" he asked, talking in hushed tones. "How the hell did you get in?"

I held up the spare key to his reinforced lock and smiled.

He laughed. "No shit! I forgot you had that!"

I made a show of slipping it back into the pocket of my jeans. "I snuck right in. No one noticed 'cause you were too busy getting them all riled up."

"You heard that, huh?"

I chuckled. "Most of it."

Hearing him talk made me more impressed. He was a good public speaker. People hung on every word he said. I couldn't even blame them; I did, too.

"I wanted to beat his ass," Trent growled and dropped on the edge of the mattress. "When I walked in, he was trying to convince everyone how great he was."

"Judging from the stuff I overheard, no one really bought the bullshit he was selling."

T made a sound and glanced over his shoulder. "I thought you went home."

"Have you seen the way you fill out my shirt?" I teased. "I'd follow you anywhere."

Trent's white teeth flashed. "I'm glad you're here."

"Me, too." I rubbed my hand over this head and trailed my fingers down the back of his neck. Of course I'd be here. There wasn't anywhere else I wanted to be. The second he disappeared into the house and out of sight, there was this spot in the center of my gut that began to ache.

The idea of him in that house, basically full of vultures, left me feeling cold. Yeah, I knew T could handle himself. But not knowing… anticipating… lying in bed all night alone, just waiting for the next time I'd hear from him to be sure—I couldn't handle that.

I parked down the street in an overflow lot most of the houses around here used when they had parties and needed extra parking. I put the Fastback in the back of the lot, in the dark—something I didn't like to do because I was afraid someone would mess with it, or worse, try to steal it.

But it was a risk I was willing to take tonight.

I walked right in the house and moved swiftly up the stairs and let myself into his room. It took maybe thirty seconds.

I was gonna have to get up hella early, something I hated, but at least when I woke, he'd be beside me.

Damn. I was turning emo. I needed to drive. Fast.

"You're right," I said, trying to keep things light. Trent would never say it or even allude to it, but he was in pain.

He frowned. "Right about what?"

"This bed is too small for you."

The sound of his low chuckle vibrated beneath my skin. "Sorry you snuck in now?"

I'd sleep in a cardboard box in the pouring rain if it were beside him. "Nope. We'll just have to sleep extra close."

"Best idea I've heard all day."

"Take off your shirt," I ordered.

"I feel used, Forrester. You're just here for my body."

I gave him the finger, then reached for the hem of the shirt to slowly peel it over his head. I did it extra slow—you know, because of his ribs. And because the way his abs rippled when he lifted his arms was something I needed to stare at longer than two seconds.

"I want to look at your ribs, jackass."

"They look the same as when you saw them an hour ago." He grunted.

I tossed the shirt onto the floor, and he reached for mine. I let him pull it off but then turned my attention to his midsection. He was right; it looked pretty much the same as earlier.

"I really wish I'd been here," I whispered, ever so lightly caressing the worst of the bruising.

He caught my hand. "I'm glad you weren't."

I slid off the bed and made my way around the narrow space between the mattress and the wall, around to the side where T sat. I kneeled at his feet and pulled off his shoes.

Neither of us said anything as I worked, but I felt his eyes the entire time. Once the shoes and socks were gone, my hands slid up his legs and thighs to hook around the waistband of the sweats. Our eyes locked, and Trent lifted his hips and ass so I could slide the pants down and work them over his legs and feet.

"How do you like those boxers?" I asked, a little cheeky. I sure as hell liked looking at him in them.

"You're not getting them back." The depth of his voice and the way his eyes roamed over my face and chest made me flush. God, he was sexy.

"I can live with that."

He smirked because it was so obvious by my throaty tone he made my body hum.

"Get your head out of the gutter, frat boy. You look more uncomfortable than a horse with a mouthful of bees. Lay down," I said, trying to hide the desire I felt being this close to him.

"Frankly, I'm offended your head isn't in the gutter with mine."

I made a rude noise and pushed him back onto the pillows. "It is. After last night, my head should pay rent to the gutter 'cause it's gonna be living there."

Trent smirked and crooked a finger at me. When his crooked front tooth flashed, fondness and desire battled within me. I never knew I could be so incredibly charmed and turned on at the same time.

Giving in, I pulled off my sweats and T-shirt. T was on his back, so I straddled him, hugging his hips with my thighs and giving him all my weight. I didn't have to worry about crushing him; the guy was just as strong and muscular as the pro football players I lived with.

I was sorely tempted to grip his cock and tease it with some stroking, but I held back. It wouldn't be fair to him or me. I wasn't going to do anything about either one of our hard-ons. Trent was way too exhausted, and I knew he was in pain. All the soreness from what happened to him last night was in full swing.

"I gotta say I like the way you look under me." My palms flattened on his chest and rubbed upward, stroking his well-defined pecs.

"Wanna see how I look over you?" His hands covered mine.

"Right now, it's my most anticipated moment," I confessed.

"Mine, too."

Just thinking about sex with him caused my hips to rock. Trent smiled lazily and palmed my waist.

I shook my head. "No way."

He lifted a brow.

"I didn't come here for sex," I explained, keeping my voice very quiet.

We were in a house full of men.

"Then why are you here, Forrester?"

I liked when he called me that. I don't know why. It was just my last name, but when he said it, it was more.

"Because I love you."

Against my skin, his hands went slack, and his eyes closed. "I wish you knew how amazing that sounds to me." The emotion in his voice almost made me forget about my no-sex-tonight rule.

"I do." I promised. "It's the exact same as when you say it to me."

He shook his head once. "No." He looked up, the amber of his eyes blazing with vulnerability. "You're stronger than me, Drew. Deep down at the core." He paused to swallow and look away.

I watched the emotion play across his features. I watched him search for the words to explain what was going on inside him, and then I watched him weigh them, as if he measured exactly what each one would cost.

"I've… I opened up a part of myself that was so private it physically hurt, the deepest place I feel things, the place where my most exposed feelings lie. That cost me a lot, Forrester, and I was scared. *You* are the biggest risk I'm ever going to take, so when you say you love me, it's the biggest reward I'll ever know."

I grabbed his jaw and rubbed the pads of my thumbs over the skin there, reveling in his words, the moment… and the way he looked at me. "Don't ever underestimate the power you have over me, frat boy. I promise you I'm just as powerless when it comes to you."

"I love you," he rasped.

After that, no more words were said. There was honestly nothing left to say. When you understood the depth of feeling and the level of connection we had, words just didn't compare.

My head buzzed as our lips moved together. His fingertips were unsteady when they stroked over my scruff. Our tongues and mouths made love, but it was never about anything more. It was just us simply being together, exploring each other in ways we'd been deprived of until just recently.

When at last our lips stopped moving, I rested my cheek on his shoulder and flung a leg over his. The languid feeling of his fingertips dragging up and down my spine made me drowsy and lulled me to sleep.

Turns out I kinda liked a bed Trent was too small for because for us together, it was just right.

I called in sick to work.

Not because I didn't want to get up early (though, who the hell ever wants to do that?), but because I wanted to drive.

I wanted the open road, my foot against the gas pedal, and the feeling of flying. I needed it, too—the solitude that came over me when I drove. There was a stillness that came with driving fast, a sort of mental clarity. It didn't make much sense to say, but the only way I could describe it was the ability to literally speed up the world around me allowed my mind to only see what really mattered. All the scenery whipping by blurred together, leaving all that remained the stuff that mattered most, the stuff no amount of speed could ever blur.

I was happy—no, I was fulfilled being with Trent. But that fulfillment wasn't without strife. I still had things to work through in my head. Decisions to make. And let's face it. I was still beyond pissed about him getting jumped. Maybe some speed would shake loose some of the anger weighing me down.

Maybe the adrenaline rush would give me some courage.

"If I could skip classes today, I would," T said, looking at me still tangled in the sheets.

I was enjoying the view. Though I could tell he was still sore, he was moving a little bit easier today… or at least putting on a good act.

It reinforced that what he really needed last night was rest, not us going at each other for hours.

It was early, but not as early as I usually had to drag my ass out of bed. The second my alarm went off, the familiar sense of dread about sitting in that cubicle all day with the damn noose—*I mean tie*—around my throat was too much.

I waited until more of a decent hour and called in. I told them I was sick, likely some kind of food poisoning from something I ate over the weekend. They believed me. There was no reason not to. I didn't like my job, but I showed up and did the work well.

This was only the second time I'd called off since starting that job, the first time being when Ivy had Nova. I wasn't even worried they would see me out because I was going where people I worked with never did.

After that, I settled back against T and drifted back into this weird but utterly comfortable place between deep sleep and consciousness. It was the place where my body and mind was totally relaxed, but I was still aware. I felt the rhythm of Trent's breathing, the hardness of his body but the softness in which his arm wrapped around my waist. Those sounds were like rainfall pattering against the windows and overhead on the roof. Soothing, comforting, and the stuff that made you snuggle in a little tighter.

The second he worked his body from beneath mine, I was awake, fully and totally. Not even my lazy-ass brain wanted to sleep without him.

I watched through slumber-heavy eyes as he moved around the tiny room. When he disappeared to the bathroom, I listened for any sound he might make or any kind of disruption to what he was doing in the bathroom.

I wasn't supposed to let anyone know I was in here, but so help me God, if anyone fucked with him, I'd fly out of this room so fast they wouldn't even see who was beating their ass.

Luckily for all the fuckers in this house, no one caused an issue and I didn't have to whoop any ass.

Trent let himself back in the room within minutes. His hair was of course styled into place, not so neat it looked anal, but not messy like mine usually was. Sometimes I'd almost dare to call his style preppy… but I couldn't. His overall demeanor wasn't preppy. He was too laidback for that label.

Besides, I hated labels. Any kind. And I wasn't about to label my person with one so silly it was associated with the way he looked.

Trent wasn't wearing a shirt, a fact that sort of made me crazy. This wasn't an empty house. Who knows who saw him here on a daily basis without his shirt? It never bothered me before when guys walked around half naked. Hell, it was natural.

But it bothered me now.

Correction.

It only bothered me in relation to Trent. I didn't want anyone looking at *him*.

He saw me watching and smiled. His lip was no longer puffy; it just had a healing cut. His eye was still slightly swollen but would likely be back to normal by end of day. The bruising was still heavy, that blue-ish purple shade that would soon start turning that ugly shade of yellow.

The Band-Aid on his head was gone, but the butterfly bandage was still in place. Personally, I would have preferred it to be covered completely, but I knew it needed air.

The button on his slightly faded jeans was undone, the band of my boxers visible, and I smiled. I guessed he hadn't showered. His waist was tight and defined, and it made me think of how it felt to run my fingers up the ripples of muscles last night as I straddled him.

"You have time for breakfast before class?" I asked, still surveying his body. My eyes were just as hungry as my stomach.

"If we go now." He picked up a shirt lying nearby, and it made my face pull up like the Cheshire cat.

"Wearing my shirt again today?"

He flashed a quick smile. "I like it better than mine."

It was my favorite, but it was clear I'd never get it back. Which oddly made me like it more. The fabric was faded blue cotton, what used to be a vibrant shade now more subdued from wash and wear. The front of the shirt had the outline of a Mustang on it, kind of like a drawing but just the bones of the car without any details.

It fit Trent tighter than me, and the sleeves clung to the rounded muscles of his arms. Once it was on, he stepped to a dresser and rummaged around to pull out a pullover sweatshirt. Instead of having a hood, it had some kind of funnel neck, which bunched up around his jaw in a casual way. It was white, and the ends of my blue T-shirt stuck out from the hem, giving him some kind of stylish double-layered look.

When he was done getting dressed, he pulled out another shirt and tossed it at me. It landed on my face, and I was momentarily blinded by cotton. I took that as a hint I was taking too long, so I slid out of bed.

The sweats I'd worn here last night were lying on the floor, and I pulled them on. They were a shade of charcoal and kind of slouchy. The shirt Trent tossed me wasn't the one I wore last night, but one of his. It was black, my favorite, with a silver Under Armour logo on the chest.

Maybe this one would replace the one he stole.

Once I was dressed, I ran my hands through my hair and called it done. I'd grab a shower and shit later.

"Ready?" Trent grabbed his book bag and slung it over his shoulder.

I stepped up to him, welcoming that little sizzle I always felt between us, and held his stare. My deft fingers reached between us and found the undone button at the top of his pants and easily put it how it belonged.

"Oops," Trent whispered.

My fingers lingered a little longer than necessary down by his fly. His breath smelled like mint.

"You did that on purpose." Slowly, I drew my hands back and pulled his shirts back into place.

"I would never do such a thing." He winked.

He was a charming bastard.

"Come on," he murmured and caught my hand. "Let's go eat."

At the door, he paused and opened it a crack to peer out into the hallway. "Move fast," he said, coming back inside and handing me the keys to his Mustang. "I'll drive you over to your car."

I nodded.

Before turning back, he swooped in and kissed me hard and fast.

Somehow we got lucky. I made it out of the house without anyone seeing me. We rushed across the front walkway like we'd just broken the law.

Soon as we were in T's Mustang with the engine running, we looked at each other and laughed.

Before pulling out of the lot, Trent grasped my hand and put it on the stick shift. "I'll drive, you shift."

"Think that will work?" I asked, wondering how my shifting would match up to his footwork with the clutch.

"Everything else about us does," he quipped and gripped the wheel.

Anticipating his action, I put the car in reverse. We slid back in the lot. Then I put it in one, and he spurred us forward.

It was actually a pretty cool thing. It was like proof we were as in sync as I thought. But even though the driving came natural to us, something about what he said bothered me.

Everything else about us does.

I wanted to believe that was true. I wasn't so sure.

There was something I sensed that wasn't exactly working for us. Our engine could be running just a little smoother.

I had some not-so-easy decisions to make.

Twelve

Trent

The point of no return.

I was there.

For so long, I felt I was standing on a precipice. Looking back, but longing to gaze forward. You can't walk forward when your eyes are looking back.

I stumbled. I fell.

I got back up.

I tried to prevent the future from becoming the past by pushing Drew away. Drew wouldn't go. Even my family seemed to sense I had one foot out the door.

They rallied around me. Around us.

I accepted Drew's heart and tucked it right next to mine.

So here I was. Standing in the present, turning my back on the past.

Our r*evol*ution began with love.

Thirteen

Drew

It felt like forever.

Being in my car and speeding down the road seemed like a distant memory in my rearview. Really, it had only been a few days. However, when the minutes between now and then were filled with so much else, it was easy for the feel of the clutch beneath my foot and the sound of the rumbling engine to cease to exist in my mind.

But never in my heart.

Fast cars and driving would be in my heart until the day it stopped beating. It could live right next to Trent.

After breakfast, T went to class, and I hit the road.

Driving alone was sometimes therapeutic. It gave me a good chance to really think and let my mind drift.

It was also damn good practice.

I could make mistakes, I could try out new maneuvers, and I did it without the watchful eye of those I might be competing against. I also could fly in an even less-controlled manner than I usually drove.

Ron Gamble would probably have a fit. If he thought I was too uninhibited when I tried out for him—when I was actually holding back—well, he'd likely fire my ass if he saw me now.

Oddly, that just made me push harder.

I went to the back roads Trent and I drove a lot. I coasted up and down hills, powered around corners, and drifted around curves. After that, I hit up a couple straightaways and opened up the engine. The Fastback needed some work. I'd been driving her hard lately and hadn't really babied the engine as much as usual. I'd been too busy.

After I spent a few hours on the asphalt, I drove across town to an auto parts shop to get some of the stuff I needed beneath the hood. I liked an auto parts store; it was what a bookstore was to a bookworm. I liked the smells, the crowded shelves, the chrome (oh yeah, the chrome). I even liked shooting the shit with the guys behind the counter. They all knew me by now.

So we talked parts and sometimes they gave me deals or the inside scoop on new shit before it hit the shelves.

My hands were full when I stepped out onto the sidewalk and let the door swing shut behind me.

The sound of a smooth engine caught my attention, and I looked up. Lorhaven's black Camaro slid into the parking spot right beside my Fastback.

Goody gumdrops.

As I was stepping off the sidewalk, his driver's door popped open and the dyed blond head of Arrow emerged.

I was relieved it was him and not Lorhaven himself. In fact, I kinda liked this kid, even if he was a Justin Bieber lookalike and my rival's kid brother.

I felt his eyes even though I didn't look at him. "Hey, kid, give me a hand," I called behind me as I went around to my trunk.

He appeared beside me, and I lifted one finger off the box in my hands and wiggled it so my keys would jingle. He took them and popped open the trunk.

"Thanks," I grunted, piling in my stuff.

"That's a lotta shit," Arrow said, poking around in it all.

"Thank your brother for me. All that money I won at his last race sure has come in handy."

"I'll be sure to *not* pass on that message," Arrow said pointedly, then turned to walk away.

"Loyalty, huh? I like that."

He stopped between our two cars and turned. "He's my brother."

"Your brother teach you how to drive?"

Beneath the light-gray plain and oversized hoodie he wore, his shoulders shrugged. His jeans were tight yet still seemed to fall past his ass. How was that even possible? I guess it really shouldn't matter because the sweatshirt and T-shirt beneath it hung so low it covered his boxer-clad ass.

At least I hoped it was boxers. Tightie whities would be fucking wrong.

Nobody needed to see that.

His tight yet too large jeans were ripped at the knees, but his shoes… his shoes were pristine. White high-tops of a very designer brand.

Kid had priorities I supposed.

"He shows me some stuff."

I nodded and slammed the trunk, leaning a hip against the back end. "So you drive 'cause he does, or is it something you love, too?"

His eyes narrowed. "What's with the twenty questions?"

I held up my hands and pushed off my car. "Just making conversation. Contrary to what your brother says, I'm not that bad."

I walked around the Mustang toward the driver's side. I wanted to get home and get to work. The driving had been awesome; now I just needed some grease under my fingernails and I'd feel back on track. Besides, the sky was looking a little gray and moody. I wanted to get some work in before rain ruined it all.

"He doesn't talk bad about you," Arrow said.

I glanced over the roof; I know I looked surprised.

He smirked. "At least not to me."

I respected a guy who didn't teach his little brother to disrespect other people.

"Shouldn't you be in school?" I asked.

He rolled his eyes. "I'm almost twenty."

A little older than I thought. I cocked my head to the side. "You not in college?"

He glanced away. "I don't like school."

Why did I feel like there was more to it than that? In fact, why did I suddenly feel like there was a *lot* more to Arrow than just bleach-blond hair and ill-fitting clothes?

"So you're more like a free-range chicken." I nodded.

"A what?" he echoed.

"You roam free. It's what you do." I finished.

He laughed. I think it was the first genuine laugh and maybe smile I'd seen from this kid.

"I don't roam. I drive."

I chuckled. "All right, kid."

"I'm not a kid." He half growled, the annoyance clear in his face. In fact, the way his eyes whipped up to me and flashed said a lot more than his words.

"All right, *Arrow*." I put emphasis on his actual name. Seriously, though, was that his real name? "You doing anything right now? Wanna drive?"

"With you?" His voice took on a curious tone.

"Sure. How about a friendly race?"

"Friendly?" He scoffed.

I felt my face crack into a smile. "Yeah, as in we won't run each other off the road and I won't take your money when I leave you in my dust."

Arrow sneered. "I'm not that easy to beat."

"Why do you think I'm asking you to ride?" I lifted a brow. "No one likes an easy win."

Truth was the kid—*I mean Arrow*—was a good driver. I wouldn't necessarily say beating him would be easy, but I'd be surprised if I lost. He just needed some practice and a couple more years.

"Where?" He lifted his chin.

I grinned. "Your turf. You pick the road, and I'll follow."

He shrugged. "Yeah, okay."

I smacked the top of my Mustang. "Oh, hey, not downtown."

"Why?" He glanced over his shoulder curiously.

"'Cause I'm supposed to be at work right now."

"You a free-range chicken, too?" he cracked.

"Just on days I'm sick." I made a bogus coughing sound.

He tossed back the long hair falling over the side of his head and laughed. "Let's go."

I followed him… Okay, I rode his ass a few miles away to what looked like an old airstrip that wasn't used much anymore. There was a chain-link fence around the wide, open area, and as we drove closer, I could see the long tufts of brown grass that had grown up and since died between some of the cracks in the pavement.

There was an old, all-white pretty jenky control tower that looked more like a lighthouse perched down the strip, with windows all around the top.

Parked near the fencing in the overgrown grass were planes that were old and looked abandoned. They weren't the big commercial planes; most of these looked like they were (or had been) privately owned.

On the far side of the strip were some metal buildings, all with rounded tops and huge doors that opened. Basically, they were barns for planes.

Arrow pulled up to the gate and got out. My car idled behind his as I watched him jog over where it was locked. For as abandoned as most of the place looked, the lock and security was state of the art. After he flipped up some kind of latch, he moved to a sleek-looking keypad and punched a few buttons.

Seconds later, the chain-link gate swung inward. Arrow made a motion for me to follow him before getting back into his car and driving through. After I followed, the gates swung closed behind my car.

Maybe this place wasn't as unused as I assumed. If so, why would anyone bother with such a nice lock?

I followed him across the pavement toward one of the longest looking strips. He stopped at a white painted line (not faded and chipped, but freshly painted), so I did the same.

He didn't bother to roll down his window; he just revved the engine.

I did the same.

We took off seconds later, and I opened her up, but like always, never going as hard or fast as I knew I could.

It was awesome.

We did a couple drag runs up and down the strip. I beat him every time.

The fourth time I beat him, he hit his brakes and fishtailed to an immediate stop. I was a little more delicate.

He slammed out of the car and glared at me. "Why the fuck do I keep losing?"

I grinned. "You're trying too hard."

He cussed at me some more.

"You're too worried about what I'm doing. Start putting all that energy into what *you're* doing."

He gave me a look and crossed his arms. "Aren't I supposed to pay attention to you?"

"Yes and no." I began and then straightened away from my car. "Obviously, you need to know where I am so we don't collide. And obviously, you want to be able to anticipate my moves. But this is a private road. It's just you and me here, and we're dragging."

"So?"

"So a lot of variables are taken out. Pay less attention to me."

He nodded, thoughtful.

"And stop letting off the gas at the finish line."

"I don't," he argued like I was insulting him.

"The fuck you don't." I chuckled. "Maybe you don't realize it, but you do. Keep that foot pressed down all the way through the line."

"I drive through the line every. Single. Time," he growled.

"Yeah, and that's good. Keep that shit up. But don't slow down. Keep going, even if you think you'll lose."

He studied me like he was trying to decide if I was bullshitting him. I didn't plead my case. I didn't have to.

"Why would you help me?" He challenged.

"Why wouldn't I?"

"Let's go again."

We lined up again and gunned the engines. We both tore off the line at the same time, and he did better. I don't know if it was frustration at losing so much or maybe he took my advice, but he punched it more. He was more involved with his own driving.

This time I barely beat him.

(Maybe I slowed down a little.)

He didn't hesitate at the end.

When he pulled up beside me and rolled down his window, the grin on his face said it all. "Almost!"

"I'm tired of driving in a straight line," I told him. "What's over there?" I pointed toward the plane barns.

"Race ya!" he yelled as his tires squealed away.

I gunned it and caught up to swerve around him and slide my car right in front of his. He swung out, and I hit my emergency brake and drifted into a wide circle. Doing this always made me feel a little off balance. Kind of like being on a ride at some theme park. The kind you loved but also made you want to hurl.

A feeling of Trent overcame me.

He didn't flash behind my eyes. He wasn't a picture in my mind.

He was a *feeling*.

Trent made me feel as if I were drifting in a circle. It was like catching a whiff of some cologne off a complete stranger at the mall, but the scent transported you back to something utterly familiar.

That slightly dizzy, somewhat nauseous but thrilling sensation filling me was no longer just a side effect of driving tricks.

It made me homesick for him. It had been only hours, but I missed him.

My car jerked to a stop. Smoke from the tires floated up around the body of the car and disappeared into the air. Without thought, my palm rubbed my chest. A little of the homesickness went away.

I pulled my hand back. *Wonder what the fuck I was thinking.*

Then I realized.

I'd been rubbing the mark he'd left on my chest. And it made me miss him less.

Well, damn.

A horn cut through the air, and I jerked. Arrow was already way over by the barns.

"Shit," I muttered and hit the gas. I tore over the pavement and parked near the Camaro.

"So what is this place?" I asked as we both climbed out of our rides.

"It used to be the town airport, like back when I was a kid," he explained.

I suppressed a laugh. I was very proud of myself.

Arrow went on. "But they built that new one on the other side of town."

"You just have access to it?"

He shook his head. "My father owns this place. Keeps his planes here."

I knew Lorhaven had money and he was born into it, but they had their own private airstrip. With planes?

"Good place to drive." I looked around, choosing not to acknowledge the fact they were obviously crazy rich.

They weren't the first I knew. Hell, I didn't grow up poor. And I lived with two NFL stars. Money wasn't new to me just because I wasn't rolling around in it. No one wanted to be judged or even befriended based on cash anyway.

"Good place to work on cars, too." He pushed away from the black Camaro and walked over to the nearest "barn." I watched him click a button on his keychain, and the door to the thing swung wide.

Inside the dome-shaped building was a full-on garage. Man, was it sweet.

It was basically #CarGoals.

Before, Trent I would have said it was #Lifegoals.

I whistled beneath my breath. "This is a sweet setup." I felt Arrow watching as I walked in and wandered around. My fingers itched to touch all the tools and the parts out for cleaning or just on display.

In the center was a freaking car lift. Like the kind you saw at car repair shops. Damn, that would be so nice to have. It would make oil changes and undercarriage work so much easier.

On the walls hung a bunch of ribbons and awards. There was even the title to the Camaro, Lorhaven's Corvette, and a couple other cars I'd never seen them drive.

"So where's all the cars?" I asked, motioning at the titles.

"In the next hanger."

Large stainless-steel tool lockers and toolboxes on giant rolling casters lined the walls.

"Your favorite is the Camaro, though, huh?" I swung around to look at him.

He nodded. "It's tough."

I don't know why, but to me, that seemed like an odd response. Did he need a tough car because he didn't feel so tough himself?

God. I was turning into Oprah.

I needed some fries. A beer. And my person.

Not necessarily in that order.

I pulled my hands out of the pockets of my leather jacket and pivoted toward the entrance. My eyes caught a display nearby, and they about fell out of my head.

"Is that a vintage Benford sparkplug?"

"Yep."

That sparkplug had its own gravitational pull. I couldn't resist going over and letting my hands hover over the space above it. "I've never seen one of these in person," I said, awed.

Serious car junkies sometimes collected rare or vintage car parts. Sparkplugs could be very sought after, including this one. It was plated with twenty-four-carat gold.

"You can touch it," Arrow said from close by.

I hadn't even noticed him approach. I was too blinded by the vintage beauty.

"Where the hell did you find this?" I asked, picking it up and cradling it gently. I smoothed my thumb over the sides.

"Not sure. It's my brother's."

I grimaced. I'd forgotten about Lorhaven.

Reluctantly, I put it down and resisted the urge to pull out my phone and take a selfie with it.

Please. It would be better than those horrid bathroom selfies people post all over social media. Like, dude, no one wants to see your toilet.

"I'm sure your brother would blow a gasket if he knew you brought me here."

"He's not that bad."

I leveled my eyes on his. "I still have the dents in my fender from when he tried to run me off the road."

Arrow grinned.

"Anyway…" I began and stepped back from the sparkplug. "You're doing better with the driving. Just remember what I said."

"You're leaving?" he asked.

"I got places to be." T's classes were letting out soon.

"I can help you with those dents if you want." He offered.

I glanced up, and he looked away shyly. Poor kid probably didn't have any friends. His brother likely scared them all away.

"Maybe another time," I said.

I was almost to the door when he spoke again. "So what's up with you and your manager?"

I stopped and turned. "What do you mean?"

"Haven't seen him around much lately."

"He's been busy."

"So he's still around?"

I hesitated. "Yeah…"

"What about that pro driver? The girl?"

"Joey went back home."

He was full of questions suddenly.

"Cool." He shifted. Awkwardness was like his new best friend.

"I'll catch you later," I said, lifting a hand and waving.

"See ya," Arrow called back.

That was weird, right?

In the car, the first thing I did was check my cell. There was text from T.

Class over. Stopping by the frat b4 I find you.

Want me to meet you there? I texted back.

No. I'll come to you.

I knew he'd say that. *Everything okay?*

No.

My fingers spasmed around the black case on my phone. *What the hell does that mean?*

I turned the key and fired up the engine while I waited, impatient for a reply.

I miss you.

It was a good thing I was alone, because the goofy grin on my face when I read that would have been embarrassing.

Me, too.

I'll hurry.

I dropped the phone in my lap and sped home. I even ran a couple lights just for fun.

Just as I turned onto my street, the sky opened up and rain literally dumped from the clouds. "Seriously?" I yelled upward.

A crack of lightning and the rumble of thunder replied.

"Assholes," I muttered.

No one was home when I pulled in the driveway. Romeo and B left to do some NFL stuff this morning and wouldn't be back until the day after tomorrow. Rim was probably at the shelter, and Ivy could've been anywhere. Probably at the boutique or shopping for her fashion channel.

Since Romeo wasn't home, I took advantage and opened up the garage and drove in. He always parked here, but since him and his Hellcat would be gone tonight, I could do the work on my car inside, rain be damned.

The sound of the heavy drops splattering against the driveway (the door was still open) was kind of nice. After shedding my jacket, I got to work unloading the car parts and pulling out tools.

As I worked, my mind drifted to the place it always seemed to go lately.

Trent.

Fourteen

Trent

The sky seemed to open up out of nowhere. One second, everything was calm (but gray), and the next, heavy sheets of rain pounded my windshield.

I didn't mind the rain so much, though. It had a sort of cleansing effect on things. Washing away the worst to give way to a clean slate.

Today had been long. People stared, people asked me about my bruises, and rumors flew. I didn't do anything to dissuade any of the talk. Why should I?

Let the fuckers who worked me over get a nice heap of oh fuck. Let them hear it all, see it all, and get nervous. I saw one of the four on campus. The second he saw me, he turned and hiked the other direction.

The second classes were over, I went to the frat, did some obligatory shit, and then swung by a drive-thru on the way home. It wasn't dark yet when I pulled into the driveway, though everything outside was shrouded in shadows and the sun was nowhere to be seen.

The garage door was open, and the Fastback was parked inside. The hood was propped up, and I smiled because I knew Drew was there leaning over the engine.

Almost as if he heard my thought, the top of his blond head poked up and stared out through the heavy rain to my car.

I cut the engine and pulled my black baseball hat a little lower to shield my face. Rain pelted me the instant I lurched out of the dry interior of my car, and water splashed up my ankles as I ran into the garage. Once there, I stopped and shook myself like a dog fresh out of the bath.

"What took you so long?" Drew griped, coming around the car. His blue eyes slid up my body and latched onto my face.

From beneath the rim of my hat, I watched him, taking in his familiar, welcome form. "Brought you some fries." I held up a white paper sack. The coffee I'd gotten myself was still in the Mustang, long forgotten. Who needed caffeine when I had a dimple-wielding car addict in front of me?

Drew snatched the bag out of my hand and reached in to pull out a bunch of fries. I watched him shove them all into his mouth. The side of his cheek puffed out with the food, and his eyes rolled back a little while he groaned. "I needed these."

Just like that, my day didn't seem so long anymore. In fact, I stood there and prayed the minutes—no, the seconds dragged by from here on out because I wanted as much time with him as humanly possible.

"What about me?" I scoffed, mock indignation in my voice.

Drew shoved another huge bite of fries into his mouth. "Fries before guys."

"Your priorities suck, Forrester," I told him.

He set aside the sack and wiped the salty grease from his food on the shoulder of his shirt. Correction, *my* shirt.

The toes of his shoes hit mine when he stepped up close. His hands reached for my hat and spun it around backward on my head.

Excitement curled low in my belly, and I had to force myself to stand there and not grab him close. I liked the anticipation. Of waiting to see what he would do. Of not being the one to always make the first move.

I wasn't opposed to it. In fact, if someone asked, I would likely answer I made a lot more first moves than he did.

That's what made this moment so much sweeter.

"My priorities are exactly as they should be." His voice was low. I had to strain to hear him over the pounding of the rain.

I lifted an eyebrow. "Fries before guys." I reminded him.

"You're not a guy."

"No?"

He closed the distance between us. Our chests bumped when he advanced. Any bystander might glance at us and assume we were measuring the other, possibly even challenging the other… but there was no challenge here.

Only desire.

His lips came close. "No," he whispered. I felt the brush of his mouth more than I actually heard the word.

Then he was kissing me, and I forgot all about fries and anticipation. I sank into the kiss. I actually felt my soul tug inside me, swaying toward Drew.

Unable to help myself, I wrapped one arm around his shoulders and held him tightly against my body. Drew's hands wound around my waist and dipped low, fingertips pulling at the hem of my shirt, and my back muscles contracted waiting for his touch.

Instead of going up beneath the fabric, his hands slid down, diving right into the back pockets of my jeans so he could palm my ass.

I groaned into his mouth and tilted my head a little farther. Drew intensified the kiss, his tongue delving deep, and we battled it out for who could explore more of the other.

A crash of thunder literally shook the roof, but it didn't matter. We were creating our own storm right here in each other's arms. When at last he retreated, he did so slowly, pulling my lower lip as he went, tugging it out and sucking gently.

My heart was thumping when we pulled apart and the air brushed over my kiss-slicked lips and made them feel cold.

Drew smirked like he was proud of himself for kissing the shit out of me and reached down to adjust the hardness beneath his jeans. When he was done, he reached over and adjusted mine.

Blazing hot need pulsed through my veins. "Be careful, Forrester," I said, hoarse. "Your virginity is at stake."

He scoffed and grabbed the bag of fries to shove some more in his face. His lips were slightly swollen now from kissing.

"I hate to break it to you," he said, chewing loudly, "but that ship sailed a long time ago."

"Not the ship I'm talking about."

He paused in chewing. The second he realized what I meant, he glanced down at my cock.

"I took your virginity." The possession and pride in his tone was just a little arrogant.

"I gave it to you." I corrected.

"Would you do it again?" His voice was curious, if even a little abrupt.

Was that a little vulnerability? I smiled. "That's something I can only give once."

He made a face, and the white sack crumpled when his hand clenched around it.

"Yeah, Forrester," I said low. "I'd do it again."

Just like that, the confidence he always wore like a second skin came back. His smile was quick and satisfied. His hand dove back in for the food. "I'm not sharing my fries."

"There's ketchup in the bag," I told him, amused. Like I even entertained the thought of him sharing those damn fries. "And I do have a burger in there… You gonna eat that, too?"

He made a face. "You probably got extra tomato on it."

"Nah, I'll just add the tomato off yours to mine."

He grunted and moved to the front of the car. "Come look at this. I need a hand with the engine."

Just like that, we transitioned into best friend mode. I loved it. I loved the layers to our relationship. I loved how one minute, he was adjusting my junk because he was the one who made it hard, and the next, we were eating burgers and arguing over the best way to fix an engine.

It was everything. And though our relationship had many layers, they weren't separate. Like my feelings for him weren't kept in a neat little box beside the one where our friendship was.

We swirled together. Like chocolate and vanilla soft serve, like ketchup and mustard on a burger.

Our friendship was better because of our love. Our love was better because it blossomed out of friendship.

"You need some muscle," I told him after a few minutes of watching him work. "Step aside." I used the flat of my hand against his shoulder to push him over to wedge myself above the engine where he'd been showing me what he was doing.

After a few seconds, I loosened the cap he was struggling with and also flipped a few other things open and pulled out a bad sparkplug.

"See?" I held the plug up with one hand and patted his cheek with my other. "I think Mr. Magazine Cover is turning into a pretty boy."

Drew slapped my hand away. "Asshole."

I laughed and went back to work. The garage was dim because there was only one overhead light and the sky outside was darkening quickly. The rainstorm added an extra gloomy quality to the light, but it wasn't a hindrance. We were two guys hunkered down amongst tools and greasy food. Just the two of us without the outside world to bother with.

A little while later, my hands were dirty and the scent of oil filled the air. Both our heads were bent low and a bare bulb was lit and clipped to the underside of the hood, giving us some much-needed extra light.

I felt Drew move slightly, his elbows hitting the edge of the car. "So this is what you had in mind for dinner tonight?"

I moved back and grabbed a nearby rag to wipe off my hands. "Do you need more romance, Forrester?" I teased.

"Do you?" He wasn't teasing. Slowly, Drew pulled back, propped a hip against the car, and crossed his arms over his chest.

I watched him closely, trying to hear what he hadn't said. "Why would you think that?"

He shrugged. "You're not the best talker, T. That's cool, but I don't want you sacrificing your own happiness for mine."

I dropped the rag on the workbench and stepped closer, mirroring his position. It hit me in all the soft spots. He was asking if I was happy like he was worried I wasn't.

As if I could be anything but happy with him.

"All I want is who we are." I gestured between us. "Burgers and fries, engines, bad jokes, and maybe you beside me in bed at night."

"That's all?" He tilted his head.

I nodded. "But if you need more separation… like more friend time and more… person time, then I'm down. Say the word. I'll even get you some flowers and pretend I'm nervous when I pick you up at the door."

I'd totally be nervous. But he didn't need to know I was serious. But joking aside, this was something I needed to know. I thought the way we blended was perfect, but what if he didn't feel the same?

"Flowers?" He cocked an eyebrow.

"You can be the girl in the relationship." So maybe I wasn't done joking. On the outside anyway. It helped cover some of the nerves bunching low in my belly. Even though we made it past a lot of hard parts, it didn't mean any of this was easy. It might not ever be. But some things in life were worth the struggle.

He laughed and shook his head. The blue of his eyes sparked with amusement, and I relaxed a little. "You know how I feel about labels, frat boy."

"My bad." I pretended to be sorry.

Drew chuckled and rubbed a hand over his face. He had some grease smeared on his fingers. I thought about snatching his hand and cleaning it up for him. "I don't want you to think I'm ashamed of you. Of us."

I stiffened, and although I didn't make a sound, I still heard a low whistle in my mind. That was a heavy sentence to drop. It blew up all traces of jokes and sarcasm. "I don't think that."

He glanced up, held my eyes. I liked the way we'd grown together. How once we skirted around the way we felt, ran from our thoughts. Now we looked each other in the eye and dealt with it.

"I had some time to think today."

I nodded so he would continue.

"You noticed how I reacted when everyone looked at us when we came downstairs, how my instinct was to pull away. I haven't told my father, my brother, or Gamble."

"Drew—" I started, but he cut me off.

"You've been shouldering our relationship alone. You got attacked for it. You faced the frat and when you told the family you were gay. You. Not me. You probably wouldn't have told them about me at all if I hadn't spoken up. Would you?"

Slowly, I shook my head. Of course I wouldn't. That was his decision to make. I'd never take something like that out of his hands.

Drew pressed his lips together before continuing. "You've kept me out of it. You've been shielding me."

"And I'll keep doing it. There's no timeline on this. There's no rule that says you have to spring out of the closet and shout our relationship to the world. You don't have to declare we're dating. You don't have to hold my hand in public. You don't have to do anything you aren't ready for."

"I called Ron Gamble before you got here," he said.

I jerked upright. "What?"

"I asked for a meeting. I'm going to tell him."

"If you're doing this because you somehow think I want you to…"

"Don't you?" He pressed gently.

I sighed. "Have I thought about it? Hell yeah, but not because I think you're ashamed. I think the unknown of people's reactions is a heavy burden for you to bear. In some ways, it would be easier if we could walk into a room and not worry about how we looked at each other."

"People are gonna see regardless," he mused.

I smiled. "Yeah, probably. But I can back off, stay in the background of your career."

"No." His voice was hard and finite. "You've spent almost all the time I've known you in the background, T. You don't belong there, and I'll be damned if that's where I put you."

"What are you saying?" I asked, trying not to be totally won over by his burst of resolve.

"I want to live like I drive. Full throttle. I don't want to back down. I don't want to put my career above our relationship. I don't want a line drawn between my life with you on one side and everything else on the other."

"Tell me what you need, Drew. You'll have it." I kind of felt like I was walking a tight rope. Walking that line Drew mentioned he didn't want to have. It was unsteady, and I was scared, but I had to keep my balance. I had to make it across.

"As determined as I am…" His voice faded away and his face turned down so I couldn't look at him.

"You're scared." If he couldn't say, I could. I knew what it was like to be scared. I knew what it was like when you weren't supposed to be scared. My joke about Drew being a girl aside, we were both men, strong ones, ones who would never want to show weakness.

The truth was everyone in life was sometimes afraid. It was how one reacted to that fear that defined a person.

He nodded but didn't look up.

The need to make the bubble Drew and I lived in a little bit bigger, a little more secure, grew tenfold. The distance between us was minimal. I grabbed him, not really caring if he was ready or not. Sometimes I liked to move slow with him, cautious so as not to scare him away.

But now wasn't the time for that shit.

Now was the time for action. I knew what it was like to be scared and to fall into a black hole of not knowing how people would react to the way you felt inside. I didn't want him to feel that. I knew it was likely inevitable—it was a natural almost automatic response to falling in love with your best friend—but he wasn't alone.

He didn't have to be alone.

His big body collided with mine, and I wound both arms around him to hold him close. My heart ached a little when his forehead hit my shoulder, like it was a relief I was offering to hold him up.

"You aren't alone," I whispered.

"Do you ever get scared?" he whispered back.

All the fucking time. "Not when you're beside me."

"Liar," he muttered.

I tried to suppress my laughter, but my body quaked with it, so I know he felt it, too.

"I'm coming to the meeting. I'm gonna be there at your parents' house," I told him.

His body, which was pliable in my arms, went rigid.

"Don't bother," I said, lazy, tightening my grip. "It's not up for discussion. I don't have to talk, but I will be there. I just said you aren't alone, and I meant it."

"What if he throws me out?" Although the words weren't whispered, they were low, and they ripped from the deepest part of him. A part so deep I had no idea it even existed.

He gave me something else with those painful words. Something I didn't even know was missing.

He was mine entirely now.

He might have given me his heart before, but it wasn't just his heart I wanted.

I wanted the place I thought only I had inside me. That place that hid behind the heart. As tender as the heart was, this place was more so. A place so fragile only the heart could protect it.

He showed it to me.

Now it wasn't just his heart that would protect it.

I would, too.

For all the fierceness that rose up inside me, I couldn't lie. "I don't know," I replied and hugged him a little tighter.

The sharp grip of his fingertips pushed into my lower back, and I let him cling. It reminded me of all the times I tied a knot in the straw paper he always blew across the table at me.

Sometimes in life you had to tie a knot and hold on. I would be his knot.

Of all the obstacles Drew and I faced as men who'd fallen in love, the biggest hurdle for Drew was his father. I didn't know what it was like to want to please someone so badly, because my dad had never been around.

It seemed like a lot of pressure to not only be who you were, but who everyone else wanted you to be.

Oh.

Maybe I did understand that better than I realized.

Drew shifted, but he didn't pull away. His head turned to the side and his cheek rested against my shoulder. It wasn't often I got to hold him. It wasn't often he seemed to need this kind of reassurance.

Even though it was for reasons that were difficult, I relished in it. A light, almost giddy feeling somersaulted around inside me. It was still new between us, or maybe the chemistry was just so raw it would always be this way. A million butterflies knocked around inside my stomach, bouncing off the walls and making everything feel like an earthquake.

"You smell like leather," I murmured, tucking in just a little closer. I had to get my feels in while I could get 'em.

"You smell like home."

Aanndd holding him wasn't enough anymore.

I wrenched away, his fingers dragged over my sides as I yanked and practically tossed his ass on the edge of the open engine. The hood was propped up just enough to allow his head room, and I lunged forward between his open knees to attack.

My fist twisted in the front of his T-shirt, bunching the fabric the way he bunched up my heart. My chest rumbled like a souped-up engine as my lips latched onto his.

He tasted like salt and French fries, his lips full and warm.

I licked deep, so deep his body swayed backward, but he wasn't about to get away. I slammed my hand down on top of the engine to brace my weight while both his hands clamped around my shoulders.

If he were a snow drift, I'd be the plow. I wasn't gentle, but really, I didn't have to be. I kissed him like I always wanted to but never actually did.

I lost count of time, of the sound of the rain. Everything around me distorted down until the only thing in focus was the burning need to satiate the way he made me feel.

But kissing Drew was like drinking water from the sea. The more I drank, the thirstier I became.

So I kissed him endlessly; I devoured his mouth with relentless appetite.

There was no way a woman could withstand the potency of passion between us. We were like two forces of nature crashing together at unmatched speed. But Drew could. Speed was practically his specialty, and his strength matched my own.

I released the grip on his shirt, palmed his hip, and pulled him right up against me. Our centers met. His dick was stiff beneath his sweats, and the friction of it rubbing against my jeans made me shudder.

I wrenched my mouth away and pressed my lips together. My balls were drawn so tight up against my body I wanted to shove my hand down the front of my pants and massage them.

So careful. I'd always been painstakingly careful with Drew. Until now.

"I think I might be high," Drew said, breathless, his body swaying a little.

I hid a smile. I was feeling a little high myself. "Too much?" I asked.

"More." He scoffed. "I want more."

I rubbed my thumb across his lower lip. Back and forth. Back and forth.

Just as I was about to suggest we take this inside, a sound snapped me back to reality, and reality brought an unwelcome guest.

"Well, well, what do we have here?"

My head whipped up as Lorhaven stepped into view.

Fifteen

Drew

Panic hit me first.

It wasn't my finest moment and I wasn't proud. But I didn't have control over my immediate reaction to a surprise.

It was so incredibly easy to feel secure with Trent. I didn't even have to try.

So when Lorhaven stepped into view and no doubt saw how Trent and I were wrapped up in one another, I felt like a volcano I didn't even know was active erupted inside me.

The panic was hot. It burned beneath my flesh; like lava, it wanted to cling to everything it touched, and I knew if I let it, then it would cool into cement and I'd never fully shake it free.

Fuck that.

"What the hell are you doing here?" Trent said. There wasn't a trace of panic in his voice, only anger and annoyance.

He didn't even indicate he wondered what Lorhaven saw. But I knew he was thinking about it, trying to read me without looking back. His body turned in the direction of our visitor, effectively blocking me from sight.

As much as I wanted to declare I didn't need even just a second to recover, I did. I was grateful for a moment's reprieve.

"After today, I thought I had an invite to drop by anytime I wanted. Maybe I should have called first?" Lorhaven quipped.

I straightened from the car. T was so close our bodies brushed together.

"After today?" Trent echoed.

I stepped around him, up to his side.

Lorhaven barely glanced at me before giving Trent all his attention once more. "What the fuck happened to your face?"

Trent crossed his arms over his chest. The acknowledgement of his battered appearance made me wonder about his ribs. I hadn't even asked about them yet.

Trent ignored him entirely and swung to me. "What happened today?"

"I did some driving with Arrow," I replied.

"And you thought that gave you an engraved invitation to our house?" Trent asked Lorhaven. I don't think he even realized what he said, how he called this place *our* house.

But Lorhaven noticed. He smirked. "Where I come from, if I let you into my place, then your door is open as well."

"Arrow took me where they keep their cars." I explained a little further.

"You guys have your own garage?" Trent asked, curiosity winning over the anger. He didn't like my rival, but information was always handy to have.

Lorhaven grunted. "It's an airstrip. We have several hangars."

"But you don't *live* there." Trent pointed out.

"Arrow does."

And that explained the bed I saw in the back of the hangar. Damn. I'd been right. *That kid must be hella lonely.* I felt bad for leaving now.

"Your brother lives at an abandoned airstrip?" Trent scoffed.

"It's not abandoned," I answered, thinking of the security and the planes. I folded my arms over my chest. "Why does he live there?"

If their father had all the money I knew he did, why was his son living at a garage?

"What happened to his face?" Lorhaven ignored my question to ask his own.

"I decked him," I lied.

Lorhaven looked between me and T. His stare was divided between scrutiny and interest. "Didn't look like you were fighting when I got here. At least not the kind with fists."

"You son of a bitch," Trent growled and lunged forward. Within seconds, he had Lorhaven pinned against the wall, his forearm pressed right at his throat.

To my surprise, Lorhaven didn't fight back. He let himself be restrained. Correction, he didn't try to get out. Maybe he knew it would be a waste of energy. The power Trent was clearly pulsing with was no bluff. It was real, and he was pissed.

I had no doubt in any part of me that when T was finally pushed to the edge of that careful control he always imposed on himself, whoever was on the receiving end wouldn't stand a chance.

Even so, Lorhaven didn't know Trent like I did. He didn't know the private fight he'd been battling since I met him. Lorhaven couldn't possibly know just how dangerous Trent would be if pushed to protect the one thing he valued most.

Us.

Yet he still put up no fight.

Why?

"I don't know what you think you saw…" Trent warned.

"I think we both know what I saw." Lorhaven's voice was strained, like the pressure on his windpipe was starting to wear him down.

"Trent…" I stepped forward.

"If you—" He began, not listening to me at all.

Lorhaven tried to smile, I think, but it was more of a grimace. His body shifted. The black leather jacket he wore scuffed against the wall. "I don't care."

Adrenaline was already pooling into my limbs, tingling my fingertips and readying my body in case I had to pry T off, but those words tripled my heart rate.

Did he mean what I thought he meant, or was it just wishful thinking? Was it me being so freaked that someone found out about us before we were ready to tell?

"Don't you fuck with me," Trent growled.

Lorhaven held out his hands like he was surrendering.

"T…" I recovered just enough to speak. "He's not fighting you, frat boy. Step back and find out why."

A funny feeling was starting to climb up the back of my neck. I wasn't sure if it was intuition or just a rush from standing here at the ready.

Trent backed off with a huff, but he didn't retreat very far.

"I underestimated your guard dog, Forrester," Lorhaven said after he straightened off the wall. "I wish my brother were that lucky."

Snap.

Just like that I understood.

I stared into Lorhaven's eyes. "He does. Isn't that why you're here?"

"I thought he was wrong about you." His head shook a little.

"Are you two speaking Japanese?" Trent cut in.

"Arrow's gay, T," I said, blunt.

Trent reacted physically, drawing back, surprise widening his hazel eyes. "No shit?"

Lorhaven nodded.

"He was hitting on me," I whispered to myself. The questions, the offer to help me fix my car, bringing me back to his place… He was trying to feel me out.

"What!" Trent gasped.

"Down, boy," Lorhaven pushed away from the wall and stepped back into the conversation, not threatened in the least Trent might lose his shit again. He gave T a look. "Your boy here is slow on the uptake just like you."

I scowled. "I've never been hit on by a guy before."

"So I'm assuming this is your first, uh, relationship with a man?" Lorhaven asked, glancing between me and Trent.

"How is that your business?" Trent snapped.

"We're making it his business," I said mildly. "Isn't this what we were just talking about? Coming out?"

By the way? What the fuck kind of term is *coming out?*

Coming out from where? Hiding? The closet? La-La Land?

I never had to "come out" when I was dating a girl. I wasn't hiding my relationship with Trent... Okay, fine. Maybe I was. But it was a defense mechanism.

Kinda pissed me off I had to be defensive for falling for my best friend.

I looked back at Lorhaven and nodded. Seemed like starting right here, right now and telling him what was between me and T was as good a place as any. Besides, Lorhaven was an asshole. Maybe his reaction would give me some practice for the rest of the world.

"Makes sense. That's probably why I never pegged you as gay."

"I'm not gay," I said insufferably.

"You know what I mean," he rebutted and rolled his eyes.

Okay, so maybe he wouldn't be great practice because it really seemed he didn't give two shits.

"So the Biebs is gay." Trent mulled it over.

"Watch it," Lorhaven growled.

"Like you don't agree he totally looks like Justin Bieber." Trent scoffed. "And you're here because he's into Drew."

The black boots on Lorhaven's feet planted a little more firmly into the concrete, his weight settling into an almost alert stance and his fingers flexing. This guy was a lot of things, but clearly, he was loyal to his brother.

And this was why his brother was loyal to him.

"He's never brought anyone back to our place before," he said, his voice a little vulnerable compared to his body language. I understood that paradox far better than he likely realized.

It was the way a man acted when he felt vulnerable but, even so, would fight to death to protect himself and anyone else he cared about.

Trent looked like that a lot.

Looking between the two now… Trent and Lorhaven had a lot in common.

"He's young, he's trying to figure shit out, and for some reason, he likes you." He looked at me straight on.

"And you're afraid I'm going to hurt him," I surmised.

"It hasn't always been easy for my brother. I came to warn you off."

Trent made a sound. "You mean scare him off."

Lorhaven shrugged like there was no difference between the two.

"And now?" Trent asked.

Lorhaven lifted an eyebrow.

"Now that you know about me and Drew?" He elaborated.

Lorhaven's dark, intense gaze came back to me. "He said you gave him some pointers today. Worked with him on his driving."

I shrugged. "A little. He's a good driver. Seems like he really wants to learn."

"I've always been into cars," Lorhaven said. "It's more recent for Arrow. Racing is an outlet for him. A place to channel his energy. It's become a passion. I think it's good for him."

I understood that. There was nothing quite like the freedom of flying down an empty stretch of road.

"And Drew gives him a hard-on," Trent said.

You know, if we were a bunch of women standing around, everyone would be all offended by that. Good thing we weren't women.

"Pretty much." Lorhaven shrugged. "He told me you left kind of abruptly today. He didn't seem to think too much of it, but he always wants to believe in people." He shook his head like the idea made him sad.

"You thought I figured out he was hitting on me and couldn't get away fast enough."

"Pretty much. There's a lot of bigoted assholes out there."

That's what I was afraid of.

"Now you know you don't have to worry about me or Trent making it hard on him. We get it," I said.

His stance changed. It was like this invisible weight lifted off him. He looked between me and T again, studying us. "I'm guessing the bruises on your face and the reason your favoring your one side is because you've met some of those bigoted assholes."

"Yeah," Trent replied.

"Look, I know we have the whole rivalry thing going on…" Lorhaven motioned between me and him. "And you and I…" Lorhaven turned back to T. "Well, we kinda hate each other."

"Why the hell do you hate each other?" I wondered out loud.

They both shrugged.

Unbelievable…

"That shit doesn't have anything to do with this. This isn't something I would use against you. There are some lines a man just doesn't cross. You don't have to worry about me. You have my support."

"You support me and Drew," Trent reiterated like he wanted to be sure.

Lorhaven nodded. "You gotta let people be who they are."

"Your brother is lucky," I said.

"No. He struggled for a while before I realized what was going on. I was caught up in my own life, my cars, women… but I know now, and I'm trying to make up for it."

"You can't make up for it," Trent said nakedly. "But being there now counts."

"It's hard," Lorhaven whispered. It was like Trent's truth allowed him to speak his own.

"I know," Trent replied.

Are they getting along? Bonding?

Was that a little bit of jealousy stirring in the depth of my belly?

"I'd like to maybe hang out with Arrow again," I said. "If that's okay with you?"

"Yeah." Lorhaven rubbed a hand over his head and blew out a breath. Again, I felt a feeling of relief tumble off him. "Yeah, I think that would be good for him."

"For sure," Trent said, leaning back against the side of the Fastback, finally relaxing. "But I am gonna have to tell him Forrester is spoken for."

I suppressed a smile. Kinda made me proud Trent wanted to stake his claim.

Lorhaven grunted and then offered me his hand. I shook it.

Then, to my surprise, he did the same to Trent. For a second, I thought maybe T would rebuff him, the way he looked down at the outstretched hand. But then he straightened and slid his palm against Lorhaven's.

"You ever need some backup dealing with the douche nozzles that pounded your face, call me. Some guys just deserve a good ass kicking," Lorhaven said as they spoke.

"I got it handled," Trent replied.

"I figured."

In the wide doorway of the garage, Lorhaven stopped and turned back. "Maybe let him down easy," he said to me.

I half smiled. "Done."

Trent made a sound. "Drew's too old for him anyway."

Again, that sad smile crossed his features. "Arrow's a lot older than the calendar. Wise beyond his years in a lot of ways."

He jogged out into the rainstorm, not even wincing when the splattering rain attacked his shoulders and head. I watched him until he disappeared into his Corvette and the headlights cut across the pavement.

Trent leaned back against the Fastback, his eyes focused on me. "That was the last thing I expected today."

"No shit." I agreed.

But as far as surprises went, it was pretty good one.

Not only did I have the people I lived with and Trent by my side, but now I had an ally in the racing world.

An ally in the form of my rival.

Which, oddly, made the fact he offered us alliance a lot more legit.

Today was a good day for me. So much support. So much acceptance. It wouldn't all be like this. I wasn't so naïve to think that.

However, I wasn't as alone as maybe I'd thought.

Sixteen

Trent

That confrontation with Lorhaven pushed me off the ledge I was teetering on. The second he looked at Drew and me and the realization hit his eyes, I stepped.

No. I didn't just step.

I leapt.

Something in me snapped. It was an audible sound inside my head.

I was reminded exactly who I was.

Exactly who I wanted to be.

I was strong. I was capable. I might not be what everyone thought, but I was better.

Possessive and protective. That was us.

There was no turning back now. We'd come too far. My love was too deep. The point of no return was an interesting place. It was a state of mind, an acceptance of the future and a vow to leave the past exactly where it belonged.

Behind me.

All that was left now was to move forward.

The week went fast. I had to admit watching Con and his three little accomplices squirm was a special kind of fun. Some might say I was playing with my food…

But didn't they deserve it?

Did knowing punishment was coming, but not knowing when or how, make it worse?

By the looks on their faces every time I saw them… oh yeah.

Those weeks Con spent chirping in my ear like an annoying little insect, whispering dirty words and intentions… Now I was giving him a dose of that, too. Every chance I got.

On Wednesday night, we had a frat party. Not a new occurrence. But this was a special party because my brothers were using it as a recon mission, trying to figure out who jumped me.

And me? I was very hospitable.

I handed out beers, taking care to make sure I gave one each to my four special friends. *Ah,* the dubious way they stared at those beers, silently wondering what I'd put in them when no one was looking.

Of course I stood there and waited for them to drink them. There was no way they could get out of it. What kind of blasphemy would it be to deny a personally poured beverage from your leader?

Suckers.

I admit I thought about slipping a little special something in their drinks.

But almost as soon as the idea occurred, I nixed it. Something like that was done to Ivy once. That shit wasn't funny, and doing it would only pull me down to the level of the creep who did it to her.

Plus, I'd rather they be conscious and alert for my payback.

By the weekend, the bruises on my face and body were yellowed and fading. The cut on my head no longer needed a butterfly. My ribs still hurt, but at least I didn't favor my opposite side as much.

I gave some credit for my healing to the Wolves coach. Even though technically the season was over, he was still committed to his players.

I walked into his office busted, and he made it his mission to make sure every time I walked out, I was a little bit stronger. It was the football way of life.

Busted happened. Healing happened, too.

The Wolves had a damn good medical and training program for the players. I had access to the trainers, the physical therapist, and all the equipment in the state-of-the-art gym.

I'd seen the trainer three times this week. The therapist dropped in the first day to help write out a plan and approved exercises that would help accelerate the healing, but still be safe and not make my rib area worse.

Coach asked me once what happened to me. I gave him the same exact story I told the frat. I knew he smelled my bullshit, but he didn't call me on it.

Once word got around I was training in the gym, some of the other players came around, and we'd all work out together. So in a way, getting jumped was a blessing.

A fucked-up blessing, but one all the same.

I missed my football brothers. Sure, I saw them on campus and they came to the frat parties, but I missed the comradery of the team. The sounds and echoes of the locker room.

I had that back now. I had them rallying around me because someone beat my ass. I even got several of them involved in the charity football game we were putting together.

It was going to be sweet. Romeo, Braeden, and the boys all back on the field together again for one last time.

Hells yeah.

But, yeah. I often wondered if the Wolves would still come if they knew I was gay. I wished I didn't have that doubt whispering in the back of my head. I knew someday I wouldn't.

Someday soon, like *very* soon, I would know the answer.

It would be a defining time in my life. In Drew's life. We would find out who our true friends were.

We checked into the same hotel we stayed at when Drew met with Ron Gamble the first time. We didn't even bother driving up to the valet; there was no point. Drew would never let anyone drive his car (besides me of course), and I didn't need dropped off at the door.

Once the Mustang was parked in a relatively safe spot, we grabbed our bags and walked to the entrance. I recognized the valet right away; it was the same one from before. I didn't expect him to remember us, but he did.

"The Fastback right?" he asked, looking at me, not Drew.

I grinned. "Hey, man. How ya doing?"

"Another day, another dollar," he quipped.

Drew looked between us, confused.

I reached into my pocket and pulled out some cash. "You remember the deal from last time?" I asked, holding up the green.

The valet inclined his dark head. "Of course. Your car will be safe."

"Thanks, man." I slapped the cash into his hand and pointed to the spot where it was parked. He nodded and pocketed the money.

When we were out of earshot, Drew looked at me. "What the hell was that?"

"Insurance. Making sure the car doesn't get jacked while we're here."

"You paid the valet to watch my car last time we were here?"

"Yeah." I shrugged and pulled open the door leading into the muted gold tones of the hotel lobby.

"Always looking out, aren't you?" he asked, warmth lighting his eyes.

"Always." I agreed.

His fist appeared between us, so I bumped it out.

After we checked in, on the way past the large fountain with the couple beneath the umbrella, Drew's phone went off.

He ignored it.

In the elevator, I gestured to his pocket. "You gonna check that?"

"Nope."

My phone went off. I pulled up the text message. It was from Joey.

You in town? Why isn't Drew answering his phone?

@Hotel now, I texted back. *He's checking in.*

Yep. I lied. My loyalty would always be with Drew. I had a good idea why he was ignoring his phone, even though the only thing he was actually doing was making the fixation on the fucking thing worse.

Telling Joey what was going on inside my person's head was not on my to-do list. If he wasn't ready to talk about it, then he wasn't ready.

We have dinner plans. I'm coming to pick you up.

Wait. What? First I'd heard of this. "We have dinner tonight with Joey?" I asked as the elevator slid to a stop.

Drew gave me a *WTF* look.

What dinner plans? I texted. At the same time, I said, "Maybe if you picked up your phone one of the hundred times it's gone off, we might know what the hell's going on."

I'll be there in twenty. Send me your room number.

I shot off a quick reply with our room number as we walked down the empty, swanky hall and stopped in front of our pristine white door.

The puzzling fact we had some surprise dinner plans fell off my map for a moment. Instead, as I watched Drew unlock the door, a giddy kind of feeling washed over me. I was nervous. A whole night alone in a hotel room with him.

No worrying about anyone on the other side of the walls. No frat brothers to sneak past, no family members to wake. Showering together and leaving the bathroom door open.

The same bed.

Him beside me.

Breakfast in our boxers.

Little things that were the big things. Moments I'd been waiting for.

The last time we were in this hotel, I'd been wound so tight I'd barely slept. Knowing he was so close, knowing I couldn't touch him how I wanted. It wasn't like that anymore. Our relationship grew into something I honestly only thought I would imagine and never get to live.

This time, when I sank into the cloudlike king-size bed, he would, too.

I felt like I did the morning of my first college football game. Scared and excited at the same time. I felt like a kid on at date at the movies, thinking of a sly way to pull off the "movie move."

So many firsts. So many feelings and experiences that were new. With Drew, it was sort of like I was learning to live all over again, so even the simplest of things felt firsthand.

"What'd she say?" Drew asked, holding open the door from inside the room and patiently waiting for me to enter.

Slipping the phone into my pocket, I stepped in, and the definitive click of the door latching behind us made the hand curled around the handle of my duffle spasm just a little.

"Said she'd be here in twenty."

"I didn't make dinner plans with her," he muttered.

"I don't think she cares," I cracked and headed through the main room toward the bedroom.

The room itself looked almost identical to the one we stayed in before.

Like we were getting a do-over.

The door opened into a square sitting area with a large dark-gray couch (that pulled out), a coffee table, rug, and lamp. Against the far wall was a small brown table that could seat four, and there was a huge flat-screen on the wall.

Near the door that led to the bedroom was a wet bar with a granite-topped counter and sink. There was a mini fridge, coffee maker, and all the other usual stuff hotels laid out for guests. I bypassed it and stepped into the ample square bedroom.

The bed was in the center, made up all in white. Still looked as fluffy and comfortable as the first time. There was a flat-screen, some other furniture I barely even looked at, and a door that led into the bathroom.

Everything in the suite was done in muted shades of gray and white. It was a clean design, and I was glad there wasn't a bunch of granny decorations. You know, mauve flowers and shit.

My duffle hit the floor near my feet.

"You gonna share that big-ass bed this time?" Drew asked, watching me from the doorway.

I turned and matched his sly smile with one of my own. "I'd have shared it last time, too."

His duffle joined mine, and he dove on the bed. He was wearing a pair of jeans—for once they weren't nearly black. These were faded and soft-looking; around the hem, they were starting to fray just slightly.

When he rolled and stretched his arms beneath his head, the long-sleeved blue T-shirt he was wearing rode up and exposed a sliver of skin at his waist.

I couldn't stop staring at that peak of skin. I daydreamed about leaning over him and tracing the area with my tongue…

"Are you listening to me?"

"Huh?" I said, snapping out of the fantasy.

His smile was slow and knowing. "I was planning on room service, some TV, and clothing optional."

"Shower with the door open?" I added.

"I like the way you think, frat boy." His dimple flashed, and he patted the mattress beside him.

Instead of lying down, I dove on the bed. Right on top of Drew.

"Ugghhh," he groaned when I landed. "Are you trying to kill me?"

Ignoring the protest in my ribs, I pushed up onto my elbows and hovered over his face. "You need mouth to mouth?"

I didn't bother waiting for an answer. I didn't really care. I was the one who wanted mouth to mouth.

The deeper I kissed, the farther I sank into him. We molded into the bed as a single indent, one of his legs pushed through mine, and I kissed just a little deeper. As we fused together, I rubbed my chin against his stubble, letting the rough sensation send goose bumps down my spine.

I liked him beneath me. It made me hungry… It made me want a lot more than mouth to mouth.

In what was slowly becoming a signature move, I ripped my mouth free, grasped his chin, and pushed his head back so I could kiss across his jawline and suck down his neck.

Drew's fingers delved beneath the waistband of my jeans and kneaded into my flesh. I came back to his mouth, licking past his teeth and rubbing both my lips fully against his.

"Cancel dinner," he quickly said before letting me take his lips again. "Let's stay in."

I groaned and, without lifting my mouth, I fished a hand into my pocket to try and find my phone.

He ended up trying to help me, except I don't think he was helping me at all. He kept finding something that was *not* my phone. Damn, his hand felt good. I loved the way my skin seemed to ripple every time he brushed against my dick.

It was like throwing a pebble into the center of a lake. The waves it created stretched far and wide across the surface.

Thought left my brain. I forgot about my phone. Need hammered throughout my body and made me drunk. My hips thrust into him and would have kept the rhythm, but his palms settled on my hips and he pulled his mouth from beneath mine.

"Frat boy," he groaned.

"Forrester," I replied.

"Someone's at the door."

I stilled and looked down. "What?"

Drew smiled and tugged my lower lip with his fingers. "Someone is at the door, big guy."

"Big guy?" I laughed.

"Would you rather I say little guy?"

I was alert and amused enough now to hear the insistent knocking on the door in the other room. *Damn.* Had it already been twenty minutes?

I shoved off Drew and stood. My cock was practically bursting out of my jeans. "Little clearly doesn't apply here." I gestured to my fly.

"Maybe I should text Braeden, tell him size matters."

I laughed out loud. "He'd probably ask for pics."

On my way to the door, I adjusted myself, trying to conceal the fact I was sporting some serious wood. Thankfully, I was wearing my Wolves T-shirt and it was a little big, so it hung low enough to cover what needed covered.

Joey's wild, curly hair was the first thing I saw when I pulled open the door. "Took you long enough," she said and stepped around me into the room.

"Come on in, Joey," I said dryly.

"Where's Drew?" she asked, swinging around to look at me. Her eyes widened. "What the hell happened to your face?"

"How many laws did you break on your way over here?" Drew drawled, stepping into the room. I noted his hard-on was also effectively concealed.

Before Joey could turn to steal his attention, our eyes met, and they held a lot of promise for later.

"You've been ignoring my texts!" she exclaimed. But regardless of how "mad" she was, she went straight in for a hug.

"What's this about dinner?" Drew asked, avoiding her words and wrapping her in a bear hug.

Joey was dressed casually in a pair of black leggings and some kind of tight, hot-pink tank with a black cropped T-shirt over it. Curves, that's what Joey was… all curves. Her dark, wild curls practically attacked Drew.

When she pulled back, her eyes bounced between us. "Change of plans," she announced. "Instead of meeting with my father in the morning, we're meeting him for dinner tonight."

"What?" Drew's eyes widened, and I watched him try to bank his shock.

"*We're* meeting him?" I questioned Joey but still kept an eye on Drew.

"You asked for this meeting so you could tell him, didn't you?" She waved her finger between me and Drew. "About you two."

"Yeah, that's why we're here."

Joey nodded once at his reply, like it proved what she already knew. "Well, I want to be there. And talking about it outside of his office is better. Too many gossip hounds."

"So you want to have dinner at a public restaurant…?" I drawled. Correct me if I'm wrong, but that didn't seem like the brightest idea.

"Nope," she said. "Let's go. I'm driving."

"Where are we going?" Drew asked.

Joey gave us both a dazzling smile. "Home."

And here we were, at another first.

Not only were we going to his home, but we were going to be openly admitting we were in a relationship to the man who had every ounce of ability to make or break Drew's racing career.

Seventeen

Drew

Gamble's house wasn't a house. Joey's "home" wasn't really.

It was a freaking estate.

With gates. And security.

Hell, I wouldn't be surprised if there were snipers hiding in the well-manicured bushes.

The second the yellow Skyline pulled up to the large wrought-iron gate, a security guard stepped out of a small white hut and up to the car. Joey rolled down her window and called a greeting.

The guard smiled and opened the entrance so she could drive onto the grounds.

The place was of course hella nice, but honestly? I expected it to be more austere, almost untouchable. Of course, the entire residence bespoke of wealth, but it wasn't as arrogant as one might assume.

"It's a Colonial Revival style house," Joey said, taking the liberty to give a brief "tour" as we pulled up. I'm sure the way Trent and I stared out the windows was all the interest she needed. "This one my father had built to resemble a nineteen-thirties Bel-Air estate."

The entire house was white and sprawled out before us. The middle of the home was one large square building with a two-story portico at the front and huge white columns that stretched up to a balustrade roof. There was an imposing front door with an impressively large chandelier hanging above it.

Coming out on either side of the main building was another wing, also white with lots of windows lining the front framed by black shutters. The roofline was traditional and dark but was accented with small dormers rising out of the top in a row across the entire home. Each dormer had a darkened window in the center.

The driveway stretched right up to the wide, white front steps. On either side was immaculate landscaping and small trees, which gave the home the feeling it had been there a while.

Joey parked right near the stairs and cut the engine.

"He knows we're coming?" Trent asked.

"Definitely," she replied. "I told him I wanted to be at the meeting and asked if maybe the housekeeper could make my favorite dinner."

"Joey," I teased, "are you a daddy's girl?"

"Let's just say he doesn't often refuse me," she replied and got out.

I was nervous. How could I not be? I thought I had all night to kind of get used to the idea that I was coming out to Gamble.

Just because I was determined to not hide how I felt about Trent didn't mean I sometimes didn't want to. Opening yourself up to harsh judgment is never easy. No one wants to be scrutinized and stereotyped based on the way they feel or the life they lead.

And let's face it; my career was on the line.

Just because Joey accepted T and me didn't mean her father would. He was older, "old school." In my mind, trying to gain acceptance from someone who was older, more set in their ways and beliefs, and had grown up in a less open-minded time in America was sort of like trying to milk a cat.

What if he rejected me? What if the disgust on his face was so transparent it was impossible to deny? What would it do to me?

To Trent?

I told myself to suck it up. I was doing this.

As we walked up the wide steps, I felt Trent's stare. I glanced at him.

Behind Joey's back he mouthed. "You okay?"

I nodded.

There was no butler or maid that answered the door. We didn't ring some gonging doorbell and stand there forever to wait to be granted entrance.

Instead, Joey flung open the door and walked right in. "Dad!" she yelled through the broad, fancy entryway. The floors were black-and-white marble, there were classic white statues lining the walls, and a black chandelier lit the space.

It was quiet in here, but really, I didn't expect it to be loud. As far as I knew, it was only Gamble who lived here and possibly Joey.

"You live here or over at the apartments by the track?" Trent asked, looking around.

"Here," she said. "There's really no point in having an apartment. This house is so big, and my room is on the opposite side from my dad's."

She motioned for us to follow her out of the entry, passed a sitting room, and continued down a wide hall to an open wooden door. "He's probably in here," she said as she went.

I just concentrated on making sure my shoes didn't make a squeaking sound against the really clean floors. That would be embarrassing.

"There you are," Gamble's deep voice came from inside the room.

Right before I could follow Joey over the threshold, Trent's hand snagged mine. "You ready for this?" he whispered.

"Are you?"

He gave my fingers a light squeeze before releasing me. "Yeah."

"Drew!" Gamble said when I stepped in. The room was what I would call a gentleman's study. All polished wood paneling, heavy furniture, and a large fireplace. There was a desk on one side, but it wasn't the focal point. I actually really appreciated that because it spoke volumes about the man standing in front of me.

Yes, his work and business was a large part of his life. But there was more to him than that. His job wasn't everything. If it was, his desk would be huge, it would be front and center, and the atmosphere in here would be stuffy instead of comfortable.

I think it would be hard for a man like Ron Gamble to do anything but intimidate people. That seemed like a heavy cross to bear.

Sort of like falling in love with your best friend.

There was so much room for misinterpretation. For assumptions.

"Scotch or whiskey?" I asked, gesturing to the glass in his hand.

"I'll get you some whiskey, son, but you're gonna have to drink it out of a baby bottle."

Trent laughed.

Joey rolled her eyes and finished crossing the room to give her father a kiss on the cheek. He smiled at her warmly, and it was just another flash of the man behind the image.

Joey glanced at me before going over to pour herself some scotch. Clearly, in this house, whiskey was for pansies.

Is this why she expertly took control of this meeting? Setting it up in the evening, after traditional business hours and in Gamble's personal home? Was she trying to show Trent and me there was a whole other side to Gamble people rarely saw? Was it her way of telling me without saying the words that he just might understand more than I thought?

Trent went across the room before me and held his hand out directly to Gamble. "Thanks for meeting with us."

Gamble shifted the glass into one hand and offered the other to T.

"A meeting is overdue," he said. "Joey, pour the men a drink."

"Women's rights," she reminded him, sipping out of her own.

"Hospitality," he rebutted.

"Yes, sir." She moaned and set aside her glass to pour two neat glasses of scotch.

I sidled up to her and leaned close to her ear. "That's a good girl."

"Screw you," she said fondly and shoved the glass at me.

I chuckled and sipped at the dark liquid. It was smooth all the way down.

"Have a seat." Gamble gestured to the seating options around the fireplace. There were several leather club chairs, a couch, and a few other options of chairs with wooden frames.

I sat in one of the club chairs, and Joey sat on the couch. Trent sat nearby in another of the leather chairs, while Gamble took up one of the wooden-framed ones.

Frankly, I wondered if it made his ass sore. Looked uncomfortable as hell.

"As I said…" Gamble went on. "I'm glad you called. I wanted to give you an update on the new division and give you a schedule of some of the preliminary races. Also, a few endorsement deals have come in, so you'll need to look those over, Drew, and see if any of them are a good fit."

"You can send that stuff to me," Trent said.

Gamble nodded. "Once you decide, I'll have my legal team make sure the deals are solid. Also, because the preliminaries are being scheduled, we need to get some kind of driving schedule down so you'll be ready. We also need to talk about the car you're going to be driving and assembling a pit crew to travel with you."

"I need a pit crew for preliminary races?" I asked. How big were these events going to be?

"Maybe not as full of a crew as you'll need once the actual racing season starts, but I'd never send you to qualify without a team to troubleshoot your car."

"I want to be on the team," Trent said.

Gamble nodded around his scotch. "That's a given."

It was all so real and so goddamn exciting. My racing career was literally blooming in front of my eyes. It was everything I always wanted.

"And of course, we need to discuss your salary. You're not going to be able to hold on to your day job much longer. I'm going to need you here to train."

No more day job? No more neckties, staring at the clock 'til five and dragging my ass out of bed so I could get there on time?

Hells yeah.

I found myself grinning, like one of those big stupid grins people wore on lame-ass TV commercials, but I couldn't help it. Life was falling together.

Or was it?

My grin vanished with the thought.

"Before we get into all of that, I need to make sure I'm still the racer you want," I said.

The glass in Gamble's hand lowered toward his lap, and his eyes belayed some surprise. "And why would you think I changed my mind?"

"You haven't yet. But you might after I say what I came here to say." Tension built low in my stomach. It sort of felt like it was chewing up my insides and making them ache. Around the glass, my palm was sweating, and I griped harder because I was worried the drink would literally slip out of my grasp.

Please don't let my career slip out of my grasp either.

The words were right there, lodged in my throat. I wanted to say them. I wanted to boldly tell him I was in love with Trent, but the syllables were sticky, thick, and clung to my esophagus like a bad case of mucus.

You could hear a pin drop in the few seconds that followed my words. Everyone was waiting with bated breath.

As I struggled, Trent cleared his throat. "Drew and I are in a relationship."

All the air in my lungs whooshed out silently. The pressure in my chest and the thickness in my throat suddenly let go.

I didn't even look at Gamble. I was too compelled to look at Trent. He spoke so calmly, so matter-of-fact. He could have been reading a grocery list. I admired that so hard. I loved him for it.

He glanced at me, and the single connection I felt when our eyes met was all I needed. I wasn't giving up a life by admitting my relationship.

I was gaining one.

Amazement, the kind that made you feel gobsmacked and woozy, gripped me. It wasn't Gamble's reaction to Trent's admission I was even concerned with. I hadn't even looked at him yet. The first person in this room I sought out was my person. It proved everything I needed to know.

I was gonna be okay.

I swung toward Gamble and relaxed back into the leather. "Trent and I aren't just friends. I'm in love with him."

Gamble calmly looked between us. His eyes gave away nothing. His face gave away nothing. He sipped his scotch. Joey fidgeted on the sofa.

I kept my eyes trained directly on him. I wouldn't let his silence unnerve me. I wouldn't let it make me doubt myself.

There was no doubt.

Trent was it for me.

"I see," Gamble said after a moment. "And how long has this relationship been going on?"

"Only a few weeks," I replied. "It's new, but that doesn't mean it won't stick. This isn't a phase."

"You knew about this?" Gamble addressed his daughter.

She nodded. "It was obvious when I was in town, driving with Drew."

"And what do you think about these two?" Gamble asked.

God, the man had a fucking poker face. It was virtually impossible to know what he was thinking.

Joey didn't seem alarmed, though, so I told myself to chill the fuck out.

"They're real," she replied simply. "I like real."

He nodded as if he heard what she didn't say.

Gamble glanced back at me. "Must have been hard coming here tonight. Now I see why my daughter wanted to have this conversation at home."

I nodded. "Look, I know this probably isn't what you signed on for. You're a businessman first, and you're basically building a new racing brand from scratch. I would have disclosed my, uh, relationship to you in the beginning, but it wasn't as it is now. Having your main driver in a relationship with another man might not be good for business. Maybe you don't want a gay man as the face of your team. If that's the case, tell me now. There are plenty of other good drivers that would be willing to take my place."

"You would choose him over your career?" he asked, speculation in his tone.

The question pissed me off. I knew, *knew* without even looking at Trent it was a kick in his gut. Trent would internalize those words; he would feel like he was taking something from me instead of giving.

I sat up, holding my body firmly, and stared right into Gamble's eyes. "I already did." I yanked my gaze from the older man and looked at Trent. "There's no choice."

T lifted his glass, and I watched the liquid slip past his lips and slide down his throat. He did well keeping his reaction contained, but I felt it. I knew it was what he needed to hear.

"And how do you feel about keeping your personal life personal?" Gamble asked.

My back teeth came together. "I like my privacy. Trent and I aren't the type to go skipping through a forest holding hands and making out on the street. But I won't deny him. I won't act like he's a dirty secret. People will see anyway, just like your daughter did. The pull between us is too strong. That's why I'm telling you."

"The interviewer at *GearShark* already saw," Trent remarked.

Gamble's eyes shot open. "She did?"

Trent nodded. "Seemed to think it would help Drew's career."

"She didn't print it…" he mused. Then glanced at me. "She respects you."

"I threatened her with a lawsuit." I clarified.

Gamble chuckled. "My boy, lawsuits are a practical daily occurrence to journalists. They push the envelope. Even if she didn't print the story, she would have whispered. She would have started rumors. The industry would be abuzz right now, and she'd be collecting off it. But I haven't heard a single word."

"Why don't you cut to the chase?" Trent said, his voice out of patience. "You want us to leave or not?"

Gamble laughed. "I always have liked your bluntness."

"Well?" Trent replied and stood.

Could he feel my budding agitation? The frustration welling inside me because Gamble wasn't really saying anything? Instead, he was just wearing my patience.

The guy should have been a politician, answering questions without actually giving an answer.

"Dad," Joey warned as if she were getting frustrated as well. "Put them out of their misery."

Gamble tossed back the rest of the scotch in his glass and stood. He was dressed comfortably in a pair of what I assumed were dark-colored rich people lounge pants. They were too nice-looking to be considered sweatpants. Paired with them, he had on a light-blue polo that looked like it was made out of cashmere.

Ivy would probably drool all over this guy's closet.

"Hopper's gay," he announced.

I felt my mouth literally fall open. Of all the shit he could say, I never thought it would be that.

"Hopper. Your pro driving coach," Trent reiterated.

"The one you called a dick." Gamble agreed.

I glanced at Joey, and she nodded.

"You didn't think I might like to know that?" I asked.

She shrugged one shoulder. "I knew what my father would say on a personal level, but on a business level? I never have any idea."

The sound of light footsteps approached, and a woman with dark hair pinned back poked her head in the room. "Dinner is served."

"Thank you, Ellen!" Joey chimed out, fondness in her voice.

Ellen (who I figured was the housekeeper or cook or something) smiled. "Anything for you Josephine."

"Josephine," Trent echoed.

Joey whipped around and gave him an evil eye.

He grinned.

"Thank you, Ellen. We'll be right there," Gamble said, and when she was gone, he set aside his empty glass. "Shall we eat?" He gestured toward the door.

"I'd like an answer first," Trent said, stubborn.

"I'm starving," Joey said dramatically.

Gamble faced me, and I felt Trent step up to my back, silently offering support.

This was it.

The future of my career.

"Your relationship with Trent is of no consequence to me. I might be an old man, but even I understand the heart chooses who it wants."

"You're not that old, Dad," Joey rebuffed.

"And the racing?" I asked, my heart still squeezing. The lightest touch grazed my lower back. I could feel the heat of it through my shirt. Trent.

Gamble glanced at Trent. "I'll be blunt. I agree with the reporter."

"What?" I asked, blinking.

"I think it will help your career."

"I'm not exploiting our relationship," Trent said, his voice firm.

"No one said anything about that. But you already made it clear you have no intent of being shy about it either. I like it. In a division where the drivers go against all the rules, do what they want, and represent the underdog? Frankly, you being gay makes you a *better* face for the brand."

"For the revolution." Trent corrected. He brushed his fingertips a little more firmly in a soft caress over my back before pulling away.

"That is what you called it in your *GearShark* interview," Gamble said to me. He shook his head slowly, mulling over possibilities. "A revolution of racing meets a revolution of the way people view athletes."

"If you think me announcing I'm with a man is going to make everyone in this world magically accept gay people, there must have been some expensive, exotic shit in that scotch."

Gamble laughed.

"All you need for a revolution is a spark." Trent's voice was soft but meaningful. He'd been thinking about this. More than I realized.

"Are you quoting *The Hunger Games*?" Joey wondered out loud.

"The what?" Trent asked.

"We need to have a movie night," she muttered.

"Exactly." Gamble nodded. "The demographic for this division is young. The young are far more open-minded than most, and not only will this barely register on their radar, but it will give a lot of them something to identify with."

"Is the gay population really that large?" I wondered.

"It doesn't even have to do with sexual orientation. Not really." Trent spoke up. "Like Gamble said, the underdogs, those who feel singled out, whether it be because of who they love, how they look, what they do… People everywhere feel different. Here you are, this amazing driver. You earned your way into a meeting with Ron Gamble and convinced him to start a new sport for people who'd been discriminated against for years."

People who were discriminated against = indie drivers.

"You're breaking down walls. And you're doing it with speed. And now you're also admitting—no, *we're* admitting to being in a relationship. Frankly, it's one more thing for people to admire."

"And hate." I reminded him. Not that I thought he needed a reminder. I thought he knew better than I did. He was the one walking around with cracked ribs.

"Oh, there will be hate." Gamble agreed and looked at me. "I guess the real question is, are you sure you're up for this?"

I never wanted to be a role model. I never wanted to be someone to break down walls or even give a voice to people who felt like they were somehow less.

But that's where I found myself.

I looked at T. The lines and angles of his face were so familiar to me. So strong. He was my best friend and he was my lover. Underneath all that, though, he was a man.

A man with doubts and feelings. With vulnerabilities and insecurities.

I was, too.

We all were.

It didn't make me less of a driver—less of an athlete. If anything, it made me better.

So while, no, this wasn't where I expected the road to lead me, here I was. I was lucky. Trent and I had each other. We had family and friends rallying around us to support us.

What about the people who didn't have anyone? Could I somehow give someone else some kind of hope, even from the cover of a magazine?

I could. I would. But someone else would do it better.

I swung around to Trent. "I think you should do it."

"Do what?" he asked.

"Call the reporter at *GearShark*. Start the revolution."

"What about you?" he asked.

"I'll be there," I replied, my attention condensed down to only him. "Always."

"I like it." Gamble approved.

"Beef Wellington tastes better hot," Joey said.

Everyone laughed.

"We're having beef Wellington?" Trent asked, suddenly more interested in food than anything.

Beef Wellington was good, but it wasn't French fries.

"It's Joey's favorite," Gamble said.

"So we're going to do this?" Trent said, setting aside his glass.

"All you have to do is say the word," Gamble said. "We can go sit down and talk numbers and details while my daughter eats me out of house and home."

"Yes," I said.

My heart squeezed again, but this time it wasn't because I was nervous or even scared.

I was excited.

Eighteen

Trent

Ron Gamble was a man who got shit done.

After one evening in his impressive home, talking business with him, I knew exactly why he was the richest man in the state.

There weren't many people like him.

He was cunning and quick but still had an uncanny eye for detail. It was like his mind processed things twice as fast as most others. The conversation we had over beef Wellington, creamy mashed potatoes with a hint of horseradish, and roasted root vegetables reminded me why I decided to major in finances at Alpha U.

It was exhilarating.

Most people thought of finance as stodgy and boring. It was all numbers and spreadsheets. Yeah, obviously, that was part of it, but there was so much more. A person in finance had to be good with people, personable.

Some might argue charm was a definite bonus to have. Why? Because people needed to feel comfortable with you. Money made the world go round. Some didn't like it, but it was a fact. So becoming an advisor on something as big as their finances… well, trust was one of the most important components.

Not only that, but in finance, you learn to not only look at the equation, but at the bigger picture. Numbers are fluid; you can manipulate them to put you on a path to a specific outcome. You must have a clear goal for what you want to achieve, so all the pieces can be laid in place to make a complete picture.

To me, that was exciting. It wasn't just crunching numbers. It was building something. It was taking risks for big payoffs.

Finance was basically just a narrowed-in business degree, a specialty, but a broader sense of business was still required.

While racing was a sport, and I spent a lot of time beneath a hood lately with Drew and watching him on the track… that wasn't all there was to it.

This new division was a business. It took a lot of strategic planning to put it together, to get it going, and to make it work. It was fascinating to me, listening to Gamble talk about how it was all being started.

For the first time in a long time, I didn't feel like I needed a break from my major or even my chosen career. I felt challenged and motivated to roll up my sleeves and pitch a few ideas of my own.

What impressed me more about Gamble was his willingness to listen. Even though he was extremely successful, he didn't sit at the table and act like he knew it all. He was eager to bounce ideas with me. Hell, he even asked my opinion on a few things. I wasn't nearly as experienced as him; I was basically still in diapers compared to him. But it didn't seem to matter.

He liked blunt, so that's what I gave him. I asked him why.

His response?

I was young and hungry. I was almost fresh out of college, and I had a vested interest in this budding revolution of racing because Drew was at the center of it. In his experience, sometimes actual work experience wasn't as good as a fresh eye and a new outlook.

Beyond that, I'd been in the circles with Drew for a while now. I'd been in the indie world, and since I wasn't a driver, I probably had a different perspective, a perspective that would be useful on the business side.

He was right.

Instead of making me feel like I was the shit and maybe had an inside track to some hotshot job in the division, the whole night talking with Gamble lit a fire inside me. I wanted to prove myself. I wanted to show Gamble he was right—I was young and hungry. I was motivated, and I did want to look beyond just the drivers at the business as a whole.

After all, a man isn't defined by his words, but by his actions.

It was late when Joey dropped us off at the front entrance of the hotel. It practically glowed with a golden halo because of all the lighting. I wondered if they did it on purpose so the outside hue went with the gold accents used inside.

Even though we ended up meeting tonight, the meeting for tomorrow was still on. It ended up a good thing we had some extra time because after all the talking we did at dinner, there was more work to be done.

Drew and Joey were going to go out on the track for some drive time, and I was going to spend some time in the pro headquarters, which was also being used for the new division. I wanted to look over the endorsement deals coming in for Drew, his schedule, and his financials. I knew he wanted to quit his job, but I wanted to make sure it was a smart move first.

We were both quiet on the way up to the room, walking past the front desk, small kitchen that offered coffee and water around the clock, and the "business" center, which was basically a section of the huge lobby walled off with large sheets of glass with several computers, printers, and free Wi-Fi for the guests.

The second we walked into the room, my eyes went right to his cell, which lay left behind on the wet bar. I wasn't sure if he turned it off, and I didn't ask. It really didn't matter. He was ignoring it regardless.

Maybe I'd ignore mine, too.

On impulse, I strode across the room, pulled my phone out of my jeans, and tossed it down beside his.

When I turned back, Drew was leaning against the closed door with a grin on his face. The way he was leaning made the black leather jacket fall off the sides of his body and accentuate his long, lean waist. His jeans rode low on his hips and skimmed over his thighs, emphasizing the strength in his lower half.

I couldn't see his hands because they were behind him, but I imagined his palms flat against the door, like he was bracing himself for me.

Because he knew.

He knew I was coming for him.

My eyes ripped from his body and flashed up to his. The dimple in his cheek deepened, and my tongue ran over my teeth. Blond hair fell over his forehead, threatening to conceal one of his blue eyes.

Sexy. Powerful. Unshaven.

And there was this thread… a small imperfection at the hem of his jeans. Even though he literally made a mouthwatering sight standing there in our private room, my eyes kept going back to that string.

The hem was slightly too long, so the bottom of the material (at the back of his heel) dragged the ground. Over time, the fabric began to fray with the repeated action of rubbing against pavement.

Right now, one small, white string stretched out across the floor beside his foot.

Everyone's jeans did it. Mine, his, yours. It wasn't anything new. It wasn't anything that deserved so much thought.

Except the presence of that string made me want to tug it. To see what would begin to unravel if I did. I rather liked the thought of unraveling Drew.

Of pulling that thread until there was nothing left.

"You know how I was talking about having a clothing-optional night earlier?" Drew's voice was like a good bottle of wine. Smooth, slightly sweet, and didn't go to your head until after you'd drunk it all.

I nodded. There was a fire building low in my stomach. This tingling, burning sensation that was sort of addictive in the sense I wanted it to spread. I wanted to be consumed.

"I changed my mind."

I lifted one eyebrow. I had a feeling I knew what he was going to say. But I wanted to hear it anyway.

"No options anymore. Naked. Now. All night."

Well. Wasn't he a bossy bastard?

I liked it.

I really fucking did.

I pushed off the floor. I needed the extra momentum to push me closer to him faster. As I prowled toward the door, I started peeling off my clothes.

I took pleasure in tossing the fabric all over the space, owning it all, littering the entire room with sexual intention.

When I reached him, all that remained on my body was a pair of unbuttoned jeans. One of Drew's hands appeared between us, and one finger dipped beneath my boxers and rubbed over the wiry hair leading down to my cock.

While he teased, I unbuttoned his jeans with deliberate care and then took my time sliding the zipper down over his already erect dick.

Once his pants were fully open, I helped him pull of his jacket and shirt. Before sliding down his body, I pressed my palms against his shoulders and dragged them down his arms, all the way until our hands linked together and we stood there chest to chest, holding hands.

"There's a lot of shit I like about you, Forrester," I spoke. "But right now, my favorite is when I stare into your eyes, you stare right back."

"I see you, Trent," he answered.

"Even if I went blind right now, I'd still see you," I echoed.

The side of his mouth curved up. "Always gotta one-up me, don't ya, frat boy?"

I laughed low and pulled my hands from his. The chain he always wore around his neck, the one with the speedometer pendant on the end, was my target. I lifted it, and he dipped his chin so I could pull it over his head.

"We're not gonna need speed tonight." I set it aside.

His back hit the wall when I slid down his body. Knowing what I was going for, his hips jutted out, and I laughed deep in my throat. Drew loved getting head. I might even argue he liked it more than French fries.

My knees hit the floor once his shoes and pants were gone, and I knelt before his steely dick, which stood out from his body at attention.

The weight of his balls in my palm was now familiar, and I squeezed gently, cupping them and using my fingers to gently massage the base of his cock.

He made a satisfied sound, and his palms flattened on either side of his hips against the door. I took his cock slow, wrapping my lips around the taut flesh and slipping down, taking him deep.

When his tip hit the back of my throat, he muttered something incoherent. I pulled back slightly and began to work his rod, making sure it was good and slick and he was good and worked up before pulling back almost completely to suck just the head past my lips and graze my teeth on the sensitive spot on the underside.

He shuddered in my mouth, and I grabbed his hips. Using my hands, I started guiding his body into a rhythm that allowed him to essentially fuck my mouth.

After a few minutes of my guidance, one of his hands slid into my hair and gripped while his hips took over all on their own.

As he thrust himself into my mouth, I massaged his balls and caressed his inner thighs. The hand tangled in my hair started to tremble, and his hips moved faster. My lips tightened around his quivering dick, and he whispered my name.

I liked when he whispered my name.

His orgasm exploded across my tongue. His cock literally pumped like its life depended on it. Drew collapsed against the door, and I moved with him, gripping his hips and taking over since he was no longer able to move.

I drank him down. Taking in a part of him was natural to me, as if he were an acquired taste I never had to actually acquire.

I sucked him dry and then lifted my head. His chest heaved, and the instant my mouth released him, his body began to melt down the door, sliding into a practical puddle until his ass hit the floor.

I sank back onto my ass, sitting directly in front of him, spreading my legs so he was in between them.

"We need to get our own place," he said, a little out of breath.

"It definitely would have some advantages." I agreed.

"Tonight was a good night." His chin came down so we could meet eyes.

"Yeah." I let myself grin. I honestly didn't expect it to go so well. Trying to guess someone's reaction to a male-male relationship was like trying to figure out why a dog's farts smelled so bad.

Though I tried not to show it, I'd been worried. How could I not be? Drew was risking everything. I honestly didn't know what I would've done if Gamble had turned him away.

It probably wouldn't have been pretty.

"You up for the interview with *GearShark*?" Drew asked.

"Absolutely." I was looking forward to it. It was what I wanted to begin with, a chance to carve out a place in this life for Drew and me.

"You were on fire tonight at dinner. You really like all that business stuff."

I made a face. "You get your adrenaline from cars; I get mine from closing deals."

"Graduation is coming." He pointed out.

"Amen."

He smiled, then turned serious. "So how about it?"

"How about what?"

"How about we get our own place."

One minute my heart was beating along just fine, and then it stuttered. I felt it trip and then restart. He wanted to move in together.

A serious case of homesickness washed over me. Just the idea of permanently occupying the same place as him made me long for that home. As if all along I'd known that's where I belonged, but I'd only just gotten the directions.

"You just want me to blow you every day." I joked because it was the only way I could process what he suggested.

It was so intensely craved, I almost hurt.

To belong somewhere, to someone, and for that blessing to meet me every day at the door...

"You already do that." Drew pointed out, humor in his tone.

It sounded odd, the humor, because even though I'd just made a joke, there wasn't anything funny about this.

"You really want to get a place?" I asked.

"I really do."

"Me, too." *Damn.* My voice was hoarse.

Drew stood and held out a hand to me. "C'mon, I feel like taking a shower with the door open."

I chortled and placed my hand in his, allowing him to pull me to my feet. I started toward the bathroom first, but he pulled me back around.

His arms were strong when they wrapped around my shoulders and pulled me in for a tight hug. I stepped in a little closer to soak in as much of Drew as I could while returning the hold.

"Thanks for being there tonight," he whispered in my ear.

Like I'd be anywhere else.

"I'll always be here for you. Best friend's honor," I vowed. Because even though tonight was about us and the part of our relationship that was more than friends, the kind of support we needed for something like coming out to Gamble could only be the kind a best friend could give.

Drew pulled back but kept hold of my hand to lead me past the king-size bed and into the bathroom. "I hope you didn't plan on sleeping tonight." He reached out and grabbed my cock right through my open jeans.

As if.

With Drew, sleep was always the last thing on my mind.

Drew

A single touch.

It contained enough power to move mountains.

Enough power to rip apart families.

Twenty

Trent

I'd never seen him like this.

While I welcomed all the firsts I experienced with Drew, I wished this didn't have to be one of them.

In some ways, I'd grown used to living in the moment with him. It seemed for a while, it was all we had. Stolen moments, shared looks. Minutes of unrestrained feeling and unbridled chemistry. Ever since he sat beside me in Screamerz that first time, our relationship was defined by moments.

Moments were fleeting… weren't they?

Not really.

Because the feelings and impressions single moments left as imprints stayed long, long after the moments were gone. It was those imprints we carried into future moments. They shaped us, influenced us. Conditioned us.

I was afraid.

Not really a new feeling, I know, but just because I knew it didn't mean it was any easier. If anything, the fear got harder. I was in so deep, tangled so tight, I'd never get out, and that's what scared me. Because if today went terribly wrong, I'd be twisted in a lot of upcoming moments that would break me.

I didn't know Drew's father, not enough to make any kind of guess on how he'd react to us. Sure, I'd met his parents a couple times when they came to town, but it was never more than a casual introduction.

I knew they were good people. Of course they were; they raised Drew and Ivy, who were both awesome. They'd been strict as parents, and they had remarkable ideals. They loved their kids, though, and to me, that was most important.

Still, the closer we got to Drew's North Carolina home, the more I began to doubt love was enough. I knew firsthand sometimes all love did was complicate things and hurt people more.

By the time we stepped off the plane and climbed into a rental car, Drew became more withdrawn as the miles between us and his childhood dwindled. Though it worried me, I knew it wasn't me he was withdrawing from. It was from the situation, from the emotions erupting inside him. Right now, all he could do was retreat inside his head; it was the only way he could try and process.

At first, it freaked me out. I'd asked him a question, and he didn't reply. So I asked him again. When he still didn't answer, I wondered what I'd done to piss him off. Nothing. Even if there were something, he wouldn't give me the silent treatment.

No offense to the ladies, but men didn't operate like that.

Fine, that was a broad generalization. Drew and I didn't operate like that.

He simply hadn't heard me. He was deep in the confines of his busy mind. So I left him there. Trying to pull him out would be like waking a sleepwalker.

I used the time to think. What would I say if they didn't accept us? What would I say if they did? Would this be awkward? Would they look at me as someone looks at a stranger when Drew told them he loved me?

That's what I feared the most.

Becoming a stranger to people to whom I would have otherwise just been me. It's like everything I was, the college student, the athlete, the friend, the son… the man—all of that would somehow be cancelled out when people found out where the heart inside my body lay.

I was still the same.

Drew was still the same.

So far, we'd been lucky. We'd yet to become strangers to people we knew. How long would it last? How much luck did one man get?

Surely I'd used up my lifetime allowance. I had Drew; he was like the jackpot of luck.

After our meeting at Gamble Speedway, we'd driven to the airport for the quick flight to North Carolina. The Fastback was parked at headquarters where the pros kept their cars. There was no way we'd leave the car in the long-term lot at the airport, so Joey had driven us, dropping us off right at the curb near the terminal.

It wasn't going to be a long trip. We were catching a plane back tomorrow night. I had classes Monday morning and frat shit all next week.

GearShark jumped on the interview when we called. Well, technically, Emily, the journalist, jumped on the interview. Even though we didn't say what it was about, she knew, and of course she wanted the scoop. I wasn't surprised. I expected it. I was surprised she wanted me as the main feature of the article. I wasn't the racing star. But it was what we'd all discussed Friday night at dinner, and it was what Drew wanted.

I was waiting on a call back from her on the schedule and details. However, the interview would be soon. Emily didn't want any chance one of us would get cold feet.

I glanced at Drew and frowned. *Is he getting cold feet right now?*

Drew grew up in the mountains of North Carolina where the trees were tall and thick, the landscape was green, and the dialect was unmistakable. His parents were well off, not millionaires or anything, but they lived a comfortable life. They didn't live in a totally secluded area; it was definitely within driving distance of a more populated area, but the land they owned and the fact their home sat deep on the property made a man forget they didn't have to drive hours for a gallon of milk or a pizza.

I wouldn't necessarily call where they lived a farm because there weren't livestock roaming around and tractors in the field, but there was a definite feel of country here.

The road stretching across their property was paved and well maintained. I drove slow across it so I could gaze at the open fields, tall grasses (yes, even coming out of the winter season), thick areas of tall pine trees, and a distant view of majestic mountains.

The speed I'd chosen was also of benefit to Drew. He needed all the time he could get.

Soon, a ranch-style house came into view. It was a big house, only one story so it sprawled out horizontally. It was a nice place with a natural stone exterior and wide porch with an arched cover over the double front door. On the cement porch were oversized planters filled with greenery that spilled over the sides and didn't appear bothered that it wasn't quite summer out. 'Course, around here it didn't matter. This was the South. It was sunny and bright and approaching eighty degrees.

There was no garage attached to the house. Instead, the cars were parked on a paved driveway that ran alongside the house instead of in front of it. There were two cars there, and my stomach twisted a little. Both his parents were here. Waiting.

I knew they had questions.

Drew literally called them up a few days ago and told them he was coming to visit. He didn't offer much by way of explanation. While I knew they were excited to see him, parents wouldn't be parents if they didn't know when something was up.

I had a very strong suspicion this was the reason he suddenly hated looking at his phone. He didn't want to have to try and explain via text or voicemail why he was coming. He just wanted to ignore his mother's questions.

I didn't say shit about it. When he powered down his phone and shoved it inside his duffle before we went through security at the airport, I pretended not to notice. He didn't need me harping on him. He didn't need me to tell him he was wrong or, hell, tell him he was right.

Who was I to say?

Drew got to deal with this the way he knew how. He got to feel whatever he wanted.

There was no right and wrong for this. Even if there was, I wouldn't know what it was. I was here to back him up. I was here to validate him and remind him it was okay.

And if need be, I'd be here to protect him.

"Park over there," he said, the sound of his voice almost startling against the silence. He gestured to a giant shed that could have possibly been considered a barn. It was shaped like one, with the traditional barn doors on the front. I imagined it was where they kept their lawn equipment and anything else a property this size needed. Basically, it was a detached garage.

I pulled in close to the building, driving right up onto the grass. I felt like maybe parking on the side where the car was out of sight from the house might give Drew a little bit of relief, make him feel they weren't standing inside, staring out from the windows, watching and trying to figure out what the hell was going on.

I shut off the engine but left the keys in the ignition. Once I adjusted the baseball hat on my head (I knew it didn't really shield my healing bruises, but it was an effort), I rested my head against the seat and stared out the windshield.

His hand reached for mine. He didn't move or look at me, but he sought me out. I opened my fingers and turned my palm up. Drew's hand slid home, entwining with mine.

"We used to play football in the field over there," he said quietly, pointing through the windshield. "And that hill, just beyond over there"—he pointed again—"is where I used to race my modified Big Wheel down the slope."

My heart squeezed. I could almost envision a small version of the guy holding my hand running through the grass with sunlight glinting off the blond in his hair. How carefree he must have been, how innocent.

I wanted to tell him we could just forget this. My fingers actually trembled with desire to turn over the ignition and put the car in reverse and leave this place.

But there was no going back.

There was no *never mind* or *cancel* button on the way we felt. Drew and I made a choice.

We chose to accept the decision our hearts made for us.

So even though I felt like running, even though my heart splintered when he reached for my hand for comfort, we were doing this. Once this was done, we would do it again with my family and then the entire world.

"I don't want to disappoint them." His quiet voice filled the car.

"I know."

His eyes turned to me for the first time in what felt like hours. The blue was sort of icy, like maybe inside he was feeling cold.

No, not cold. Numb.

"I don't want to disappoint you either."

I made a choked sound and forced my body around to face him. My knee lifted, bending between us and falling over the cup holders in the center to make more room for my new position.

I cupped his jaw with one hand. "You will never disappoint me."

"What if I do?" he whispered.

"I'll love you anyway."

He smiled. I rubbed my thumb along his jaw, lightly scratching over his stubble.

"I didn't tell them I was bringing you," he admitted, a grimace pulling at his features.

I drew back and pulled the keys from the ignition. "I know." If he had, he would've had to explain why I'd be with him, and that was something he avoided until the very last possible second.

With a deep breath, Drew got out of the boring sedan we rented and reached into the back for his duffle. I did the same. Before we even hit the porch, the polished-wood door swung open, and a woman stepped out.

Drew's mother was of average height, not tall and not short. Her hair was a medium shade of brown that she wore in a shoulder-length style. Today she was dressed in a pair of jeans and a plain white T-shirt. Over the shirt was some sort of flowy-looking sweater with draping arms in a gray-and-pink flower pattern.

She wasn't wearing shoes, but slippers that looked kind of like loafers, but they were pink and had fur poking out from the inside.

Her eyes were blue like Drew's and Ivy's. Her smile was quick, and when she noticed her son wasn't alone, it didn't dull. I thought that was a good sign.

"Andrew!" she exclaimed happily and held out her arms.

"Mom." Drew grinned and jogged up the stairs to wrap her in a hug. He was a whole head taller than her.

When he pulled back, she turned to me. "Trent, it's great to see you again. I didn't realize you were coming."

"Mrs. Forrester," I said and quickly gave her a hug. "Hope you don't mind me crashing your visit."

"Not at all!" she said. "And you know better than to call me Mrs. Forrester. Call me Adrienne."

"Is Dad home?" Drew asked, fidgeting a little.

"Of course. He's inside. We've both been waiting for you to get here. I wish you would've let us pick you up from the airport."

"Ivy sends her love," he said as we headed for the door, choosing not to acknowledge the fact he'd been ignoring his texts and avoiding a car ride with his parents.

"She called this morning." Adrienne went on, heading inside. "Nova's getting so big. I was just telling your father we needed to plan another trip out there to see her."

"I'm sure she'd like that."

The inside of the house basically looked like it could be in a magazine. It was contemporary but comfortable, with a touch of country. The room we walked into was one huge great room. The floors were hardwood with various scrapes and dings that gave them character. The walls were painted a light but warm shade of tan, and there was a giant stone fireplace on the far wall that stretched all the way to the ceiling.

Wooden beams crossed the ceiling and were stained the same color as the floor. Area rugs in muted tones and patterns defined different areas of the room and provided a guide for where to look.

A huge leather sectional sat near the fireplace, above which hung a huge flat-screen TV. There were candles everywhere, most of them lit, and the entire room smelled of melted vanilla and sugar.

Artfully arranged on one wall near the front door was a huge collage of family photos. In the center were black letters that spelled out the word *family*. My eyes went instantly to all the images of Drew at various stages of his life, and a knot formed in my throat.

The kitchen was open to the great room as well, separated by a huge granite island with high-backed stools lining the front. The cabinets beneath the counter were painted a rustic red, adding a pop of color in the otherwise fairly neutral space. Behind the island, the rest of the cabinets were made of distressed wood in a creamy finish. The hardware on them wasn't black, but more of a bronze brown. The appliances were all stainless, and the stovetop was sunk right into the countertop, making it look like it had been there all along.

"Burke! Drew's here!" Adrienne called toward a hallway that led out of the great room and then went ahead toward the kitchen.

"Office is that way," Drew explained as we passed. "Dad's probably working."

"Can I make you boys a sandwich?" his mom offered.

"No, thank you," I said, and Drew shook his head.

I wanted to reach out and stroke my hand down his back and remind him to breathe. I'd caught myself twice already reaching out to touch him before remembering I couldn't.

Drew's father appeared out of the hallway and stepped into the kitchen. "Son!" he said, rubbing his hands together like Drew was a delicious meal. "Good to see you!"

"Hey, Dad," Drew said and stepped forward for a quick hug.

Drew's father held out his hand to me, and we shook. "Trent."

"Sir," I said. Even though I'd met these people before, I couldn't help but feel awkward, like this was a movie and I was in high school picking up this guy's daughter for her very first date.

But this wasn't high school. This wasn't my first date… and Drew wasn't a girl.

"Wasn't it nice of Trent to come along with Drew so he wouldn't be alone to travel?" his mother said.

That's when I really knew this wasn't going to go well. I liked Drew's parents, but, man, they were old school and lived in their own little world. I was also beginning to see how Drew was so good at ignoring things (like his phone, like the way we felt for each other for so long), because I was beginning to think his mother was the same way.

Honestly, there was nothing wrong with that. I respected it. I lived in my own little world, too, I supposed. Everyone did.

I just wished the worlds we occupied weren't so incredibly different.

Burke crossed the kitchen toward a large coffeepot taking up a spot on the counter. The red light on top was lit and dark liquid filled up the pot about halfway.

"Coffee anyone?" his mom asked us.

We both shook out heads.

"Well, don't keep us in suspense anymore, son. Give us the good news!" his father said, turning from the pot with a mug in his hand.

"Good news?" Drew asked.

"You must have some. After all, you did come all the way home for an awfully short visit." His mother agreed.

"I did come because I wanted to talk to you about something." Drew hedged.

"Let's go sit down," his mother directed and headed toward the sofa.

I sat on the end near the armrest and propped my elbow on the cushion. I was surprised when Drew sat right beside me. He didn't touch me or even glance my way, but I knew.

I knew he needed my closeness, because in his position, I would need the same. Again, I fought the urge to touch him but consoled myself with the knowledge he knew I was here.

Drew's parents sat nearby, on the other side, so we were almost facing each other.

Burke took a drink of his coffee, then set the cup on a polished wooden table in front of the couch. "How's the job going?" he asked.

"It's, ah, fine," Drew replied.

His father heard the hesitation in his voice and nodded like he understood. "You're too qualified for that place. You need more of a challenge. I called Simon, my contact at the large software company that rivals the one I work for, and they're going to be hiring this spring, soon. I put in a word. Just send over your resumè—"

"Dad." Drew cut him off. "I live in Maryland now."

"Of course." He nodded. "There are plenty of great software jobs there. That's probably why you're here. Who hired you?"

Drew took a deep breath, and I reined in my patience. "I'm driving now, for the new racing division."

"That's not a full-time job," his father argued.

"Actually, it is. I've just come from a meeting with Ron Gamble. He owns the new division I'm racing for. He's going to pay me to drive full time. I'm going to be training and touring to different races. I've also got some endorsement deals coming in. It's lucrative, pays well."

"Computers pay well," Burke rebuffed.

"You know my passion is cars, Dad."

"Ever since you were a little boy," his mom mused.

I kept my eyes trained on his father, measuring his reaction.

His lips thinned. "Cars is a hobby."

"It doesn't have to be," Drew argued. "I told you when I moved up there with Ivy I was going to pursue a career in cars."

"But you still work in computers."

Drew sat back, a little stiffer. "You didn't think I could do it." He huffed. "You thought it was just a dream."

"Cars are not a career, Drew," he replied in a no-nonsense tone. "We discussed this. This is just a phase. Your degree, your skill set at software and technology is your future."

"That's not what I want."

I wondered if anyone else heard the hurt deep in his voice.

"What do you mean it's not what you want?" his dad said, incredulous. "You've been working toward this for half your life."

"No, Dad!" Drew spit out. "You have. You've been shoving your chosen profession down my throat since I was just a kid."

"Andrew," Adrienne said, shocked.

"Haven't you been listening? I know you've heard me when I said it before. We had this conversation when I moved to Maryland. You were disappointed then, too, Dad. I can't keep living the life you want me to live. I've tried…" His voice faltered, then came back. "My whole life I've been trying to please you and live up to everything you wanted me to be. I can't anymore. I can't be who you want."

God.

How could they not react to the pain in his voice, the absolute anguish? How the fuck could they just sit there and stare at him?

I couldn't.

It was physically impossible.

"Forrester," I whispered and reached out a hand. My palm slid over his thigh, a touch meant to comfort. A touch meant to let him know not only did I hear what he said, but I was *listening*.

Drew made a sound, and his hand fell over mine. He grasped at my fingers like they were a lifeline, like I was the only thing keeping him grounded.

You could have heard a pin drop.

The silence in the room was so loud it muffled my ears. Suddenly, everything seemed to happen in slow motion, like were in a movie and someone hit the wrong button.

Both Burke and Adrienne looked down. Their gazes zeroed in like arrows on a bull's-eye right to where we touched. Confusion crossed their features, and it slowly gave way to horror.

That single touch told them exactly what Drew had yet to say. It wasn't that I was trying to hurry it along. I'd only been wanting to give the person I loved some support.

"What the hell is this?" his father said, glancing up from our hands. His voice was dangerous and low.

Drew let go of my hand, and I pulled mine away.

"It's why I came," Drew replied. "I do have news." He cleared his throat. "But I don't think it's the kind you were hoping for."

"Andrew," his mother said, pressing a hand to her throat.

"I'm in a relationship with Trent. We started out as best friends, but we've become more."

I admired the way he went right to it. He didn't try to explain in a roundabout way. It was hard, but he did it.

"What!" Burked exclaimed and leapt up off the couch.

Drew nodded. "I know it's a shock, which is why I came home. I wanted to tell you in person. We've been together for a few weeks now… I wanted you to hear it from me before *GearShark* breaks the story."

His mother made the sign of the cross over her chest and sighed.

Seriously.

His father, on the other hand, appeared murderous. He was angry, almost beyond angry, like he thought Drew was just saying this to hurt him. "You aren't *gay*."

"No." Drew agreed. "I'm not. But I'm in love with Trent. He makes me happy, just like racing."

"Why are you doing this?" Burke erupted and stalked toward the fireplace. "Are you that angry with us for pushing you, for wanting our son to reach his full potential?"

Ah, the guilt trip. I hadn't seen that coming.

"I'm not angry with you," Drew said. "This isn't about you."

"But I don't understand," his mother said. She at least didn't look angry.

"I know, Mom." Drew rubbed a hand over his face.

Suddenly, Burke swung around, his blazing eyes locked on me. "How dare you?"

I pulled the hat off my head so I could meet his gaze head on.

"How dare you try and turn our son against us?"

Drew went rigid beside me, but I forced myself to remain calm. "I'm not turning Drew against you. Clearly, you don't need help in that department."

His mother gasped, and it made me feel contrite.

"Is this the kind of influence you've allowed into your life?" Burke raged at Drew, jabbing a finger toward me. "You move up to Maryland to be with your sister, and now you want to turn your back on your career, drive cars, and… and… *sin* with a man?"

Aaannd here we go.

"No one is forcing me. No one is trying to influence me, except you," Drew replied, tired.

"We just want the best for you," his mother said.

"Then let me live my life the way that makes me happy."

"This can't make you happy," she replied.

"I forbid it!" Burke demanded.

"I'm a grown-ass man. You can't forbid anything," Drew snapped.

"Language." His mother gasped.

I wanted to laugh. I couldn't, though, because this was pretty much everything we'd been afraid of. They weren't going to accept this relationship. Drew was going to suffer for it.

His father turned his glare back to me. I wanted to flinch because there it was. That look. The one someone gives a stranger. I was no longer the man they met several times in the past. I was the enemy. I was a bad influence, and I was trying to take their son.

"How do you live with yourself?" his dad implored. "Are you jealous of my son? Jealous his life was better than yours? Is this some sick game to you? Do you get joy out of ripping away another man's life, driving a wedge between him and his family?"

"That's enough." Drew cut in and stood. Gone was the weariness and even the sadness. In its place, anger was taking over.

Drew was as tall as his father, so when he closed the distance between them, they were eye to eye. "Don't talk to him like that. Not ever. This isn't his fault. He didn't *make* me turn gay and certainly didn't rip away my life."

I wasn't sure what to do. It seemed I didn't have a place to speak, like I needed to let Drew handle this his way. But honestly, Burke's words stung. How could they not?

Hadn't I worried for weeks and months about how my love might ruin Drew's life?

"You weren't like this until you moved up there."

"Yes, Dad, I was." Drew pinched the bridge of his nose. "I'm the same person I've always been. It's you who never wanted to see. I've spent my entire life trying to live up to your expectations, being the son you always wanted. But this is me. Who I've always been. You and Mom just never saw because I didn't let you. I've never wanted to work in software. I hated college, and my day job makes me feel like I'm dying inside. I've always felt a little different. I've always felt like the son you wanted just wasn't who I was. But I tried." His shoulders sagged. "I tried so hard."

"Andrew," his mother said sadly and got up from the couch.

"When I went to see Ivy and walked into her house, it was the first time I felt like I truly belonged, like I didn't have to be who someone else wanted me to be. It was so... It was a relief. So I stayed. And I know it looks like being there changed me, but it didn't. It just made me more *me*."

Burke turned away. I couldn't tell if he was listening, and frankly, it made me want to deck him. I knew how hard it was to pour out a piece of your soul, to admit to being more or something different than people thought.

It was fucking excruciating. The least the man could do was look at his son while he spoke.

"Honey, we love you no matter what job you work in," Adrienne said and hugged him. Drew returned the embrace, squeezing his mother tight, but over her shoulder, his eyes sought out mine.

He was breaking inside.

Drew stepped back from his mother and looked in her face. "Do you love me no matter who I love?"

Her breath caught. Mine did, too.

Her eyes filled with tears. "What you're asking us, Andrew… it goes against the Bible."

"Do you think God loves me less because I love another man?"

Did you hear that sound?

It was the sound of my heart cracking.

It was a sound I knew well because it was the same sound my ribs made the night I was attacked.

Adrienne's tears trailed over her cheeks, and she reached for Drew's hand. "How could anyone not love you?"

"It's impossible," I said.

Drew and his mother looked in my direction. I offered them a smile. His mother tentatively returned it.

"You'll move back home."

Everyone's eyes widened when the deep, authoritative voice filled the room. Burke's back was still turned and his posture was rigid. Both hands were folded behind his back, one lying over the other. It looked like he was in the military and standing at parade rest. So formal. So rigid…

So unaccepting.

"What?" Drew asked.

"You'll drop out of racing and move back home. I'll get you that interview at the company here in town. It's not too late to fix this, to be the man I raised you to be."

Drew's mouth thinned. "No."

Against the small of his back, Burke's hands clenched together. "You will. Or you will no longer be welcome in this home."

Adrienne gasped. "Burke!"

I jerked up off the couch. "Are you fucking kidding me!" I went off.

Burke turned around to pin me with a stare. "You are not welcome in this house. *Ever.*"

"What kind of father would disown his own son?"

"And what did your father say?" He lifted an eyebrow.

I felt like he'd thrown a rock at my chest. I cleared my throat. "I don't have a father."

Drew glanced at me sharply. He knew my dad wasn't around, but he seemed surprised anyway.

"Maybe if you did, you wouldn't be so depraved."

Drew moved fast, like lightning. One minute he was staring at me, and the next he was flying across the empty space between him and his father. His arm swung back, his fist clenched.

"Drew!" his mother gasped.

His father's eyes widened in surprise. Just before he delivered the punch, he deflated and dropped his hand. "All my life…" Drew began. "I wanted to be just like you. You were the man I measured everyone against."

His father lifted his chin, and Drew shook his head sadly.

"But now I'm ashamed. I knew I was going to disappoint you today, and I've been struggling with it for weeks. But it's me who's disappointed. Disappointed I put so much faith and energy into wanting to be like you."

"Andrew," his father said, more emotion in that one word than I'd heard all day. It made me see deep inside that man, he really did love his son.

Too bad he wasn't better at showing it.

"You won't bully or threaten me into the life *you* want me to live." Drew went on. "I wish you could see how happy I am, how excited. I wish when you looked at Trent, you saw the man I did. A man who is passionate about business, who is loyal to his friends, and who feels more deeply in his little finger than you do in your entire body. You might be disgusted that I love him, but I'm proud. I'm proud to love someone who loves me enough to walk into this house and take the abuse you've so casually thrown at him. You want to make me choose? I choose him. I choose *my* life over the life you want me to have."

My heart swelled, filling in that crack I'd suffered earlier. There was so much beauty in Drew's heartbreak. Probably because he was determined to overcome.

Drew turned his back on his parents and looked at me. "I want to go home."

Without another word, I went to the front door and picked up both our bags. The door was heavy when I pushed it open and stood, holding it ajar.

"Andrew," his mother called after him when he started my way.

Drew stopped, the pain in his eyes naked and real. He blinked and turned back to his mother. "I'm sorry, Mom."

She was openly crying now, and he wrapped her in a hug. "My door is always open to you," he whispered against her hair.

She sniffled against his shirt. I looked up at Burke, who was watching his wife and son embrace. There was guilt in his eyes. Guilt and pain.

Had Drew's words sunk in?

Now that he was faced with the truth he was literally disowning his son over a lifestyle choice, was he beginning to see the error in his ways?

I hoped so. For Drew's sake. I hoped this man could find it inside him to remember the child he raised, to remember the person Drew was at his core.

He must have felt my stare because our eyes locked.

The regret vanished, and in its place came hardness. Wrath.

Even though it stung, I wanted him to blame me. I'd rather take the anger and let Drew have the regret.

Unblinking, I held his stare. I didn't look away until he did.

Drew brushed by me on his way out the door. I stiffened slightly because I didn't want to accidentally touch. It was my touch that set off the events before. It was probably best if I didn't touch him again until we were alone.

Assuming he would want me to touch him then.

Yes, yes, I knew he'd chosen me. I knew he said he was proud to love me. But later, when we were in the quiet of the hotel room we were going to have to go and find (we were supposed to stay here), things might feel different. His veins wouldn't be pumping with anger and challenge. The stinging hurt from his father's rebuff would be felt deeper… and perhaps Drew would begin to feel regret.

Instead of letting the door slam behind me, I carefully pushed it closed. It seemed far harsher to leave quietly than to bang away. Sometimes silence carried more impact than noise.

At the car, Drew climbed in the driver's seat. I didn't say a word. I tossed the bags in the back and took up shotgun. He fired up the engine, and threw it in reverse.

We weren't in the Fastback, and this car wasn't equipped for mad speed. But he needed to drive; he needed the release.

I rolled down my window to let in the air, and he floored it all the way across the property. The wind whipped through the interior, pulling at my hair and clothes. The air smelled like sunshine, and the rumble of the engine was familiar.

Just before we took a turn that would lead us out onto the main road and toward town, where I assumed we'd find a room for the night, Drew pulled the emergency brake and drifted to a stop.

The engine ran idly, and his hair was a windblown wreck.

In one motion, he leaned forward, draped his forearms over the steering wheel, and bowed his head. His shoulders shook.

I hesitated for long seconds, my hand hovering over the broad expanse of his back before settling firmly between his shoulder blades. I felt the breath hitch in his body, and I searched for any way I could somehow take away his pain.

In that moment, it seemed maybe not having a father was a blessing in disguise because at least when a man didn't have one, he didn't have to worry about being disowned.

I rubbed gently against his back.

Drew stilled and slowly pulled back off the wheel.

His eyes were damp when he looked at me. My chest squeezed.

"C'mere," I whispered and opened my arms.

He came, tucking himself right against my chest. The tip of his nose was cold, and he pressed it to my neck. I ducked my head and folded my arms around his body.

His fingernails dug into my back and his body shuddered.

And there on the side of the road, I held him.

Twenty One

Drew

Some hurt burned.

Some hurt ached.

And some hurt was so potent it left you feeling numb.

I'm not sure what was worse: telling my parents about Trent or finding out they were only human. In a way, I'd walked through life disillusioned just like most children. From the day we're born, parents aren't really people. They're pillars of strength, examples of humanity, and somewhat exempt from the cruelty of the outside world.

Until they aren't.

Until the illusions are shattered and a child turns into an adult.

It's hard to look upon your parents with the childlike ideals you grew up with when it's through eyes of experience.

The disappointment of learning my parents weren't everything I thought they were was a bitter pill to swallow. In fact, I think that pill was still stuck in my throat, lodged there and refusing to go down.

I couldn't even be angry, but I wanted to be. Part of me wanted to rage and yell. To declare how unfair life was and how dare my own father deem I wasn't worthy enough to be his blood anymore.

All I felt was sadness. Like a part of me was in mourning. Like I'd just spent my day at a funeral… for a piece of my life.

I knew not everyone would accept T and me. I anticipated it. But I expected better from them.

Maybe my father thought his "tough" love approach would somehow make me see reason. It didn't. All today managed to do was drive me closer to Trent. It was him, after all, who wrapped his arms around me when all was said and done. It was him who didn't demand I choose or draw lines in the sand.

I learned something today in the midst of that fight.

All love was not created equal. It wasn't a birthright. It wasn't earned by blood. Love wasn't guaranteed.

Really pure love was hard to come by.

It didn't matter where it was found. All that mattered was that we held on when it was.

I chose a local hotel that wasn't nearly as swanky as the one we stayed at in Maryland. It was a mid-range place that was clean and close to the interstate. It would be an easy drive back to the airport tomorrow.

Our room was a typical one-room place. In the center was a giant king-size bed with a flat-screen on the wall, a couple dressers, and a small desk and chair near the window.

Not too far from here were lots of restaurants I hadn't been to in years, some bars, an outdoor mall, and a movie theater. There was also a place where you could go hiking and take in some of the scenery.

I didn't feel like doing any of that.

I knew my parents would likely be disappointed, but I never honestly thought they'd *disown* me.

You're not welcome in this house.

"I think I might call the airline, see if there's an earlier flight back to Maryland tomorrow," I said. I don't know why, but my voice sounded strange to my own ears.

"You sure you wanna do that?" Trent asked from over by the window.

"They aren't going to change their minds," I said.

"I can call them," he offered. "Order some food, too. You wanna go take a shower?"

"How do you do it?" I asked.

He turned away from the window and looked at me. "Do what?"

"Shove down all the hurt I know you feel and try to shoulder mine, too."

He half smiled. "Shouldering yours makes mine feel lighter."

"About what he said to you…" I began.

Trent shook his head. "Forget it. You don't owe me an apology. His actions aren't yours."

"He was an asshole."

"Yeah, he was."

I smiled. "Maybe I will take that shower."

Our tickets were in the pocket of his duffle, and he went for them. At the same time, I pulled out some fresh clothes from mine. Before I was even in the bathroom, he was already dialing the airline to see about changing our flight.

For a standard hotel, the water pressure was actually pretty good. I turned the temp a little hotter than usual because my body was understandably tense. I stood underneath the spray, letting it pelt me, and goose bumps rose along my arms because it felt so good.

I tried not to think about my parents. Doing so wouldn't change anything. But it was hard to just move on and let it roll off my back. Especially when I felt so betrayed. It would take some time, time for me to maybe make sense of how they reacted.

No.

I would never be able to make sense of what they said. But maybe I would learn to accept it, accept them for who they were, even if they couldn't accept me for who I was.

I grabbed the tiny bottle of shampoo and dumped some in my palm to scrub my hair. The suds were rinsing down my body when I heard T enter the bathroom.

"Tickets are changed. There was a fee, but I paid it."

I grunted. Good. It was better we got home early anyway. At least Trent wouldn't be in the car half the night while we drove home after picking up my car, and he'd actually get a decent night's sleep before having to be in class Monday morning.

And shit, I had to go to work.

I didn't think it was possible, but I hated that place even more now.

"What do you want to eat?" he asked. "Besides fries."

I smiled, and water ran in my mouth. "Forget food. Get your ass in here."

The curtain was yanked back, and T stood there naked as the day he was born. "Thought you'd never ask."

I laughed. It felt good. Even after everything, it seemed okay to laugh with him.

We took turns washing each other's bodies, which turned out to be a very good distraction from the thoughts trying to take over my mind. Even though his body was hard and strong and the soap clung to all the contours, it was his eyes I kept going back to. The lashes were wet, so they appeared darker than normal. The hazel looked more like deep, liquid gold, and when he looked at me, all the tightness in my limbs didn't feel so tight.

Water droplets clung to his lips and made me thirsty, so occasionally, I'd lean forward and suck the moisture across my tongue. Trent's back was under the water, but he wrapped his arms around me and spun so it was me beneath the spray.

"Turn around," he instructed, so I did, and his wide hands settled over my shoulders and began to massage the knotted muscles there.

I groaned and slapped a hand against the shower wall, leaning in a little and succumbing to the intoxicating feel of his massage. His fingers worked expertly, like they automatically knew exactly where to spend the most time. When his hand closed around the back of my neck and squeezed, I moaned.

He kept kneading the muscles, using his strength to work out the worst of the stress. As he did, my body became languid and more relaxed. The sound of the water falling from the showerhead and the feel of it rushing over my head and coating his fingers as he worked gave me a freaking hard-on.

I swayed a little, and one arm came around my waist to tug me back against his body, giving me some support.

He was hard, too. His stiff cock pressed right against my ass, and I shivered.

"Had enough?" he asked, still working the side of my neck with one hand.

"Not nearly," I groaned.

Trent turned us so we faced the back of the shower, the wall that was the longest. He put both my hands up on the tile so I could support myself and then went back to massaging, working his hands down my back and up again to my shoulders.

His hips stayed close, though. His rock-hard rod rubbed against my ass and hip. I found myself arching in to it, wanting to feel more, anticipating his slick, smooth head against my skin.

His massage turned a little deeper, and his hips started rocking against me in a gentle thrusting motion.

Breath hissed between his teeth, and I smiled secretly. Slowly, his hands worked down to my waist and dipped to my front.

His hand latched onto my dick and jacked me lightly.

"Time to get out," I rasped.

He gave my head a little squeeze and then shut off the water. My head felt a little foggy and my body was relaxed—yet stimulated—so before I knew it, Trent was wrapping a white towel around my shoulders and roughly drying off my chest and arms.

When that was done, he took some time to dry my cock, my balls, and between my thighs. As he drew back, our eyes met and he smiled. Even though he was turned on as fuck, and so was I, it didn't dilute the care he always showed me.

"Bed," I demanded and took his hand to lead him out of the bathroom and toward the king.

He was still wet when we stopped beside it, so as I dried his body, he rubbed his towel over his hair and then mine, too.

When I was done, I grabbed his towel and threw it on the floor with mine. It only took a second to yank back the heavy white comforter and blankets to reveal an equally white set of sheets.

I was the first to climb in the bed. The butterflies I always felt with him were shaking my insides and making my body quake. I reached for him, pulling him over me as I sank into the mattress. I wanted him over me tonight. I wanted to feel his weight, see the broad lines of his shoulders, and basically feel the protection he always wrapped around me.

I liked having a person who was so strong; that way I could borrow some of his strength when I was feeling depleted.

He seemed to know what I wanted without me speaking a word because his body came down over mine instantly. The feel of his chest against mine was perfect, and the way his powerful thigh slid between my legs made me want more.

We rubbed our dicks together as we kissed, going at each other like we hadn't touched in days. I licked across his crooked tooth and bit his lower lip. He gripped the back of my neck when his tongue delved deep and swallowed my moan of pleasure.

Our hips were working as we humped against each other. The tip of my cock was weeping, so I slid a hand between us and used the moisture to caress that sensitive spot at the base of his head.

"Drew," he whispered, pushing his body closer and reaching down to cup my balls.

His dick was weeping, too. I felt the silky desire slip across my lower abs.

"I want more, frat boy," I rasped when he stroked a finger over my taint. His fingertip gently caressed my rim, and my eyes rolled back in my head.

Both his arms wound back around me and rolled so I was the one on top and he was beneath me. Instantly, his legs parted wide and he grabbed my hips.

He was inviting me into his body.

I fucking loved being inside him. It was literally the closest I think a man could get to heaven on earth. I'd been inside him a few times since that first night. Once I took him from behind. Just gripping his ass as I sank deep into his body had been enough to make me come.

He was so accepting of me. So willing to give me anything I wanted.

I loved him, and nothing anyone said would make me stop.

I kissed down his chest and across his abs as I slid to the end of the bed. Quickly, I went to my duffle and pulled out the small bottle of lube and a condom.

When I came back, I didn't move over him. Instead, I sat beside him. He glanced at me with question in his eyes.

I held out the foil packet.

Instantly, the golden hue of his irises sparked as he caught my meaning. "Forrester…" He began. I could already hear the doubt in his tone.

"I want you inside me, Trent. I want to feel you move within me."

His teeth sank into his lower lip. "Are you sure? Maybe you should take some more time. Today was—"

"I don't need more time. I just want you."

He closed his hand around the packet. I lay down, and he moved to his knees.

"Which way?" he asked, trying to give me as much control as he thought I would want.

But I didn't want control, not right now. Not with him. I trusted him.

"I want you over me," I said. "All I want to see and feel is you. I don't care about anything else."

He laid aside the foil packet and picked up the lube. I spread my legs, and he settled between them. Before, I always thought of girls as the ones who needed "time" to get ready for sex. Guys walked around with instant hard-ons, literally ready to plunge in.

But men needed time to get ready, too. Entering anyone's body, be it a man or a woman, wasn't an instant thing. Well, unless you were an asshole lover.

Trent was a generous lover. He always gave and often didn't take. I learned a lot about intimacy from him, far more than I'd ever learned from a woman.

Intimacy didn't come necessarily from the actual act of sex. It came from the way you treated the act, the way you approached it, and the way the person you were with cherished your body.

His hands were gentle and quaked with desire when he started touching me. His lips were like soft pillows when they lit upon my flesh. Even though I'd given him an invitation to enter me, something we'd yet to experience, he didn't rush.

Trent took his time, sucking my nipples into his mouth, nibbling at the side of my neck, and raking his fingernails over the insides of my thighs.

When his fingers started probing the sensitive nerves just beyond my taint, he took my dick deep into his mouth and sucked, making me lift off the bed in pleasure.

I wasn't new to ass play; he'd definitely been in the area before. I liked it, more every time we did it. When he first breeched my body with the tip of a well-lubed finger, it felt like I was sort of cresting a hill on a roller coaster. Like tension was building as I went up and up.

He moved slow, caressing my cock with one hand and working me open with the other. Every so often, he would pause and apply more lube, rubbing it between his fingers to warm it before massaging it all over my sensitive areas.

When he worked up to two fingers, I moaned, and he wrapped an arm around my bent leg and held on to my thigh as he slid in and out of my body.

My cock was so hard it throbbed, and I ached for him to touch it, to give me the release I so desperately wanted. My hand went for it, but Trent laughed low and knocked my hand away.

"Oh no, you just lay there. Don't you worry. You're going to come."

"I want more, Trent," I begged.

His fingers slipped out of me and traced around my rim. My ball sack was drawn up tight against my body, and I spread my legs just a little bit wider.

Once more, he came back, and I knew he added another finger because the tightness was back when he slid in. I liked it, though. It made my cock twitch.

"Deeper," I urged and wiggled my ass. His fingers delved deep and rubbed against my prostate. Breath hissed between my lips. I rocked against him again, rewarding myself with another epic tremble of bliss.

Blindly, I felt around until the condom was in my hand. I thrust it at him, and he took it. I watched through half-closed eyelids as he rolled the latex over his impressive length.

I knew it might hurt the first time he entered, and yeah, maybe I was a little apprehensive, but I knew I'd like it. He did. He always came twice as hard when I was inside him.

"Your feet might tingle," he warned. "That's normal."

I nodded.

I heard him apply more lube to his cock and then rub his fingers down along my crack and tease my hole. Both hands hit the mattress on either side of me, and my eyes sprang open. He stared down at me intently, and I was unable to look away.

"I love you, Drew," he whispered, but I didn't hear those words with my ears. They whispered directly into my heart.

"I love you, too."

His mouth covered mine, and he kissed me thoroughly while rocking his hips and the tip of his cock against my ready hole.

Every time just the very tip slid in, I shuddered because it felt so good. Seconds later, he drew back, lifted my legs so they bent at the knees, and positioned his dick at my entrance.

"You sure?" he asked, his voice throaty with desire.

I rocked against him, and the tip of his head slid in. He moaned.

Trent moved little by little, pushing his thickness into my body. At first, I wanted to panic, but he was there to grab my dick and stroke it.

Suddenly, it was like my body gave way, and he slid the rest of the way so he was buried deep.

His fingers dug into my legs, and I felt his balls against my thighs.

"You're so tight," he breathed, holding himself still.

"You feel good, frat boy."

His eyes cleared and met mine. I nodded.

He started moving; I started moaning. Thank God we did this for the first time in a private room. There was no way in hell I'd be able to keep the moans of pure pleasure inside me. Someone would have heard.

Trent moved gradually, keeping up a steady assault on my prostate, until I started to swear I was going to blow. Suddenly, he changed rhythm and pulled almost completely out but then surged back in deep and swift.

I opened my mouth, but no sound came out. His strong hand wrapped around my rock-hard dick and pumped.

I exploded all over my chest and his hand. White light burst behind my eyes, and my back arched up off the mattress.

"Don't stop," I begged even as I came. The orgasm seemed to go on and on. Just when I thought it was ending, he would rub against that fucking magic spot inside me, and more jizz would shoot out onto my chest.

I was completely weak when he finally let me finish, drained in the best possible way. My back hit the sheets, and I looked up at his strong, wide body over mine.

"Yes?" he asked, smug.

"Oh, hell yes," I replied.

Trent thrust his hips, and his eyes closed. He was still rock hard inside me. I knew he'd held off on his own orgasm until I was completely spent.

"Take it, frat boy," I growled and shoved my ass down onto his cock.

His arms wrapped around my thighs, and he started moving. He wasn't rough; it didn't hurt, but he did move with some speed.

Even though I'd already had an orgasm, it still felt good. I loved the way he felt stretching my inner walls and making all the nerve endings sing with glee.

A few seconds later, his body went rigid and his eyes flew open.

"In me," I whispered so he knew he didn't have to pull out.

Before the words had even fully left my lips, his body started convulsing as release ripped through him. The pulsing of his cock was my new favorite sensation, and I wiggled around a little so I could milk every last drop out of his shaft.

When he was done, he relaxed back onto his haunches, leaving himself still cradled in my body.

Beads of sweat dotted his hairline, and we both were breathing erratically. Trent eased out and collapsed beside me.

My head turned in his direction. "So much for my virginity," I joked.

He grinned up at the ceiling, then rolled to kiss me. His eyes were serious when he pulled back. "I didn't hurt you, did I?"

I shook my head. "You don't do anything without protecting me."

He glanced away.

"What?" I asked, brushing the backs of my knuckles across his bare chest.

"I wish I could have protected you better today."

"There's nothing you could have said or done. It would have only made it worse."

"That's why I just sat there." A muscle in his jaw ticked, and I knew today was a test of patience for him.

I knew he told me not to apologize. I knew he said I didn't have to be responsible for what my father said to him. I said it anyway. "I'm sorry about what he said to you."

Trent threaded our fingers together and lifted my knuckles to his lips. After a few minutes, he said, "It's easier to blame me than you."

"There shouldn't be any blame at all," I said. "Why does it feel like such a crime, such a hurdle to love you?"

"I don't know, Forrester," he murmured, kissing the backs of my fingers again. "I'm not sure I ever will."

"I'm gonna go clean up," I said, choosing to change the subject.

He released my hand. "I'll be there in a sec. I'm gonna order some room service."

The rest of the night, we watched TV, ate room service, and made out. We kept the conversation light and didn't talk about my parents anymore. It was a good end to a shitty day, at least until it was intruded upon.

Trent's phone went off with some frat business, and he spent some time on the line dealing with whatever Omega's newest drama was.

It reminded me of the four men there I hated and vowed to get revenge on.

The football game was set for next week, but I wasn't sure that was going to be enough payback. I thought about all the ways T protected me and how much abuse, physically and verbally, he'd taken because of our relationship.

Maybe because I'd witnessed the verbal abuse firsthand today, I lay in bed beside him that night and couldn't sleep.

I plotted instead.

And I came up with a plan.

So while Trent was sleeping soundly, I crept out of bed and grabbed the room key. Now was as good a time as any to put my plan in play.

Twenty Two

Trent

Game day.

Have a little fun at some asshole's expense day.

The pressure Omega was raining down to find the guys who jumped me was getting real. They put out word far and wide on campus and made it clear there would be serious retribution for whoever dared mess with the fraternity.

And the Wolves?

They were applying their own pressure because one of their own was jumped.

So not only were the four guys in Omega feeling the pressure and hearing the smack talk *inside* the house, but *outside,* too.

Just call me Trent, king of the head game.

They were squirming, almost jumpy. After today's charity game, they would likely be hurting. After that?

I was thinking it might be time to let the house in on what they didn't know.

As much as I liked to play with my prey, it was getting old. Seemed like there was a hell of a lot more important things to deal with.

Since arriving back home from the meetings with Gamble and the suck-fest with Drew's parents, he'd been a little quiet. I figured he had a right to it. I mean, his parents literally threw him out of his childhood home.

A couple times, I'd woken in the middle of the night to find him missing. When I'd crept through the house, I'd found him downstairs on the couch with a laptop. Both times, he'd told me he couldn't sleep and didn't want to wake me with the light of the computer.

He hadn't withdrawn from me. The very air between us still burned with friendship and intimacy, but still, I worried about him.

Last night, he stayed at the frat with me. We fell into a pattern of alternating whose place we stayed at. The obvious best choice was our house, where we didn't have to sneak around, but I was still president of Omega for a few more weeks, and my presence around here needed to be known. For many reasons, including keeping an eye on Con and keeping him on the verge of pissing his pants all the time.

I was wearing Drew's boxers (well, technically, they were mine now), and he was wearing a pair of mine (which were his now), and his body was pressed up tight against mine. He fit against me like a glove, or the perfect pair of football pads. I'd grown so used to sleeping with him beside me, the one night a few days ago we slept apart, I'd barely slept at all.

I was so surly the next day from lack of sleep and agitation from not getting to cop a morning feel, I'd nearly ratted out all four dickheads in this house and then stepped back to watch the house react.

I didn't, though. I reined it in and thought about today.

But I did whisper some sweet nothings in Con's ear all through breakfast.

Sweet nothings = veiled threats

After that night, I told Drew there was no way in hell we were sleeping apart again. My bossiness earned me a blowjob. That got rid of my shit mood real fast.

The football game was set to take place at the indoor field where the Wolves practiced and sometimes held scrimmages. It was smaller than the actual outdoor field, so it was never used for actual college games. We could have used it today, but we scheduled it under the dome just in case there happened to be some weather.

Since it didn't start until later in the morning, I planned on spending some quality quiet time in bed with my guy.

You know what they say about best laid plans?

Me either.

Anyway, half the house was woken up when someone started acting like the doorbell was a freaking piano and pressing on it like he was Mozart.

I sat up in bed, Drew's arm still draped over my waist and him still totally asleep (I swear the dude could sleep through a freaking alien invasion) and listened for a moment, trying to make sense of what the hell was happening.

Some footsteps in the hall and on the stairs made me think maybe they guys would tell whoever the hell it was to go the hell away.

Instead, all I heard was the slamming of the front door and someone bellowing for Con.

What. The. Fuckity fuck?

A few more doors opened, and some voices echoed in the hall. I kicked off the blankets, and my feet hit the floor.

"Wha—?" Drew said, lifting his bedhead off the pillow and cracking open one eye.

He looked like a surly pirate.

It was hot.

"Someone's at the door," I whispered. "I'll be back in a few."

His head hit the pillow again, and then his middle finger lifted off the mattress. I grinned, figuring the gesture wasn't for me, but for whoever was at the door, and picked up the first pair of sweats my hand closed over. They happened to be his.

They were gray and really soft inside.

Damn. Why did all his clothes feel so much more comfortable?

I didn't even bother with a shirt, just went to the door, unlocked it, and pulled it open a crack. Before shutting it completely behind me, I reached around and locked the handle—you know, just because.

By that time, the front door slammed again, and Con's agitated voice carried up the stairs. The insistent ringing of the doorbell started up again.

"What the shit is going on down here?" I snapped, jogging down the stairs. It caused a little tweak of pain in my ribs, and it only made me more irritated.

I was pretty much healed from the number Con and the three stooges pulled on me, but my ribs were still healing and the bruising around them was slightly yellow.

"Con's pissed off some biker," said one of the guys standing in the entryway.

I glanced at Conner, who had an angry, flushed look. "I told you I have no clue who that guy is!"

"What guy?" I said as the doorbell rang again about fifty times in three seconds.

That was some talent right there, making that much racket with a damn doorbell.

I stalked over to the front door and yanked it open.

Sure enough, there was a biker standing on the other side with his finger pressed to the button. He was close to six feet tall, with a stocky, wide build and a bit of a beer gut. His full beard (which was nowhere near as sexy as Drew's scruff) was peppered with gray to match the dark hair on his head. He was wearing a pair of jeans and leather chaps. To match, he had a black leather jacket and a T-shirt beneath it with the Harley Davidson symbol on it.

"Who the hell are you?" I asked.

"Where is he?" the biker demanded, trying to see around me. I was bigger than him, so he wasn't having much success. "That little weasel hiding behind you?"

"Which weasel is that?"

"The one who promised me a Harley Davidson Seventy-Two."

I crossed my arms over my chest and leaned against the doorjamb. "You mind explaining a little bit more?"

"Who the fuck are you?" he growled, trying to look behind me again.

I did him a favor and shoved the door open wide.

All the brothers standing around in the entryway stared out at him.

"What the hell, Con?" one of them whispered loudly.

"He in there!" biker man demanded and started forward.

"Whoa," I said and put a hand out to stop him. "Sorry, this is private property, members of the Alpha Omega fraternity only."

"Says who?" the biker challenged.

I straightened and dropped my arms at my sides. "Says me," I growled. "I'm the president of this house, and if you got a problem with one of my guys, talk to me."

"You rich types are all the same," he muttered.

"Excuse me?"

"I shoulda known better than to do business with some well-to-do college boy. But these bikes were designed for the moneyed, so I figured that's where I'd get one."

I stared at him blankly.

He sighed. "That kid in there, Conner something-or-other, owes me a bike."

"I don't know him!" Conner yelled from behind the door.

I reached around and pulled him out of the space and face to face with the angry man. "This kid?" I asked.

The man pulled out a piece of folded paper from inside his leather jacket, smoothed it out, and handed it to me.

I laughed out loud.

"Something funny?" the guy griped.

It was a listing on BikeList.com, which was sort of like the eBay of motorcycles, dirt bikes, four-wheelers, and jet-skis. It was well known for buying and selling a lot of really good and sometimes rare small engines. Including Harley's.

I took the paper and held it so I could read it, and I felt Conner looking it over as well. The listing was for a Harley Davidson Seventy-Two. The description listed the bike as: *Mint condition Harley with a fully rehabbed body. This bike is especially sought after because it doesn't represent any specific body type, but instead represents an entire era.* It went on to boast the extras and features, which were frankly impressive.

There were even two pictures of the bike, and right there in the background was the Omega house.

The price was listed, which I found to be an impressive number, and then the deposit, which was marked paid in full, was subtracted from that total.

Five hundred bucks.

The seller listed was Conner.

Stapled to the front listing was a printout of what looked like message or email traffic between this biker (whose username was Hog_Heaven) and Conner (whose username was plain Conner). I skimmed quickly and caught the gist of what was happening.

Conner listed some fancy bike on Bikelist.com, got a bite from an interested buyer, strung him along, and then charged a five hundred-dollar deposit (nonrefundable) to hold the bike until this man could come test drive it and hand over a full check.

Only there was no bike.

So when this guy showed up this morning, expecting to drive home a new piece of hog heaven (hey, his words, not mine) and got the door slammed in his face, he was understandably stubby.

I glanced at Conner. "Why would you sell this nice man a motorcycle you don't have?"

Conner flushed. "I didn't!"

"It's all right here. You can't deny physical proof."

Some of the guys behind me stepped up, and I passed the listing back. We were all brothers after all. It was their business.

"He's lying!" Con shouted.

"You little bastard!" Bearded man lunged at him.

Since I was still half asleep, my reflexes weren't that great, and I wasn't fast enough to pull him out of the way.

Oh darn.

Con was snatched up by the front of his white T-shirt and literally dragged out onto the porch.

"Where's my bike?" the man growled.

"Get off me!" Con demanded, struggling to get away. "I told you I don't have a bike!"

"I gave you five hundred dollars for a deposit on a bike you don't have?"

"No—" Con began, and the man shook him.

"You little thief. I want my money back."

"I didn't take your money!" Con looked at me, a plea in his eyes. "I didn't!"

I smiled at him. "Just give him the cash back."

"I don't have it!" Con wailed. "I barely have twenty bucks."

"Prove it," the biker growled and shoved Conner back. He slammed into the door casing and bent forward.

"Just show him your bank balance," one of the bothers suggested.

Conner's face cleared, and he pulled out his phone. We all watched as his fingers flew over the numbers.

I knew the second he was in his account and the news would not be helpful because his face went stark white. "That's not right," he muttered.

Biker dude snatched the phone and glanced down at the screen.

"Argh!" he yelled and threw the phone, then a punch.

Con's head snapped back, and I admit I enjoyed his pain.

When the biker went back for another, I stepped between them. Letting Con take one hit was fine, but any more than that and I'd look like a pansy prez.

"Look. This kid doesn't have a motorcycle. He was clearly trying to scam decent people like yourself out of their hard-earned money."

I glanced over at Conner. "That's a really low thing to do, man."

"I didn't do it!" he roared.

"It's all right here," one of the frat members said, passing the papers back up front.

"Sir, on behalf of Alpha Omega, I'd like to sincerely apologize for the cruel and thoughtless actions of this boy." I held out my hand as I spoke.

He stared at my hand like I had two heads. "I'm calling the cops."

"We'd appreciate it if you wouldn't." I inclined my head. Secretly, I was having a dance party in my mind.

Karma. That's what this was.

"I'll give you the money back!" Con said, desperate.

I lifted an eyebrow. "So you admit to conning this man and taking his money?"

"No!" Con faltered. "Yes… *Fuck!*"

I glanced behind me at all the brothers. They all wore grim and annoyed looks. I made eye contact with them all. Each of them nodded slow.

I turned back. "Conner, you know as a brother of this house, your actions reflect on us all. You've disgraced the fraternity."

"I didn't do it," he growled.

"That's not what you just said," the guy behind me said.

"You did this." His eyes lit up and malice dripped from their depths.

I drew back. "What?"

"You somehow set me up, all to get revenge."

I plastered an innocent, shocked expression on my face. "Revenge for what?"

Our eyes connected. We had a silent conversation no one else heard.

You did this as payback. Conner's eyes accused.

Karma's a bitch. My eyes laughed at him.

"For what I—" He stopped abruptly.

I smothered a smile as satisfaction filled me. He almost ratted himself out.

What a loser.

I sighed sadly. "Conner, I really don't know why you think I would do something like this to my own brother. I take my role as president very seriously, and I would never do anything that would reflect poorly on this frat. I can promise you I had nothing to do with this." My words rang out with truth because the truth was what I told.

Although I did wish I was responsible.

Conner's chest was heaving. I pushed the listing into it. "Pay the man back and try to convince him you being a dick shouldn't punish us all."

I started back in the house.

"Wait!" Con yelled out in fear.

I glanced over my shoulder and pinned him with a knowing stare. "Surely you don't need my protection. It's only one man. It isn't as if you're being ambushed."

His eyes widened.

I stepped in the house and shut the door behind me, leaving Con to clean up his own damn mess.

"First, he tries to overthrow you as president, and now, he blames you for something as childish as this?"

one of the house members said in wonderment. "What the hell is that guy's problem?"

"I don't know, guys. I really don't." I spoke like I felt regret about Con's and my relationship.

"You did the right thing," Jack said, slapping a hand on my shoulder.

"Thanks." I looked up to address everyone. "All right, assholes. I've got a charity game to get ready for. I'll see all of you at the field in just a few hours."

I hid my smile all the way up the stairs, but when Conner's shriek carried through the door and to my ears, I just couldn't suppress my emotions.

I grinned.

The door was unlocked when I put my hand on the doorknob to my room. I pushed it open and went in. Drew was going to love hearing what kind of trouble Con had gotten himself into.

But he was gone.

In his place on the bed was a note.

Sneaking out while everyone is occupied. See you at home.

PS: Couldn't find my pants so I took yours.

PSS: I miss you like a fry misses ketchup

—F

I read his scrawled words three times just because he wrote them. After I tucked the note into my nightstand, I quickly got ready.

Twenty Three

Drew

Could you hear that sound?

It was me laughing.

I might not have used my fists, but I could still hit.

Man, I would have loved to see Con's face when the biker showed up asking for him. I also would have loved to see him take a couple punches, because there was no way in hell he wasn't going to get at least a couple.

Asshole.

After the commotion started downstairs, I snuck down an old service stairway (thank God this was an old house) and crept to the back door. No one saw because they were all too busy being secretly amused Con was such a douche.

I stood there and listened as long as I dared. I mean, it was funny as shit. That kid was probably having diarrhea in his PJs. I knew he'd probably try and blame T, but it wouldn't go that far because he'd have to rat himself out in order to explain.

He was too interested in self-preservation for that.

Besides, Trent had no idea I was the one who totally set up Con. He had nothing to do with it, so when he said so, everyone would believe him. The family was very adamant at the family meeting I not burst in the house and throw some punches.

No one said I couldn't put my computer skills to good use.

It was earlier than I liked, so I drove to a Dunkin Donuts and ordered a coffee, and then on impulse, I grabbed a bunch of donuts and a second cup of coffee. Today was game day. I knew everyone at home (well, the guys) would be gearing up for some fun, and I was anxious to get home and join them. Hopefully, T would come over so we could all go to the field together—you know, as a united front.

Up until this point, the guys that attacked Trent thought he was keeping their identities to himself. Today, they were going to learn otherwise. They would know he told, and they would also know this little charity game wasn't only benefiting the organization the frat voted on, but also our need to exact some physical pain.

I didn't drive home, though. Not right away. Instead, I pointed the Fastback in the opposite direction and drove to a place I'd only been once before. The private airport looked the same as the last time I was here, with the large fence all around and the top-notch security on the gate.

Since I didn't know the code and I didn't see a buzzer, I pulled up close to the entrance and laid on the horn.

It was so loud it annoyed even me.

As I held my palm over the noisemaker, I consoled myself with some coffee.

A minute later, there was some movement across the way, and I eased off the horn to flicker my headlights.

A second later, the gate opened, and I nosed the Mustang through and sped over to the hangar where Arrow lived.

The wide door on the front was still closed, but there was a small man-sized door on the side, and he was standing in it, watching me. All he was wearing was a pair of loose sweats, his chest bare. He was definitely tall and lanky, but maybe not quite as skinny as I originally thought. He did have some definition to his chest and arms, but his abs were flat.

Arrow also had quite a few tattoos; almost his entire left shoulder was covered in them, and he had some on his chest as well. I wasn't about to stare long enough to know what kind of designs they were. He might think I was checking him out.

I carried over the extra coffee I'd gotten and held it out between us.

He glanced at it, then at me before taking it.

"You drink coffee?" I asked.

"Doesn't everybody?"

I wondered what his conversation with Lorhaven was like after our talk in the garage at home. I wondered if Lorhaven told him about T and me. I wondered what Arrow thought about us. I wondered if he was embarrassed because he had a crush on me.

Oddly, I wasn't embarrassed by it. It was kind of flattering, I guess. Mostly, it kind of endeared the kid to me. (Yes, I know I'm supposed to think of him as a man, but it's hard, okay? He's kind of like the baby brother I never had.)

I felt this odd sort of kinship with him even though we were nothing alike. Well, at least I'd thought that before.

Now?

Now I was starting to think maybe he and I had more in common than either of us realized.

"Thanks," Arrow said, gesturing to the Styrofoam cup, and took a sip. Then he gestured with his head to the door, and I followed him inside.

It smelled like oil and car parts. You know, that sort of metal tinge to the air.

"What are you doing here?" Arrow asked, blunt, as I glanced around, looking into the back of the hangar toward the bed he slept in. Clearly, I'd gotten him up. The sheets were still tangled and there was an indent in the pillow.

"Going to a football game this morning. Thought you might wanna come."

"Why?" His eyes were suspicious.

I had a feeling Arrow was suspicious of people a lot, and it was because he'd been conditioned that way.

I remembered Lorhaven saying something to the tune of Arrow always wanting to see the best in people, and I wondered how he balanced that with the wariness.

I shrugged. "Might be fun."

"Trent gonna be there?" he asked.

I nodded. "My whole family will be there. You'll like them."

"I don't think so," he said.

I lifted an eyebrow. "You don't strike me as the type to judge people before you meet them."

"I meant I don't think they'll like me."

I lowered my coffee away from my face. "They like me. They like Trent. They're totally cool with our relationship."

"So you *are* in a relationship with him."

I nodded. "Your brother told you, didn't he?"

"I thought he was making it up. Trying to keep me away from you."

I laughed. "He would do something like that."

Arrow grinned.

"Your brother is a lot of things, but I don't think he would intentionally hurt you. He wants you to be happy."

"I know." He looked away, giving all his attention to the cup.

"My father kicked me out, too," I said softly.

His head snapped up.

"That's why you live here, right? You told your father you're gay, and he kicked you out."

"He hates me now."

My stomach clenched. I knew exactly how that felt. I knew exactly what it was like to be suddenly unloved by people who said—*no, who were supposed to*—they always would.

It sucked real bad. But something whispered in my ear that as rough as I had it, Arrow had it ten times worse.

I at least had a family who loved me, a whole house full of people who cared. And I had Trent. With him, I would never, ever have to feel alone.

Who did Arrow have besides Lorhaven?

"I don't think he hates you. I just think he doesn't understand, and it scares him."

"The result is still the same." His tone was matter-of-fact.

Oh yes, Lorhaven was right. This kid was definitely beyond his years.

"You're right." I agreed. "And it doesn't make it suck any less. But for every person who is narrow-minded, there's one who isn't."

"Yeah? Where are they?"

I held out my arms. "Right here."

He ran a hand through his blond hair, pushing it over to reveal the ultra-short side.

"What about Trent?"

"What about him?" I asked.

"He know you're here?"

I smiled. "He will if you come with me."

The look on his face made me smile. "I'm the possessive one, not him. Besides, he likes you."

"I hit on you."

I couldn't help it; I laughed out loud. "Dude, you need to work on your game. I had no idea."

"Way to crush a man's ego," he said and pressed a hand over his chest.

"I'm here, aren't I?" I said. "Look, I'm all in with Trent. That's not gonna change. But I got room in my life for friends."

Arrow stared at me for a long minute. I saw the debate rage in his mind. He wanted to be friends, so badly. He was almost desperate, but it was that desperation that made him hesitate. He was asking himself if he could trust me. If this would only come back to bite him in the ass.

It made me ache for him.

"You can invite your brother if you want," I offered, barely able to say the words without choking. Obviously, his brother was the closest person to him, and his loyalty went beyond the bonds of blood.

To trust.

Seemed like Lorhaven might be the only guy in Arrow's life that actually cared and wouldn't screw him over.

"Yeah." Arrow nodded. "Okay."

I grinned. "Get some clothes. Trent's not possessive, but if I show up with a half-naked gay dude, he might learn to be."

Arrow laughed, and I thought I saw the tinge of a blush across his cheeks.

Did I just kinda flirt with him?

Like for real?

I was getting good at being gay.

No, strike that. I was getting good at being who I really was.

I wasn't interested in Arrow, not like that, but it felt pretty good to give him a little boost of confidence. I didn't think he got those very often.

Maybe this good deed would help counteract the bad one I put into play at the frat this morning.

Not that I cared. Con deserved exactly what he got.

And it would be good for Arrow to see the bigots of the world didn't always win out.

Trent

The scent of brewing coffee and the sounds of a lively baby greeted me when I walked into the house.

Ivy's blond head poked out of the kitchen when Prada came rushing toward me, her nails clicking a ruckus as she came.

"Hey!" she called.

"Hey."

"Where's Drew?" I called out. She'd already disappeared back in the kitchen.

"I thought he was with you!"

That stopped me in my tracks. What the hell? He wasn't here? A sick, panicked feeling wrapped its icy-cold fingers around my heart and squeezed. I wasn't a paranoid person, but now I knew how one felt. The irrational but totally authentic thoughts running rampant through my mind literally made my palms break out in a cold sweat.

Flashes of the night I was jumped played behind my eyes like a B-rated horror movie. Had someone seen him leave the frat this morning? Had someone jumped him? Was he lying somewhere unable to call for help?

I yanked out my phone and dialed him.

It rang and rang. Just when I was about to throw my phone, he answered.

"Hey," he said like he didn't know I was having a mini heart attack.

"I thought you were dead in a ditch, asshole," I yelled.

There was pause on the line. "You at home?"

"And you aren't."

His muffled curse didn't make me feel any better. And then the sound of a muffled voice that was *not* Drew's grabbed my attention.

"Forrester!" I demanded. "Where the fuck are you?"

"I'm on my way home. I'm fine." He sounded a little guilty.

I blew out a breath. "You okay?"

"Yeah, frat boy. I'm fine. I should have texted you."

"Ya think?" I snapped.

"I am a big boy," he muttered.

I made a rude sound. "Yeah, so am I, but I still got fucked up."

Silence.

"Yeah… I'm sorry, T."

My anger deflated, and the panic I felt was draining away. "It's fine. I shouldn't have freaked."

"I get it."

"I'll see you in a few?"

"Definitely."

I cut off the line and walked into the kitchen. Ivy was standing at the island with some coffee and a bagel in front of her. Nova was in her little seat with dry Cheerios all over the place.

She grinned when she saw me and held out her arms.

"Hey, midge." I unhooked the little buckle around her waist and pulled her up. There were Cheerios all over her, too, and some of them fell onto my chest and decorated the black T-shirt I wore.

Nova reached down and picked one off my chest and held it out to me between her two tiny fingers.

"For me?" I asked and then snatched it out of her fingers (gently, of course) like I was starved.

She laughed like it was the greatest thing she'd ever seen.

"Mushy," I commented as I chewed. "Just how I like my Cheerios."

Ivy laughed.

I snuggled the baby close and kissed the top of her head. She decided she liked feeding me, so she started picking all the Cheerios off us to shove them in my mouth.

It was gross. I ate them anyway.

She liked it.

"Where's my brother?" Ivy asked.

I glanced away from the baby. She was looking good as always in a pair of skinny jeans, a long floaty-looking white top, and a colorful scarf draped around her neck. Her blond hair was wavy and pulled into a high ponytail that bounced when she moved around.

"On his way home."

"He okay?"

I grimaced. Obviously, she heard me reading him the riot act. I wasn't exactly quiet. "He's fine. I just overreacted."

"You're very protective," she said. "I like that."

"He's been through a lot," I muttered and ate another Cheerio.

"So have you."

"He told you what happened in North Carolina, right?" I asked. This was the first time I'd been alone with Ivy since we got back. Since Drew's parents were also hers, I wanted to know what she was feeling about the way they treated him.

"I had to drag it out of him."

I nodded. "Probably didn't want to upset you."

Ivy set down her coffee and looked straight at me. "How bad was it?"

Braeden walked in the room, but it was as if he knew we were talking. He said nothing and just went right to the coffee. On his way, he did stop to kiss Nova on the cheek. When he tried to lift her out of my arms, she clung to me and shook her head.

She loved me.

And she loved that I ate her nasty used cereal.

"It was bad," I said. "I don't think I've ever seen Drew that upset."

She nodded. "My father doesn't understand."

"He disowned him. Kicked him out and didn't even try."

Braeden slapped the coffeepot down a little harder than necessary but otherwise said nothing.

Ivy's eyes filled with tears. She glanced at Nova in my arms. "I just don't understand how a parent can do that to a child."

"He's been kinda quiet this week. You think he's taking it harder than he's letting on?"

She sniffled. "I don't know. Dad's approval has always been something Drew always wanted."

"Does your brother know yet?"

She nodded. "I called him and told him. I know it wasn't my place, but I wasn't about to let Drew do it and have him react like Dad."

"It's your place," I told her gently. "You're his family."

"You are, too." She reminded me.

I didn't think these people knew what it meant to me to have their support. Maybe it was time they knew.

Maybe it was time Drew knew. It might make what he was dealing with seem a little less isolating.

"You can butt into my business anytime," I told her.

Nova made a sound, and I looked down. She couldn't find any more cereal to feed me.

"All gone," I said and shrugged.

She pointed to the pile on her tray.

"You teach this kid to be so smart?" I asked Ivy.

Nova pointed again, and Ivy laughed.

I scooped up a handful and held them between us. She proceeded to make me eat more.

"Only for you, midge," I told her. "You know I love ya, right?"

She leaned forward and kissed me. My heart melted just a little. I glanced at B. "You're already buying guns, right?"

"Bullets, too," he quipped.

Ivy rolled her eyes, then returned to the topic. "He wasn't upset like Dad. He was surprised, but once he has time to think it over, I think he'll be fine with it. You and Drew don't need to worry about him."

"Thanks," I said, relieved.

"My father, though…" Her eyes darkened. "I don't know what to do,"

Ivy was in a tough spot. She probably felt caught in the middle of her brother and her parents. I didn't want that for her, and I knew Drew didn't either. She wasn't the one in a relationship her father considered depraved.

"You don't have to do anything," I said.

She made a frustrated sound. "If I do nothing, it looks like I agree with my father, and I don't! I told him what an ass I thought he was being."

My eyes widened.

Braeden laughed. "Gave him hell, she did."

"I love my parents. I really do. But they're wrong. And I want Nova to know her grandparents, but I won't raise her around people who would disown their own son over who his heart chose."

I glanced at Braeden, worried. Was Ivy really contemplating severing her relationship with her parents over this? Nova's relationship.

Braeden shrugged. "She has a point."

I didn't want that. I didn't want the relationship I essentially set into motion to affect not only Drew and me, but hurt everyone around us.

I was about to tell her that when the door to the garage opened and Drew stepped in. The second he was in my sight, my eyes swept over his body, assessing and making sure he was definitely okay.

He was looking sexy in my sweats, uncombed hair, and a coffee in hand. His blue stare found mine first, and I felt something click inside me, back into place where it belonged. That's how I felt when we weren't together, like a piece of me had shaken loose and was missing.

Nova was bouncing around in my arms at the sight of her favorite uncle.

"There's my favorite girl!" he said, grinning at her.

Arrow walked into the house behind him, carrying an identical coffee. Surprise shot through me. *So that's whose voice I heard.*

Arrow appeared out of his comfort zone and like he wasn't sure where to look. Drew gave me a meaningful look, and I understood. For whatever reason, this kid had grown on Drew. I understood why;

he was sort of like a stray without a home that just needed someone to adopt him.

Yeah, I knew he had Lorhaven.

Maybe the guy wasn't as bad as I originally thought, but I still didn't like him.

"What's up, man?" I stepped toward Arrow and held out my fist.

He bumped his against mine. "Hey, Trent."

"You gonna play some football with us today?"

He seemed a little taken aback by the easy way I greeted him, but he recovered fast. "I thought we were watching."

"I'm going to smash heads," Braeden quipped and stepped around Ivy to introduce himself to Arrow.

I made the introductions while Drew went for Nova. She held her arms out to him, and he snatched her up.

"Traitor!" I told her.

Nova gave me a toothless grin and picked up a Cheerio out of my hand and held it to Drew's lips. He ate it of course.

His face screwed up. "Why is it mushy?"

"Baby slobber," I told him.

Ivy was inviting Arrow to sit with her at the game and asking him about his style. "You remind me of someone…" she was saying.

"Kid looks just like the Biebs," Braeden announced.

I laughed, and Arrow blushed.

Nova kissed Drew, and it stole my attention. Then she leaned toward me, so I bent and she kissed me, too. Then, to everyone's surprise, she put her hand on my cheek and tried to push it toward Drew.

"Uhhh…"

"She wants you to kiss," Ivy explained. "That's her new thing. Kisses."

Drew and I looked at each other. Yeah, everyone knew about us, but we never kissed in front of anyone before.

Ever.

Nova made an impatient sound and patted my cheek.

I glanced around the room, not sure what to do.

Braeden made a rude sound. "You telling my daughter no?"

Drew rolled his eyes.

My eyes asked him a question.

He nodded.

I leaned forward and pressed our lips together. It was meant to be a quick peck, but the second we touched, I got a little lost. My lips clung to his a little longer than necessary, but it couldn't be helped.

When I pulled back, Nova clapped between us, but all I could look at was Drew. No one else seemed to give a rat's ass I just kissed another dude in the kitchen, but I sure as hell cared.

I loved kissing him.

"What's going on in here?" Rimmel said, entering the kitchen with Romeo right behind her.

"Oh, nothing. Just Trent and Drew making out," Braeden announced. "Oh, and Justin Bieber is here."

"I'm changing my hair," Arrow muttered, which launched Ivy into a full-on lecture about the latest hair trends for men.

Basically, it was a typical morning at home. Everyone talked over each other, we were loud, and Braeden was rude. After a few minutes, Arrow seemed to relax and fit right in. He was still a little quiet, but he was obviously still trying to check everyone out.

After we devoured most of the box of donuts Drew brought home, we snuck up to his room for the only few minutes of alone time we'd probably get all day.

"I should have texted," Drew said the second we were alone.

"Yeah," I said and then attacked his mouth. That short kiss we shared before was a teaser, something that left me wanting more.

He opened for me instantly, and our tongues slipped against each other's while our lips moved in sync. I reached around and grabbed his ass, wishing there was a lot less clothing between us. He must have felt the same, because he was pulling at my shirt.

I let it go and slid it off and tossed it on the bed. "We don't have time for this." I reminded him.

"I know," he said even as he ran his palms over my chest and down my abs.

I kissed him again. Hard and deep. He groaned into my mouth, and I swallowed the sound.

Grudgingly, I pulled back and licked at my lips so I could get every last taste of him inside me. "Arrow, huh?"

"I like him."

I nodded. "Me, too."

He started pulling off his clothes and rummaging around in his drawers for fresh ones. I watched, admiring the strong lines of his body and remembering the way his skin felt beneath my fingertips.

I wanted to touch him. I thought about it over and over, but I didn't. This time if I did, I wouldn't be able to stop. I'd want to take him completely, and he was loud when I had sex with him.

Kissing in front of the fam was one thing; letting them hear him moan my name was another.

"Stop it," he said, turning toward me.

"What?"

"Thinking about being inside me. You're making me crazy."

"I can't help it. I want more."

"Me, too." His voice dropped.

It still kind of amazed me that he felt the same way I did, that his body responded to my touch like mine did his. What were the odds really? What were the odds I'd meet someone who not only was a friend, but then had the capacity and the open heart to become my everything else?

Without thinking, I crossed the room and snatched him to me. Our bodies pressed tight, and I knew he could feel my erection between us. I smiled against his head because I could feel his, too.

"Later." I promised myself out loud.

"Tonight?" Drew lifted his head.

I kissed him again even though I wasn't supposed to.

I mean, really, our entire relationship was a giant "wasn't supposed to." We did it anyway, and it was the best decision I ever made.

"Tonight." I promised and then let him go.

"I'm gonna jump in the shower. I'll be down in a minute."

I nodded. "I still haven't told you what happened this morning at the frat."

He turned from the door, grinning. "Oh, I know what happened."

My eyes narrowed. "You heard all the shouting?"

"That, too."

Realization dawned. Holy shit balls. Drew totally set Con up. Mr. Computer Savvy himself.

"How the hell did you pull that off, and how did you put the five hundred in his bank account?"

Drew sniffed and looked smug. It was sexy. "Don't ever piss off a hacker," he said. "And *especially* don't go after the person a hacker is in love with."

I laughed. "You sneaky bastard."

His smile was sly.

"You covered your tracks, didn't you?" I worried. If this was somehow discovered…

"Taken care of."

"How?" I pressed, still concerned. I started imagining ways I could take the blame if he got caught and make it sound like I actually knew how to hack.

"I used computers with IP addresses not linked to me or you. Internet cafés, libraries, even a hotel in North Carolina—not the one we stayed at. I used one in Maryland, too."

I grinned. He was smart.

"Plus, I know how to move around a computer undetected. I know how to do things without leaving a trace. I might not like my day job, but I do it very, very well."

"I fucking love you," I told him.

"How bad did Con come down on you?" he asked.

"Not very. He couldn't." Which was exactly why he never said anything to me about his plan. I had nothing to do with this.

Drew nodded. "Good."

"Should I assume there's more involved than just Hog Heaven?" I inquired.

"You shouldn't assume things."

I took that as a yes.

Twenty *Five*

Drew

The media came to the football game.

I don't know why I was surprised about it, but I was. I really should have been used to them being around, especially since the new racing division was set to blow up at any minute.

I had two endorsement deals with the ink dry, a magazine cover under my belt, and very soon, T and I would likely become a major media interest.

Maybe that's why I was surprised. Well, not surprised as much as cautious. The press didn't know about Trent and me yet. I knew we agreed to tell them, to basically "come out," but we hadn't yet.

We were going to have to be careful today.

Careful how we interacted, how we looked at each other. How we were together.

I hated it.

Yet I understood.

Ah, the paradox that was Trent and my relationship reared its ugly head.

I wanted to be free to love him, but I didn't want to make it a thing. I just wanted to be. It wouldn't be a thing if I were with a girl. No one would bat an eye.

I could sit here and think about how unfair it all was, how frustrating it was, and how sometimes it hurt, but really, what would it change?

Nothing today.

Tomorrow? Maybe. The interview with *GearShark* had the potential to maybe change a few things.

So today it was what it was. We would be careful. We would have been anyway because the frat didn't know; the Wolves didn't know.

But my parents knew. I could still taste their reaction in the back of my mouth. It tasted like rotten eggs and barf.

I knew what that shit tasted like. I've played the game Bean Boozled.

Bean Boozled = that disgusting game of jelly bean roulette where you had no idea what disgusting flavor you'd eat until it was exploding across your tongue.

Their reaction and even sometimes looking at Arrow made me feel incredibly insecure to tell anyone else about my relationship.

But then I looked at Trent.

The doubt didn't go away; it would probably always be there, but it no longer seemed like something I would allow to hold me back.

The game was Omega versus the football team. I was playing with the football team. Yeah, the scrawny racer was playing with a bunch of literal pro athletes.

Hopefully, I wouldn't die.

The football side was comprised of some Maryland Knights players like Romeo and Braeden, along with a handful of other guys, and the rest were guys from the Wolves. Even though Trent was one of the Wolves, he was playing with his frat.

Since I wasn't a football player, it was explained to everyone who asked (which was a lot) that the reason I was playing was to represent the new racing division. Because Ron Gamble owned the Knights and the new division and he cut a huge check to the charity we were benefiting today, he requested I (his new face of racing) be allowed to play as well.

It was good press after all.

Really, I was just here so I could legally cause some bodily harm to four guys on the opposing team, but no one needed to know that except the family.

The turnout today was more than I expected. I always heard how much Alpha U loved football, but to see it was something else.

And holy crap, did people like Romeo. He was literally swallowed whole by a huge crush of fans the second he walked onto the field. More than once, I glanced up at Rimmel in the stands, but she didn't seem fazed by it at all. It was like it was nothing new.

Braeden was getting almost as much attention, but then again, Ivy was, too. She had her own fan base now because of her column and YouTube channel.

The vibe of the game was casual, meaning people who'd bought tickets were allowed on the field before the game started to meet and greet the pros. It was madness, but it explained why so many tickets were sold.

Even though this idea was born out of the need for revenge, it really was a great event and supported a worthy cause. We raised a shit ton of money for the charity. Trent looked like a hero, and the frat was cast in a really good light.

The game wasn't supposed to be full contact because obviously, the frat would get their asses handed to them. It was officially flag football with tackling allowed.

Unofficially, I didn't care.

Before the game was set to start, the fans were told to find their seats, and once the field was clear, the teams retreated to their sides. It felt weird to be on the opposite side from Trent, but it was a necessity. I found him in the group across the field. It was easy because he was the biggest one.

Or maybe it was because I loved him.

When I started thinking about the way he kissed me earlier and how he said he wanted to be inside me, I had to look away. If I didn't, I was going to look like one of those cartoon characters with hearts in their eyes.

Lame.

The press would have a damn field day.

Romeo and Braeden approached and took up position on each side of me. They both had their flags already fastened around their waist. We were wearing Knights colors, and the frat was wearing Alpha U colors.

"Crush 'em, but don't break 'em," Romeo said quietly.

"You're getting soft in your old age," Braeden told him.

"At least make it look like an accident." Romeo conceded.

Braeden offered me his fist, and we bumped it out.

The entire team got together and talked strategy. Obviously, Romeo was the quarterback, and most other positions were filled. I was put on defense. Strange because I wasn't that big, but no one questioned Romeo.

Our game wasn't going to be as long as a real football game, but the fans didn't care. They cheered and flocked to the stands like nobody's business.

I avoided the press, who was especially interested in our side of the field like a plague, and breathed a sigh of relief when they were escorted away so the game could begin.

Our team won the coin toss, so we got the ball first.

I smiled under the helmet when I saw three out of the four guys who attacked Trent were playing offense, including Con. I wasn't sure where the big one was, the one who'd been friends with Trent up until he started thinking T was gay.

I looked for him earlier but had yet to lay eyes on him.

The ball was snapped and the game began. I knew the basics of football, but I wasn't an expert. It really didn't matter anyway. I went right for Conner.

He was in my direct line of sight, and I charged him. I sank low like I knew Trent did and didn't hesitate. I bulldozed into him and took him down. He landed with an *ooomph* beneath me. I quickly "scrambled" up and "accidentally" kneed him in the balls.

"Ugghh…" He rolled to his side.

"Man, you okay?" I asked. "My bad."

He rolled onto his back and glared at me. His chest was heaving, probably because his boys were barking.

I offered him a hand to help him up, but he knocked it away.

I smiled. "Have a good game."

The distinct flare of panic in his eyes when I spoke made me extremely satisfied as I turned to walk away.

Braeden lived up to his "Hulk" status during the game. That guy was a freaking beast on the field. It was quite the contrast to the guy I saw with my niece and sister. But it sure was hella fun to watch. He took down guys like nobody's business, and by the end of the first quarter, one of the guys who jumped Trent was escorted off the field with a limp.

As the quarterback, Romeo wasn't really in the position to tackle, but he still managed. He ran the ball a couple times and used his upper body as a battering ram when Conner or a few other guys got in his way.

Of course, we couldn't make it look like we were targeting a few players rougher than the others, so we couldn't take them out every play, and we had to actually play the game.

It was fun actually.

Watching Trent in his element was awesome. The only other time I saw that kind of passion in his eyes was when he talked business with Gamble. He played quarterback for the frat. It wasn't his usual position, but he was the best choice. Plus, it was a little less "contact" for his ribs.

I had a feeling Romeo pretty much warned his Knights players to back off Trent, and of course, the Wolves already knew about his injury because they'd been training with him while it healed.

A couple times, T got sacked, but not hard enough to reinjure him. Still, each time he went down, my heart skipped a beat. Shit, I had no idea how Rim and Ivy dealt with this all the time.

Romeo seemed to realize how I was feeling, which made me wonder if I was being obvious. Before Trent took the field again, he was at my side. "Why don't you play out there this round?"

I glanced at him. "Why?"

"You notice Con's out there this go around?" He hitched his chin toward the field.

"What the fuck?" I muttered. "He wouldn't take down someone on his own team. That would look shady."

"Unless it was an accident," Romeo said.

I wouldn't put it past him. He'd already taken a bunch of cheap shots at Trent. "I'm going," I said.

Romeo called in one of the other guys, and I jogged out to take his place.

Trent glanced at me momentarily, but his eyes didn't linger.

The ball was snapped into Trent's hands. He held it, looking for an open pass. When he found one, he threw the ball. Most players followed the ball, but my eyes stayed on T. I even let the player by I was supposed to be blocking.

It's a good thing. I wasn't the only one whose eyes stayed with him. Conner cut across the field toward Trent. He shoved one of the opposing players back, and it looked pretty legit.

I knew better.

I took off in a sprint toward my person and Conner. T's eyes locked on me and widened. Then he saw Conner, and his expression changed.

I increased my speed and ran full on, full throttle right into Con. I ran like I drove.

Balls to the wall.

We slammed together and fell in a heap. Both of us laid there stunned for a minute and then I started to pull back. Conner grabbed the front of my jersey and pulled me back.

"What the fuck is your problem, fag?"

Like oil and water, I let the slur roll off my back. "I think you know," I snarled.

I stood up and stepped back. Con leapt to his feet and lunged at me. Our arms locked together, and we started to struggle. He tried to kick me, but I twisted away.

Trent yelled and ran forward.

I ripped off my helmet and threw it on the turf. "Come on!" I challenged Con.

Con whipped off his helmet, too, and took a step. Frat members grabbed him by the waist and restrained him.

No one restrained me, but they all gathered at my back.

"All right!" Con yelled. "All right, I'm good."

Everyone holding him let go.

"Play!" one of the Wolves yelled, and players started to fall into position.

I took one step, a single step away, and Con rushed me. I was expecting it, though. He was a little bitch and wanted to get in at least one hit. I plated my feet and swung around, using my momentum to propel my fist.

It caught him right in the face. He went down hard.

Blood covered his nose, and he lay there, dazed.

"You're gonna pay for that you faggot," he slurred.

I lunged at him again, but Trent appeared and wrapped one arm around my waist to restrain me. "Down, Forrester," he whispered beside my ear.

I pulled back, but my muscles quivered with readiness.

I wanted to punch him again so bad.

Braeden appeared and picked up Con off the ground by the front of his shirt. "The fuck you just call my brother?" he asked, holding Con up so his feet dangled.

"I called him a dirty faggot," Con spat.

Trent tensed, and I gave him a warning look.

Braeden glanced at the nearby ref. "You gonna eject this asshole, or should I make it so he can't play no more?"

Con started to struggle, and B batted away his attempts.

"Ejected," the ref called, "for use of derogatory comments. Unsportsmanlike conduct."

The crowd cheered.

"What about him? He punched me!" Conner yelled.

"You deserved it." Braeden let go of Con, and he fell on his ass.

"Back to the game!" the ref demanded, and everyone started moving around.

A couple guys hauled Con off the field and sat him on the bench.

Before walking back to the sidelines, I gave Trent a look.

"I know," he said softly. "I know."

I wanted badly in that moment to reach out and touch him. Just to give something tangible to what always seemed to be between us. We couldn't, not just then.

It actually kind of hurt.

It hurt way more than anything Conner's mouth could spew.

We parted ways. As we walked, I felt the invisible tether between us stretching, but it didn't break.

Romeo clapped me on the back. "Nice save, Drew."

"Thanks," I said, watching Con dabbing at his nose with a towel. Though in that moment, it didn't feel like a save.

Sure, I kept Trent from taking a hard hit to the midsection, a totally illegal hit considering he already got rid of the ball.

But…

Maybe I kind of understood why Trent wanted me to just stay away. I had this tingly feeling on the back of my neck now.

Like maybe I'd just made everything worse.

Twenty *Six*

Trent

Before the game…

All the Omega members were gathered, changing before the game, laughing and giving each other shit just like always. It was a good time, but I sort of felt like I was viewing it all through a window, like an outsider looking in.

But I wasn't an outsider. I was the president. I was the leader of these men.

I didn't want to be.

Not anymore.

In fact, I was sort of embarrassed I had to be here—with them.

I'd changed in the past few years here at Alpha U. Most of my changes happening within the past year. It was a natural progression of life, growing from a youth into an adult.

For me, it felt like more.

I guess I always used to feel like I was renting the space inside my skin. Like I was borrowing it or it wasn't really mine. I was the football player, the jock. I was the frat boy, the playboy, the college student who knew what he wanted.

I was who everyone saw when they looked at me. I met their expectations—no, I exceeded them.

I'd always been a good friend, the kind who listened and faded into the background. The wingman. The sidekick.

Things started to change. There was a gradual shift inside me. I fought that shift for a long time. But eventually, a crack in a foundation spreads and then everything sitting on it is in danger of sinking.

My foundation didn't just crack. It shook. It experienced an earthquake…

And it was that earthquake that rebirthed someone new.

The real me.

I no longer rented space inside my skin.

I owned it free and clear.

I wasn't completely changed, but I wasn't the same either. Maybe a hybrid? A combination of the past and the present, which would carry me into the future.

Like every new build, the walls and plaster would take time to settle. I was new, and I still felt scared.

I was resolved.

Not resolved to accept life, but resolved to *live* it.

As I stood here in the locker room, surrounded by men I once considered my brothers, I realized my circle was getting smaller. Not because four men in this group ruined it for everyone, but because I no longer needed to be here.

After today, after I dealt once and for all with Conner and the three other guys who attacked me, I could phase out of the fraternity. I could hand over the reins to Jack and not look back. It was time.

This wasn't an experience I regretted, because it brought me to where I stood today.

"You're late!" one of the members hollered and snapped me back to the here and now. I looked up. It was Daniel.

I think of all the four guys who jumped me that night, it was him I was most disappointed by. There are some people you just expect better from, so it royally sucks when they turn out to be a lot skeezier than you thought.

Daniel and I rushed Alpha Omega together. We went through Hell Week together. We even had a couple classes together back in the day when we were still taking basics. He'd been a friend. We partied together, drank together. We were brothers.

And then he held me down and whispered things like, *"People like you belong in hell,"* while I was beaten.

Conner was a real shit-bag. But somehow, Daniel seemed worse.

I guess because with Conner, you always expected something like that, but not from someone you thought was your friend.

He'd avoided me since that night. I only ever saw him during frat events and meetings. I saw him once on campus, and he physically crossed the street to get away from me.

I liked to sometimes think it was because he was ashamed of what he did. But I knew the truth was because he thought I was disgusting.

So how come I was the disgusting one, but he was the one who acted out of his own disgust?

Daniel was looking a little rough around the edges and a little dazed and confused. His short, dark hair was mussed, and he was gripping a paper in his hand like his life depended on it.

"Where the hell you been?" Jack called, who was standing off to my left.

Daniel glanced up at him. "Sorry. I had a meeting with my career counselor."

"On game day?" Jack questioned.

"It was sort of an emergency."

"What kind of emergency?" I spoke up.

Daniel looked at me and frowned.

"There's an issue with my transcript," he replied. It was like he was so distracted he forgot who he was even talking to.

"What kind of problem?" someone beside him asked.

Daniel sat on the bench. "I'm on academic probation."

I kept my face smooth and didn't react. He didn't deserve my surprise. Just because he wasn't the type of guy to ever get low scores didn't mean he didn't actually get them. He was never the type of person to beat anyone up either…

"They're just now telling you now?" Jack asked.

"Apparently, there was some kind of error and their system never caught it. Anyway, the school realized it today, and I got called in." He rubbed a hand over his head. "I'm failing two classes."

It was late in the semester. If he really was failing, there was no way he was going to have time to make that up.

"What about graduation?" I asked.

"They won't let me." He sounded hollow, like he was in shock.

"You're not going to graduate?" Jack said, incredulous.

"No!" he shouted out, frustrated. Everyone who wasn't paying attention before sure was now. "My school records show I'm failing two classes. All my assignments are turned in, but half of them all got shitty grades. And my midterms? Apparently, I barely passed those."

"If you were struggling, why didn't you ask for help?" Jack pressed. "You know the fraternity has access to free tutoring. Any of the brothers would have helped."

I nodded because Jack was right. One of the requirements of an Omega charter was he perform well in all classes and maintain a passable average.

"I didn't know!" he exclaimed. "No one said anything to me until today. I thought I was passing. This has to be some mistake."

"Maybe their computers are malfunctioning," someone offered.

"They aren't. The office checked. And rechecked. Then my career counselor called the professors and had them access their online gradebooks. I'm fucking failing."

"What does that mean?" Jack asked. He was looking at me, not Daniel.

"It means he won't graduate. He'll have to retake these two classes and graduate next semester," I answered.

"I'll have to reenroll for next fall!" he hollered and punched a locker.

"Summer classes?" someone offered.

"Not the ones I need," he replied, bitter.

"Can you make up the work? The assignments?" I asked, knowing he couldn't.

"Don't you think if I could, I'd be doing the work right now?" He fumed and looked at me. "You're probably loving this."

What goes around comes around, fucker. "Of course I'm not."

"I can't play in the game. I'm suspended from campus activities. I'm on probation with the school."

"That seems awful extreme for failing two classes." Jack crossed his arms over his chest.

"I might have made a scene in the office," he muttered. "And they had to call campus security."

"This calls into question your charter at Omega," I said.

His nostrils flared. "What?"

"This is grounds for being dismissed from the brotherhood."

Beside me, Jack nodded, grim. The men all standing around averted their gazes and went back to dressing.

"You can't kick me out of here. If I go, I'll take you with me."

I yawned. "Since you aren't playing, you can leave. Maybe you can convince the teachers to give you extra credit."

His lips thinned into a straight line.

"We'll have a house meeting and vote on your status, and I'll let you know."

He slammed out of the locker room like the Tasmanian devil.

I wondered if maybe Drew had gone a little further with his hacking skills or if Daniel just really dropped the ball.

Either way, I didn't really care.

One down, three to go.

After the game…

We got our asses handed to us. On a nicely decorated platter of La-ooser.

Not like I expected anything else, though. I mean, damn, the Wolves and the Knights together on one team?

#Epic.

It was fun to be out on the field again, although I missed being alongside the Wolves. The game ran a little longer than expected, but no one complained. The fans there seemed happy to stay.

We raised a lot of money, so I counted the day as a success.

Not only that, but the three guys who needed a little extra tackling all got what was coming to them, and by the end of the game, they knew damn sure why they seemed to be so accident prone on the field today.

One guy was already gone, off to the campus clinic because he popped his knee out of socket and had to have it popped back in. Conner's best friend was probably going to be black and blue with bruises tomorrow, and Conner…

Well, he had a busted nose, a busted ass, and a bunch of grass stains all over his clothes. If he'd actually hit Drew like he'd intended, he wouldn't have gotten off so lucky. The fight wasn't totally a surprise, but I'd hoped Drew would keep his cool.

He only did what I would have done, which was taken out the threat he saw to me.

Conner was pissed, though. He was sitting in the corner of the locker room, drilling holes in the back of my skull with his stare.

After I gave a short, "We lost, but we won because of all the good we did for the charity," speech, the guys all hit the showers and began changing.

I just left on my sweaty, stained clothes. I'd wait and shower at home. There was no way in hell I was getting naked in here in front of Con and his last remaining co-conspirator.

Even though I wasn't showering, I hung in the locker room a bit, talking shit and laughing with the other guys. At one point, most everyone was hitting the showers, and a few had already left when Jack approached.

"Today was planned for a reason, wasn't it?" He spoke very low.

I glanced up from my phone. "Duh."

"It was them, wasn't it? Con and some friends."

I heard it in his voice, the surety. I lowered my phone and slid it into my pocket and leaned one shoulder against the lockers. "What do you mean?"

"Our own frat brothers jumped you."

How the hell did he figure that out? I hadn't told anyone.

A pinched look came over his face. "I'm assuming your silence is an agreement."

"You might be on to something." I hedged. He was the almost president. He had a right to the information.

"It's because you're gay, isn't it?"

I jerked upright and reared back slightly.

Some laughter filtered in from the direction of the showers, and I grabbed Jack by the arm and led him even farther away, over near the entrance.

"Why would you say that?" I asked when we were totally alone.

"That night a while ago when you left brothers' night to go with Drew. You asked me if I cared you were leaving with him. It got me to thinking. Then the rumors started whispering through the house, and Drew hasn't come around since. Not to mention your family sure was rough on a few particular players today."

"Was it that obvious?" My tone was sheepish.

"No, but I watch and observe, just like you."

I blew out a breath. "Fine. I'm in a relationship with Drew. I never confirmed it to Conner, but he suspected, and he turned those other three against me. He thought if he could beat me up and scare me bad enough, I'd leave the house and he could swoop in and take control."

"Push me right out." Jack mulled that over.

"Pretty much. And we both know if that happens, Omega is screwed."

Jack nodded. "We should tell the house, let them take care of it."

I nodded. "That's the plan. I was just letting them squirm a while."

"Devious." Jack nodded. "I approve."

"So you're okay with it?" I whispered.

"With having you as president? Of course."

"You know what I mean." I levelled my eyes on his.

"Yeah, I know. I'll tell you what I said back then, when you left to go with Drew on brothers' night. I don't have a problem with it. Love is love."

I held out my hand, and we shook on it.

"You're going to make an awesome prez. How would you feel about taking the reins a little earlier than planned?"

"You know I'm up for it."

I nodded. "Good. I'll keep you posted."

Not long after everyone started filing out of the locker room, everyone was pumped for the giant party we were having at the house tonight to celebrate the game.

On his way past, Conner stopped to stare at me.

"How's the nose?" I asked with a smirk.

"You think you're so clever, don't you?" he asked. "Enjoy it now, because when everyone finds out you like dick, they'll be singing a whole new tune."

"Maybe." I conceded. "But if they do, you probably won't still be around to see it."

He made a rude sound, then stepped back. "Tell your boyfriend I owe him one."

I leapt forward to grab him by the shirt, but a damn bench was in the way, and the little pecker turned and ran.

Done.

That was it.

No more head games. No more hacking.

No more playing with my food.

He threatened Drew. I'd do anything, and I do mean anything, to keep something like what happened to me from happening to him.

It was time to eat.

Twenty Seven

Drew

I was getting old.

Like I might as well put in an order for a cane and a rocking chair.

Well, maybe not *that* old.

But old enough that a party didn't sound like fun. 'Course, maybe it was because of the tension I felt at this particular party.

This was the first time I'd been in the Omega house at a party since before Trent was beaten up. It was the first time I'd been here at all since that night as far as everyone else was concerned.

It would be odd if I didn't show. My absence would be more notable than my presence. I knew people in the Omega house whispered about Trent's sexual orientation, and I knew it was me they all suspected him being with.

It didn't bother me. Not like that. Not anymore. It seemed like after facing my father, facing a room full of douche bag frat guys was the equivalent of having gum stuck to the bottom of my shoe.

Let me make it clear, though. Just because I didn't care they suspected or whispered and just because I didn't care what their opinion was on who I loved… it still made me nervous.

I'd already witnessed what some of the guys in this house would do. After the game and the way Conner and I went after one another, I was afraid of making it worse. Trent still lived here.

Plus, we'd yet to come out to the press and to T's mom.

Something I was very curious about. I didn't know much about that side of Trent's life. He never talked much about his mom, his dad… anyone. The only thing I knew for sure was he was an only child and his dad wasn't around.

At least I wasn't alone tonight. Romeo and Braeden were here; a lot of the Wolves players were here. It wasn't just the frat and me. This was a post-game party and a huge one at that. The house was packed, so much so that people spilled out into the backyard where there was a small bonfire burning and lights strung around the old trees.

There was a keg in the yard and one in the kitchen. Coolers with liquor and beer sat like every two feet, and the music was so loud I had no doubt campus security would get a noise complaint.

Of course, maybe not. Everyone on the entire street was here, so there weren't many people left to actually call and complain.

We were out in the yard, the massive crowd around Romeo, Braeden, and a couple other Knights players. Rimmel and Ivy went home with Nova, and I was thankful. This was no place for them.

The bonfire was against my back, which I was glad for, not because the darkness brought some cold air, but because if I had flames at my back, I couldn't have frat assholes sneaking up behind me.

Trent was inside, still making his rounds and doing his job as president. I knew he was trying to make his way out here, so every few moments, I would scan the crowd for his familiar face.

People were interested in the new racing division, which I thought was cool because it meant word was getting out, so I ended up talking cars while I nursed my beer.

"Hey-hey!" Braeden called out a little bit later, and the crowd parted around them as Trent stepped through.

My heart fluttered a little at the sight of him in a pair of beat-up jeans. I liked the worn look on him; it was sexy. With it, he was wearing a plain white T-shirt that molded to his impressive chest and over was an olive-green, army-style jacket.

He grinned, flashing his crooked front tooth, and bumped fists with just about everyone he passed.

"To our host!" Romeo yelled and lifted his beer.

Everyone cheered and did the same. I laughed because I could only imagine what it was like when Romeo actually went here.

Trent grinned and drank to their cheers. His eyes met mine over the rim of his red cup, and the fire at my back reflected off the gold flecks in his gaze. He took up position between me and B, leaning close to my ear.

"Daniel is on academic probation. Couldn't play today. Won't be graduating."

I sipped my beer. "I wondered why he wasn't on the field."

My little field trip into Daniel's college record sure paid off a lot better than I thought. Hell, I had no idea the fuck would have to defer graduation. Oh well. He deserved it. It was a shame, though, he wasn't on the field to take a few hits today.

Trent caught my eye and lifted a brow, silently asking if I was responsible.

I smiled.

"Good game, loser." Braeden butted into our private conversation. "How'd it feel to take a loss today?"

Trent laughed. "Strange. I'm used to being on the winning team."

We all settled into a conversation, mostly about football, because you know, the NFL pros were in our presence. There was some smack talk about how bad we smoked the Omegas and, of course, some beer drinking.

I noticed Trent seemed to be drinking the same as I was tonight, as in not really. There was no way in hell I'd let my guard down around all these people. Especially with guys like Conner running around.

I'd yet to see him, but I knew Trent had. He was in the house, and I'd pretty much stayed out in the yard.

In a perfect world, it would have stayed like that.

We all know perfection in life is very rare.

Unless of course you're a crispy, warm French fry dunked generously in Heinz ketchup.

Jack appeared, breaking into the circle where we all were standing. Trent was on instant alert. Must have been the wary look on Jack's face.

"Thought you might wanna know," Jack said, trying to keep his voice down, but it was a party and he wasn't leaning close. So obviously, people could hear him. "Con's in the house. He's talking a lot… Saying some shit. Getting people riled up."

Trent let out a curse. "He drunk?"

Jack nodded, grim. "Want me to handle it?"

"Nah, man." Trent clapped him on the back. "It's time I deal with him once and for all."

Braeden was already starting for the house, Romeo right beside him. Trent turned to me. "Just stay here."

I laughed.

Trent's eyes stared unflinchingly into mine. "I'm not gonna lie in there."

I stared unflinchingly back. "I don't want you to."

Trent measured me a second longer and then nodded. He walked right through the path B and Romeo were cutting, and I followed right behind. T was the first to walk in the back door of the house.

In here, the music was so loud it actually made my body vibrate. People danced all over, and there was a game of beer pong set up near the kitchen.

Trent went right through toward the main living space. It's like he had radar for the guy, like he knew exactly where Conner would be.

The vibe the four of us gave off as we moved through the house got a lot of attention. All of us were impressive in height and build. I was the smallest, but I wasn't so small I'd get lost in the crowd.

It was Romeo who garnered the most attention. He was intimidating when he wanted to be. His quiet power and blue-eyed stare were enough to make even the drunkest person sober enough to get the hell out of the way.

And Braeden… well, he simmered with temper. He was a hothead, had been since the day I'd met him. I knew he'd throw a punch. Hell, we'd exchanged a few ourselves.

Conner was in the center of the living room. His eyes were blackened from the hit I gladly delivered to his nose, and it was puffy and painful looking. Probably explained why he was self-medicating with the excess alcohol tonight. Maybe he was trying to dull away the pain of getting punched in the face.

He was talking animatedly to a group of mainly Omega members, but there were girls hanging on some of the guys, too.

Their gazes all shifted to Trent when he approached. Tension in the room spiked, and some people turned a wary eye.

"I hear you're in here talking shit again, Conner," Trent said, his voice icy and hard. He never talked to me like that. To anyone. "How many times have I told you if you got something to say, then say it to my face?"

Conner's face screwed up into a mean look. His eyes swept toward the family standing at Trent's back. "I see you brought backup."

Trent shrugged one shoulder. "I know you like to fight in groups."

Conner's face paled.

Jack appeared, stepping around me, B, and Romeo and moving to stand near Trent and all the Omega brothers.

Conner sneered. "Had to run and tell, didn't you?"

"I think maybe our president has a right to know what you've been saying about him. Don't you?" Jack replied.

"He knows exactly what I've been saying about him," Conner said. "He's just too chicken shit to admit it."

"Like you were too chicken shit to come at me in a fair fight?"

Conner laughed. "Your threats are getting old, Trent."

"No threat. I think you've seen some action." Trent raised his voice. Everyone around us grew quieter. Out of the corner of my eye, I saw Romeo gesture for the music to be turned down.

Just like that, the music settled into a much lower tone.

"I knew it!" he yelled, pointing at T with an accusatory glare. "That was you! You're the one who brought the biker over. And that game today?" He held out his arms. "That was just an excuse so you could thrash me!"

"I know it's hard to believe," Trent said, "but not everything is about you."

"Admit it." He pressed. "Admit the shady shit you've been pulling."

"I can honestly say I haven't done one shady thing. If you got knocked around in the game today, it's because you're a wimp who can't handle himself."

Conner's eyes flared, and he threw his beer across the room. The cup hit the wall, and the tawny liquid splattered everywhere.

"But you…" Trent continued mildly, like Conner's outburst was nothing at all. "You've been throwing all kinds of shade, haven't you?"

"You deserved every last bit of it."

I stiffened because that was a clear admission. One punch to his face just wasn't enough. Nothing I'd done to this kid would ever be enough.

Trent kept his cool. I had no idea how or even why, but he did. "Conner's been trying to get me out of here for months. He tried to do it by the book, and when that didn't work, he resorted to other, more unorthodox methods," he announced.

More of the Omega brothers gathered around. In fact, the party had pretty much come to a screeching halt.

"He's been talking. You've been whispering. If someone has something to ask, then why don't you just fucking ask it?"

One of the brothers stepped forward. I think his name was Josh. He'd been standing here with Con when we walked in.

"Are you gay?" he asked point blank.

Conner started laughing. "He won't—"

"Yes," Trent said, cutting him off.

Conner's eyes widened in shock. "I told you! He's been lying—"

Braeden moved so fast it was like no one realized it until Conner was no longer talking and on the ground. Braeden stood over him and shook out his fist. "Shut the fuck up."

Conner moaned and sat up. Braeden planted himself in front of him and crossed his arms.

I couldn't help it. I grinned. Romeo did, too. I also wished I'd done it.

"Did you say yes?" Josh asked.

"Yes," Trent repeated. "I'm gay, and yes, I'm in a relationship with Drew." He gestured at me with his thumb.

Murmurs and talking started working around the room.

"I wasn't lying about it like Con would have you believe. I was trying to figure it out, trying to learn how to balance me with the person everyone wanted me to be." He went on. "But I did lie about something."

"Ha! I told you!" Conner yelled. "Liar."

I started forward, and he flinched, his lips pressed together.

Trent rolled his eyes but then turned toward me and held out an arm, blocking me. To the room, he said, "I lied about not knowing who jumped me a couple weeks ago. I do know."

More murmuring went through the house. "Who was it!" a couple Omega brothers demanded.

"What the fuck, man!" someone else yelled.

"It was my own brothers," Trent said. "Conner was the ring leader. Daniel, Michael, and Jeremy helped him. They held me down in the parking lot right outside this house and beat me. For weeks, when Conner's had a chance, he's whispered taunts at me."

I watched Trent's shoulders tighten and his chest puff out with a deep breath. On impulse, I stepped up closer, presenting a united front. It was time I shouldered some of this as well.

"Dick licker, faggot, sinner, pervert, gay boy, you name it; I've probably heard it. He also suggested on more than one occasion that I kill myself."

"Are you fucking kidding me?" I spat. Anger so hot it was white burned through me. There was no fucking excuse. None.

Braeden's face turned red, and he reached down and lifted Con by the back of the neck. Romeo moved and buried his fist right in his gut.

Everyone stood there in shock.

But it wasn't good enough.

I lunged forward and grabbed Conner by the front of his shirt. My vision was tinged with red and my chest heaved with breath. "You're the one who doesn't deserve to live," I growled and punched him in the face.

He crumpled to the ground, and I leapt on top of him.

What if Trent wasn't so strong? What if Trent didn't have all the support around him? What if Conner managed to get in his head…?

What if T actually took his suggestion and ended his life?

I hit him again, and there was scuffling and movement all around me. Braeden grabbed my arm, and I swung at him, too.

Conner's lip was split and bleeding, and his eyes were wide with fear. Maybe he finally realized he pushed things too fucking far. Maybe he understood I wanted to kill him.

A set of vise-like arms wrapped around my chest and dragged me off the asshole. I fought to get free until Trent's voice penetrated my murderous fog.

"Stop, Forrester," he said against my ear. The brush of his lips turned me slack. I stopped fighting and let him pull me back. "He isn't worth this."

"You are," I said, my chest still heaving.

Conner was getting to his feet, watching me with fear in his eyes. I gave him a cold look, and he tried to run. A few nearby Omega brothers grabbed him and forced him to stay.

"He'll get his." Trent leaned in and said low, "I'm okay. You and I are okay."

I nodded, focusing on his face and his resolve. Someday I was going to ask him how he stayed so calm. Someday I wanted to know why he was so much more protective of me than himself.

Because he loves you more than himself.

That thought made me want to pound Conner all over again. But I didn't. I stayed at Trent's side, and he continued talking.

"I didn't say anything because I felt betrayed, and it would cause a divide in this house. But clearly, I can't keep putting up with it, and I won't lie about who we're sharing a house with. Before you knew who it was and the reason I was attacked, you all wanted revenge. You were pissed off on my behalf…" Trent's words trailed off.

"I've already spoken to Jack. He's going to take over presidency. I'm going to step down. I understand not all of you want a man who's in love with another man to represent this fraternity. But," he said, drawing everyone's attention back, "I'm still president tonight, and until I hand this house over. I could have run to the dean when I was attacked. I could have had this entire frat shut down. I didn't. We take care of our own. I was loyal to you even when you weren't loyal to me. Think about that." He stared at Conner.

The three guys who helped Conner jump him were shoved into the room by angry-looking Omega members. The three guys appeared scared and uneasy.

Trent ignored them and continued to talk. "I'm going to hold a house meeting in the morning, an official Omega meeting, and we're going to put it to a vote. Will the four men who attacked me lose charter? Until tomorrow, this shit is over. You can stop whispering. I'm gay, and I'm in a relationship with Drew. Accept it or don't. Just know if you come at me, I won't back down."

Romeo cleared his throat. "Just know," he boomed over the room in a loud but calm voice, "that anyone else who comes at Trent, my brother, will also deal with me."

"And me," Braeden echoed.

"And me," I added, even though I thought my attack on Conner spoke louder than my words.

"And the Wolves!" a guy hollered.

A bunch of howling and cheering erupted behind us.

Trent turned and looked. I followed his lead. Almost the entire Wolfpack was standing behind us. They were all wearing their jerseys, and they all stood in solidarity with Trent. With us.

"Seriously, guys?" Trent seemed surprised.

I wasn't. Trent was the kind of guy who inspired loyalty.

"One pack united!" someone yelled.

Everyone in the room started cheering.

When it died down, I glanced over at Con. He looked like he'd swallowed a lemon.

"Fag!" someone yelled from over by the doorway.

Everyone whipped around to see two guys who I didn't know standing there glaring. They weren't Omega. They must have just been here to party.

"Trash needs taken out," Romeo said.

Just like that, the Wolves swarmed the two men and literally carried them out of the house and threw them on the lawn. When the sound of the slamming door echoed through the building, people clapped.

"Remind me to take those jackasses off my Christmas card list," Braeden muttered. Again, he grabbed Con by the back of the neck. "Speaking of, what shall we do with this one?"

Some of the Omega brothers were standing around, looking conflicted. It pissed me off and made me sad at the same time. Why couldn't these guys be as quick to accept T as the Wolves?

"Nothing," Trent said.

Braeden made a face. "Dude, no."

"Let him go. This is his house. He's still an Omega. Same with the other three," Trent ordered, holding his ground.

"Until tomorrow," Josh quipped.

I smiled. That guy wasn't so bad.

Trent nodded. "House meeting tomorrow morning. Pass the word."

I was pretty sure almost the entire house heard, but I guess it was better safe than sorry.

"Now you know!" Trent called out loudly as everyone was still staring at us. "Party it up!"

Just like that, the music blasted through the house again and people resumed like someone un-paused a movie. It didn't totally go back to the way it was. I mean, people were staring and talking. Omega members were still standing around, looking a little shell-shocked.

Trent went over to Jack and did some kind of hand shake. "Thanks for the heads-up and for the support."

"I admire the way you've handled this," Jack said. "I hope I'm half the president you've been."

Trent didn't acknowledge the compliment. "Hey, I'm out for the night. I'm gonna disappear, give these guys some time to think about everything. I'll be here for the meeting tomorrow."

Jack nodded. "See you then."

Outside on the front lawn, Trent stopped and turned to Romeo and Braeden. "You had my back in there tonight and today." He cocked his head. "You've always had my back."

"Family takes care of family," Romeo said.

"Thank you." The sincerity in T's voice was real. Even though he'd only said two words, he was acknowledging a lot more.

"Give me some man love," Braeden joked and held out his arms.

Trent hugged him. Then he hugged Romeo. Then they both hugged me.

It was like a man hug-fest.

"Seriously, though," Trent said when we were done handing out the hugs. "I've never had much of a family. I didn't really know this was possible."

"Now you do," Romeo replied.

"Yeah," Trent echoed. "Now I do."

We spilt up into separate cars. Romeo and Braeden were in the Hellcat, and T and me were in his Mustang. The second we were alone, I reached for his hand. Our fingers linked and settled over the gearshift.

"How about we shift together tonight?" Trent whispered.

"Together is good," I whispered back.

That's how you know you have a love that will last forever. If you can literally fight your way through obstacles for an entire day and be faced again and again with strife and still be able to sit in a car when all is said and done and not only want to shift together, but know you wouldn't have it any other way.

I'd probably never, ever say it out loud, but there was a name for what T and I had.

It wasn't just love.

It was #TrewLove.

PS: Get it? That's our ship name. #Trew.

PSS: Don't tell anyone I gave us a ship name.

Trent

Have I ever mentioned blowjobs make everything better?

No?

They do.

Today was going to be a long day.

Not just long, but challenging. After yesterday and knowing what today had in store, sleep had been a very elusive thing.

It wasn't frustrating, though, like lying in bed usually is. I didn't stare at the ceiling and become increasingly agitated as I counted the hours of sleep I wasn't getting. Instead, I lay there listening to the sound of Drew breathing. I felt the way his body nestled into mine and the way our body heat mingled together to create the perfect temperature.

When we got home last night, we went straight up to the room. When we first started telling people about our relationship, I thought maybe it would impact the way were when we were alone.

Like there might be some awkwardness, some hesitation. I worried maybe the comments we got about how we were depraved or somehow wrong for our feelings would intrude.

It didn't happen. Drew and I were beyond mind games. When we were alone, it was like nothing else mattered. No one else came into play. I was my most authentic when I was alone with him, and I thought it might be the same for him.

It seemed like the further "out" in the world we got, the closer it pushed us together.

We had sex again last night. I entered his body from behind. He dropped to all fours on the mattress in front of me, and I stood behind him and slid right home.

Goddamn, the way he felt around my cock was unlike anything I'd ever known. Seeing his long back and broad shoulders stretched out on full display in front of me as I speared him over and over made my stomach quiver with butterflies even as my balls tingled.

I had to press a hand over his mouth when I took him because he was just as vocal as before. Hearing him moan like my cock was the most satisfying thing he'd ever experienced was pretty much the most satisfying thing I'd ever experienced.

He came with his teeth biting my fingers and my hand wrapped around his cock. Just feeling him explode beneath my touch was enough to make me erupt inside him.

Now here I was, lying against the pillows in a bed filled with our body heat, his full lips sliding down over the very length he allowed inside him last night.

'Course, there was no condom between us now. Now his tongue swirled around my base and licked up my shaft.

Today was going to be a long day, but the way it was beginning sure was sweet. I thrust up a little and palmed the back of his head. Both his hands slid beneath my ass and lifted my hips off the mattress so he could take me deep. As he did, his palms kneaded my ass cheeks while his fingers slid along my crack.

I reached for the lube on the table beside the bed and slid it beneath me so it came into contact with his hands. He grasped it and pulled back but kept my head in his mouth and swirled his lips around it while he opened the slippery liquid and covered his fingers.

A little while later, I was panting with the need to come, and his hard-and-ready cock was standing up off his body, wrapped and eager. He didn't say anything when he laid on the mattress, just like I didn't say anything when I handed him the lube.

He didn't have to ask me to enter my body; he was welcome inside me anytime. His heart already had permanent residence in my chest anyway.

I straddled his hips and grabbed onto his dick.

I knew I didn't have to ask; this was exactly what he wanted, but I couldn't not be sure. He was my entire life, and I was going to treat him like it even if I didn't have to.

"Like this, Forrester?" I asked low as I positioned myself right over him.

He nodded, and I sank down.

This was a first for us, a new position. We'd been trying more lately, exploring all the ways we could drive each other to distraction. I sank low, taking him deep. Drew's chin tipped back and his eyes closed when I rotated my hips and rode him.

I leaned down, bringing us chest to chest, and kissed up his neck to rake my teeth over his scruffy jaw.

We started to move together. Between us, my cock rubbed against his abs, and I dropped my forehead onto his shoulder.

I kept up a steady rhythm, and his hips moved in tune with mine. My body began to shudder with the sweet torture of my dick rubbing against him.

Drew wrapped an arm around me and pressed his palm against my back, pushing my body closer against his and increasing the pressure on my cock. With one hard surge, he pushed deep inside me and hit my prostate.

A moan vibrated my throat, and an orgasm burst over me. He kept me pinned against him and the pressure on that magic spot as I quaked and spilled out all over his stomach and chest.

When I was finally spent, he grabbed my hips and held my body so he could pull out and thrust back in at exactly the angle he wanted.

Our eyes collided; intense emotion built as I rode him. I knew when he was close because his eyes started to drift closed. I grabbed him by the chin and squeezed, forcing his eyes to stay on mine.

"Let go," I demanded and sank all the way down. Keeping him deep inside, I rocked in small movements, and he came apart beneath me. His eyes went wide, the blue flashed, and a look of awe stole not just one, but two consecutive beats of my heart.

Afterward, I rolled the condom off his cock, and I cleaned up his chest and mine. Because the hour was still early, we snuck down the hall and took a shower together without making a sound.

I had moved some of my clothes over here. They were tossed in the same drawers as his. He told me I wasn't getting "a drawer." Instead, I was getting them all, and I had to share them with him.

I liked it better that way.

I dressed in the same jeans I wore last night but put on a long-sleeved polo with royal blue and orange stripes. It had a white collar and some kind of embroidered logo on the left sleeve. Drew wore his usual outfit of black jeans, messy hair, and a long-sleeved T-shirt he could throw his leather jacket over. Not that I was complaining. I liked the way he looked.

We glanced at each other strangely when the scent of freshly brewed coffee hit our noses the second we stepped out of the bedroom. Why would anyone else be up this early, especially after all four guys were out so late the night before?

Downstairs in the kitchen, I really thought I'd find Ivy up with Nova, but it wasn't her blond head I saw.

It was Romeo and Braeden.

They were both looking surly and half asleep, with giant mugs of steaming coffee in their hands. Their mugs were the travel kind…

"What are you doing up?" I asked.

Braeden practically growled at me, and Romeo rolled his eyes. "Did you really think we'd let you two go back to Omega today for a vote about the fucktards who beat you up?"

"Uh, yea?" I said, going for the coffee. I grabbed one of the travel mugs sitting nearby and poured it almost full. Then I added some cream and shit and handed it to Drew.

He gave me a grateful look and wrapped his hands around it.

Then I went back for mine.

"Get your head out of your ass," Braeden said. "We're going. And if anybody even breathes wrong, I'm kicking their ass."

"I'm not some little girl," I reminded everyone. "I can take care of myself."

"Until they decide to hold you down," Drew rebutted.

I was never going to live that down. A guy gets his ass beat one time, and then he needs a bodyguard everywhere he goes.

"Look, obviously, we know you can handle yourself. We're going anyway," Romeo said.

"Fine." I poured some coffee down my throat. I wasn't going to argue anymore. Frankly, I was glad they were going. Not because I needed bodyguards, but because I needed my family.

I wasn't sure what was going to happen at the meeting today. I pretty much announced I was gay and in a relationship with Drew and then left.

Maybe Con was able to talk his way out of the fact I ratted him out. Maybe they were all plotting against me right now.

I didn't care.

This meeting and vote was a formality. My way of giving the frat a chance to be who I tried to make them. I worked hard the last couple years on Omega's image. I poured a lot of hard work into trying to hammer home the idea we didn't have to be a bunch of asshole party boys.

Party boys? Sure. But assholes? No.

I kind of felt like maybe a parent might when they spent years raising a kid and then stood back and watched them enter the world. They watched and hoped they raised them well enough to be good people.

That was the road I was on right now.

I did everything I could to make Omega a better place. A respected place. Today, I found out if everything I did was for something…

Or for nothing.

Twenty *Nine*

Drew

Everyone was already gathered when the four of us walked into the Omega house.

It was quiet and impossible to make out the vibe I was picking up.

As soon as we opened the front door, we all exchanged looks, and Trent squared his shoulders and strode through the entry and into the dining room.

"I brought some friends," he said, as Romeo, B, and I filled the doorway. "Anyone object?"

No one said anything.

Trent strode past the table and up to the podium at the head of the room. Jack was there off to his left, and everyone was sitting quietly, waiting.

Trent's large hands wrapped around the edges of the podium, and he glanced out over the room. I could see the trepidation in his eyes but also his resolve.

I don't know why, but I knew he expected the worst today.

Just like he expected the worst when he admitted to me how he felt about me, when he told the family, and even when we told Lorhaven.

For whatever reason, Trent was almost conditioned for the worst. I was beginning to see a disturbing pattern in his thinking. It wasn't that he was a negative person. He wasn't. And he always tried to reassure me, and everyone else around him, that everything would always be okay.

But I saw it now.

Deep down, Trent was always surprised when things worked out for him.

I didn't like it.

In fact, it sort of pissed me off.

After he scanned the room, his face changed. He straightened. "Where's Con and his merry band of dickheads?"

Some laughed.

A few others coughed.

Jack stepped forward. "They're in the basement. Where we take the pledges."

I leaned over toward Romeo. "Isn't that like some storm cellar with stone stairs?"

Romeo nodded. "Yep. I was down there a couple times when I was rushing."

"What the fuck are they down there for?" Trent asked.

Jack cleared his throat.

One of the other guys at the table leaned forward. "We tied them up. We weren't about to let a bunch of bigots who don't fight fair wander around this house."

Romeo and Braeden both burst out laughing.

Trent blinked. "You tied them up in the basement because they beat me up?"

Another brother spoke up. "Them and a few other assholes who don't like gays."

This time I was the one who laughed.

"It was quite a night last night," Jack told Trent.

"They've been down there *all* night?" He sounded flabbergasted.

See? He had a serious issue. He probably needed therapy.

Or maybe just some French fries.

"Well, yeah."

Trent glanced out across the room. "So all of you are okay with the fact that your president is gay?"

"You aren't gay. You're Trent," someone said.

Josh spoke up again. "You've always done right by this frat, and now we're gonna do right by you. Being gay doesn't make you any less than who you've been the past few years."

"Now this," Romeo said, "this is a frat I would have loved to join."

People began nodding.

Trent stood there a moment and cleared his throat. He gripped the podium again, and I noticed how hard his fingers squeezed. "This is a proud moment for me. To look around this room and see not only acceptance, but pride in this fraternity. It was a long road to get here. Some days I wondered if we ever would, and some days I worried there might be more of you like Conner than like Jack."

"Booo!" someone hollered from the back.

Trent grinned. It was welcome sight. He deserved to grin like that every day of his life.

"I guess I should have had more faith in my brothers. I can hand this house over to Jack now and look back on all the time I spent here with fondness, not contempt. Thank you guys for having my back and for not casting me out."

Everyone started clapping.

"Well, this went a lot better than I thought," Braeden told Romeo and me.

Romeo rolled his eyes.

When the clapping died down, one of the house members I didn't really know stood up. "Can I say something?"

"I think you spoke to soon," Romeo muttered to B.

"Sure," Trent replied.

"I just want to thank you, Trent. Thank you for coming out and making me realize I don't have to lie about who I am."

"You're gay?" Trent asked.

He nodded.

"That man love must be some good shit," Braeden cracked.

Everyone looked at him.

"He's an idiot. Ignore him," Trent said. "Anyone in this room got a problem with Sam being gay?"

Sam glanced around nervously.

Everyone shook their heads.

"Good to hear," Trent announced.

Sam looked relieved and sat back down.

Look at my guy making a difference.

"So should we put to vote the charter status of Conner and the others?"

"I think we already know the outcome," Jack said.

"All those in favor of stripping their roles and removing them from the Alpha Omega brotherhood, say aye."

Everyone said aye.

I did, too, even though I didn't really get a vote.

"I think that pretty much takes care of the meeting," Trent said.

Jack spoke up. "There is one thing…"

"What?" he asked.

"What are we gonna do with all the guys tied up in the basement?"

In the end, the assholes were brought up to the meeting and stood in front of the fraternity.

I derived an immense amount of satisfaction from the fact that they all had their hands tied behind their backs and were wearing nothing but their underwear. The three guys who beat up Trent that played in the football game all had a nice spattering of bruises, and it appeared they had a few fresh black eyes to go with them.

The handful of guys who I guess spoke up against Trent and his sexual orientation also had some black eyes. I had to admit I gained a lot of respect for the house as a whole.

Whenever I looked at T, I could see the relief in his face. How heavily this had weighed on him and how much freer he looked now.

Conner and his followers were told their fate and given papers Trent drew up a long time ago (just in case) outlining they were being released from their charter. After they were untied, they signed the papers and were sent to pack.

The guys who didn't participate in jumping Trent but didn't agree with his lifestyle choice were given an option: stay and act like a decent human being or get the hell out.

Only one chose to walk. The rest decided being gay wasn't that big of a deal after all.

Conner wasn't happy about his fate. He told everyone as loud as he could, but his words didn't carry any weight here anymore, and no one gave two shits he was upset.

When the four of them walked out of the house with their shit in their hands, everyone clapped. Conner turned back to likely sneer and deliver one last hateful comment to Trent, but he slammed the door in his face.

De-nied.

Once everything was taken care of, Romeo and B went back to the house. Trent took my hand and led me outside.

It was there, right there on the sidewalk in front of the Omega house, that he cradled my face and kissed me deep. When he pulled back, there was nothing but love in his eyes.

"Now what?" I asked, wrapping my hand around his.

"Now we go tell my mom and my grandmother."

"Today?" I questioned.

He nodded. "I've put it off long enough, and I know you're curious about where I came from."

"I am," I said as we walked hand in hand to my Fastback. "But honestly, it doesn't really matter. You're my person no matter what."

"I know, which is why I want to do this."

Inside the car, I fired up the engine and turned toward him. He kissed me again, just because he finally could. "It's about an hour drive to my mom's. We should probably stop and get some French fries."

"I like the way you think, frat boy."

We ate burgers and fries on the drive. He at my tomatoes, and I ate half his fries. We held hands over the gearshift and didn't really talk about where we were going.

We retreated into the world that only existed when we were alone. Mostly, we talked about the *GearShark* article with Emily next week, racing, and what kind of place we wanted to get when he graduated.

The miles slipped by, and soon, we were pulling up to a small two-story, split-level home. It was brown with black shutters and a one-car attached garage. Hanging above the garage door was a weathered basketball hoop. The yard was small and the landscaping was minimal, but it was neat and clean. The street was lined with other houses that looked very similar, and all the trees on the street were mature.

I thought about how I felt right before we told my parents. Just recalling that day made my stomach twist a little and a knot form in my throat. I looked beside me at Trent, who didn't appear to be struggling.

"Hey," I said, pushing aside the way my parents hurt me. "You know what to expect in there?"

He thought it over for a minute. "Yes and no."

I raised an eyebrow.

"My father left my mom when she told him she was pregnant. He didn't want a kid, and in my opinion, he must not have wanted her," he told me. "She raised me as a single mother, but I think it was more out of duty than motherly love. She wasn't the… warmest mother. She isn't like your mom. She didn't hover and she wasn't overprotective. She worked a full-time job, and then when I got older, she took on a part-time second job, and I spent a lot of time alone."

Okay, so this was hard to hear. It also wasn't what I expected. I guess I always assumed T had a pretty good life growing up. Sure, his dad wasn't around, but that didn't always mean life sucked.

"I spent a lot of time with my grandma." He smiled for the first time since bringing up his family. "I call her granny."

I nodded. That knot in my throat was back.

"So yeah." He continued and cleared his throat. "I don't expect much of a reaction because she never really gave one before. I think when I moved out to go to Alpha U, it was more of a relief for her."

I didn't understand. Maybe it was because I was raised with a mother who always cared too much (well, until I told her I was in love with a man) and a father who wanted to mold me in his image. I couldn't imagine what it was like to come home from school to an empty house. To not have my parents show up for school stuff and award ceremonies.

"She ever been to one of your football games?" I asked.

"Not even one."

I took those words like an arrow to my chest. He played college football for *four* years. In those *four* years, she never found time to go to *one* game?

No wonder he held so much inside. He'd only ever had himself. No wonder he always seemed surprised when our family showed up for him.

No one ever showed up for him before.

As if he sensed his answer upset me, he said, "But Granny watched all my games on TV. She even got a satellite dish so she wouldn't miss them."

It was like even now, when he was telling me about *his* life and the not-so-great life *he* had growing up, he was trying to make *me* feel better.

How the hell did a man turn out so fucking selfless when he grew up with a woman who wasn't?

"She ever come to Alpha U?" I asked, not wanting to voice any of the thoughts tumbling through my mind. They would upset him. And maybe I was jumping the gun. Maybe I was reading this wrong and his mom wouldn't be as bad as I was imagining.

He shook his head. "She doesn't get around too good. She has multiple sclerosis. She actually lives in a center for the elderly nearby."

"A nursing home?" I questioned.

"No, it's different. Kind of like a big apartment complex. The residents have their own places, but they have people who work there, a full staff plus a resident doctor that helps them with day-to-day stuff. She likes it there. She has her independence but still has the help she needs."

It made me even sadder that the one person who seemed to give Trent the love he always deserved was a woman who was somehow afflicted with a painful disease.

Life just wasn't fair sometimes.

"So you don't think your mom is gonna act like my parents?" I asked.

He reached for the door handle and popped open his door. "Only one way to find out."

Thirty

Trent

I called ahead to tell her I was coming. It had been a while since I'd been "home," and I wanted to be sure she'd be here. I didn't know her schedule or even her routine. My mom and I just weren't that close.

She didn't ask why I was coming or if everything was okay. She just told me she'd be there, and I said okay.

When you walked into my childhood home, there was an immediate choice to go up or down. Downstairs was the doorway that led to the garage, the laundry room, and a family room. Upstairs, which is where we headed, had three bedrooms, the kitchen, a living room, and a bathroom. The living room was open to the stairs, with a traditional wooden banister separating the spaces.

"Mom?" I called out when I saw she wasn't sitting in the living room.

"In here," she said from the other side of the wall where the kitchen was. Drew glanced at me, and I smiled. He seemed more nervous than I did. 'Course, he was probably afraid this would be another situation like the one we dealt with in North Carolina.

The top of the stairs looked directly into the eat-in kitchen. In front of us was a wooden dining table that seated four and a set of sliders that led out onto a small wooden deck. Off to the right was the kitchen space, with a U-shaped layout for the appliances, cabinets, and countertops.

This house hadn't changed since I was a kid. When she had the walls repainted, it was always in the same creamy off-white color. The carpet in the house was a neutral shade of tan, and all the finishes were standard for an older mid-priced home.

"Your room down there?" Drew asked, pointing down the hallway where the bedrooms were.

"Used to be the first door on the left."

"Used to be?" he asked.

"She made it a sewing room when I moved out."

I knew by the look on Drew's face this displeased him. I was going to tell him it didn't matter because this wasn't my home anymore, but I didn't get the chance.

"Oh, you brought a guest," Mom said, and we both looked up.

My mom was a short woman, probably only about five feet three. She was thin and had hazel eyes like me. Her hair was light brown with golden highlights she probably got at the salon, but I really had no clue. She never bothered much with makeup, but she really didn't need to. She had smooth skin and was still pretty young because she had me before she even turned twenty.

"Mom, this is Drew. I've mentioned him before," I said. "Drew, this is my mom, Rebecca."

"It's nice to meet you, Ms. Mask," Drew said, holding out his hand.

She surrendered hers but said, "It's actually Wallace."

"Mask was my father's last name," I explained.

"Sorry about that," Drew said.

My mom smiled politely. "You didn't know."

Drew gave me a look that said, *Why didn't I know?*

Because it wasn't important. Because I thought it was odd my mother gave me the last name of a man who didn't even want me instead of her own.

Maybe she didn't want you, either.

Can I get you boys a drink? Iced tea?" she asked. "I was just slicing some apples for a pie I'm taking in to work tomorrow."

"What do you do?" Drew asked.

"I work at the local credit union during the week, and then on the weekends, I work at a local bakery."

"Ah, so that's where Trent gets his love for finance. Must run in the family."

It was kind of painful to watch Drew try so hard with her. It wouldn't matter; she would be indifferent.

"Oh yes, that is your major." She glanced at me.

I didn't look at Drew. I couldn't.

"So how you been, Mom?"

"Oh, you know me, always busy," she replied, and I pulled out a chair and sat at the table. Drew followed my lead and sat beside me.

"School's almost out for the semester, and I'll be graduating. I've been thinking about what kind of job I might look for," I said.

"I'm sure you'll find something great. You've always been a hard worker and a smart boy."

We made small talk for a few more minutes while she continued peeling and slicing apples. When the conversation started to wane, I cleared my throat.

"So I came over because I wanted to talk to you about something."

"Oh?" she asked, not looking up.

I nodded. "About a magazine that's interviewing me."

"Well, that's exciting." She looked up. "Is it for school?"

"It's a driving magazine. Drew's a racecar driver."

She glanced up at that. "Really? Well, that sounds exciting."

Drew smiled. "It has its moments."

"Do you drive a Mustang like Trent?" she asked.

He nodded. "It's an old model."

"Mom and Granny helped pay for my car," I told him. "I saved my money half my life because I wanted a car when I turned sixteen." I smiled at the memory.

"Well, we had to get you something so you could get yourself around. With my two jobs, it was hard being everywhere at once." Mom agreed.

"Anyway," I said as I avoided Drew's stare. "I'm gonna be talking about some stuff with the magazine that I wanted to tell you about first. You know, in case you read the article."

She laughed lightly. "You know I barely have time to read."

Drew sat up; his feet hit the floor. Beneath the table, I put a hand on his leg, telling him it was okay.

"Well, you might hear people talk," I said.

"About what?" she asked, still cutting apples.

"About the fact that Drew and I are in a relationship."

She said nothing. Nothing at all. She just stood there and kept slicing. I knew she heard, though, because of the way she stiffened and the white-knuckled grip she had on the knife.

Finally, she turned, her gaze bouncing between Drew and me. "You and him?"

I nodded.

"You're gay?"

"Yes, Mom. I'm gay."

She turned her back and kept cutting. I glanced at Drew. He gave me a wary look, and I shrugged.

I really thought she'd say more than nothing.

"Mom?" I asked after a few more minutes of strained silence.

The sharp thud of the knife going into the cutting board point first was the beginning of more than nothing.

"You ungrateful child," she intoned and gripped the edge of the counter. Tension radiated off her shoulders.

"What?" I asked.

She spun. "After all the sacrifices I've made for you. The years I worked day after day to make sure you had a home and clothes and food. This is how you repay me?"

"Me being gay has nothing to do with you, Mom," I said, a little caught off guard.

"It has everything to do with me!" she shrieked and pushed off the counter. "What I don't understand is why you would want to hurt me this way."

"I'm not trying to hurt you," I argued.

"What will people think?" she worried. "What will they say about me? They'll think something is wrong with me because I raised my son to be gay."

She glanced up, anger in her eyes. "You're ungrateful and selfish."

I reared back. I might have expected more than nothing when I told her, but I hadn't expected this. "You think I'm being selfish," I repeated.

I really didn't know what to think. She was making this all about her. She never even appeared to wonder what it was like for me to come here and tell her. For me to have to come to terms with being gay.

"I know you are!" she shouted. "You're only thinking about yourself. I raised you, even after your father left! He didn't want you!" she cried. "Maybe this is why!"

That pierced. It pierced the most tender part of my heart.

Drew stood abruptly, the wooden chair clattering to the floor. "I suggest you think about what you say from here on out before you let it fly out of your mouth," he said, calm, almost deadly.

"Don't you talk to me that way in my home. This isn't any of your business. This is a family matter."

"He is my family," I said, standing. "He's been more of a family to me than you've ever been."

"How dare you?" She gasped and put a hand up to her neck. "Is this why you're trying to humiliate me? Because you think I've been a bad mother?"

Drew laughed bitterly. "You think you've been a good one?"

"You don't know anything about our life." She gave him a disdainful look.

"I don't think you're a bad mother," I said, weary. "I'm sorry this has upset you."

"Then stop it," she said, disregarding Drew. "You can stop this before it's too late."

Stop being gay?

I wanted to laugh. She acted like it was something I worked at. Something I tried to be. I could no more stop being gay than the sun could stop rising.

I could no more stop loving Drew than the ocean could stop moving.

"I can't. It's who I am."

"I'll call Granny!" she threatened. "I'll call and tell her what you're doing. She'll disown you. She'll never speak to you again!"

"She wouldn't," I argued, a sick, clammy feeling coming over me. Granny wouldn't disown me. She loved me. She'd always loved me.

Before she knew the real you.

"Don't listen to her, T," Drew said softly right beside my ear. He knew I was spiraling inward, he knew I was starting to cave in.

"All these years," she said, almost like she was suddenly disillusioned and trying to work it out in her own mind. "All these years, I did what was expected of me, and for what?"

"Mom," I said and stepped forward.

She stepped back. "Get out."

I stopped and stared. "You want me to leave?"

She nodded. "I've done my job. I got you to adulthood. There's no reason for us to have to see each other again."

Wow.

I always knew my mom was… distant. But I never thought she was mean.

Until today.

I glanced around the house I grew up in, the house I spent so much time in alone. I looked at the mother who quite possibly never loved me, and I tucked all those feelings right beside all the others that used to hurt.

I walked to the front door and didn't look back.

My hand was wrapped around the handle when I heard Drew's voice carry through the house.

"I feel sorry for you," he said. "I feel sorry that for all these years, you've had someone as amazing as Trent right here and you never even knew it. You were right when you said I don't know anything about your life. I have no idea what could make you so cold and unfeeling to a child who did nothing but wish you were there more. He's not the selfish one. You are. And what I do know is someday you're going to regret this, but by then, it's going to be too late."

My eyes were misty when I heard him on the stairs and felt his hand on the small of my back. I watched through slightly blurry vision when his fingers closed over mine and turned the handle to open the door.

Out on the porch, the sound of the door closing rang with a finality I never thought I'd hear. I just needed a minute. A minute to process what just happened in there.

"Look at me." Drew's voice called me out of my own head.

My eyes focused on him and the blue of his irises. He grabbed my face between his palms and shook me gently. "You're better than this place. So much better."

"Thank you," I whispered. "For what you said in there."

Still holding my face, his lips pressed against mine. He kissed me hard and fast before pulling away completely and taking my hands.

"We're leaving," he announced. "I hate to tell you this, T, but your mom's a bitch."

I laughed. Like a real laugh that brought everything around us crashing back in color. But just because life was back in color didn't mean it was pretty.

Even the most beautiful colors could sometimes look dirty.

"She's probably on the phone with Granny right now." I think out of everything my mother said, it was her threat to ruin my relationship with my grandmother that hurt the most.

Not only did she not want me in her life, but in my Granny's life either.

She didn't care if I was alone.

She never had.

She never would.

"What do you want to do?" Drew asked, staring out the windshield, the engine idling. I appreciated he didn't tell me what he thought I should do. I knew he was upset by what happened, by everything he learned about the way I grew up.

I knew he wanted to drive home and for me to never think of this again.

I knew because that's the things I wanted for him when we left his parents' house. He knew, just like I did, that even if we did that, it wouldn't erase our past or what happened here today.

That's why he was asking me where I wanted to go from here.

"I want to go to Granny's," I said, decisive. "If my mom has turned her against me, I want to know."

It was like a Band-Aid stuck to a hairy leg. I wanted to rip it off fast and get the sting over with all at once.

Thirty One

Drew

It was wrong to hate.

I hated Trent's mom anyway.

She did indeed make good on her threat to call T's granny and spill the beans.

Granny was waiting at the door when we walked up.

Trent was pale and shaken from what happened with his mom. But he was still strong. He still held his head high.

Granny invited us inside, and two things happened:

1.) She told Trent he had good taste in men and offered me a cookie.

and

2.) She informed Trent his Scottish accent wasn't very convincing and she always knew it was him who called, but he could call her anytime and talk

in a bad accent because she loved him.

Granny was my new favorite person.

Thirty Two

Trent

I was relieved.

Feeling relieved made me wonder if I was fucked up in the head.

What kind of son is relieved when his own mother throws a hissy fit about his life choices, calls him ungrateful, and then tells him to get out?

Me.

Maybe she wasn't the only one that forced a relationship out of obligation instead of desire. When I thought about it—*really* thought about it—I would realize I stopped being hurt by her a long time ago. Even if I still lived kind of cautiously, like her ability to hurt me was still there.

When I was a kid, I used to wonder why she wasn't like the other moms. Why she didn't read me bedtime stories, take me to the movies, or yell at me for playing too many video games. It used to cut deep when I would look around at school for her face in the crowd or in the stands at my high school football games and she wasn't there.

She never was.

She was the kind of parent who did her duty. She made sure we had a place to live, food to eat, and clothes to wear. She made sure I did my homework and paid all the fees when I wanted to play football in high school.

I couldn't say she was a bad mom, because she wasn't. She did right by me. She raised me even, after my father walked away. She wasn't mean, she didn't beat me, and she didn't bring a dozen men in and out of our lives. In fact, she didn't date at all.

She was just distant. Absent.

She kept everyone at arm's length, including her own child. Maybe she never bonded with me when I was born. Maybe she never tried.

Or maybe when my father left her because of me, it cut so deep whenever she looked at me, that's all she saw.

I learned at an early age to be self-sufficient. Instead of acting out, I internalized it all. I learned how to tuck my deepest pain and my darkest loneliness so deep no one would ever see it. I was a friend to everyone. I listened when people talked, and I kept things laidback and easy.

Why? Because that's what I always wanted for myself.

I joined the football team (and later the fraternity) for that sense of family. I was good at it, and people liked me. So I kept playing. I was the one everyone liked, and I never had to be alone.

But I was.

I grew more alone, and the place I hid my real feelings got overfull.

I met Romeo and Braeden freshman year when we all started playing for the Wolves. We were friends; I was friends with everyone. But no one ever really knew me. Sometimes I wondered if *I* really knew me.

It's easy to lose yourself when you have no idea who you are to begin with.

I used to wonder why she didn't love me. Why my father didn't want us. The only person who ever really showed me love was Granny. She came to my games, and we played checkers on rainy days. She used to tell me my mother loved me in her own way, the best she could.

I supposed that was true.

But it wasn't good enough.

As I got older and started Alpha U, I would sometimes wonder if I was like her. If my mother's inability to love was somehow my affliction, too.

Then Drew sat beside me at Screamerz.

He was the best friend I ever had. Someone I felt more myself with than anyone. Our friendship healed something in me, or maybe it just gave me the confidence to be who I really was.

I felt like he was the first person who really looked deep enough to see past the mask I always wore.

And I fell in love with him.

I fell in love with the least likely person I ever could. But in a way, he was the most obvious choice.

I wasn't unable to love; I just needed the right person to give it to.

Maybe it was okay to be relieved. It was okay to move on and let some of the old hurt go. I had a family now, the kind I always wanted.

The kind who wanted me.

They all knew who I really was now, and they loved me anyway.

I wouldn't fool myself into thinking it would always be easy for me. I would probably always still have days when I was a little more pulled in close. Days it would be easier to tuck my feelings deep and not let anyone see. There might always be that whisper deep in my head saying I wasn't good enough.

Everyone had their demons. These were mine.

But as Tennessee Williams once wrote: *If I got rid of my demons, I'd lose my angels, too.*

"What's going on in there?" Drew asked, leaning across the seats and tapping my head with his finger.

I grabbed his hand and pulled it down, pressing it against my chest. "Nothing going on up there. It's all happening in here."

"You doing okay, frat boy?" he asked softly, rubbing his palm against my chest.

He worried about me, and I loved him for it. He didn't have to worry, though, because I was more at peace than I'd ever been.

"I really am."

"I love you more than French fries."

I laughed even as my heart swelled. I was so ready for this interview today, so ready to tell the entire world (or maybe just the subscribers of *GearShark*) he was mine. After today, everyone would know, and I'd never have to worry about the way I looked at him in public ever again.

I wouldn't be ashamed, even though some people thought I should. I spent too much of my life without the touch of love to ever tarnish the love I had now with something as ugly as shame.

"Gate's open." I gestured to the opening that led into the airport.

Drew nudged the Fastback forward, and I looked around. It was kind of really epic that Arrow lived at an airport and he and Lorhaven kept their cars in hangars.

When Emily Metcalf said she wanted to come to us for the interview, I knew it had to be somewhere other than the Chesapeake Speedway. Been there, done that. We needed something new, somewhere as unique as the new racing division.

Drew mentioned the airstrip, and everything was set up.

Lorhaven and Arrow jumped at the chance because they knew they'd get another behind-the-scenes look at *GearShark*. Not to mention the last time Lorhaven got a half-page article about his driving and ended up with a sponsorship for the division. We'd definitely be seeing a lot of him at the preliminary races now.

Plus, this was good for Arrow. We'd sort of taken the kid under our wing, and that sort of meant I had a truce with Lorhaven.

He still wasn't my favorite person; he never would be.

We clashed in the most basic way. Maybe I was pissed because the second I met him, he was a lot of things I always wanted to be. Confident, unapologetic, and had a whole turf in town where everyone respected him.

He'd caught Drew's attention, and that was an automatic dislike. Part of me always worried the deeper

Drew got into racing, he would pull away from me. I never told him that. I always supported his racing and I always would. My insecurities were mine to bear, and besides, I knew it was partly those demons I mentioned trying to tell me I just wasn't good enough and eventually Drew would realize.

You can't hold so tight to people. The ones you love—hell, even the ones you hate.

Maybe I didn't hate Lorhaven after all. Maybe I just intensely disliked him. Besides, I had a feeling he was going to be an ally for Drew on the track in the coming months.

The *GearShark* team was already here and setting up. Drew parked the Fastback beside Arrow's Camaro, and we both got out.

It looked a lot like the shoot we did with Drew. The photographer had a white backdrop set up for photos, some lighting already in place. Beyond that, I saw his assistant scouting for other locations for more organic shots.

There was definitely plenty to pick from out here. The sky was blue and the temps were finally warm. It was a good day to be outside. I was hoping we did a couple shots with some of the older planes in the background. That would be kinda cool.

Even though they had a wardrobe person here, Ivy insisted on dressing me anyway. I didn't argue like Drew had. I just put on the clothes she handed me so we could leave.

She picked a dark pair of jeans, a black fitted T-shirt, and a white collarless leather jacket. Usually, Drew was the one to wear the leather, but this one was preppier and had less street style.

I was keeping it because it was obvious Drew liked it. His eyes lingered on me just a little bit more, and when I first stepped out in it, his tongue ran across the front of his teeth.

There was a big table with coffee, pastries, and fruit where Arrow, Lorhaven, and some of the crew were gathered around. I waved at them on my way to Emily.

"Let's get him into makeup," she said the second I was within earshot. I was gestured toward a director-looking chair, so I slid the jacket off my arms and sat down.

"Oh my," the makeup artist said, staring. Then she glanced at Emily. "Less is more with this one."

Emily turned thoughtful and smiled.

Drew made a rude noise. "You didn't say that about me."

"Someone's jealous," I told the girl.

She giggled.

From behind her, Drew glowered, so I gave him a wink. It only made him glower harder.

"What happened to your eye?" she asked as she started dabbing my face with a sponge. "You have some discoloration." Her finger ran over the part that was still slightly bruised.

"I got in a fight," I told her.

She drew back and looked at me. "Really?"

I nodded.

"Did you win?" she asked. Why was it women always thought it was hot when guys seemed dangerous?

Drew rolled his eyes. He was totally pissed this girl was flirting with me. I settled back a little more in the chair and enjoyed it. Maybe I liked it when he got all possessive.

"Did I win?" I mused, smiling at the memory of Con in his tightie whities with his hands tied behind his back. "Oh yeah, I won."

"Guess all those muscles came in handy."

"Oh, for shit's sake," Drew muttered.

Emily announced the photographer was going to do the photos first and then we'd do the interview. "Drew, would you mind taking a minute to talk to me while Trent's doing the photos?" she asked.

"Sure thing." He agreed. Even though technically, it was me doing the interview, he was still a part of it. This was *our* story.

"What about a cover shot of him without his shirt?" the makeup girl called over her shoulder to Emily.

"A cover shot?" I said.

Emily nodded. "We're considering putting you on the cover."

"Why does he need to be half naked?" Drew asked.

"Muscle cars, muscles on men… It sells magazines," the makeup girl mused, still dabbing that sponge around my eye.

Drew appeared silently at my side, crossing his arms over his chest. "He's with me."

The girl straightened, and her surprised expression bounced between us. "You're together?"

"Yeah, so forget about it," he quipped.

I burst out laughing. "Go get some coffee, Forrester. You're cranky."

"I'm not bringing you any," he said as he walked away.

"Thanks!" I called after him.

"I can still admire your muscles," the girl told me.

"I heard that!" Drew yelled.

Everyone within earshot laughed.

The photographer came over and looked at me. "Mess his hair up. Lose the shirt."

"Told ya," the makeup girl sang. She set aside her tools and reached for some hair crap.

"Maybe we should ask him how he feels about being shirtless on the cover of a magazine," Emily told the photographer.

"How do you feel?" The photographer looked at me with a raised brow.

I smothered a smile and thought about how testy it was going to make Drew. "I'm cool with it. But I have some bruising around my ribs."

I pulled up my shirt to show them.

"Body makeup!" the photographer yelled. "Hurry, I'm losing the lighting."

"Can you take off your shirt?"

I lost the shirt. From across the pavement, I heard Drew sputtering and Lorhaven laughing.

She applied some makeup to cover the bruising, and when I glanced at it in the mirror, I was impressed. It was all totally covered, though I admit most of it was faded so it probably wasn't hard to hide.

As I was being led off by the photographer, Drew intercepted my path. He had two cups of coffee in his hand.

"I thought you said you weren't making me one?" I teased.

"You looked cold with half your clothes missing," he slurred.

I smiled widely. "You don't like the view?"

"Oh, I like it. But I don't like that everyone else likes it, too."

I grabbed the coffee out of his hand and leaned in. "No one else will get to touch it tonight."

"Just hurry up," he demanded, but then he smiled.

The photo shoot went pretty fast. It seemed like the second I stepped in front of the backdrop, the photographer was snapping pictures. I actually wasn't as uncomfortable as I thought I would be, despite the people standing around watching.

Once we finished with the backdrop, I put on my T-shirt and jacket to follow the photographer over to the side of the steel hangar for some more "rugged" shots.

Drew hung back so he could talk to Emily, but I felt his eyes every now and then, so I knew he was making sure I wasn't stripping down to my boxers.

"Have you ever thought about modeling?" the photographer asked as he snapped away.

"Uh, no," I replied.

"You should. I do a lot of shoots for different companies. You have a pretty universal look and a good body for clothes... and no clothes."

"Modeling isn't really my thing." I'd rather close deals and stay behind the camera.

When we were done, the photographer handed me a card out of the inside of his jacket. "If you ever want to pick up some jobs, give me a call."

I thanked him and pocketed the card. If anything, this would be good to get a reaction out of Drew. Maybe I'd tell him I agreed to an underwear shoot…

"That took a long time," Drew complained when I approached.

I smothered a smile. "How was it with Emily?"

"Fine. She's all thrilled we called to give her the story." He batted his eyes and made his voice sound higher than normal. "She just knew I was gay."

"Hey," I said, thinking maybe he wasn't in such a zesty mood just because of my photo shoot attire. "You still wanna do this?"

He reached out and grasped my hand. It made my stomach flip because it wasn't often he touched me in public. "Absolutely."

"Hey, so where's the pro?" Lorhaven asked, butting into our moment.

I gave him a look. "Who?"

"I think he means Joey," Drew replied.

"What do you care?" I asked. He got along with her almost as good as he got along with me.

"I don't." He sniffed.

I gave Drew a look. *Suuurre he didn't.*

"She's home," Drew said. "She has her own racing to do. I'll be going there to do some driving with her soon."

Lorhaven nodded. "I've got some drive time coming up, too."

"Congrats on your sponsorship," Drew said. "I knew it wouldn't take long to get one."

"Yeah, well, my father offered, but I don't let Daddy buy my way."

"Joey's a damn good driver," Drew snapped.

I gave his hand a squeeze and then took a moment to be surprised we were still standing there holding hands.

Like a couple.

"Right, 'cause Daddy didn't pay for this airport and your hangars. And the Corvette you're driving," I retorted.

Lorhaven gave me a sour look. "I paid for my car. Arrow's, too."

"Trust fund?" I asked.

"Fuck you."

"You two are worse than a flea on a dog's ass." Drew interrupted. Then he turned to Lorhaven. "Thanks for letting us use the place this morning. Appreciate it."

"Thanks for inviting Arrow to the football game," he said. "Sorry I couldn't come. I was working."

"You have a job?" I asked, shocked.

Lorhaven gave me the finger.

"I like your brother," Drew said.

"Yeah, me, too," I added.

"He likes you guys, too," Lorhaven admitted. I could tell it pained him to say so. "He, uh," he said, glancing in his brother's direction. "He doesn't have a lot of friends."

"He does now," Drew replied.

Lorhaven nodded. "Yeah, well, I'll let you get back to your article." He started to walk away but then came back and looked at me. "And if I haven't said it, I think it's really cool what you're doing. It's gonna make a difference for people."

I didn't make a sarcastic comment because he was being real, and I knew he was thinking of his brother and the fact that he had two guys in his life who were making their relationship work despite the reasons not to.

I held out my fist. "Thanks." We pounded it out, and then he walked off.

Drew gave me a look. "Was that so hard?"

"What?" I scoffed.

"Being nice."

"Did I tell you that photographer offered me a modelling gig? For boxers?"

"Fuck you, frat boy," Drew said fondly.

I laughed.

"C'mon. Emily's waiting." He tugged my hand, and we walked across the pavement, our hands still stuck together. I liked being with him like this.

"By the way, you aren't doing that shit," Drew said nonchalantly.

"Wouldn't dream of it." I promised, still reveling in the feel of his fingers tangled with mine.

The interview with Emily went well. We talked for what felt like a long time. She asked questions; I answered them.

Sometimes Drew butted in, but mostly he just listened. Every now and then, I'd say something and look at him to make sure he agreed or that what I said was okay.

He never once looked like the interview was difficult for him. If anything, he looked proud of me.

I'd be lying if I said that didn't mean something.

We were breaking down walls, Drew and I. Not necessarily out in the world (but maybe we would), but with each other. We'd come a long way, and through it all, we still stayed friends. Best friends.

"Hey, so, Trent," Emily said, approaching after we wrapped everything.

"Yeah?"

"It's a little unorthodox, but I was wondering…" I nodded, so she went on. "I usually write like an intro into my interviews… You know, like the one I wrote when I interviewed Drew?"

Again, I nodded. I read the article. Hell, I bought about twenty copies of the magazine.

"I was wondering if you wanted to write the intro this time? Like, you know, as another way of saying everything you want to. The interview will be great regardless, but I feel like having you start it off would have more of an impact for the readers."

"What do you want me to write?" I asked.

"Whatever you want to say."

I nodded. "Sure, I'll give it a go. If you don't like it, you can scrap it and write the intro."

She laughed. "Awesome. Thanks." She reached in her bag and pulled out a card. "Here's my email. Just send the copy over when you have it done. I'll have it edited for errors and add it to my interview and then send the final draft to you."

I added her card to the one already in my pocket.

Once the *GearShark* crew packed up and headed out, we shot the shit with Arrow and Lorhaven for a while and did a little friendly racing around the strip. It was good times.

We hadn't spent enough time just fucking around (not the sexual kind of fucking) lately, so after we left the airstrip, we worked on the cars, then watched a movie.

Finally, it seemed like shit was settling down. We weren't weighed down with the worry of telling people or hiding. We weren't stressed and looking over our shoulders. We were back to being what we always were: best friends.

Except now it was better.

Thirty *Three*

Drew

Emily emailed the draft of the *GearShark* article. She also sent the cover. Trent was on it.

Without a shirt.

Frankly, I was equal parts turned on and appalled.

The article itself turned out pretty good. Better than good because Trent was the majority of it.

I didn't know if it was going to make a difference in someone's life, but looking at it now…

It made a difference in mine.

It wasn't that long ago when I sat down with Drew Forrester for his first official interview and the first official announcement of the brand new racing division spotlighting indie drivers on a track where there are no rules.

That article and cover has been the most read and searched issue GearShark has released this year. I didn't think anything could top that issue… until now.

It seems only appropriate the magazine is essentially topping itself. I guess the only way Drew Forrester gets knocked out of the top spot is when he does it to himself. I'd say that bodes for some *interesting driving during the fast-approaching debut season of the yet-to-be-officially-named indie division.*

But Drew isn't here by himself today. In fact, Drew isn't the feature of today's article. The person who loves him is here with him.

You might be surprised to know that person is another man.

Trent Mask was here with Drew the last time we met. Not only are Trent and Drew friends, but Trent is Drew's manager. I picked up on the dynamic and somewhat multifaceted relationship between these two almost instantly.

When I asked about it (off the record), I was met with something that couldn't quite be defined as hostility. It was more shock, denial, and a high degree of protectiveness for one another.

Looking back, I can understand why I got the reaction I did. Which is also why today's article is even more special.

To say I was surprised when I got a phone call from Drew would be an understatement. When he asked if I was interested in an article that maybe focused more behind the scenes of the new division, along with a personal touch, I was intrigued.

Then I sat down and spoke to Trent. I have to say he certainly knows how to grace a magazine cover, but more than that, he just might be Drew's better half.

What resulted was nothing short of eye opening and in many ways revolutionary. I think once you read the introduction I asked Trent to write (in lieu of my introduction, which I still managed to sneak in here—What can I say? I'm a writer with a need to write), it will be perfectly clear to you why I think what I do.

Not only does this developing division have indie drivers and no rules, but it also has a lot of heart. I'm thinking that line between the pros and the indies is a line people are going to be stepping over on their way to sit in the stands.

And now, readers and drivers, allow me to hand this article over to the man who puts the rev in REVolution.

Trent Mask for GEARSHARK ©

I'm not what anyone would consider a profound guy. I'm not a journalist for a magazine or a professional writer. Maybe that's why Emily asked me to write an intro, because my words are those of just a man. A man who finds himself in a unique position, being able to speak to a lot of people who I consider to be a lot like me.

Truth be told, I'm not here, though, to speak to the masses. I'm here for one man. I'm here to be a spark, a single source of heat to possibly ignite a fire and change the way we treat one other. It's a selfish cause, really, because it's Drew I think of. It's Drew I'm really asking you to treat kindly. But maybe if you discover giving one man who deserves acceptance easy, it will be easy to give across the board.

It isn't an easy thing to look in the mirror and see a face you essentially hide behind. It's not easy to want to be liked—even loved—for who you really are. Have you ever felt like an outcast in the center of a room? Have you ever felt alone but been in a crowd of people?

I have. I don't want that for Drew. For anyone.

Don't judge others because they sin differently than you. If you haven't walked in someone else's shoes, don't pretend to understand.

Racing is a sport, but it brings people together. Let it. Let it be the thing that binds us. Let it be the thing that represents something greater.

All I'm really asking is that you keep an open mind as you read ahead. I'm asking that you let people live the way their heart asks them to.

Be part of the revolution.

GS: You have to know you aren't our usual interview here at *GearShark*.

TM: Sometimes it's nice to take the more scenic route.

GS: Does that mean you don't like speed?

TM: There are people who don't like speed?

GS: No one who reads this magazine.

TM: There are people who don't read *GearShark*?

<Have I mentioned this one is just as charming as Drew?>

GS: So what's it like behind the scenes of a budding racing phenomenon?

TM: Exciting. There's a lot that goes into racing besides driving a car.

GS: Like what? Give me an example.

TM: Endorsement deals, sponsorships, making sure a car is ready to perform.

GS: What about dealing with the drivers? Is Drew a handful?

TM: Only when he doesn't get his French fries.

<For the record, this one smiles a lot, and his front tooth is slightly crooked.>

GS: French fries are his favorite, then?

TM: Definitely. And he's most definitely *not* a morning person.

GS: Have any other secrets on Drew you can dish?

TM: I'm in love with him.

GS: Does Drew know how you feel?

<Note: Drew is sitting right beside Trent for this interview. He's listening, and his reaction is not one of surprise. In fact, I'd say he rather likes hearing Trent is in love.>

DF: I know. I feel the same way about him.

GS: So you're in love with Trent?

DF: Yes, I'm in love with Trent.

GS: Are you two in a relationship exclusively?

TM: Yes, we have been for several weeks.

GS: So when I asked you about your relationship at our last meeting, were you together then?

TM: We were still trying to figure it out.

GS: Was the attraction there from the beginning? Have you always been gay?

TM: We were best friends first. I think the chemistry we have together is what made us so easily friends. I've always felt stronger for him than I have anyone else, but I denied the way I felt, uh romantically, for a long time. I thought being friends would be enough. *<pauses>* But it wasn't.

GS: Is Drew the first man you've dated?

TM: Yeah, but I think I always knew I was interested in men. *<He totally glances at Drew, and I feel the sparks between them.>* He was just the only one I was willing to admit it for. Up until him, I dated women.

GS: Mind if I ask Drew a question?

TM: Not at all.

GS: Drew, what about you? Have you always been gay?

DF: I don't consider myself gay. I always dated and was interested in women. But like Trent said, being friends with him just wasn't enough.

GS: So you're bi?

DF: No. I'm a guy in love with another man.

GS: Trent, is Drew it for you?

TM: Yes.

GS: Were you scared coming here today? Is this hard for you both?

TM: I'd be lying if I said no. I think even people who are straight can understand why we would be hesitant to come out about our relationship.

GS: What makes you say that?

TM: Because love is complicated and messy. For everyone. But it's especially hard when you love someone that most people think you shouldn't. We're basically opening ourselves up to a lot of judgment, and we don't want that. No one likes to be judged. Indie drivers are judged because they aren't pro. They're seen as somehow less because they don't have big sponsors and a set of rules. My relationship with Drew is seen as somehow less because people think love between two men can't be as strong as love between a man and a woman.

GS: Is it?

TM: I think love between two men has the ability to be stronger.

GS: Why?

TM: Because there is so much working against us. Love has to be really strong to withstand the hate.

GS: Have you and Drew experienced hate?

TM: Yes. People in our lives we thought would always love us turned their backs. A few friends don't want to be in the same room with us anymore. *<clears his throat and his face darkens>* I was jumped by four men and beaten.

GS: How have you dealt with it? Why are you still here talking to me today?

TM: We're here because we want the revolution of racing to be about more than just the racing. This is a sport for the overlooked, the drivers who were told they weren't good enough. As Drew said before, it's a division of underdogs who are determined to make a mark, to show the world they are just as good as the pros. We want people to know in this division, everyone is welcome and no one will be made to feel like they aren't good enough.

GS: You've felt like that? Like you aren't good enough?

TM: Most of my life.

GS: I have to say that's hard to believe. I look at you, and you're like the poster boy for the all-American jock. Good-looking, confident, a hard body… I think a lot of people are going to scoff when you say you feel like you aren't good enough.

TM: Did you miss the part where I said I was held down and beaten? But yeah, I get what you're saying. I know how I look, but that's just on the surface. I think a lot of people will identify with the fact that they might look one way but feel another.

GS: Kind of like judging a book by its cover?

TM: Something like that.

GS: So you said people have turned their backs on you both? Have people been supportive?

TM: Absolutely. We have an entire family that supports us. Ron Gamble supports us. Other indie drivers support us. We're hoping your readers will support us.

GS: I don't see how they couldn't. So you've drawn a lot of parallels between the new division and your relationship with Drew. Drew, are you worried coming out with something so personal about yourself will hurt your budding career? You said Ron Gamble, your sponsor and founder of this division, is supportive, but were you afraid he wouldn't be?

DF: This is my absolute dream job. I've always wanted to race for a living, so of course I'm worried this could hurt my career. I definitely was nervous Ron Gamble would cancel our sponsorship. He didn't have to keep me on. But he did. He's a smart businessman, but he's also a good human being.

GS: You could have kept your relationship a secret.

DF: *<sits forward>* You just heard Trent say he sometimes feels like he isn't good enough. I love him. I can't help loving him. Would we have chosen this? Maybe not, but there isn't a choice here. It's him. I would never put him in the shadows and treat him like he was a dirty secret. He's not. If people want to think lesser of me because I love someone, then maybe I don't need them in my life.

<At this point in the interview, Trent reaches beside him and holds out his hand. Drew responds immediately by linking his with it. I have to say seeing two strong men resolved to love each other kind of makes my heart speed up just a little.>

TM: Since coming out with our relationship, we've met a few others who have been struggling with the same kind of thing. Everything I do is for Drew, but this is for those people, too. Like I said, sometimes we need someone—anyone—to come forward and make being different okay. Drew and I are in a unique position because of the division. Thanks to Ron Gamble, Drew has the ability to kick ass on the track and prove he doesn't have to follow the rules to do it.

GS: I think you have that ability, too. You're both easy role models.

TM: No. We're men. We're human just like everyone else. We just want to live our life and not hide.

GS: What would you say to all the haters out there?

TM: I don't have anything to say to them.

DF: I have something to say.

GS: Okay, what?

DF: Don't be an ass about it. *<pauses>* Can I say ass?

<Trent laughs, and I do, too.>

GS: So what you're really saying is not everyone has to like your life choices, but you don't want to hear their opinion?

DF: Well, if you want to be all politically correct about it.

GS: *<To Trent>* I can see what you mean about him being a handful.

TM: I think I deserve a raise.

GS: Is it hard to balance all the roles you have in each other's lives? Friends, co-workers, and romantically involved?

TM and DF: No.

<I admire the way these two know exactly what they want and don't apologize for it.>

GS: I don't know if it makes a difference, but for the record, everyone here at *GearShark* supports you both.

TM: It makes a difference. Even just one person can make a difference.

GS: So what else can you tell us about the new division?

TM: Preliminary races start next month. There has been a huge turnout and interest, so we expect to see a completely full track when season one starts. More specifically, Drew has signed two endorsement deals with major corporations.

GS: Which are?

TM: We're going to let those businesses be the ones to announce first. After all, it is their contract.

GS: Drew, what about the rivalry with fellow driver Lorhaven?

DF: As we agreed, we're keeping that rivalry on the track. You'll definitely be seeing him, though. He's picked up a sponsor.

GS: Does he know about your relationship?

TM: Yes. He supports us.

GS: Rivals become friends, perhaps?

TM: Perhaps.

GS: Before I wrap this interview, I was hoping you could each tell me one thing on your bucket list.

<Note: they both responded, and you can read their answers in my Bucket List Confessions! article in the back of this issue. Their answers will appear alongside yours. Thanks to all the readers who sent in submissions!>

GS: So what's next for you both?

TM: Hopefully, a championship trophy for Drew.

GS: And for you?

TM: Happiness.

I think these guys deserve happiness. Don't you?

Thirty *Four*

Trent

I used to wonder what I did to deserve the life I had.

I wondered why I was being punished.

Deep down, I wasn't really happy.

Now I wondered how I got so goddamned lucky.

I realized everything I ever felt and went through was to bring me here.

To Drew.

To who I really was.

Deep down, I knew true happiness.

Epilogue

Several months later...

Drew

The airport was bustling with busy people and the sound of beeping golf carts as they sped past. Not my favorite sound.

Three days was too long, too long to go without seeing my person.

I was attached to his face. To seeing his eyes first thing in the morning and hearing his throaty growl when I slid under the covers and took him into my mouth.

French fries didn't even taste the same when he was gone.

A group of passengers starting filing out of the security point, and I searched their faces, anxious for a glimpse of the one I wanted to see. The more people that came out and the more that weren't him the more impatient I grew.

Finally, I caught a glimpse of sandy-colored hair and a snippet of a wide shoulder. Adrenaline spiked in my bloodstream and relief poured into my chest.

He glanced up at the exact moment I did, as if our eyes were two magnets with an intense pull. He smiled wide, and I bounced from foot to foot, waiting for him to get his ass over here.

The second he was within arm's distance, his duffle hit the ground at my feet and we reached out at the same time. It wasn't a quick embrace. I'd waited what felt like endless hours for the feel of his chest against mine. His arms were my favorite place to be, and I didn't care who was uncomfortable at the sight of two grown men embracing in the middle of the airport, because I needed the feel of him like I needed oxygen in my lungs.

The softness of his shirt was welcome against my forehead when I pressed it against his shoulder. The tips of his fingers dug into my sides, and I felt the brush of his lips along the side of my hairline.

"I kinda fucking missed you, Forrester," he murmured.

"I'm not doing this again, frat boy." I vowed, and I truly meant it. The next time he had to travel for work, I was going, too.

"C'mon," he said, releasing me and tossing his bag over his shoulder. "Let's get the hell out of here."

We held hands through the crowds; we held hands almost everywhere we went these days.

Some people stared. Some people made faces. A few made lewd comments.

Some people smiled.

Sometimes it still bothered me, but most of the time, I felt sorry. Sorry for the people who were so closed off about everything that they would never get to experience the kind of love I felt with Trent.

The best days, though, were when no one even noticed at all. As if two people in love weren't anything to even notice, as if it were a natural occurrence.

Maybe someday it would be like that always.

"So," I asked as we headed out into the warm sunshine, "how was your first official business trip for the NRR?"

The NRR was what the division settled on as a name. New Revolution Racing. I liked it; it fit. After Trent's article and cover ran, the word *revolution* took on a life of its own in the indie community.

We were a revolution on many fronts, and the new division was taking over, the popularity of the "new" sport even more than Gamble anticipated. The preliminaries were huge, the competition was fierce, and with the actual racing season about to begin, I knew it was only going to get bigger.

Trent's passion and smarts for business and finance earned him a job offer from Gamble himself. He was now employed by the NRR and handled a lot of the financials but also some of the business side of the division. When Gamble first offered him the position, he was skeptical for two reasons:

1.) He didn't want the job because of who he knew. He wanted it because he deserved it.

and

2.) He still wanted to be my manager.

I told him the only way he could prove he deserved the job was to take it and do it well. So he accepted on the condition he still be allowed to manage my career and be at all my races.

Gamble accepted because, after all, I was just another extension of the racing and one of his investments. What was good for me was also good for him.

Gamble wasn't the only owner of the NRR; it was too big for just one man to own. Now there were three different investors, and they all had a vote in how it was run, so technically, Trent wasn't working for Gamble, but for a corporation Gamble partly owned.

I didn't care really. I just wanted T to be happy, and it seemed like he was.

"It was good," he answered, throwing an arm around my neck as we entered the short-term lot where I'd parked the Fastback. "Busy, but good. I'm excited about this season."

"Me, too," I said. "But no more business trips without me. If you can travel to all my races, then I can travel to all your meetings."

"I can live with that."

At the car, he didn't get in. Instead, his duffle hit the hood and the sound of the zipper brought up my head.

"What the hell are you doing, frat boy?"

"I got you something." He grinned.

"Yeah?" I abandoned the door and came back around.

Nodding, he reached inside his bag and pulled out what looked like a rolled-up T-shirt. It was gray, and he held it out.

I took it and let it unravel, shook it out, and held it up. Laughter bubbled up as I stared at the front. It was a vintage-looking tee, and in the center was the huge label for Heinz ketchup.

I lowered it enough so I could look at Trent. He was smiling wide. "You had to have it."

I tossed the fabric on the hood and ripped the T-shirt I was wearing right over my head in the center of the lot. Trent ripped the tag off the new shirt and handed it over, and I slid it home.

"Looks good." T nodded.

"You owed me a new favorite shirt anyway," I said, taking in my old favorite shirt, which was stretched across his chest.

"I got you something else," he said, reaching back in the bag.

"How the hell did you have time for shopping? I thought you were working."

He shrugged. "I missed you."

Sometimes, Trent's voice still dropped with vulnerability. Sometimes, I still heard the hesitation when he expressed his deepest feelings.

I walked around the hood where he stood and squeezed between him and the front fender. My ass hit the car, and I spread my legs to make room for him to step close.

I didn't care we were in the parking lot at a busy airport. All I cared about was making sure the vulnerability that sometimes haunted him was put back in its place.

"I love you," I told him. Those three words seemed the best in combating anything Trent might feel. "It's not gonna change."

He wasn't insecure. He believed me when I told him how much I cared. He wasn't clingy either. He spent too much time being alone; he knew he'd be fine if he had to do it again.

He just felt so deep, it sometimes hurt him, and I knew without him saying it, I had the ability to ease that pain.

His hazel eyes warmed. "I love you, too."

A warm early summer breeze blew through the air and ruffled the tips of his hair. Trent's hand appeared between us, and he opened it up to reveal a small box in the center of his palm.

"Oh, I hope it's a diamond!" I cracked.

"Shut up and open it, wiseass."

I lifted the lid to the black velvet box and looked down. In the center was a round charm, one that could be worn on a chain.

"It's a St. Christopher medal," he said. "You know, to protect you while you're driving. Figured it might come in handy during your first season while you're kicking everyone's ass."

I was totally gonna kick ass, just like I did in all the preliminaries. And right there on my bumper was Lorhaven.

"You got me a medal for protection?" I asked, still looking down. It looked like it was made in stainless steel and had the familiar image of St. Christopher in the center. Around the perimeter were the words: *Behold St. Christopher and Go Your Way in Safety.*

Trent reached into the box and flipped it over. The back was engraved.

Watch Over Drew

"Figured you could add it to the chain you always wear with the speedometer on it," Trent added.

I blinked down, still staring at it. My finger brushed over the words.

Sometimes it overwhelmed me how much he loved.

How much I loved.

I pulled it out of the box and palmed it. We added it to my chain right then, but instead of tucking it back beneath my shirt, I left it out with the round medal on top.

"I'm never gonna take it off." I promised.

"That's the idea." His fingertips brushed across my jaw.

"I didn't get you anything," I murmured, wishing I had.

"You get me something every day just by being in my life."

"Braeden's right," I said. "We're like a damn Nicholas Sparks movie."

He laughed.

I grabbed the front of his shirt and pulled him down. He came willingly, the look in his eyes changing from amusement to desire.

"Thank you," I murmured against his lips, then kissed him.

He kissed me back softly. It was a meeting of the lips, a whisper from the heart. We didn't kiss as long as I wanted, but we were in a parking lot.

After we made it past the toll booth, I turned onto the main road. "Ivy wants us to stop by the compound."

"Yeah?" Trent asked. "Now?"

I felt his pain. I was horny as hell. Three days was the longest I'd gone without some form of sex since T and I got together.

"She's waiting for us."

He groaned. "Fine. What's she want to show us this time?"

"I think the kitchen," I said, shrugging.

The compound was the house Romeo and Braeden decided to build after Nova was born. It was basically just several acres of land all sectioned off by a stone fence (or wall, however you wanted to look at it) with a giant house for the four of them to live in. It was a necessity considering their celebrity status in the state and the fact the press never left them alone.

When T and I told the fam about our plans to get a place once he graduated and they were ready to move into the compound, shit hit the fan.

Another family meeting was called.

They assumed we would be moving in with them.

Six people plus a baby under one roof? Didn't anyone want any privacy?

The house they were building was big, big enough that everyone had their own wing. Trent and I didn't want that, though. We liked to live in our own little bubble as much as we could.

But we did love the family, and honestly, I wanted Trent to have them nearby. He spent too much of his life alone already. It was time he had what he always deserved.

The solution was to build a place of our own on the property, within the walls of the compound. It was kinda perfect really. The press didn't exactly leave T and me alone either.

We'd sort of become a hot topic in magazines and papers. The press loved any shot they could get of us together, added bonus points if we were touching.

Mostly, we were accepted by the racing world. The fact we were part of a "no rules" division of underdogs was exactly as everyone hoped. It worked in our favor.

Of course, we got the hate. We got the comments, the nasty emails, and occasionally, we got hassled in public. That never ended well. Trent didn't take kindly to anyone approaching us.

Especially me.

The last time I had some words with an abusive photographer, the guy got too close and Trent knocked him out.

So yeah, walls around our private residence were a good thing.

We could afford it because I got a fat paycheck from Gamble for the season. Then I got a bonus because I won so many preliminaries. If I made it to the championship race at the end of season one, there was quite a paycheck waiting at the finish line.

At first, Trent wasn't too keen on me slapping down the money to build us a place. But it wasn't as if he didn't bring in income. He did. He got paid for managing my deals and he got paid well for his job with NRR.

We definitely weren't rolling as deep as Romeo, but money wasn't necessarily an issue.

Besides, buying a house was an investment in our future, the one we had together. Trent couldn't argue with that.

Ivy was designing the place because when we were asked about finishes, I said I liked black and Trent announced he didn't care.

Ivy was appalled, so she took over. I made her promise not to make it look like a bunch of girls lived there, and from what I'd seen so far, she was doing a good job. Until the houses were finished, we all still lived where we always had. Trent had moved in right after he handed the presidency over to Zach.

He graduated last month, and his mom didn't come.

But Granny did.

I went and got her and drove her to campus myself as a surprise.

It was the first time I'd ever seen T cry.

She cried, too, and then she asked me to floor it because she liked to drive fast.

Yeah, Granny was still my favorite person for life.

I still hadn't talked to my father, though my mom called me every once in a while. I talked to her because I loved her, but it wasn't the same. I knew she called when Dad wasn't home and she probably didn't tell him. She told me my father missed me and followed my career in *GearShark* and in the papers. She also said he cried when he read the article on Trent.

I wasn't sure I believed her, but I hoped maybe someday he would come around.

Overall, we were happy and I had no regrets. Regret was a waste of time.

Trent's hand settled over the back of my neck as I drove, and he played with the short strands of hair.

"Hey, Forrester," he said.

"Yeah, frat boy?"

"I'm so glad my heart chose you."

Reaching around, I pulled his hand around and pressed my lips to center of his palm. *Not as glad as I am.*

"I'll take care of it, T." I vowed.

I'd take better care of it than my own.

It was the easiest promise I ever made.

The Finish Line

#TrewLoveForever

Turn the page for *Bucket List Confessions!*

Bucket List Confessions

We asked our readers (and our cover model!): What's on your list?
The answers came flooding in from all over the world!
Check out the submissions below!

written by Emily Metcalf
©GearShark Magazine

"To be the first NRR champion driver. Oh and to see how many French fries I can fit in my mouth at once."
– Drew Forrester

"I just want to be happy. Oh and I want to fit one more fry in my mouth than Drew."
– Trent Mask

"It has been my dream, since I was a freshman in high school and saw some beautiful photos from a trip our vice principal took, to visit the Greek island of Mykonos." - Raquel Auriemma

"Traveling around San Francisco discovering all the amazing things the city has to offer." - Cushla Gera

"Visit Ireland!" - Paula Guarneros

"Have a book published." - Savannah Sharp

"Meet Nick Bateman!" - Debi Goldberg

"Travel to every state as well as Ireland, Italy, France, Germany, and Switzerland, while there visit bookstores." - Ashley Dunning

"To travel all over Europe!" – Jordan Noonan

"Travel to Santorini, Greece." – Aubrie Brown

"Learn to ride a motor bike and I've always wanted to visit Venice but have a big fear of water but have promised myself I'd go. So one day ☺" – Tracy Bradd

"Visit all 50 states!!" - Shaquala Dalambakis

"Alaskan Cruise (also see the Northern Lights 'Aurora Borealis')." - Carol Workman

"A trip to Australia to see the Great Barrier Reef." - Rachel Bowes

"Drive across America on historic Route 66." - Jessica Johnson

"To go to Paris, Italy, and London." – Amanda Edmunds

"Ride an elephant." -Sophie Bethany

"Visit Disney World and Cocoa Beach Florida." - Mandy Hall

"Run all 3 spartan races in a calendar year to earn my trifecta- the sprint (4-5 miles) super (8-9 miles) and beast (12-13 miles) 💪☺!" - Alli Parker

"A trip to Vegas and get a helicopter ride to the Grand Canyon." - Katie Montgomery

"To run as the Incans ran in Machu Pichu." - Rachel B.

"White Water Rafting!" - Julie Sodergren

"To travel to each state in the United States." – Stephanie

"Kiss the Blarney Stone (or maybe just visit it because I heard stories about the locals ;-))" Jeanine Denzer

"To visit England and to go zip lining." - Traci Hoffman

"Write a romance." - Tessie G.

"Attending the Readers and Writers Unite conference in Houston, Texas. It will be my first conference." - Jenny Needham

"In my bucket list, one of the things I want to do is conquer my fear and go bungee jumping at least one time." - Crystal R

"To have a Big fairy tale wedding with the love of my life "Mr. Right" and live happily ever after." - Mario A Sandoval

"I would love to go skiing in the Alps!" - Heather Chrisco

"Take a road trip all through the US, hitting all the tourist attractions along the way."

– Kathryn Jacoby

"To go anywhere out of the country." – Sada Maciel

"Airboat across an alligator infested swamp." – Joelle Schnorr

"To travel out of the country. Two places I would love to go are Italy and Canada."

– Tracey Milito

"Go to Egypt and see the pyramids." – Yvonne L

"Travel." – Lisa Arrieta

"Have a baby." - Kim Walker

"Take a Hawaiian cruise to see the Pro Bowl." – Shelly Paxon

"Seeing the castles in Ireland." – Kristen

"To travel to places of historical importance. Egypt, Rome, London, Philadelphia, Washington DC, etc." – Marquita

"Maybe It's sounds stupid, but since I had a car accident a few years ago, I've not been able to drive, (I mean not more that a block), I've been dealing with severe panic attacks every time I'd try, so I'm on it! I really want to drive again, I used to love it." - Paola Cortes

"To go to Ireland." – Stephanie Garza

"Kiss the Blarney Stone!" - Vanessa Johnson

"To move to a warmer climate!" – Karen Voitik

"Visit the Great Wall of China." - Elizabeth Farrar

"To visit Machu Picchu." – Dawn Strickland

"To travel the world as a photographer." - Jennifer Strahan

"To go to Australia." - Kara

"Climbing a snowcapped mountain." - Katie Anderson

"Backpacking through Europe." - Kimberly

"Take a trip to the Maldives and stay in one of those huts over the ocean." - Felicia Gerdes

"Drive a NASCAR race car in the Richard Petty driving experience." - Bridget S.

"I would like to be a foster parent before I die." - Caitlin Mahoney

"Swim with great white sharks!" - Stephanie Bass

"To get over my fear of heights and skydive." - Jennifer Gurrola

"To travel out of the country." - Mia Wagner

"Go to Ireland and kiss the Blarney Stone." - Andy Currey

"To go skydiving!" - Lisa Lajcarov

"I would love to learn how to play the piano." – Gina B.

"I want to buy an Aston Martin DB9 and take it to race at the Nurburgring!!!" – Samantha C.

"Ride horses in Paris France!" – Kaydence Hebert

"Go to Universal Studios and swim with sea turtles." – Nathan Hebert

"Enjoy a two week family vacation at St. John, United States Virgin Island." – Shawn Hebert

"Take a trip to the Maldives and stay in one of those huts over the ocean." - Felicia Gerdes

"Drive a NASCAR race car in the Richard Petty driving experience." - Bridget S.

"Fly to Paris France. To be able to stroll down the Champs Elysées with my baguette in hand. Possibly reading under the Eiffel Tower. Riding a bike through the streets of Paris exploring everything that the city has to offer. Thank you GearShark team!" – Amy Callahan

"To travel to many amazing cities across the world!!" - Paige Walker

"To backpack through Europe for a summer." – Tina Garcia

"Ride on a hot air balloon." – Hazel

"To head back to my parents' home country of Ecuador and stand at La Mitad deal Mundo I.e. The middle of the world and enjoy being in both hemispheres at once." - Jess Acosta

"After winning lottery & purchasing Winnebago, I would love a trip to every state in the USA & doing fun things with hubby & fuzzy daughter!!!" - Kim Jelinski

"I want to publish a book inspired by my experience dealing with Polycystic Ovarian Syndrome (PCOS)...If I ever get the courage." - Jenny Rose

"I would like to be a foster parent before I die." - Caitlin Mahoney

"Swim with great white sharks!" - Stephanie Bass

"To get over my fear of heights and sky dive." - Jennifer Gurrola

"To travel out of the country." - Mia Wagner

"Go to Ireland and kiss the Blarney Stone." - Andy Currey

"I will love to hike at Queen Charlotte Track, New Zealand... Beautiful country and More important is near the famed wine growing region of Marlborough.. 😁.” - Francheska Auquilla

“To move to a warmer climate” - Karen Voitik

“Visit the Great Wall of China.” - Elizabeth Farrar

“To visit Machu Picchu.” - Dawn Strickland

“To travel the world as a photographer.” - Jennifer Strahan

“To go to Australia.” – Kara

“Climbing a snowcapped mountain.” - Katie Anderson

“Backpacking through Europe.” – Kimberly

“To own a 1967 Chevrolet Impala and cruise some of the same roads they drove on in any of the Fast and Furious movies!” - Stefanie Lewis

“To take a trip to Fuji with my husband.” - Lesley Koke DeWig

“A Europe road trip!!!” – lanie

“I would really love to visit Ireland, Scotland, England and France to trace my ancestry in person.” - Margay Leah Justice

“Travel to all 50 states. :)” - Melanie Brunsch

“I want to write a book. A tattoo with my children's name and birthdate.” - Ardra Lukens

"I would like to walk across the United States of America. I've never been to the U.S, and would like to walk from the west coast to the east coast." - Sarah Hageman

"One winter, I want to stay in the Icehotel in Jukkasjärvi, Sweden. While I'm there, I want to make a tripto Aurora Sky Station in Abisko National Park, so I can witness the Aurora Borealis." - Caroline Frimston

"Have season tickets to all my favorite sports events." - Jennifer Alfaro

"My father, who passed away in 2005, loved trains. Unfortunately, I have never been on a train. I would like to take a train ride across the country and try as many bbq ribs in different states as I can." - Janelle F.

"Be a contestant on a gameshow." - Valentina Rodriguez

"Travel to Scotland." - Heather McCalmont

"Take my mom and kids to Korea to see family that I haven't seen since I was 3." - Sylvia D

"Spend a couple of months traveling the world." - Tabitha Adkins

"To drive the Autobahn one day. No speed limits!" - Melissa Stickney

"My number one item on my bucket list is to drive with a professional NASCAR driver in an Indy 500 track." - Brandie Thiel

"I want to see a concert at Red Rocks in Colorado." - Sarah Symonds

"To go skydiving!" - Tamsin

"To visit Ireland." - Amanda Anderson

"Meet Drew. Get A Paperback Copy of #Junkie. Get more paperbacks…" - Saumya

"Go to a NASCAR race. My dad was a huge fan and we always talked about going together. Now that he is gone I want to go and do it in memory of him." - Danielle Lewis

"The absolute without a doubt #1 on my bucket list is to adopt a child." - Crystal Hammond

"Jump into a hot convertible and take a leisurely tour across America on Route 66, stopping at all the attractions along the way." - Lisa F.

"Open a bookstore that gives readers a wide range of books to read from, but also specializes in helping unknown authors to get their work discovered." - Jessica

"Travel the world." - wassila

"Be in two places at once." - Jamie Vining

"To travel to places of historical significance. I love history." - Marquita

"Owning and restoring a 1960 Chevelle by hand...or a 1969." - Emma Reverie

"To skydive!" - Juli Faulkner

"My favorite car is a '69 Mustang Boss and on my bucket list is driving it, fast, with all the windows down the entire length of the PCH (Pacific Coast Highway). That would be an amazing experience." - Miranda Vescio

"I would love to visit Antarctica and take a dancing video with penguins." - Aarati

"To visit and swim in Lake Hillier, the Pink Lake, in Australia." - Ashley Ehlers

"Indie publish my first book "Yellow Sunbird" that will be part of the "Finding Me" series." - Tammy Hamilton Green

"Visit England and Ireland." - Jennifer Malotke

"To find my Romeo Anderson #goals ☺." - Deniz N.

"It's corny, but I want to go to The City of Love and kiss under the Eiffel Tower. The hopeless romantic at its finest." - Amanda G.

"To own and restore 67 Chevy Impala." - Brenda Parsons

"I want to snowboard all best mountains in the world. I'm currently going through my North America list and have crossed off 6 mountains so far." - Cynthia Amora

"Visit all 50 states." - Dawn Stefanski

"To go freaking Skydiving! That would be AMAZING!!" - Rosie

"To climb Mount Everest." - Shannon V Mummey

"Skydiving!" - Shasta Mosley

"I would love to make it to every track and watch a NASCAR race." - Sunny W.

"To visit the Eiffel Tower!" - Jade Hyland

"Travel the World!" - Tiffanee Wylie

"To move to a warmer climate." - Karen Voitik

"To kiss my person under the fireworks." - Robin Geary

"Sail around the world on a cruise ship." - Jan Zevallos

"Doing a couple boudoir photo shoot with my significant other." - Samantha

"Travel to America and ride shotgun on the saltflats races. Woohoo!" - Stephie Batten

"Experience Weightlessness aka Zero Gravity." - Elizabeth A. Alvarez

"To tour Italy." - Angie Schexnaildre

"I love to ride horses and I've been riding since I was a girl. Girls and horses, right?! I'm Irish and more than anything, I want to ride horses in Ireland that's number one on my list in life."

- Joanna Mueller

"To have sex in a fast car!" - Rebecca Ross

"Snow; to see snow in real life, to experience it all: play, build a snowman, have a snow fight and make a snow angel. But overall to touch it for the first time and feel it and get cold. I live in California and I only seen snow on tv and social media. thank you." - Chelsea Deri Guzman

"Go to Australia and scuba dive at the Great Barrier Reef." - Gina Behrends

"Travel across Europe, taking extra time in Italy. I'd love to experience the food, drink and culture there." - Evan Grace

"To travel around Europe." - JoAnne Garcia

"Hope to see The City of Lights one day. 🗼" - Cynthia Corona

"Zip lining over the giant majestic Redwood trees in the Santa Cruz Mountains. A little speed and a lot of beauty!" - Melissa Rutherford

"To see the Fairy pools on the Isle of Skye, Scotland." - Lindsey Westenhouser

"Swim the Great Barrier Reef." - Jennifer Harrington

"One day when I'm able, I'm going to Greece to meet the family I have there for the first time." - Traci Smith

"Write and publish a book." - Bethany Elaine Macielag

"Photograph the coast of New Zealand." - Karin Anderson

"Doing a cross-country road trip! - Momo Xiong

"Swim with dolphins!" - Laura

"Move to a foreign country for at least 6 months to learn about a new culture." - Trish

"Go to Ireland." - Shey Houston

"Ride in a Race Car." - Andrea Figard

"I want to head down to the race track and be driven around the track as fast as possible. I feel the need, the need for speed!" - Deb Carroll

"Travel. I would love to travel and visit every state!" - Lora Murphy

"See each of my sons find their true love." - Leanne Michele

"BASE jumping. I'm addicted to adrenaline and a bit of risk. BASE jumping is perfect."
- Kristen Piersa

"I want to cage dive with great white sharks." - Elisia Goodman

"Visit Bora Bora and stay in a suite built over the water." - Jennifer N.

"I want to go to Santa Monica." - Heather Kirchhoff

"To get married even if it's a drunken night in Vegas." - Angelica

"I know most people put different places in Europe for their bucket list. Not me. I am a huge country music fan and I would love to go to Nashville!!" - Traci Bishop

"Attend an NHL game." - Audrey Eaton

"Conquering my great fear" - Shadow

"Driving a 57 Chevy Bel-air and road tripping around the country to visit all the best food and libraries." - Melana

"To race around the Nuremberger ring in Germany at top speed." - Michelle strange

"Take my family on vacation to the Bahamas" - Lucy Cariez

"Going to Grand Prix in Monaco. I love racing, especially drag racing since I grew up around it, at Coastal Plains Dragway, and to me that is one of the most exciting race you could ever attend. Just the location the people you would be around, the quality of drivers and the whole racing atmosphere would be worth the money to me." - Heather Fesperman

"To succeed in the fire department and make the world a happier place." - Madison

"Go diving with sharks." - Melissa Huie

"My father, who passed away, loved trains. I would like to take a train ride across the country." - Janelle Fluker

"Travel the world." - Luisa Ramirez

"Swim with free dolphins in the middle of the ocean." - Laura

"Publishing my book and be on NY best seller." - Marlyn Ruiz

"Travel to New Zealand." - Evelyn

"To travel to Italy and visit Juliet's tomb in Verona." - Cheyenne Davis

"One night stand." - Syl

"I saw in a movie once a girl who had wanted to be in two places at once and ever since I've added that on my bucket list. Straddle the border of two states at the same time. So simple but awesome." - Nanette Bradford

"Have a reading with Theresa Caputo." - Mary Ashley Deeb

"Swim with great white sharks in South Australia!" - Ashleigh Hardy

"1. To go explore the ancient ruins in Greece (Athens)." - Catherine Bates

"Visit Texas." - Shaz Dawson

"Sky diving!" - Monique

"Jumping out of an aeroplane." - Sonis

"I would love to travel across Europe and visit as many literary landmarks as possible, such as Westminster Abbey, Keats House, Fitzroy Tavern, and the Charles Dickens museum." - Jennifer Partridge

"Swimming with the dolphins in Hawaii." – Darlene

Note: these reader submissions have not been edited and reflect the way they were submitted to GearShark. Please forgive any typos!

I didn't know until the last page how this book was going to end. I debated and I went back and forth on how many books to give these two. But really, it's not my decision. It's theirs.

What they've told me is they've said everything they needed to say. I feel it and I'm proud of them. I'm proud of this book.

I'm not saying we won't see Trent and Drew again. We will. But perhaps not in their own full-length novel.

I feel like it's time for these two to just be happy. To have all those moments Trent wants to have. I think we all know it might not ever be easy for them in some respects, but that just makes their happiness that much sweeter.

It's a beautiful thing for people to be happy when sometimes life gives them reason not to be.

I can't say this book turned out the way I thought it would. I wasn't really sure what to expect going in. Although, part of me expected more racing, more cars, and maybe more Joey. But as I said above, it's not my decision. It's theirs.

Trent and Drew's main focus was each other. They can't really move on to the things they want in life until they know where they stand with each other. They are the foundation on which everything else sits. Because of that, I feel like this book is relationship heavy. It focuses a lot on them and how they deal with being in love.

There isn't as much racing in here as in #Junkie, but I do still think it has that flavor. I am right now considering a book for Lorhaven and maybe one for Arrow (who, by the way, totally wormed his little way into my heart in this book). If those books come to fruition, they will focus a lot more on racing.

And of course, there will be romance…

I think for right now, I'm going to kind of revel in Trent and Drew. In their story. In their love. I never set out to write a book about two men who fall in love, let alone two books.

I'm so glad I did.

I think they might be my favorite books I've written. I'm proud of these books and of these two men. They will forever have a special place in that deep spot right behind my heart.

I hope you enjoyed this book and feel it did justice to these two. I have to say the feedback for *#Junkie* is overwhelming. I have never had so much feedback (all good, too!) so fast with any other book. The fact that so many of you were willing to give *#Junkie* a try even though this isn't your normal genre means more to me than anyone will ever know.

I've cried a lot of tears over your emails and reviews and messages.

It shows me how capable people are of acceptance and open-mindedness.

Saying thank you just doesn't seem like it's enough, but really, I have no idea what else to say. So thank you for reading these books and for loving Trent and Drew like I do. I may not have hit lists or made it a bestseller, but I got something better.

I got your support.

See you next book.

XOXO,

Cambria

About CAMBRIA HEBERT

Cambria Hebert is an award winning, bestselling novelist of more than twenty books. She went to college for a bachelor's degree, couldn't pick a major, and ended up with a degree in cosmetology. So rest assured her characters will always have good hair.

Besides writing, Cambria loves a caramel latte, staying up late, sleeping in, and watching movies. She considers math human torture and has an irrational fear of chickens (yes, chickens). You can often find her running on the treadmill (she'd rather be eating a donut), painting her toenails (because she bites her fingernails), or walking her chorkie (the real boss of the house).

Cambria has written within the young adult and new adult genres, penning many paranormal and contemporary titles. Her favorite genre to read and write is romantic suspense. A few of her most recognized titles are: *The Hashtag Series, Text, Torch,* and *Tattoo.*

Cambria Hebert owns and operates Cambria Hebert Books, LLC.

You can find out more about Cambria and her titles by visiting and following her here:

Website: http://www.cambriahebert.com.

Email: cambriahebert@rocketmail.com

Facebook: http://smarturl.co/CambriaHebertFanpage

Twitter: https://twitter.com/cambriahebert

Instagram: @cambriahebert

Sign up for my Newsletter: http://eepurl.com/bUL5_5